Out of This World

A FICTIONALIZED TRUE-LIFE ADVENTURE

SONIA JOHNSON
&
JADE DeFOREST

WILDFIRE BOOKS
Estancia, NM 87016

Published by Wildfire Books.

Inquiries should be addressed to:
Wildfire Books
Star Route 1, Box 55
Estancia, NM 87016
(505) 384-2500

Typesetting: Fox

Cover Photograph: Jantina Eshleman

Printed in the United States of America
First Printing October, 1993

Library of Congress Cataloging-in-Publication Data

Johnson, Sonia
        Out of this world: a fictionalized true-life adventure/Sonia
Johnson and Jade DeForest
        p.   cm.
        ISBN 1-877617-10-5 $12.95
        1. Gay communities—New Mexico—Fiction. 2. Lesbians—
New Mexico—Fiction. I. DeForest, Jade, 1952- . II. Title.
PS3560.038643093   1993   93-23517
813'.54—dc20   CIP

Acknowledgments

With deepest appreciation to Paki Shivani, a most remarkable editor, and our lovers Amber, Eleanor, Jeanette, Margaret, Marilyn, and Saralena who made us think and kept us laughing through 'the Year of the Book'. Also warmest gratitude to the women of the original Wildfire community who taught us so much about ourselves, and for Harriet Lerner's presence in our lives.

o o o o o o

Other Books by Sonia Johnson:

From Housewife to Heretic $10.95

Going Out of Our Minds: The
Metaphysics of Liberation $12.95

Wildfire: Igniting the
She/Volution $10.95

The Ship That Sailed into
the Living Room: Sex and
Intimacy Reconsidered $12.95

Available from:
Wildfire Books
Star Route 1, Box 55
Estancia, NM 87016

Please add $2 per item for shipping and
handling.

June 1982. A sweltering day in Springfield, Illinois. Streets and sidewalks jammed with people of all ages, colors, backgrounds. Traffic rerouted so the march can wind through the streets to the state capitol building. Placards and banners—"Ratify the ERA now!"—swaying above the heads of marchers. Inside the capitol, the legislature holding hearings that will determine the fate of millions of American women.

Sitting in the rotunda, eight women on day 36 of a fast for ratification. Several now confined to wheelchairs, and one, Sonia Johnson—the woman excommunicated by the Mormons over this issue—a mere skeleton. Under the banner, "Women Hunger for Justice," eight women willing to die for it.

Outside the capitol building, a male reporter stopping two women marchers—one's T-shirt with QUESTION AUTHORITY, the other's with QUESTION EVERYTHING—asking them why they want the ERA.

Question Everything: "We want the same rights as men. Equal opportunity, equal pay, equal justice under the law. No more second-class citizenship."

Question Authority: "We want men to respect us, to treat us as human beings, not sex objects."

Reporter not getting it. "Hey, what you got to complain about? You can vote, you got day care centers, automatic washers and dryers, dishwashers, microwaves, frozen foods, television—easy lives. You're doing men's jobs—taking jobs away from us, actually. You can even go braless," leers at T-shirt fronts. "You never had it so good!"

Half an hour later reporter joins throngs inside the rotunda as the legislature adjourns for the day. Recognizing Sonia Johnson, he approaches, asks, "Why are you doing this?"

Looking him straight in the eye: "I want to change the world."

○ ○ ○ ○ ○ ○

Nine years later in the spring, twelve women were sitting around a campfire in the Gila Wilderness Area of southwest New Mexico. Some of them had been friends for years, some had never met before, but they were all connected in some way to Marian who had invited them on this camping trip.

Until late afternoon, they had been warm enough in shirtsleeves, but then the shadows of the huge ponderosa pines chilled them and they donned sweaters and jackets. The blazing fire helped keep the cold and shadows at bay.

"I don't want to change the world," Sonia said, tossing a pine cone into the fire. "What I want to do is make my own."

"Great," Lynne moaned. "Another ivory tower resident heard from." A gangly woman of twenty-seven, she was the single parent of two children, a boy and a girl. Her job as a legal secretary barely supported them, she was overworked, always tired and irritable. She and Marian had become friends four years earlier at an anti-nuclear rally.

"What exactly do you mean, Sonia, when you say you want to make your own world?" Marian asked, holding a long-handled wire basket of popcorn kernels over the flames.

"Just that. That I want to create a world that reflects me and what I love for a change, since nothing in mensworld does," Sonia answered. "A world of joy, peace, beauty, abundance, and health."

Lynne laughed mirthlessly. "I hate to burst your bubble, but it'll never happen. You'd be better off putting some muscle into making the existing system work."

"Hey, Lynne, women have been trying that one since men appeared on the planet. I don't want to be hasty, but I think five thousand years is long enough. I feel like stopping women in the street and pointing out that our little millennia-old experiment has been a failure from day one, so that if they want any joy at all, they'd better get out there and make it. 'Sisters,' I want to say, 'give up your illusion that men are going to change, stop nagging them, and make your own life!'"

"But dropping out never did any good," Angel objected. Blond with emerald green eyes, Angel was the owner of the New Age Boutique in Las Palomas, and Marian's lover. "Look at the hippies. They're back in the system now, respectable citizens who vote and write letters to their congressmen. They finally realized that if they wanted change, they had to get in there and demand it."

Sonia sighed. The same tired old argument. Reluctant to get embroiled in it again, she tried to keep her response simple.

"Since that's what you believe, Angel, obviously that's what you should do. But I can't put anymore energy into trying to change a system that's so male it has a permanent erection. All my passion is focused on femaleness—what it was before men came, how I can recover it in my life. To me, that doesn't feel like dropping out; it feels like finally dropping *in*—to the only thing that matters. But I don't expect you to agree, or to want to join Jean and me in our experiments at Wildfire."

Wildfire was their big old house in the mountains. At first they had lived there with others, but now there were just the two of them. Marcy, Sonia's lover, kept threatening to move in, but Sonia noticed that that event never got any closer.

Initially, the house had been a catastrophe, but they were slowly making it habitable. At times—such as when the drywall dust flew thick and the walls to be insulated and painted seemed endless—the temptation was strong to put out the word for others to join them. But mostly they were content to wait for exactly the right women to come along; they would know them— of this they were certain now. They also knew that if such women never came, they would be happy without them. There was endless, fascinating work to do on themselves and hundreds of experiments yet to lead them out of mensworld.

So they had hired Barb, their friend and neighbor, to help them revamp the house. A retired army sergeant, Barb had excellent building skills and enjoyed using them. And as she had pointed out, she spent almost as much time at their place as at her own, anyway. She lived on thirty acres further up the canyon with her pet pig, Ashley, in the cabin she had built herself. A tall, hefty woman of sixty-four, she cropped her gray hair with nail scissors and wouldn't be caught dead wearing anything fancier than clean jeans and flannel shirt.

"You're right about the hippies and back-to-landers," Marian told Angel. Marian was short and muscular with jet-black curls that made her look younger than her 50 years. A former nun, she had left the religious life nine years earlier, entered into a relationship with another ex-nun, and wandered from job to job until she found her true passion: the wilderness. On her forty-fifth birthday, she celebrated the opening of Wild Women Adventure Tours, a combination business/pleasure venture that had become an overnight success. But this trip was different. This week of camping with her friends was a gift she was giving herself. And an excuse to get her lover, Angel, out into the wilderness.

"The same can be said about all the alternative communities that sprang up back then," she continued. "Many of them failed, and those that have managed to limp along have done so only because the turnover's so great; few residents last more than a year or two."

Sitting next to Sonia, Jean nodded. "Exactly, Marian. The prognosis for women's communities is poor because it isn't enough to get away from men and out of their system. To succeed, we have to get their system out of us. And we haven't."

Noticing Angel's puzzled look, Jean explained, "When Sonia and I talk about men's system, we're talking about sadomasochism. Since we want women's world—total anarchy, wildness, and freedom—what we're doing at Wildfire is examining our every thought and act for evidences of sadomasochism; that is, for the need to control and for the feeling of well-being—the rush— we get from doing it. What we've discovered is that almost everything we think or do is underwritten by s/m, down to the tiniest, most seemingly insignificant."

Sonia chuckled. "That reminds me of my ludicrous self at lunch the other day. Jean and I were playing Yahtzee, a simple dice game. I noticed that after I took my turn, I always gathered the dice up and put them neatly in front of Jean, whereas she just left them all over the table when she finished. For an instant, thinking how much more thoughtful I was than she, I got a real s/m hit of pseudo-self-esteem. I caught it immediately, and we had a good laugh about it. But, shoot, what we won't do to be on top!"

Jean grabbed a handful of popcorn from the bowl Marian was passing around. "Thousands of times a day we unconsciously compare ourselves with others so we can get an s/m fix; it works whether we perceive ourselves as superior or inferior. Every time we do it, we reinforce mensystem in us. That's the kind of thing I meant we had to get rid of, Angel.

"Women say they know that before communities can succeed everyone needs to do a huge interior clean-up: toss out addictions, attachment to men and their institutions, incest trauma, self-hatred, and the victim mentality that prevents so many of us from taking strong hold of our lives. But too few realize that in the end, what this all boils down to is getting rid of the need to control and be controlled—the universal sadomasochistic pattern of human life."

"Tell me about it," Sonia sighed. "Before my brief community experience, I thought I'd done a pretty decent housecleaning job. But you know what? Even though I was writing a book on relationships, I watched myself doing Ship behavior with everyone there. Having expectations, for example; expectations are highly controlling, madly male, and destructive as hell. I think communities fail because everyone's doing relationships with everyone else all the time: making rules and commitments, compromising, having expectations, making assumptions, being passive aggressive, doing things to get others' approval or attention—oh, the list of how we scramble to get on top or wallow on bottom is endless.

"One thing we know about relationships: they fall apart. Since communities are great pots of seething relationshipness, they fall apart, again and again. And they'll continue to until women figure out for themselves the standard equation: patriarchy = sex = relationships = sadomasochism = control = nonfreedom = destruction."

"Frankly, it's beyond me why any woman would want to live in community," Harper said, refusing the popcorn bowl. She was an elegant, anorexically-thin woman of thirty-six who radiated confidence. A stockbroker and financial advisor, she had moved to Las Palomas from Boston with her lover, Lauren. They had recently purchased a country home only twenty minutes from Sonia and Jean. "I tried living in co-op housing when I was in college and barely endured it for a year. Never again!"

"I've been trying for the last year and a half to organize other single mothers into a co-op living situation," Lynne said wearily. "I'm so sick of doing it all myself, worrying about the rent, the car breaking down, leaky faucets and overflowing toilets, not being able to do anything fun because I can't afford a sitter. I don't want to marry again, but I sure would like to have some support.

"Join the military," Barb suggested. "That's what I did. I wasn't interested in traditional family life, especially the husband part, but starvation didn't look all that good to me, either. The military offered me almost endless possibilities—and the chance to live with women. What more could you ask?"

Marian grinned mischievously at Lynne. "The convent's as good as the army, you know. If you don't want marriage and do want to live with other women, it's the obvious choice."

Lynne made a face at her.

Dana brushed popcorn debris off her knees. "I think most women are interested in community of some kind." Petite and boyish, Dana lived in a small rental near Harper and Lauren and was a photographer by profession. "Even those who'd never actually consider doing it have certainly thought of it at some time. Women are social beings, we love to be together, we crave companionship and closeness. Also, we're always looking for ways to make our lives and the lives of those around us easier. That's the seduction of community living: companionship, and fuller, more leisurely lives."

"Did you break your vows of celibacy while you were in the convent, Marian?" Winnette asked irrelevantly.

"Winnette!" Lynne hissed, jabbing her friend with her elbow. "Jesus Christ!"

"Well, a lot of nuns are coming out with stories about sex in the convents," Winnette said defensively. Housewife, mother of five, and occasional babysitter of Lynne's children, she was feeling very daring to be on this women-only camping trip.

Marian didn't mind the question; she was used to Winnette's naivete. "Most people wonder but, unlike you, don't have the guts to ask. The answer is yes, I had two sexual relationships. Short, painful ones, because we lived in terror of discovery. I don't think sex has any place in the convent."

She pulled her jacket closer around her and turned to Jean and Sonia. "Getting back to what you were saying. It seems to me part of the trouble is that most feminists think they've done their internal work and are ready to live in a women's community. But if what you're describing is the sort of thing they have to do to succeed, then the truth is, they haven't even begun."

Sonia nodded. "It's clear why, too. It's the hardest, scariest work in the world. But the most satisfying, at least to me. It's all I want to do from morning to night, every day of my life. Even when I'm so shocked and depressed about the quantity and depth of s/m in me that I can hardly raise my head, nothing could stop me from going on."

"Challenging beliefs isn't easy or comfortable, either," Jean said, running her fingers through her short, coppery hair. "We're discovering that nothing we've believed is true; nothing. It's all lies, the results of thousands of years of brainwashing. Looking at what we've been conditioned to think about women is particularly painful. Every day I'm re-shocked at how thoroughly we've accepted men's view of us and how little we know about ourselves, about what it really means to be female."

"Now wait a minute," Angel protested. "You make it sound like a bunch of guys got together one night over poker and decided they were going to go out the next day and brainwash all the women. That they sat there and wrote out what they were going to say so they could . . . what? What would they have had to gain by that?"

Dana broke in. "Only everything, Angel: power, control of women, control of the world."

"Not power," Sonia disagreed, absentmindedly stroking Jean's arm. "Men don't have it, and their history tells us they never have. People with power are so self-loving that they don't have to control anything or anyone to feel good about themselves, never need to harm another living thing. This, I hardly need to point out, is not a description of men."

As she spoke, Marcy quietly rejoined them in the circle, a blanket draped around her shoulders. In her early forties with glossy brown hair hanging in a heavy braid down her back, she was a physician who had gained an impressive reputation in sports medicine. At the moment, she was watching Sonia curiously. She had never before had a lover who so freely touched other women. While Marcy never doubted Sonia's fidelity, she was not quite able to reconcile herself to her affectionate ways with women she liked.

Sonia smiled at Marcy and patted the log next to her. As she took Marcy's hand, she felt a pang of sympathy for the younger woman. Their relationship couldn't be easy for her. Marcy wasn't interested in community. She didn't really want to be with anyone but the woman she was having a relationship with at the moment. That was her predicament now. She was such an expert at relationshipping, so obedient to all its rules, that she was having to profess an interest in what Sonia cared about even though it went against her grain.

This camping trip was another case in point. Sonia knew Marcy would be much happier in a luxurious resort hotel than in a tent, that camping was the last thing she would have chosen on her own. But because Sonia had wanted to come, Marcy had acquiesced. She was always willing to compromise to make their relationship work and, Sonia thought, it didn't always turn out to be much fun for her.

Her thoughts moved on to Clare, the woman sitting next to Marcy. She had written to Sonia and Jean a few weeks earlier requesting permission to visit, and Marian had been glad to have her come along on this trip. She was looking for a women's community to take the place of the one she had just left. Although Sonia and Jean had both told her they were not actively seeking women to come to Wildfire, Clare seemed hopeful. She told them she could not conceive of living outside of community. Sonia wondered why. From everything she had told them, her twenty years of communal living in various places had been pure hell. Only forty-one years old, she looked sixty, with her deeply-lined face and gray hair. She joked that the women in her family aged early, and that her mother's hair had turned snow white when she was only thirty-five. Still, there was something almost ravaged looking about Clare, as though life had treated her harshly.

When she turned her attention back to the conversation, Marian was saying, "By the way, Jean, when I told a friend about this trip, she said she'd been a client of yours and was very sorry you'd left your practice. Her name's Stella."

Jean remembered her.

"She claims you're not only a great herbalist but a psychic as well. She told me that as a channel for spirit guides, you helped her with a lot of problems."

Jean winced at the words 'spirit guides' but Marian didn't notice. She was smiling at her lover. "Angel here, of course, has had all kinds of experiences with spirit guides." She turned back to Jean. "But I've been a patient of yours for years and never would have suspected that you were into this stuff."

"You're right, I'm not into spirit guides at all. The spirits I know are just friends."

"What's the difference?"

"They don't offer advice unless I ask for it, they don't try to guide or teach me. In fact, they urge me to listen to my own wisdom. Sometimes they share their experiences and feelings with me, or help me remember what I've forgotten, but they never set themselves up as my superiors, because they're not. Being in that other realm gives them a broader perspective, but other than that, they're just like you and me—no wiser, no better.

"Stella's was an unusual situation. I'm not a channel or a psychic, either as a career or hobby. These spirits—all women, by the way—are simply my friends. Occasionally they ask if I'll help them communicate with another woman, but not often. Sometimes a woman will ask if I'll help her contact her spirit friends, and if mine are willing, fine. But I don't do it often, I won't do it for men at all, and I won't accept payment."

"Well, I have to hand it to you for that, at least," Harper said sardonically. "I can't stand the New Age carnival scene that prevails in Las Palomas. Psychic fairs where the naive can quickly

be separated from $500 by I Ching readings, spirit guide chan-
nelings, past life regressions, and chakra balancing—all bullshit."
Angel's head snapped up, and leaning forward, she said, an
ominous edge to her voice, "Just a minute, Harper. Not everything
New Age is a carnival scene. Sure, there're some nuts out there,
but every movement has its crazies, and it's not fair to generalize
from them. The Movement should be judged by its purpose: to
help people get in touch with long-forgotten or buried aspects of
themselves."

"Besides, Jean isn't like that," Lauren reproved Harper. A
divorced mother of two grown sons, Lauren, at 53, with her short,
plump body, her pleasant face framed by light brown hair, and
frumpy wardrobe, could best be described as matronly. She and
Harper had been lovers for three years, Lauren's first lesbian
relationship.

"What she's doing isn't part of any movement or fad. It's
genuine and her spirit friends are really just that: friends. I know
because they befriended me, too, and helped me a lot."

Harper glanced at her sharply. "What do you mean, they
helped you?"

Trouble, Dana thought, watching Harper's face cloud over. *She
doesn't like finding out that Lauren hasn't told her everything, that
Lauren might possibly have a life outside their relationship.*

"They just did," Lauren answered evasively. "And it was real,
all right, because they knew things about me that no one else in
the world knows, things that are deeply private. My session with
them the day I went to see Jean and Allison was a turning point
in my life. Without giving me advice or trying to lead me, they
helped me make some very important discoveries."

Harper fought the fury that threatened to erupt into bitter
words. She had believed Lauren had no secrets from her. Although she knew this openness was one-sided—that she kept
many things from Lauren—the fact that Lauren had never mentioned this maddened her.

"I was skeptical, too," Sonia said, misreading Harper's stormy
face. "Very skeptical. Over the years, I've consulted a couple of
highly-recommended psychics, and though they said an interesting thing or two, I didn't like the feeling of them. My experience
with Jean and her friends is very different, and my instinct tells me
it's genuine."

Marcy put her arm around Sonia and drew her closer. "I don't
doubt that, Jean, knowing you," Marcy smiled at her. "But I know

there're a lot of opportunists out there with enough textbook psychology under their belts to be really slick con artists."

"You can say that again!" Barb snorted. "I went to one who gave me a great reading. So on my say-so, my friend Lucy went, too—and got told exactly the same stuff. That lesson cost me thirty bucks. Hell, I'm in the wrong profession!"

They laughed, trying to imagine brusque, down-to-earth Barb with a crystal ball.

"In women's world we won't have psychics," Sonia said, "because every one of us will be able to communicate freely with all other women—earth women, star women, spirit women. We'll have total peerness with every woman all the time."

Angel turned to Jean. "You say you don't have spirit guides, just friends. But you're wrong about that. We all have guides—spirits who are willing and able to lead us in the direction we once chose but have forgotten."

"I disagree," Sonia stepped in. "Everything in me resists the idea of being 'guided' by anyone but my inner wise Self. Women have been listening to voices outside ourselves, *other* than ourselves, for as long as men have ruled the earth. It's way past time for us to start tuning into *us*.

"And, you know, Angel, Jean's right. Spirits are just human like you and me. They can be wrong about things, they can be controlling and manipulative, and they can be downright evil. Just because they're in the spirit realm doesn't mean they're trustworthy. If a spirit gives me unsolicited advice, for instance, I'm immediately on guard; there's enough sadomasochism to deal with among the living. That's why I hugely prefer the peerness of Jean's spirit friends over the hierarchy your spirit guides seem to ascribe to."

Angel gave her a strained smile. "I don't think you understand me, Sonia, but that's okay. You've got spirit guides all around you. I can see them and hear them. One of them is a beautiful native American man, a medicine man. He's a patient soul and he'll be there if and when you decide to call on him."

Sonia resisted the urge to yell, 'Yuck!' Instead she opted for what she perceived as diplomacy. "Then he's wasting his time. I'll never listen to any man again, dead or alive, Indian chief or prime minister. Maleness is maleness, totally antagonistic to my well-being as a woman. Any male spirit hanging around me is invited—no, *ordered*—to shove off—now!"

Angel was aghast. "Don't talk like that, Sonia. They can hear you." She looked around fearfully.

"You're afraid of them, aren't you, Angel. I'll tell you why. Because they're male. Because like all women you know that maleness, no matter where it is, is harmful and dangerous."

Back under control, Angel said contemptuously, "Really, Sonia, I can't believe you're saying this. Aside from the gross over-generalization about men, surely you're intelligent enough to know that in order to become a guide, spirits must transcend the earthly body, and that once they do, gender is irrelevant."

"Gender is never irrelevant," Clare broke in. "I agree with Sonia. I've paid my dues to men's world. Now more than anything I want our world, and I know it can't exist where there's maleness." She gazed thoughtfully into the fire for a moment. Then looking around at all their faces, beautiful in the firelight, she said softly, "I remember a time when women were totally free to be female, and I want that again."

"I remember a time when women loved and cherished their bodies," Marcy said.

Sonia squeezed her hand. "I remember a time when women knew no fear."

"And no shame or guilt," Dana added.

"I remember a time when we never hurt one another," Lynne said.

"I remember a time . . . hmm," Marian thought a moment. "I remember a time when women laughed and danced and played together all day."

"I remember a time when women didn't shave their legs, and there were no pantyhose!" Barb bellowed. Staring at her—in shorts, the thick black hair on her legs glinting in the firelight—they all laughed.

"I remember a time when big was beautiful and all women wanted to be fat!" Jean shouted.

They hooted and whooped and dissolved in merriment.

2

In the mid-80's, "Open Skies," a popular magazine for nature lovers and outdoor enthusiasts, decided to do a story on women-only adventure tours. A staff member volunteered to accompany several such tours and, after a great deal of thought, opted for three: a backpacking trip with llamas in the Colorado Rockies, a bicycle trek through southern Italy, and an expedition into Nepal. When she returned to the magazine's offices, her editor asked her what, if anything, the three experiences had had in common. "Talk," she answered instantly. "Lots and lots of talk. We rarely stopped. We all had a lot to say and a lot we needed to hear." He looked incredulous, then shook his head. "Women! You turn everything into a coffee klatch. For the life of me, I can't figure out what you find to talk about."

All the things you men don't want to hear, she thought, going back to her desk: *our fears, our desires, our loves, our lives. We talked for hours about the changes we want and how to make them.*

We talked about you men, too, how damned external you are. How you boast about your exploits, your successes, your plans— polish your images—but never talk about your real feelings. We agreed that some of you try, but that you're hopeless at it.

Yes, we talked. And I'll tell you something: I got more out of my six weeks with women than out of my twelve years with therapists. Because we opened our hearts to one another.

○ ○ ○ ○ ○ ○

The trail made another switchback along the face of the cliff. Winnette, head down and sweating profusely, had never been more miserable in her life. Her feet were blistered and every muscle in her body was screaming. But she was long past having enough energy to complain. It was all she could do to take one step after another and try not to care how far behind she had fallen.

When the trail suddenly leveled out into a wide expanse of meadow, she collapsed in an unceremonious heap, oblivious to the beauty around her. The others had spread out over the landscape, discovering exotic wildflowers, taking pictures, or just gazing at the mountains towering above them.

After a while, Jean reluctantly returned to the pile of daypacks— and Winnette—and began putting their lunch together. This roused Winnette, who gratefully accepted the water bottle Jean gave her, took a long drink, then gingerly pulled off her boots.

"How was I supposed to know not to wear new boots," she complained. "The salesman said they were the best hiking boots on the market."

"He's right. But they have to be broken-in slowly." Jean reached into her backpack and extracted a package of Second

Skin and one of band-aids. Tossing them to Winnette, she turned back to her task. She worked quickly, unwrapping sandwiches and setting out containers of fresh fruit and nuts. By the time she had finished, the hikers were already gathering around her and beginning to eat. For the first five minutes talk almost stopped as the ravenous women attacked their food. But with the sharp edge off their hunger, conversation picked up.

Knowing the Gila intimately, Marian told them a little about the geology of the meadow and its surrounding mountains. Then passing the bowl of fruit around, she fell silent, letting the others talk.

Lynne stretched out on the grass with a contented sigh. "I'm so glad I came. I didn't mind taking time off from work, but I have so much to do at home I didn't see how I could possibly leave. I needed this, sisters."

"You're not alone," Sonia said. "We're terminally afflicted by the work ethic up at Wildfire. It was almost impossible for me to justify taking time off to do nothing but enjoy myself, even though we've been slaving away in our self-imposed labor camp from dawn to past dark every day for months. When Marian first called and suggested it, we both said no, we can't stop work on this house for a second! I looked at Jean and thought, 'Good grief, this woman's obsessed!'"

"And I looked at Sonia and thought, 'Horrors! This woman's a maniac!'" Jean laughed.

"So together we looked hard at how the Puritans, long in their graves, were controlling our lives, and decided we had to go camping."

"I'm glad you did; I needed the break," Barb said. "Being up here in the clean, fresh air has done wonders for my lungs. Maybe by the end of this week, I'll be able to blow my nose without getting globs of drywall plaster."

"That's gross, Barb!" Lynne threw an almond at her.

"That was one of the problems I struggled with at No Man's Land," Clare said. "The work ethic's not only alive but raging there: lists and assignments on a dozen bulletin boards and endless discussions about who does what when. On top of that, points are assigned to each job according to its worth. If you don't contribute a certain number of points each week, you have to pay more to live there. As incentive, the rotten jobs have the most points. Another incentive is that when you've completed a job, you sign your name after it. I loved looking at the lists and seeing my name up there more than anyone else's."

"It meant you were the hardest worker and therefore the best person there," Dana interjected.

"Yeah," Clare grinned a little shamefacedly. "But I can see the reasoning behind the system. It's an enormous place with a lot of upkeep, plus a cottage industry that brings in most of the money. Eleven of us weren't nearly enough to keep everything running smoothly. That's why they've launched a world-wide campaign to bring in more women."

"And why they have such a high turnover rate," Jean added.

Marcy asked, "What's the cottage industry?"

"Salad dressing, using their own herbs and homemade tofu. It's a thriving business, but it takes a lot of work to keep up with the orders. With the dressing, they work about 12 hours a day, five or six days a week. Then they have to find time to do all the other work. Burn-out's so common they had to initiate a rest-day program: each woman is allowed to take two extra days off a month. The problem is that even though everybody can see the necessity of it, they still resent anyone's taking off because it means more work for them."

"Sounds familiar," Sonia said, "Like the sweatshops at the turn of the century. How can we even begin to create a new world when we're doing that to each other?"

"I don't think they're interested in a new world, Sonia, at least not the way you describe it. They think they're doing something different by being all women together and not allowing men on the land, not depending on men or male energy for anything."

"Well, they defeat their purpose then, because energy that comes from behaving like men is very male."

"It reminds me of the military," Barb said. "Even if you've done all your work and there isn't anything left, you'd better look busy. Real busy."

"It isn't that bad," Clare said hastily, "and they envision a time when things will let up and they'll be able to spend less time working, more time having fun."

"They'll never reach that place," Sonia said flatly. "Working as competitively and as obsessively as you say they do there, every day they deepen their middle class conditioning about work: we're only worthy and good if we work hard. We have to 'earn' fun by working like demons beforehand. And if we have too much fun for too long, we must feel guilty and go back and work even harder to atone for it.

"We've been thinking about this at Wildfire, trying to figure out how not to be bossed around by those beliefs. Since there are only three of us and mountains of work, we've hardly been able to imagine not working all the time. But this trip is a beginning, and when we get back we're going to experiment in taking whole days off while the other two are working, and just hanging out—reading, walking, playing the organ, whatever. I suspect it's going to be agonizingly difficult, but we have to do it."

Marian was thoughtful. "You're right. I know from personal experience that I'm never through, I never get caught up. Something always happens to keep me from just lazing around."

"Like you think of new projects to keep yourself busy, so you won't have any idle time, heaven forbid," Marcy added. "You're old enough to have been told when you were a child, 'Idle hands are the devil's workshop'!"

Sonia lay on her stomach in the grass with her head on her arms. Marcy played with her hair, brushing it gently this way, then that with her fingertips. Watching this conjugal scene, Clare steeled herself to talk about something that was weighing on her mind.

"Worse than the work, though, was the craziness of the couple relationships there," she began. "Since I wasn't interested in getting into a couple thing, I was looked upon as either a threat or a possible conquest; I don't think anyone ever just saw me, just saw Clare. They were doing a lot of relationship experimentation, too—nonmonogamy, multiple partners—and my refusal to participate really bugged them. They said they felt judged by my abstinence. So at one of our weekly meetings they told me I didn't belong and needed to find somewhere else to go."

"Sounds like they all had PMS," Angel said.

Sonia muttered sleepily, "Nope. PMS stands for Pre-Menstrual Sanity."

"For *what?*"

Sonia rolled over, sat up, and yawned. "Sanity. I believe that women get depressed and irritable just before our periods because at that time of extraordinary power, we aren't able to sustain the illusions that make our lives bearable the rest of the month. This means that during that time we're our very sanest selves."

She settled into Marcy's arms.

"For the twenty years I was married to Vince, every month for those few days I could see the dynamics of our relationship with devastating clarity. And so of course every month I suffered through several miserable, irascible days when I'd sit Vince down and take our marriage apart piece by piece. Every month he'd say, 'It's because you're about to have your period', and I'd say, 'You betcha! This is the only time I can see the truth'—and I knew I was right, that at that time I could absolutely trust what I saw.

"But as soon as I'd start bleeding, I'd dismiss or deny it. I'd say, 'Don't pay any attention to what I said then; I was just having premenstrual tension'. Vince would say, 'But you insist every time that what you're saying then is what's real'. And I'd be embarrassed and try to smooth things over. For twenty years!

"When I was finally able to look back on that relationship with some objectivity, I realized that every month just before my period I'd been one hundred per cent right about my life, and that those were the only times I had been.

"So I have great respect for PMS, and a thorough understanding of why manunkind wants us to defame and belittle it. Men fear our premenstrual realizations of what our lives really are and the despair those realizations cause."

Harper didn't want to hear it. "That may be true of heterosexual women, but I doubt very much that it accounts for lesbian PMS."

Sonia shrugged. "Relationships are relationships, Harper, no matter who's doing them."

Harper bit her lower lip and said nothing.

"That's what I started to say, Sonia," Clare jumped in. "If you really don't believe in doing sex or relationships, I wonder why you're doing them. I mean, I know it's none of my business, but I have to say that it seems hypocritical to me. I wanted to visit because I'd been at your workshop in San Francisco and was thrilled to find someone at last who felt the way I did. I didn't realize until I got here that you'd changed your mind."

"I haven't changed my mind, so you're right—I am a hypocrite. It made me feel pretty sleazy while I was writing the book, and it's even worse now that it's about to be published. I know it can't have power in the world unless I'm living what I wrote in it."

"Then why . . . ?" Clare stopped, confused and embarrassed.

"Because I also know that it's sadomasochistic to be hard on myself about it or force myself to get out of it before I'm ready. So I'm in a double bind. All I can do is remember how I've changed in the past: I realize what's wrong, figure out why it's collaborative with patriarchy, then suddenly, without even planning to, move out of it effortlessly, often to my own great amazement. I just have to wait and have faith that it will happen like that again."

Angel sneaked a glance at Marcy to see how she was taking this. But Marcy had heard it before and, if she felt ill at ease, gave no sign.

"There's a man," Winnette popped up brightly, "who writes wonderful books about drug addiction and alcoholism. He's considered a real authority. I saw him on the Phil Donahue show and was really impressed by his understanding of substance abuse. Anyhow, you might be wondering why he was on a show as famous as Phil Donahue. It's because he's still an addict and still an alcoholic! He hasn't been able to stop yet, but he's working on it and he keeps counseling people and writing books because he's good at it. Isn't that the darndest thing!"

"Yep, quite the goldarndest thing." Barb stood and stretched. "I'm ready to explore this meadow," she said, slinging her camera over her shoulder. "What's on the agenda for the rest of the day?"

"Just as much time here as we want," Marian answered. "I never get enough of this place. Tomorrow I'd like to take you to the hot springs on the Gila. There's a canyon on the way there that you won't believe. It's even more spectacular than what we saw today.

"But if you want to do something else, that's fine with me. I like sharing my knowledge of the Gila but I don't want to be the leader; I get enough of that on my paid tours. After reading *Wildfire*, I felt very uncomfortable with that label even on those trips, and for awhile tried 'facilitator', but that just turned out to be leader in disguise.

"And you know, when I tried to shift from conventional to more shared leadership on my tours, I met with all kinds of resistance. I persisted, though, and I think that's why they're so successful, why women make such fantastic growth in such a short time."

"But what's wrong with acting like the authority if you *are* the authority and others want you to be?" Winnette asked. "Take me, for instance. I don't know anything about the wilderness. I wouldn't have the faintest idea of how to begin on my own. But knowing you were going to be with us, I felt confident that everything would go well."

"Thanks, Winnette, but there are a couple of debatable points here. Even with me along, anything could happen. Also, I think you'd be amazed at how well you'd do, how much you'd figure out, if you were up here alone and had to survive. You'd pull together resources you've forgotten existed, and come away feeling wonderful about yourself."

"The question of hierarchy interests me a lot," Lynne said. "We talk about it endlessly in my civil disobedience group. We don't want anyone to lead, so we work out strategies together."

"But you still have a spokeswoman," Marian argued, "and she's the one who's best known, the one with a name. That's hierarchy. I've wished your group would share that responsibility, rotate the position of spokeswoman, or have more than one at a time, or something."

"People outside the group won't take any of the rest of us seriously," Lynne explained, a little defensively. "So naturally we choose the one who will draw the most attention and get people to listen. It makes sense to do what's most likely to succeed."

Leaning against a tree at the edge of the group, waiting to hear the rest of the conversation before she took off, Barb shook her head. "It seems to me that if you're really committed to democracy, you'd ignore conventional wisdom—that people will only listen to the famous. That would be a worthwhile experiment in itself, choosing women from the group to be spokeswomen who aren't well known."

"It's hardly the time to experiment with peoples' reactions when you're in life and death situations," Lynne snapped.

Sonia looked up. "I wouldn't worry about hierarchy in your organization, Lynne. All organizations are male, regardless of the gender of their members, so hierarchy is inherent in them. Since there's nothing you can do about it, I say use it the most effectively you can."

Lynne looked a little mollified. "That's really what we have to do if we're going to get people to change before it's too late."

"Unfortunately, it's already too late for most people," Sonia said. "Men can't change their ways, anyhow. So going to jail or starving or doing whatever we think will change them is pointless. That's why I say that if we want something other than this shambles, we'll have to create it ourselves. We aren't going to make a bit of difference in mensworld."

"Fine!" Lynne flared. "I heard your idealistic discourse last night. But you're way off base, Sonia. If we don't do something now to stop nuclear energy and nuclear warfare, we aren't going to have a planet to pee on let alone create another world on!"

She stared belligerently at Sonia, her eyes slits of anger. "You know something else? I'm fed up to here with all this anti-male talk. I'm sorry if I'm not a man-hater. I realize I'm in the minority here. I care about humans, about the planet. I don't discriminate."

Sonia groaned inwardly. *If men are human*, she thought, *then women are something else altogether*. But she kept that to herself, and addressed the matter at hand.

"First, let me say that I understand and admire your passion, Lynne. I felt that way about the Equal Right's Amendment. But I couldn't keep on believing for very long that women could change men's ways of being in the world. I realized that we can't change *anyone* else—not our children, not our lovers, not other women, not men. No one but ourselves. So that must be our work.

"And it began to appear ludicrous to think of relying on laws for justice. Men invented and designed law to guarantee that they would always have control; that is, to *prevent* justice. Audre Lorde's right on when she says we can't use the master's tools to dismantle the master's house.

"Having said that, now I want to make very clear that I don't hate—men or anything else. Hate is quintessential maleness, one of mensmachine's innumerable cancers of the soul. I simply have to see men for what they are and recognize that, paradoxically, like all true parasites, they destroy what keeps them alive: femaleness."

"And your solution is to ignore it, drop out, and the hell with the rest of the world!" Lynne shouted. "The fact that everyone, including you, could be annihilated by nuclear bombs right this minute isn't *personal* enough?"

Winnette took Lynne's hand. "Hey, lighten up." Lynne jerked her hand away.

"Look at the facts," Sonia urged her. "Even if it doesn't feel philosophically cozy, you have to concede that nothing has changed over your years of activism, that in most cases we're back at square one or worse."

"It's because not enough people cared, not enough people stuck in there and fought!"

"I know that's the common liberal refrain, but I'm saying that even if huge majorities did what you suggest, nothing would change. It isn't that not enough of us are protesting enough. It's that protesting, voting, marching, resisting—these are useless things to do."

Ignoring Lynne's angry scowl, she corrected herself. "No, they're worse than useless, they're dangerous. They actually promote what it is we're fighting against. They're collaborative."

Lynne looked at the others and drew circles in the air around her ear, but chewing thoughtfully on a twig, Sonia ignored her mime.

"You think I don't care, Lynne, but the fact is that I quit fighting because I *do* care. Fiercely. For this earth and the women on it. It's obvious to me that men don't care and that we can't make them care, now or ever. They're going to keep on raping and killing no matter how much women plead and teach and resist, because this is what men do, this is maleness. Their own history tells us this without equivocation."

"Yeah, I know. You don't hate men," Lynne said sarcastically. Then waving that aside, "If you're so damn smart, tell this poor dumb working woman what *is* going to save us."

Sonia answered quietly, "I'm not trying to tell you what you should do, Lynne. All I'm saying is that *I* can't focus on men's horrors anymore, *I* can't bear their world anymore. Since at the moment there isn't anything else, all I can think of to do is to *create* something else—the world I long for, the one I have to have in order to live. I want everything men's world can't give me: beauty, peace, intimacy, love, nurturance.

"I know without doubt that women are capable of doing anything we can imagine. Well, I can imagine another way of thinking, feeling, behaving—a different way of being—so I know I can create it. Out of my Self, my femaleness, as men created this monster out of their maleness.

"Though I believe with all my heart that this is what will save the world, frankly, I'm not interested in saving the world anymore. I want this for *myself*—because I ache for it, because I deserve it, because I can't go on without it. That it will benefit every woman, that's frosting on the cake. But it's not the main course, not what nourishes my spirit. Besides, I can't save anyone else. That's something each of us has to do for ourselves."

"Listen, Sonia, what you're proposing isn't a new world," Lynne said scornfully. "It's the same hard, uncaring world men have already made. 'Let's just sit around with our cohorts and coo over our lovely belly buttons.'

"What all your fine flowery talk really comes down to is selfishness—not caring about anyone but your own precious self. Maybe the rest of you think it's time well spent getting to know your 'inner child' or something equally obnoxious, but it really matters to me that others are suffering and that we're all on the verge of extinction. And I intend to do something about it!"

"I hope you will," Sonia said, meeting her glare steadily. "But before you rush off to the crusades, consider this. You think I'm selfish. I think you're reacting to my breaking a taboo. It's taboo in men's world for women to put ourselves first. When I say that my foremost responsibility is to myself, to get for myself what I need—when I say I want a new world for myself—I'm making the most subversive statement possible for women: that I consider my happiness important enough to do seemingly impossible things for it, that I am worthy of my own undivided attention and deepest love."

"Right on!" Dana cheered. "Where would men be if we used our power for our own lives instead of theirs? Since they don't have any of their own, they couldn't survive without our generators to plug into. So naturally they condition us to put everyone else first."

"And to feel wickedly self-ish when we don't," Sonia added, "when in fact we're being gloriously self-full. They teach us to feel guilty for thinking first of our own lives and well-being, because when we're self-full, we're also power-full."

Marian leaned forward eagerly. "My experience bears out what you're saying. Every time I focus on molding the behavior of someone else, or controlling them in any way, I come away feeling drained and powerless."

"Because power and control are antithetical," Jean concluded. "I also think the message we give when we protest, not just to the guys in control but to ourselves as well, is that they're strong and we're weak—just the opposite of what we think we're saying. The very act of protesting is an admission that we accept the myth of their power, of their right to be in charge. It's bowing to their assumptions."

Marian nodded fervently. "I started Wild Women Tours because I was sick of being afraid of everything, sick of men's lies about the world. Especially the 'natural' world that they claim is dangerous and unpredictable. Life in the convent did little to allay those fears. I needed to come to grips with the wilderness for my own emotional health, although I rationalized that Wild Women Tours would benefit other women, too. And it has."

She looked straight at Lynne. "I've taken women who were afraid of their own shadows on trips like these and watched them transform themselves. It gives me a high like nothing I ever got in my years of anti-nuclear work.

"All the while I belonged to various activist groups and was busy fighting those guys in Washington, I knew they were laughing at us—if they even noticed us. I'm not willing to give them any more of myself to ridicule. Like Sonia, I want to put my energy and time into creating what I want, not fighting against what I don't want. And what I want is a world of and for women. That's what Wild Women Tours is about."

Barb applauded. "A most edifying lunch hour, all, but now I'm off to become one with the wilderness." She reached a hand out to Lynne and pulled her to her feet. "I'll show you my canyons if you'll show me yours," she quipped, as they started across the meadow.

"Hey, Marcy," Dana called. "Come on. Let's figure out that killer camera of yours." Marcy had purchased a new camera for this trip, and not having the remotest idea how to use it, had asked Dana for help. Standing up, she looked questioningly at Sonia.

"I'll be along," Sonia said, wishing Marcy had just got up and gone without waiting for permission. *It's a relationship, all right,* she thought resignedly.

One by one women stood, stretched, and wandered away, until only Jean and Sonia were left. Jean slipped over and sat beside Sonia, resting her hand on her knee.

"I'm so glad to be through with relationships," she said, watching Marian and Angel as they crossed the meadow.

"You're serious, aren't you."

"Sonia, when my last relationship ended, I knew I wasn't going to try again. I'd never been able to do them anyway, and I realized suddenly that I was glad, glad that the fortune I'd spent trying to learn had been totally wasted, glad beyond belief that I didn't have to try anymore. Of course, I thought it was just me—that I was deficient in some way—but I didn't care.

"I've never even thought of relationships since that day, either with longing or aversion. They're simply and finally out of my life. I could no more do one now than I could shoot a hawk. I don't know how to explain it. It's not bitterness or resentment. I'm just constitutionally unable to 'relate'."

"I'm impressed, Jeannie. No, more than impressed—overwhelmed with admiration. You know, in the face of constant and prodigious conditioning to believe that relationships are about love and intimacy, that they're natural and healthful, and that we're seriously deprived if we don't have one, your arriving at the truth is pretty damned amazing."

"I have you to thank for that, Sonia, at least in large part. That workshop I went to in Las Palomas a couple of years ago, when you were first beginning to talk about sex and relationships. Remember? I couldn't sit still because as soon as you said it, I felt as though someone had hit the focus button on a camera. I could see everything with absolute clarity, and I knew what I had to do.

"Besides, I'd suffered enough. It wasn't worth it anymore. All the therapy in the world hadn't made me any better at being half a couple. My last therapist was right on when she said she thought I didn't really want to be. That sounded right, but why didn't I? Well, I got the answer in your workshop. It wasn't abandonment or incest issues—the reasons therapy gives us. It was just as you said: sex and relationships are perversions for women, totally unnatural acts.

"When I was finally alone, I was so relieved and happy I didn't care if I spent the rest of my life up in those mountains with just the dogs and coyotes. I was not going to put myself through another relationship nightmare."

"That's the problem, Jeannie. My relationships haven't been nightmares—until maybe right at the end. This one with Marcy has seemed particularly sweet. And I say 'seemed' because I know enough to know that it isn't what it seems to be, enough to recognize illusion in myself."

Jean knelt behind Sonia and began massaging her neck and shoulders, over her head taking in the extraordinary beauty of the place. When Sonia began to resemble an overcooked noodle, Jean said softly into her hair, "I'll bet it feels wonderful to have the book out of the way."

Sonia shook her head. "No, actually it doesn't. It's not what I hoped it would be. I hate it when someone tells you all the reasons not to do something but doesn't offer any alternatives. And that's exactly what I've done."

"It'll come to you, and you can write it in another book."

"Not good enough. I want the answers now. I want to put them in *this* book, not the next one."

"I didn't know you were so discouraged. When you sent *The Ship* off to the typesetter, you seemed euphoric."

"Just massively relieved. There wasn't any reason to wait. I didn't—and don't—seem to be getting closer to a solution. And I won't until I get out of this relationship with Marcy. I'm sure of that. So—you might well ask—why don't I get out of it?"

"Maybe it's love," Jean answered matter-of-factly. "Marcy's a fine woman. It's easy to see why you'd love her. She's fun to be with, she respects and supports your work, and I think she really likes the way you are. Most women would give a lot to have what you and Marcy have."

"Just what would you say that is, Jean? What do we really have? It's true, what I wrote in the book: relationships make intimacy impossible, their very nature demands lies and pretense. This means Marcy and I don't even know each other, so how can we love each other?

"But, you might answer, love is what relationships are about, right? Wrong. Since that's what men tell us, we know damned well it's a lie. We know they're about control, pure and simple, like everything else in patriarchy.

"Anyhow, here I am, feeling that I love Marcy but knowing in my head that I'm just experiencing what I've been taught to experience, just doing the robotic relationship dance. Hell, I don't even know what love *is*. I know that's a cliche, but honestly I don't think that through all these millennia of male hatred and terrorism women have been able to hold onto a shred of the real thing. Maimed and broken things that we are, what we're left with is 'love' as our captors have programmed it into us: the excitation of the chase, the seduction, and the capture; the excitation of the daily conquest and defeat; the sadomasochistic pleasures of dependence, of owning someone else's body, time, energy, and attention, of desires to control or to rescue, or to be controlled or rescued; the illusion of belonging, of being secure, of being accepted; jealousy, resentment, and vengefulness that make us feel 'alive' in the time-honored s/m mode.

"But then ultimately sadomasochism stops working for us—no more excitation, only boredom and alienation and the search for another 'love'."

She had torn her napkin to shreds as she spoke, and now carefully gathered the pieces and put them in her pocket.

"This is men's 'love'—oh, not how they describe it, of course, but how it turns out for every one of us, whether we have the courage to face it or not: ownership, bondage, loss of self, anesthesia, boredom, jealousy, heartache. Vastest, deepest, most miserable sadomasochism.

"I know absolutely that what all the propaganda out there tells us is love is not love. It may be the best men can do, but it sure as hell isn't the best I can do. I know that never in this life or any other for 50 centuries—never since men took over the world—have I seen a movie, read a book or poem, heard a story or song that expressed what I'm capable of feeling. The way it's possible for women to love isn't even a concept on this planet anymore. It's been lost, completely lost.

"And I want it back!" she concluded fiercely. "I'm not going to use the word 'love' again until I've found it."

3

When the article about women-only adventure tours appeared in "Open Skies," it drew a record quantity of mail. Most of it was from women who were delighted that women in the wilderness were finally receiving the recognition they deserved. But an almost equal amount came from disgruntled men. Some protested that women weren't strong or capable enough to handle the endless numbers of emergencies that could occur. Others resented women's infringing on a previously male-only domain—or at least a domain where women only accompanied men, usually to cook and wash out their socks. They claimed it wasn't safe out there for women, that they had no innate survival skills. They pointed to the cases where menstruating women had been attacked by bears.

"What they really can't stand," the author confided to friends, "is that women are facing our learned fears and getting past them. And they can't stand that we were able to get along so well without them, coming back from each trip feeling more competent and powerful. But what infuriates them most is that we reported preferring the company of other women over that of men, and enjoying ourselves so much without them."

o o o o o o

The smoke curled lazily through the trees and vanished into the air.

"Fire?" Sonia asked in alarm.

"Our hot springs," Marian laughed. "They're more noticeable now that the mornings are so cool. Makes them easier to find. In the summer you have to know the exact spot."

Marian strode past Sonia and led them through the underbrush to the springs.

"Must not be sulphur," Harper sniffed the air.

"No." Marian's voice was muffled by the shirt she was pulling over her head. "I don't think they're known for any particular minerals, but they're hot, about 104 degrees. I ease in slowly and only stay submerged for five or ten minutes at a time." Kicking her panties off her foot, she slid into the steamy water.

In her underpants and man's white undershirt, Barb edged over to the pool and gingerly stuck her foot in. Then she lowered herself carefully into the water and made her way to Marian. Winnette followed in a one-piece bathing suit of basic black, looking as though she'd stopped breathing in an attempt to suck her stomach flat.

"Am I going to be the only skinny dipper?" Marian demanded.

At this, Clare, Lynne, and Dana stripped off their underwear, threw it on the rocks with the rest of their clothes, and waded in. Lauren followed, holding her T-shirt in front of her until she reached the pool. Jean removed everything but her T-shirt, waiting until she reached the water's edge to take it off. "It is hot," she told Marian, "but it feels exquisite, like silk."

As Sonia undressed, she watched Harper step out of her bikini pants and bra. *She's so thin*, she thought. *I'm afraid Jean's right that she has an eating disorder.* Then, leaving her tank top on, she joined the others.

"I've died and gone to heaven," Barb moaned, floating effortlessly in the clear blue water. "This is my idea of nirvana. Somebody drop a grape in my mouth, please. And bring me my pina colada." As nine pairs of hands doused her with water, she shrieked, "Is that any way to treat an old princess?"

"Ah do apologize," Lynne drawled. "But darlin', your horns have pushed your crown clean off your head."

Barb stuck her tongue out at her, then turned to Marian. "You really think we're safe from male eyes?"

"No one comes here this early in the season. When I checked our group in, the ranger told me we were it—except for a few elderly RVers in the modern campsites, over a day's hike from here."

"So what if men do show up?" Harper pulled herself onto a rock. "There are ten of us—ten big, strong women. They'll rue the day they stumbled upon us."

"That they will!" Barb agreed, stripping off her wet underwear and tossing it out onto the rocks.

Winnette wished Barb had kept her clothes on. She felt odd being only one of two now who weren't naked. *Thank goodness for Sonia!* she thought. Aloud, she said, "I'm sorry Angel didn't come with us."

Marian shrugged. "She didn't do any meditating yesterday, so she feels she has to do double time today. She says she needs at least five hours a day 'to access her inner being and knowledge'."

"She needs five hours a day to find herself?" Barb was incredulous. "When does she find time to do anything else? I have friends who meditate, but an hour in the morning at most."

Glancing sidelong at Marian to make sure she was too far away to overhear her, Harper muttered to Sonia and Jean, "I think it's creepy. Yesterday Angel told me she belongs to a group that meditates for prosperity. Some guy in the group wrote the book they study. He claims that if you meditate long and hard enough, you'll get everything you want. She offered to lend it to me. I told her that if it really worked, she wouldn't be trying to borrow money from everyone she knows to expand her business. She gave me a matronizing look and said she's still new at it, and it takes time. But hell, she's been doing it for over a year."

"I've known a fair number of women like her," Jean said. "A woman who rented a room from me had to meditate at least six hours a day. She was absolutely frantic if she didn't, convinced that terrible things would happen to her. The irony of it is that terrible things were always happening to her anyway. But her meditation master told her she just wasn't doing the exercises right, not putting the right amount of energy into her mantras or something. She's a mess. Her entire life centers around those meditations and there's no way she's going to see how futile they are or how obsessed she is."

Dana nodded. "I know what you mean. I worked with a woman once who could almost not move without chanting. The thing about her that was frightening, however, was that she believed that no matter what she did, even if it was harmful to someone else, chanting long enough would make it all right."

"You mean she used it to justify her behavior," Harper said.

Dana thought a second. "Yes, and sort of to atone. But even more than that. Chanting actually made her perceive her behavior as right, as if it somehow cancelled all negativity. She kept telling us how wonderful it was, how freeing, but it had her totally enslaved. She was also into prosperity consciousness, like Angel. But right after she quit working with us, she asked me to loan her enough money to pay her rent!"

Marian had joined them in the middle of Dana's story. "I try not to judge Angel, but sometimes it's hard. Like she doesn't have any particular time for meditating, so I can't tell you how many times we've had to stop in the middle of something because the urge hits her.

"But the worst is that I think it affects her judgment. For instance, a year ago she decided to get solar panels for her house. The place she called sent out a hideous guy, beyond jerk, bad enough energy to destroy the world. Angel found him so offensive that she called the company and told them they had to send someone else. But they didn't have anyone else. Turns out that, because he's the only expert, this guy is used by just about every solar company in the area whether they like it or not.

"So Angel went and meditated for hours, and when she finished she told me that everything was fine and she didn't mind having him come out again; that, in fact, during her meditation she was able to see his beauty and his pure essence—or something gaggy like that. I was there when he came back and he was loathsomely lecherous, undressing Angel with his eyes and making suggestive remarks. Angel was oblivious to it. I think if I hadn't been there he would have raped her."

Her listeners gasped.

"Seriously. The thing that upsets me is that if he had, Angel probably would have been all right with it because she would have known he wasn't really a rapist, that while raping her he just wasn't being his true self."

Sonia shuddered. "Sounds like her meditation just made her sink deeper into illusion instead of giving her clarity about what was going on. I think you're right, Marian, that a danger of any kind of meditation is that it can override a woman's instinct and judgment, and coerce her will. Pretty frightening."

"I have to keep reminding myself that it's her choice."

Jean raised herself out of the water. "The whole New Age Movement—excuse me, Sonia, I'll start again. The whole Past Age Movement is like that. It's focus is what men's focus has always been—to get women to reject their bodies as inferior and to live only in the brain."

"Because, of course, women's bodies are the core of our power, the core of our femaleness." Sonia put in.

"Right. And if you despise your body and renounce it, you can tolerate having it fucked with because it really isn't you, you're not in it. I think the Past Age Movement is the most dangerous thing to come down the pike in a long, long while. The only difference between it and heavy-duty fundamentalist religions is that it's subtler and sneakier."

Suddenly, Winnette asked, surprise in her voice, "Where's Marcy?"

"You mean you just noticed she's gone?" Harper raised her eyebrows.

"You were off bathing or something this morning, Winnette," Sonia said, "so Marcy didn't get to say goodbye to you. But she never intended to stay the entire week. She had too many clients."

"I wouldn't be surprised if she left early because of what happened yesterday in the meadow," Winnette blurted out. "I think that was horrible, Sonia, talking about your private affairs in front of everybody."

"You didn't need to stick around for it," Lynne reminded her.

Sonia only shrugged. "Marcy knows how I feel, Winnette, and she knows how I am, that I talk openly, often very publicly, about what's going on with me. She's never said it made her uncomfortable and I trust that if it does, she'll tell me."

"I'm ready for lunch," Marian announced, stepping out of the pool. Jean felt a surge of warmth as she watched her. They had been friends a long time, and although they often went weeks or even months without seeing each other, when they did, they instantly picked up where they left off.

At one point in their long history, Marian had admitted to Jean that she wanted to have sex with her, and they had talked seriously about having a relationship. In the end, though, knowing that it would ruin their friendship, they had decided not to.

Ruin our friendship, Jean thought. *Ironic that the thing we strive for most—a solid couple relationship—is a destroyer of friendship. Actually, a destroyer of everything women value.*

She got out of the pool and joined the other women in toweling off and dressing. Then they sat on the rocks and had lunch.

Winnette bit into her sandwich. "What's in this?" she asked Jean.

"Hummus and sprouts."

"It's good," Winnette said doubtfully. "I mean, I've had sprouts before, but I've never had this other stuff. Don't you eat any meat or cheese?"

Jean shook her head. "I've been a vegan for almost twenty years now, a vegetarian since I was three. When you came to see Allison and me, I told you that a lot of the trouble you had with your feet was directly traceable to animal proteins. Anybody with your problems should cut out dairy products entirely—because they're the worst—and stop eating all red meat."

"I tried, I really tried. But it's hard because Clarence expects meat at every meal and if not meat, there better be cheese or eggs. He loves cheeseburgers, and bacon sandwiches. It's just too hard to cook two different menus."

"Let him cook for himself," Lynne said irritably. "You need to go back on that diet Jean gave you. When you ate that way, the arthritis in your feet disappeared entirely, and you told me that, for once in your life, you had almost no gas."

Winnette blanched, then turned scarlet. "I'd appreciate it if you'd just keep quiet, Lynne. Remind me never to speak to you about anything personal or sensitive again." She was close to tears.

"Oh, come on, Winnette," Barb put her arm around her. "Gas is normal, we all have it and we all even have intense bouts of it sometimes. I've always said I could save a fortune in heating bills if I could bottle mine."

Laughing, every woman nodded her head.

"Barb's right," Jean said. "We all have gas, but there's a point where it becomes so excessive that it's no longer normal. People who eat meat tend to have more of it than those who don't because meat's so hard to digest; our intestinal tracts are too long to accommodate it so it breaks down in the colon and begins to putrefy before it gets out of the body. The same is true of dairy products. And putrefaction causes gas."

"Please!" Harper pointed to her lunch. "Could we talk about something else, like the life cycle of the bot worm?"

Barb poked her gently. "What's the matter? You never have any?" When Harper didn't respond, Barb said to no one in particular, "Looks like a few women around here could benefit from a Farters Anonymous support group."

"I'll be president," Sonia laughed, then turned to Winnette. "A lot of women are vegans. I've never been so healthy in my life as I have since I stopped eating animal products. I gave up meat first, years ago. Then Jean and Allison told me that dairy products cause calcium deficiency and a bunch of other dread things. I'd watched my mother lose four inches in one year from osteoporosis, so I dropped cheese and yogurt from my diet as if they were radioactive. Knowing that my body is so much better off without them, I don't miss them at all."

"Marcy told me once that her healthiest and strongest patients are vegans," Lauren offered. "She said it contradicted everything she'd learned in nutrition classes—which wasn't a lot. She said that vegans have fewer injuries and when they do hurt themselves, heal much faster."

"When I was in the military, vegetarianism wasn't what it is today," Barb said. "But there were a few who created a fuss over the meat-in-every-dish meals. They wanted spaghetti sauce without hamburger, or cooked vegetables without the pot roast. I remember that once a newspaper reporter came to our base and interviewed a few vegetarians, then talked to the base commander, O. E. Patton. O. E. was quoted as saying that vegetarians should be banned from the military because everyone knows you have to eat meat if you're going to be a good fighter. Tells you something, doesn't it."

"I can't understand why any woman would intentionally do something to harm her body, like ingesting meat and dairy and caffeine," Sonia said.

"I agree, Sonia, but how you define 'harmful' and how I define it are two different things," Dana argued.

"I think that's a cop-out," Jean said. "It has nothing to do with differences in definition. No one in her right mind would seriously try to argue that caffeine and sugar are healthful for her body; the proof that they aren't is too overwhelming. Caffeine has been tried and convicted of causing all kinds of abnormalities—heart problems and ovarian and breast cysts, for example.

"About dairy products, processed foods, chemical additives, well, their effects are murkier in people's minds. I grant that well-meaning women might eat them without understanding what they're doing. But if they continue to after they have adequate information and knowledge, I think I'm safe in saying that no matter how strenuously they insist that they love themselves, they don't. Nobody consciously destroys what they really care about.

"That's why when I see women, feminists even, who use substances that have been proven to be deadly—caffeine, for instance—it tells me that they hate themselves. It says they have internalized men's view of femaleness as the enemy and are out to kill it. Because that's what they're doing. Caffeine's a drug, a poison. It speeds up the heart, puts pressure on the kidneys, stresses the adrenal glands, and exhausts the immune system."

Dana looked pleadingly around at the others for help, rolling her eyes skyward, shrugging her shoulders, palms upward, as if to say, "Why me? What have I done to deserve this?"

Jean, deeply now into one of her favorite subjects, ignored Dana and plunged on.

"Take a look at dairy products—number one culprit on the list of allergenics, especially those affecting the upper respiratory system. No animal, no wild creature on this planet, drinks milk after weaning. And no free animal drinks the milk of another species. It's insane. There's a direct link between use of dairy products and cataracts—and fibroid tumors, arthritis, and any number of other diseases."

"I see your point, Jean," Marian agreed. "But Angel and her friends believe that a person's attitude can be a protection."

"What's attitude got to do with it?" Harper asked sharply.

"Well, they say that if you're in the right place spiritually you can eat anything and it won't hurt you. Also, they feel that if you put your hands over your food and bless it before you eat, you neutralize all harmful substances."

Jean groaned aloud. "Right. So as long as I have a loving attitude and bless her before I begin, I can beat my daughter and it's okay, it really can't harm her. In that case we couldn't call it child abuse, now could we." She was getting angry.

"Hey, don't get mad at me," Marian laughed. "I'm just telling you what Angel believes."

"I know, Marian, but it makes me sick. It's just another repudiation of the body, another way mensmachine gets us to forget the body's absolute centrality to spiritual and emotional as well as physical power. More sadomasochistic mind-over-matter bullshit, another ploy to get us to destroy ourselves. Abuse is abuse, Marian, no matter what it's called."

Marian shrugged helplessly.

Winding down, Jean continued more mildly. "My point is that we may say we love ourselves—and our bodies are ourselves—

but if we take in harmful substances, our message to them is that we really don't give a damn about them. Actually, it's worse than that, it's that we hate them. Real feminist feeling and behavior here, right? After this, why should our bodies trust us, why should they do for us what they're capable of doing?"

"You speak of our bodies as if they can think and remember," Harper said. "But those are functions of the brain. The body's great—don't misunderstand me—but it doesn't *think*."

"But she does think, Harper, and in a very sophisticated, very advanced way. In my experience, what my head knows is infinitesimal and shallow compared to my body's wisdom. She tells me, for instance, that I don't need doctors, specialists, tests and examinations to find out what's wrong. I just need to remember how to communicate with her."

"So you're proposing that we return to the Dark Ages, before medical science and doctors," Harper scoffed. "I'm sorry Marcy isn't here to defend her profession."

"All I'm saying is that men do not heal. Period. Their medical science is about manipulating, cutting, invading, tearing, causing pain and death—not to mention amassing money and enjoying god status. Women are the healers. And I'm not talking about women doctors because they're the same as their male counterparts, products of the same brainwashing."

Dana shot Harper a challenging look. "I'm with you on that, Jean."

"I know there was a time when there were no men, when there was no maleness. Don't ask me how I know, don't ask me for proof. I just know it. And I know that there was no disease then, no illness, no suffering or pain—they simply weren't concepts. Because women were joyous and free and full of love."

"That reminds me," Winnette interrupted. "The other night, Sonia, you said something about how you don't believe in making group decisions. I don't understand the reasoning behind that, or how you can even avoid it."

For a second, Sonia tried to imagine how Winnette had made the dizzying leap to this topic, but it was futile, so she simply answered her. "The reasoning behind it is simple: group decisions don't work. First, there's no way to make them that pleases everyone. That leads to the second: someone always has to compromise, and compromise inevitably causes resentment. Third, group decisions keep us from knowing what we each individually want. Fourth, they keep us from taking personal responsibility for getting it. There's more, but that should give you the picture.

"When there are no group decisions, each one of us has to take personal responsibility for getting what we want. I'll give you a hypothetical example. Let's suppose that in a few years there are ten women living at Wildfire. Of the ten, four of us decide that the road is intolerable and must be fixed. So the four of us tell the others that we want to fix the road, and that if any of them is interested, we'd be happy to have their involvement. Let's say one other woman is interested. The rest are happy enough to have the road fixed but they have other priorities for their money at that moment. So the five of us pool our money and ideas and get the road fixed. Of course, the others use it, too, and that's fine."

Winnette looked puzzled. "But what if you five alone didn't have enough money?"

Sonia shrugged. "We'd wait until we did, or try to raise it somehow ourselves. It isn't anyone else's responsibility to help us get what we want."

"Sounds cold and heartless to me," Marian said.

"Oh, no," Jean protested. "It's beautiful. No one resents having to put out money for something she really doesn't want, and no one feels owed—you know, 'I helped you get your road so now you have to help me get my swimming pool!'"

"But couldn't you achieve the same thing with consensus?"

"Absolutely not!" Sonia said. "Consensus doesn't work, either, at least not among women who are trying to be non-hierarchical because it always happens that some women's opinions are valued above others. It also implies that a decision must be made, and decision-making assumes linear time and the necessity of control. All this is sadomasochistic/sexual/patriarchal stuff. We can stay out of sadomasochism only by doing what we want."

Marian was unconvinced. "But there's a problem with making your own decisions and going for them. What if your having what you want interferes with someone else having what she wants?"

"My theory is that if we don't compromise, if we simply hold out, a third option will present itself. And not just a third, but a fourth, a fifth, a sixth, or more. Our current dichotomous world has come directly out of the male mind. Women's world, the real world, is just the opposite. In it, we don't just have two choices, our choices are infinite, if we just stay open to them."

"That happened at Cherry Tree Hill," Clare said, "the first women's community I lived in." She went on to tell the story.

It hadn't make sense for each of them to have her own separate post office box, so they decided to go in together on a large one. However, come to find out that the postmistress in the little town near them read all the mail. A couple of the women were afraid to have their redneck neighbors know their personal business, so they balked at the idea of having a box there. The only other choice seemed to be another post office twenty miles away in a much larger town.

Seven of the ten women were willing to get a box there, but the other three didn't care about their mail being read and wanted the convenience of the nearer post office. A possible solution would have been for those three women to have their box there and the others to have theirs in the larger town. But the fearful ones opposed this, afraid that the postmistress would discover their identity via the mail of the other three.

So they were at a stand-off.

While they were pondering what to do, one of the women, driving home one day from the larger town, noticed a local woman out near the road getting her mail from a rural mailbox. She stopped and asked if the women of Cherry Tree Hill could put up a mail-box next to hers. The woman gave permission, a box was purchased, installed, and the problem was solved, the solution suiting everyone far better than either of the first two alternatives.

"Talking about decision-making reminds me of something my Hopi friend, Chenoa, told me," Jean said. "She was about 104 when I met her ten years ago picking sage near my house. Without making a conscious decision, I started spending a few days a week with her. She was a highly respected herbalist and gave me a lot of information. Not just about herbs, but about everything.

"Anyhow, I'd been struggling with consensus in a group I belonged to, and was unhappy with the results. Remembering that Chenoa came from a matriarchal tribe, I asked her how the Hopi women made decisions."

Chenoa told her that every month when the moon fell, every woman who wanted to and was able came together in a specified gathering place. Jean asked what 'when the moon fell' meant and Chenoa told her it meant ovulation time—the moon being the ovum—and that all the women in the tribe menstruated and ovulated together. When Jean pointed out that there were old women who were menopausal and young girls who were prepubescent, Chenoa said that was not important. "All women who live together have the same cycle," she said, "like the moon and the sea and the stars."

Once gathered, Chenoa went on, the Hopi women held one another, stroked one another, hugged and kissed one another, licked one another all over, and rose together into the night sky.

"Licked!" Winnette flinched. "She's kidding, of course."

Jean disregarded her and went on to tell how she'd been writing all this down as Chenoa spoke, and when Chenoa stopped here, Jean waited a moment, not realizing she was finished. Finally, she said, "That sounds lovely, but how did you make decisions?"

Chenoa looked at her long and hard. Then she said again, "We held one another, stroked one another, hugged and kissed one another, licked one another all over, and rose as one into the night sky."

Jean still didn't understand but was too embarrassed to say so, knowing that as far as Chenoa was concerned, the question had been answered. It took her years to realize that what Chenoa had been trying to tell her was that the Hopi women didn't 'make decisions'. They didn't have to. Their coming together during a power time in their cycle—fully, deeply, as one—resolved everything.

"That's women's way," Sonia agreed, eyes shining. "We'll be like that together again."

"I'd love that," Lauren said, "though I'm not so sure about the licking."

Jean nodded. "I was pretty shocked, too, but I didn't say anything then. Months later, Chenoa told me that licking was a very powerful way to heal, and that through licking we could know each other so well that we could diagnose health problems before they even appeared. She also said it was a pure and honest way to be with one another."

"Well," Lauren said thoughtfully, "animals certainly seem to think so."

Pure and honest, Sonia thought to herself. *That's how I want to be with women.* Then she sighed, knowing what that meant for her this afternoon.

"Before we head back to camp," she said, "I have something I want to tell you. Something very personal and difficult. But I can't just jump into it—it's too hard. I'm going to have to ease in." She took a deep breath.

"I've been saying for years that the women's movement isn't about women's winning equal rights or equal pay or important corporate and government positions; all that does is prove that women can pass as men—and that's ridiculously easy. I'm convinced that what's going to make the only significant difference is women's changing how we feel about ourselves, returning to the knowledge and love of ourselves and one another that predates the advent of men.

"I say in every speech, every interview, every book, that our major torturer, the one that keeps us deepest in bondage, is not men's but our own implacable hatred of our Selves. And this shows up nowhere more strongly than with our bodies.

"Listening to the two of you talk," she indicated Jean and Dana, "about behavior that demonstrates that we either are or are not breaking free of this self-hatred, got me thinking."

She paused and looked around the circle. "This is the hard part. Maybe you noticed that I didn't take my shirt off at the springs this morning."

Jean felt tears sting her eyes. She knew what Sonia was going to say.

"Twenty-two years ago," Sonia's voice began to shake, "Vince insinuated that if I cared about him and our marriage, I'd have breast implants. I did it."

She could hear the group's soft intake of breath.

She went on, steadier now. "I did it because he was teaching at the university, surrounded by lovely young women—youth itself is beautiful to men—and I was afraid I'd lose him if I didn't become more sexually interesting."

"The bastard!" Barb exploded. "The lousy bastard!"

"Oh, Barb, I wish I could say he 'made' me do it, but the truth is that I didn't fight the idea. I went along easily because I knew what the consequences would be if I didn't. I don't mean that I knew consciously or that I thought it through and reached a rational decision. It's more like I knew in my bones what I had to do not to be left alone in an economically hostile world with three little kids."

Her eyes misted at the memory.

"It's been the nightmare of my life. I woke up from the surgery knowing I'd made a terrible mistake. Where my small, pretty, soft breasts had been sat misshapen, unyielding lumps—nothing like me, nothing like I'd been."

Struggling to keep from crying, her voice was harsh as she told them the next part.

"The doctors hadn't told me that no testing had been done and that for all they knew silicone could make me very ill or even kill me. They never told me I'd suffer from indescribable shame and guilt for the rest of my life."

The tears now spilled down her face and splashed off her chin.

"At first no one knew except Vince and my mother. If any of my friends wondered why I suddenly looked so different, none of them said anything. I dressed carefully to hide my new additions, loose tops with high necklines—I'd always dressed like that anyway to hide my flat bust."

"You know the rest of the story. Vince stayed around for another dozen years—a shame, really, because our marriage had essentially ended long before; I just hadn't noticed. He could have been having affairs and casual sex with other women all along for all I know. I was naive beyond belief in those days and under immense illusion about men: I thought they told us the truth.

"By the time Vince left, the church had excommunicated me and I was up to my ears in the women's movement. Every time I hugged anyone—and there's a lot of hugging in our movement, you know—I knew they'd wonder at the unnatural hardness of my breasts. I didn't let it keep me from hugging everybody anyway, but I suffered.

"Then I had my first lesbian relationship, and I had to tell her. It was hard, especially since she was a feminist. Having breast implants is about as politically incorrect as you can get as a feminist, so I fully expected her to be as repulsed and horrified by them as I was. But if she was, she didn't let on.

"By the time I got involved with Marcy, it was a little easier to talk about them. But I'm still full of shame—and fear of my sister feminists' judgment. Now I know I have to get to the place where I'm not only not ashamed of them or afraid of other women's attacks, but where I actually love them. It seems like a very long way off." The tears had stopped and dried now on her face as she looked unseeing at her hands.

Winnette broke the silence that followed this.

"Why don't you just have them out? Now that there are no men in your life, there's no reason to keep them."

"Holy shit, Winnette, why don't you just shut up!" Harper snapped, jumping to her feet and crossing over to where Sonia sat. Squatting in front of her, she took her hands in hers and spoke quietly.

"You're brave to have told us this. I've got a few demons gnawing at me that I can hardly bring myself to face, let alone tell another soul about. So I'm acquainted with shame and fear. Maybe we all have it, maybe it's women's condition. I know I'll talk about mine someday. And I think it will be easier because you did."

Sonia put her arms around Harper's shoulders and hugged her. They rocked quietly for a few moments, then Harper sat down next to her.

On the other side, Jean took Sonia's hand. "I'll bet the shame multiplied a thousand times when you became a feminist and realized philosophically what you'd done, and why."

"And a well-known feminist to boot," Lynne added for her. "The irony of that must have been pretty painful."

"You can say that again," Sonia agreed emphatically. "So I kept quiet and hoped no one would find out. I dreaded the possibility of having to undress in front of others. On the rare occasions—such as at the women's music festivals—when I couldn't avoid it, I showered late at night, when most of the women were at the concerts."

"Do you think they're really that obvious?" Jean asked. "I've worked with women who've had implants, and I know that the older ones tend to be harder, but I'm not sure I'd spot them unless I'd been forewarned."

"I'm hardly the person to ask," Sonia laughed. "Heaven knows I've never had a realistic image of them. They seem appalling to me."

"My dad wanted me to have implants," Dana confided. "He even offered the surgery to me as a gift for my thirtieth because he was so afraid I'd never get married with my flat little breasts. I almost did it."

"Why didn't you?" Sonia asked.

"I fell in love with Nancy and she thought it was crazy and barbaric. Easy for her to say: she had huge breasts. Actually, her doctor recommended breast reduction surgery to her. Such whoppers could cause all kinds of health problems, he told her, or words to that effect. She went to see a plastic surgeon. When he started to explain the procedure and she realized he was going to cut her open and take pieces of her body out, she walked out the door and started accepting her body the way it was. She was a big woman and used to shock the nell out of me when she'd walk into a room stark naked. Sometimes even when others were around." Dana smiled at the memory.

"Of course she never did it with men present, said she wasn't about to give them a free thrill. But she was more at ease with her body than any woman I've ever known. Knowing her helped me loosen up a lot, too."

"Without even knowing her I admire her attitude," Lauren said. "I know women with perfect bodies, I mean *perfect*, who are so ashamed of how they look that they won't let anyone see them naked. Afraid, I guess, that someone will notice the one tiny flaw they've inflated into a deformity. But your friend Nancy, now there was a woman who society said was not only not perfect but awful and disgusting. And she didn't care. I'd give a lot to feel that way."

"Harold wants me to have liposuction," Winnette confessed. "I'd always been pretty heavy in the thighs and hips, but after the kids were born I really puffed up. I've tried dieting but I lose it in the wrong places. He told me it's because the fat cells are so compacted there that nothing will get rid of them except liposuction. He says it's safe. He's been reading about it. But I don't know if I trust these guys."

"That's smart," Jean replied. "Liposuction is a dangerous procedure with a lot of ghastly side effects. It's surgery, major surgery, and that in itself is dangerous. I think you should suggest to Harold that he have liposuction on his beer belly. Then, if it works, you might consider it."

"And maybe penis implants while he's at it," Dana added slyly.

"Penis implants!" Harper whooped. "That's too perfect. Maybe they can implant with a substance that keeps it up all the time, give him a place to hang his hat and coat."

"That would at least be a humane use for it," Barb said caustically. "But actually, for Harold I think it would be best to start with brain implants."

Jean turned back to Sonia. "Winnette has a point, you know. You could have them removed."

"I've thought about it. In fact, I went back to consult with one of the two surgeons who did the implantation. He was very discouraging. He told me it would be virtually impossible because each one is attached to my chest wall by patches of something similar to velcro and that by now the muscles have grown over the patches. Removing them would take so much cutting it would be a massacre, he said.

"After he'd poked them a bit, he said mine were in fine shape and looked great and wondered why I was even thinking of the suicidal option of having them removed.

"So I'm trying to realize that they're with me 'til death do us part and that I have to accept them as they are, that they *are* me, and especially, that they're lovable and sweet." She pointed to her right breast. "This one hurts all the time—kind of an angry, burning sensation. I know now that this happens sometimes, but of course they didn't tell me that before.

"The other thing they didn't tell me was that they were going to cut nerves. Before the surgery I had such sensitive breasts that all Vince had to do was take one of my nipples in his mouth and I'd have an orgasm."

She shut her eyes in an effort not to start crying again. "Now I can't feel anything except a strange combination of pain and numbness. I've lost them, you see, and they were so lovely and alive."

Everyone was quiet a moment. Then Dana asked, "How are you going to love the ones you have now? I mean, I hate some of the original parts of my body and don't know how to begin liking them, let alone loving them."

Sonia shrugged and shook her head. "Ask me a year from now. Right now I'm only able to think of the very first steps."

"Such as?" Lauren asked.

"I realized today that I've been giving them minimal attention—a quick swipe with the washcloth in the shower and that's about it. So for starters I'm going to touch them a lot, stroke them, rub sweet-smelling oils and lotions into them. While I'm doing that I'm going to tell them I love them and am sorry for what I did. I'm going to explain that I didn't know better at the time, but that I do now and promise to take care of them and protect them and not let them be hurt again."

As she spoke she stroked her breasts gently, as one would a much-loved cat.

One by one the women stood and gathered their lunch dishes and scraps, filled with Sonia's story and the memory of stories of millions of women before them. In that moment, they all understood the absolute necessity of coming together to tell their stories, to tell one another the truth.

4

The tension in her body was almost unbearable. "Come on," she said to herself, "you can do it, come on. Do it. Come on. Now, now!" Then a pause—no more than a few seconds but it felt like an eternity—and the release came. She could hear the moans escape her lips, long, drawn-out relief. Partly physical, but mostly emotional relief. She had managed to do it again.

Marcy raised her head from between Sonia's legs. "You're too perfect for words." Sonia patted the bed next to her and Marcy slid up beside her.

Moonlight flowing over Sonia's bed silvered their naked bodies. In it they could see each other's faces as if it were dawn. As they smiled at each other, Sonia touched Marcy's face lightly with her fingertips. "Hello, Beauty," she whispered, reaching for her. They held and caressed each other.

"It's been too long," Marcy murmured, taking Sonia's hand and tracing the lines in it. "I've missed you, Soni."

Her lips against Marcy's cheek, she protested, "Oh, Marpoo, it was only four days. What did you do while I was gone?"

"Work, work, and more work. The warm weather gets people out exercising and hurting themselves. But I don't like being away from you so much, Soni. Now that you've finished the book, we can have more time together. I want to figure out how I can move here soon." She looked around the room in the moonlight. "You've turned this into a beautiful place. The work you've done on it is phenomenal. Remember how dark and cold and cramped and filthy it was? It's hard to believe it's the same place—so light and spacious and warm! The transformation's miraculous. I'm sorry I wasn't able to be more help, but I'll make up for it when I move here."

Relaxed and sleepy, Sonia let her own hand go where it wanted, lightly down Marcy's side to her thigh. *She's so smooth, so sleek, so shiny. Like a dolphin,* she thought dreamily. Suddenly she realized that Marcy's breath was quickening and her body moving ever so slightly. *No,* Sonia thought firmly. *No. I don't want this to turn into sex.* Rising onto her elbow, she looked down into Marcy's soft, brown eyes, bright with desire. Without thinking them first, she heard herself say the words she'd been waiting for.

"Marcy, this is the last time I can be with you like this."

"What?" Marcy sat up hastily beside her. "What do you mean?"

But for a moment Sonia was oblivious to her. She was riveted on what had just happened. *Well, I'll be damned,* she was thinking, wonderingly. *It finally happened. Just like that.*

She pulled the sheet around her. Aloud she said, "I mean I can't do it anymore, Marcy. This is the end of relationships for me, the end of sex. I knew it had to come or I couldn't do what I have to do, and that's live in women's world again."

Her eyes filled with tears. Again she was face to face with the terror of being forever alone, forever unloved, the terror that swept over her every time she challenged her conditioning about relationships. *It's all lies,* she reminded herself silently. *Hideous, damnable lies.*

"I suppose somewhere inside I'm rejoicing," she said aloud. "I must be. But sitting here, all I can feel is such an ache in my heart at saying goodbye to you that I can barely breathe." Tears streamed down her face.

Marcy ran her finger along the outline of her jaw. "Come on, Soni. You don't have to say goodbye to me. We're doing well, especially these last few months. Even with both of us so busy, we've been closer than ever, made love lots more often. Why spoil it?"

Sonia searched around on her bedside table for the box of tissues. Not finding it, she switched on the light and picked it up off the floor. With the box in her lap, she wiped her nose and face. Her eyes were beginning to swell from crying.

Looking tenderly at Marcy, she said, "I honestly believe that sex with you has been as good as sex can possibly be, and that's lucky for me—I'll tell you why in a minute. Anyway, I've been more eager for sex lately because I've had some checking out to do. Every time we've done it, I've checked my feelings: is this enough? Is this what I want? And every time—despite your wonderful lovemaking, Marcy—every time the answer is the same and very clear: no, this is not what I want. No, this is not it, not what I ache for. Every time, I realize again that I'm capable of something so much deeper, so much wider, so much *more* than can ever be possible with sex—under any circumstances, with anybody."

She wiped her nose again and looked sadly at Marcy. "I said I'm lucky that you're such a terrific lover. The reason is that otherwise I might be tempted to go on believing, as men's propaganda would have me do, that the reason sex isn't what I want it to be is because I have 'intimacy issues' or because I haven't found the right partner yet. In other words, that the fault's in me or in you, when the truth is that it's in the concept of women's sexuality itself."

She paused a moment, then feeling desolation overtaking her, she went on quickly to head it off.

"But my announcement tonight wasn't based on logic or thought; it didn't come from making a rational, conscious decision. It had nothing to do with my brain—so it should be trustworthy," she laughed a small, cheerless laugh.

"What happened is what has so often happened with me in the past. For some reason, everything I knew suddenly integrated deep within me somewhere and I am now a different woman than I was when we first lay down here."

Marcy thought that over a moment, then frowned. "Maybe so, Sonia. But I can't help but wonder if this has been brought on by the finishing of the book. You've talked about how it wouldn't have any power if you weren't living what you knew, and now you conveniently decide to break up with me before it's released."

"No, Marcy. I also said ideology couldn't force me to break up, that that wouldn't be living what I knew either, and that I'd just have to wait until it happened by itself. Well, it just happened. Inside somewhere I stripped away another layer of patriarchal muck and uncovered a woman who can't do relationships and sex. It's as simple as that—and as profound. But having said all this, I still have to admit that I hate the thought of your not loving me anymore. Crazy, isn't it?"

"You're darned right it is! Because I do love you."

"You're relationshipping me, but as for love . . . frankly, I don't think so. I think we haven't a clue yet about what love really is for women. And that's what I want to know, what love was before men came and caricatured it, what it was in women's world."

She pulled on her discarded T-shirt, and head bent, stared unseeing at the tissue box as she continued sadly.

"I had no idea I was going to tell you tonight that it was over. I'm as surprised as you are. But you're wrong that the book pushed me into doing it.

"Before I met you, I knew something was very wrong with relationships of all kinds. I'd already figured out that they keep women enslaved, and that I'd have to get out and keep out of them if I wanted to be free of patriarchy, if I wanted to save my soul. The whole time I've been in this relationship with you, I've known the day would come when I couldn't do it anymore." She looked up into Marcy's eyes. "It's come and I can't." She began to cry again.

Sonia's tears gratified Marcy. *She must care about me very much,* she thought, pleased. Looking at Sonia's wretched face, she didn't believe for a moment that it was really over, not if Sonia loved her this much.

"Look, let's talk about this some more," Marcy urged. "I know you're upset but, believe me, we can work it out."

"Listen to me!" Sonia almost shouted. "If I'm 'upset'—and you know I hate that word!—it's because you're not listening to me. I've been talking about this with you since the beginning and you keep saying you get it, you keep agreeing with me. And then you say these things and I know you either don't get it at all or that you don't believe me." A great tiredness washed over her, a recognition of the utter futility of trying to get Marcy to understand.

She continued more gently. "There's nothing more to talk about. I made my choice for freedom long ago, even before I was born. Nothing and nobody on earth can deflect me from it."

Marcy looked straight and hard into her tear-filled eyes, willing her to soften. When Sonia returned her gaze steadily, she sighed and got out of bed, pulling her rumpled T-shirt on as she went. She stooped to pick her underpants up off the floor, then started for the door, every second expecting Sonia to call her back—that's what the script said happened at this point. Reaching for the doorknob, she paused a second, waiting. When nothing happened, she turned and walked quickly back to the bed, and bent over to kiss the woman crying silently there.

"No, Marcy. Never again, you and I. Never." She turned her face away. "This is not a game I'm playing. This is the truth."

Marcy straightened up as if she'd been slapped, and abruptly left the room.

Sonia heard the door click shut. Reaching over to switch off the light, she lay back against the pillow in the moonlight, numb, not willing yet to face the ramifications of the shift inside her. Several minutes later she heard the sound of an engine starting up. Marcy was leaving. She waited until she could no longer hear the motor. Then, unable to remain anesthetized, she buried her face in her pillow and howled.

She felt as though her body were being ripped into pieces, each cell screaming with agony. Great sobs clutched at her chest, cramped her stomach, almost choked her. Gradually her wailing became the cry that is too deep for sound, her body heaving and shaking, her head pounding with pressure. On and on it went, as if the fear and sorrow had a life of their own, pummeling her, drowning her.

Finally, hiccoughing and gasping, she turned over and reached for the tissues.

It isn't so much about losing Marcy personally, she thought as she sat up and mopped her face, though surely there must be some of that . . . or at least it seems so at this moment.

What all this emotion was really about, she decided, was relinquishing forever what Marcy represented in her life—the promised happiness of a good relationship.

She knew that promise was a lie. She knew that what men called the truth was totally false for women. So their insistence that a relationship was the only way to have intimacy and joy was really code for 'relationships prevent intimacy and joy for women'.

And yet, she thought to herself, and yet . . . I know why we can't face our real experience with relationships, I know why we deny their inadequacy, their inherent and inevitable daily disappointments. In this sea of bitterness men call reality, there is one drop of honey, one particle of promised sweetness: love. Even though in actual experience the sweetness lasts a very short time—if we get even a taste of it—we go on pretending to ourselves and everyone else that it is still there because otherwise there is nothing—or so we've been led to believe, no reason to live.

She lay back down and pulled the blankets up to her chin, wishing for some way out of the pain. So I understand as well as anyone, she thought miserably, why we're so desperate to hold onto our belief in relationships. We think they're all we've got, the best there is.

But this can't be true! I know there's something else! For a moment she was comforted by the thought that maybe now, having renounced the basic tenet of patriarchy forever, she would be able to remember what it was. If she lived through this, that is. The thought sounded so piteous that she had to smile at her melodrama.

Needing desperately to go to the bathroom, she slipped out of bed on legs so shaky she wasn't sure she'd make it that far. It was with great relief that she sank down on the toilet. When she finished, she searched through the cabinet for the bottle of wild lettuce and valerian extract Jean had given her for insomnia. Ten drops in a little water, the instructions read. She measured out the ten drops and then decided to add another twenty. Just the thought of sleep gave her immense relief. For a few hours she would have a respite from the worst of it.

She made her way to her bed easily without artificial light. Sitting on its edge looking out the big window, she thought how she knew the stars were there even though they were very hard to see in the moonlight. Just as, even though she knew it was there, her joy at escape was hard to feel through her conditioned suffering. One night soon she'd look out and there they'd be, the stars, pulsing with energy, so close she could reach up and pick one out of the endless sky. One day soon she'd feel the euphoria of having wrenched men's fiercest lie out of her soul. But I'll never go to the stars with Marcy, she thought, and the pain threatened to swamp her again.

Turning her pillow over to the dry side, she crawled into bed and pulled the blankets up. How can this hurt so much, she wondered, when it's not real? I never could have gone to the stars with Marcy. Never. Our feet were cemented to the deck of the Ship. Now, without her, without sex, she comforted herself, I can finally find my heart's home.

With this, she slept.

o o o o o o

Jean met Marcy at the gate and stopped to talk a moment, surprised that she was leaving.

"Sonia's pretty tired and wants to sleep," Marcy equivocated, "and I've got a very early morning. So I decided to spend the night at my apartment. But I'll be back this weekend."

She changed the subject abruptly. "How do you like living here?"

"So far, so good," Jean replied. "I'll be glad when we finish the bulk of the work. Barb's been a great help, and with Clare here for another week, we should come close to finishing."

"Don't you miss your practice and your house?"

Jean shook her head. "Not at all. Which is strange, because I loved my work and my home and the marvelous mesa country of northern New Mexico. But I was ready to leave. Once I knew that, the rest was easy. There at the end the practice wasn't satisfying.

As soon as we fixed a patient's problem, she'd develop another. Fix that, and there was another. I realized that we weren't getting to the *root*. I didn't know what to do about it; I wanted to understand why women got sick. I knew it was about despair, but there was so much I didn't understand."

"Don't you think there's an environmental explanation? All this research coming out about pollutants, the hazards of the workplace and home. Cancer is on the increase, as is the so-called Chronic Fatigue Syndrome. I think there's a real connection."

"I'm sure there is, but I suspect something else, something that isn't so obvious or so cause-and-effectful, something enormous and deeply significant. The word 'despair' keeps coming to me. Take chronic fatigue or environmental illness, for instance. These force women to be inactive, give them an excuse for not doing the hundreds of futile things women have to do in life, including sex and child rearing. I don't mean that women are lazy. I mean that they simply can't bear to live and can't seem to die. These illnesses are a sort of limbo between. I don't blame women for getting sick. It's a mess out there and it isn't getting any better."

"Interesting theory," Marcy responded, tapping her fingers impatiently on the wheel. "In my line of work I don't see those problems. Athletes are totally focused on their careers, their injuries, their sport. There doesn't seem to be much room for anything else."

Jean nodded. "So we'll see you Saturday. Any idea what time?"

"Probably mid-afternoon. I'll call you Saturday morning and let you know."

Jean reached out and squeezed her hand, then waited until Marcy had pulled through the gate so she could lock it. As she approached the house she was surprised to see the lights off, the outside solar lights pretty much upstaged by the moonlight. She pulled her truck around to the back and realized that up on the third floor, Clare's bedroom light was on. Through the uncurtained window she could see the outlines of three sets of ears. The ears disappeared as she parked the truck. Seconds later, the owners of the ears were upon her, tails wagging frantically and tongues searching for bare skin. No matter how tired or down she might be, the welcome she received from these three always raised her spirits.

She stood as Clare called to her from the back door, asking if she needed any help. She told her no and took the two bags of groceries out of the back of the truck. She was grateful that Clare had waited for her at the door.

"Did you meet Marcy going out?" Clare asked, turning on the kitchen light.

"I talked to her briefly. Why?"

"I was surprised she left. She didn't get here until after six, and offered to take me into town with her in the morning. Barb has to take Ashley to the vet in the afternoon, and I was planning to meet her for a ride back."

"Marcy told me she had an early day and decided it would be easier to drive back now."

"She and Sonia went up as soon as Marcy arrived," Clare explained. "Marcy brought her composting toilet and they carried it to her room. She's going to install it on Saturday. I went to my room to read and the dogs followed. They were asleep on my bed when you pulled in."

"And disturbed them," Jean laughed. "Poor things. They get so little chance to rest—just all day long every day, rain or shine, winter or summer."

"Actually they had a real workout today. Sonia and I left this morning at eight and didn't get back until noon. Maggi and Tamale ran their tails off, especially when we got to the meadow. You should go up soon, Jean. It's full of wildflowers and humming-birds."

Jean nodded absently as she put on water for tea. "Maybe in the morning, if I can leave early enough. I've got a lot to do tomorrow."

Clare hugged her and went back to her room. Jean settled the dogs and sat down at the table with her tea. In a minute, Clare popped back into the kitchen, looking very pleased with herself. She had just called some friends and been invited to go with them to Carlsbad Caverns the next day. She was leaving early and wanted Jean and Sonia to know where she had gone when they got up. As they walked upstairs together, Jean wished her a wonderful time, and Clare continued up to her room. Jean paused a moment at Sonia's door and listened. All was quiet. She turned to her own door and pushed it open, switching on the blue overhead light.

This room pleased her immensely. It was large and spacious, with no walls or dividers to break up the expanse. She had chosen to have the old wood floor refinished by the woman who had refinished Sonia's floor. She was a real artisan, with an appreciation for good wood, and had done a wonderful job. The wood gleamed in the muted light.

There were two futon couches, one serving as her bed, the other easily folded out for guests. Each futon was covered in brightly colored fabric that complimented the rest of the room. Her hammock swing hung in the southwest corner. The rest of the room was arranged with carefully chosen chairs and cushions, giving the effect of warmth and comfort without sacrificing the feeling of spaciousness. Sonia had contributed various plants with the promise of taking care of them. Jean sighed with satisfaction. The room suited her.

She crossed to her desk and sifted through the pile of mail lying there. She needed to answer letters, needed to get caught up on her personal correspondence as well as the tons of mail Sonia and Wildfire Books received each week. But she was restless and wanted to talk with someone— Sonia, actually, but that was out of the question tonight. Briefly, she contemplated running up to Clare's room, but dismissed that idea.

Talk would have to wait until morning.

5

Jean finished her oatmeal and carried the bowl to the sink. Washing it, she was aware of how strange it seemed to be eating alone. They almost always had visitors, women who came to lend a hand or just to talk about their lives. Barb came down every day, and Marcy frequently stayed over.

But what was most unusual was Sonia's absence. Every morning she and Jean met in the kitchen and discussed the upcoming day, their ideas and plans. They usually walked the dogs, returning for a leisurely breakfast. She listened for Sonia's footsteps above her head. Nothing.

She checked the clock: 7:45. She wanted to go for a walk but she also wanted to talk to Sonia. She hesitated a moment, then took the stairs two at a time and stood with her ear against Sonia's door. No sound. She knocked lightly once, and when there was no response knocked again, louder. Hearing Sonia's muffled voice, she opened the door and went in.

Sonia's bed looked like a giant eggbeater had been turned loose on it.

"Sonia? I'm sorry if I woke you," seeing Sonia's flushed and swollen face, "but I just wanted to make sure you were okay before I left." She stood by the bed, unsure of what to do or say. "I'm okay, Jeannie. Dying of grief, but okay." Jean sat down on the bed and touched Sonia's forehead. It felt hot. Obviously something had happened last night, although she would never have known it from her encounter with Marcy. Keeping her hand on Sonia's forehead, she sat quietly, noting but not focusing on the tears that were beginning to run down the sides of Sonia's face.

"I was going to take the dogs up to the meadow," she said finally. "Clare told me about the wildflowers. And the humming-birds. But I'd rather be with you, if you'd like."

"No, there's nothing you can do about this. Take your walk. Right now I just want to escape into sleep as long as I can."

Jean stood up and straightened the blankets on the bed. "I've left some oatmeal on the stove if you want it. I should be back by eleven." She bent to kiss Sonia's cheek. It was feverish and she felt a pang of concern at the sunken face and obvious depression. "See you then."

She closed the door behind her, reluctant to leave but respecting Sonia's ability to take care of herself and ask for what she wanted. In the kitchen she grabbed a small backpack, filled two bottles with water, rummaged through the cabinet until she found a packet of graham crackers for the dogs, and headed out the back door. The dogs were already waiting, dancing with impatience in the driveway. As soon as the door swung shut behind her, they tore through the trees, up the path that led to the old forest service road.

It was a glorious spring morning, the sky deep New Mexican blue. Not a cloud up there, she thought, breathing deeply of the pine-scented air. The trees were alive with birds, and within a very short distance she identified western kingbirds, nuthatches, pine siskins, and a sharp-shinned hawk.

She crossed through the gate that marked the boundary of their property and entered the national forest. Here the climb began, not terribly steep but rocky enough to demand close attention. Far ahead, Tamale and Maggi were sniffing and on the lookout for something to chase. They had not forgotten the eight wild turkeys that Tamale had chased a few weeks before until her tongue was purple in her foamy muzzle.

As she walked, Jean thought about Sonia and Marcy. She could only make assumptions about what had transpired between them last night. Sonia had always known that her relationship with Marcy would be short-lived. Therefore, it made sense to Jean to assume that although the actual break-up might be painful, Sonia wouldn't suffer as much as those women who believe blindly that their relationships will never end.

So why does she look so devastated? Jean wondered. Why is she so torn apart? A second assumption slipped into place: something more must have happened, something unexpected. She could not even begin to imagine what that might be.

She thought about her own break-ups. Although she had experienced some pain, it was minimal compared with what so many women go through. For a long time she had thought she must be heartless. But lately she had come to realize that she had just had very few expectations. She never expected her relationships to work, never expected them to last, never even expected them to be pleasant while they lasted.

The 'squawk squawk' of stellar jays caught her attention and with a start, she realized she had reached the meadow.

It was breathtaking, as Clare had promised. Full of paintbrush, penstemon, vervain, lupine and columbine, all receiving the attention of the hundreds of euphoric hummingbirds. She settled herself on a rock to enjoy their intricate ballet. Mourning cloak and swallowtail butterflies flitted everywhere, and the flycatchers barely had to move from their perches for their morning snacks. A buzzing near her shoes made her aware that she was standing in the sweet yellow clover so adored by bees.

She could easily have spent the entire day there while the dogs roamed and explored, but she was eager to get back to Sonia, curious about what was distressing her, and eager to talk herself. Whistling for the dogs, she gave them each a drink and started back down.

The trip home went nearly twice as fast as the trip up, and, glancing at the clock when she came into the kitchen, she saw that it was only 10:45. The pan of oatmeal sat on the stove, now a congealed, lumpy mess. She stirred hot water into it and put it down for the dogs. Maggi and Nikki dived in, but Tamale, after a quick sniff, backed off. A street dog the first few years of her life, she had become a fussy eater. They hadn't served oatmeal at Lota Burger, her favorite hangout.

Jean couldn't wait any longer. Racing up the stairs, she knocked lightly on Sonia's door. No response. She pushed it open and stood listening, just inside. When she heard Sonia's even breathing, she quietly backed out.

Downstairs again with her restlessness, she wandered into the office and, noticing that the answering machine was blinking, pushed the 'messages' button. In a moment she wished she hadn't.

"Hello Sonia, you beautiful woman. This is Pauline Running Wolf. I'm going to be in Las Palomas in a few weeks, doing two circles. You've probably seen the flyers. Saturday's circle is for both men and women but Sunday's is for women only. I sure hope you'll come! Anyhow, I'm going to spend Monday with some women in Las Palomas and then I'd like to come to your place for a few days, visit with you, share my latest knowledge. I'd also like to offer you the gift of doing a sweat lodge. Although I can't help with the actual labor of building one, I'd be there to advise you on how to do it, and once it's constructed, to lead a sweat for you. So tell all your friends and let's get a big group together. Give me a call and we'll firm this up. Love you!"

Jean groaned aloud. Pauline Running Wolf was a controversial figure, to put it mildly. There were women who absolutely idolized her and women who couldn't stand her. She referred to herself as a Native American, old, differently-abled lesbian activist. But there was reason to believe that she was actually none of these.

Jean had met her once. During their conversation, she had told her what Chenoa had said about Native American rituals and vision quests: that they were absurd for women, that men needed these things because, unlike women, they were empty in and of themselves. They performed rituals and went on quests in an attempt to have what women innately had, be what women naturally were. "Men have to work at being spiritual, have to mimic women," she had quoted Chenoa as saying. "Women *are* spiritual. That's our definition. Rituals and formalized religions are as foreign to us as concrete."

Pauline had laughed at this, then become angry, claiming that women had lost track of their roots and it was only through Native American ritual and the leadership of women like herself that they could return to themselves. Jean had cringed at the word *leadership*. It sounded like male propaganda to her, and she had quickly got herself out of Pauline's reach.

She saved the message for Sonia to listen to and wandered back out to the kitchen, deciding she was hungry. As she was inventorying the contents of the refrigerator, Sonia came in, dressed, hair brushed, but with eyes still red and puffy and a face filled with shadows. Jean abandoned her scavenging and stood to hug her.

"I'm fixing myself some lunch," she said. "Or I'm thinking about it, if I can find something appealing. I'd be glad to resurrect something from the ruins for you, too."

Sonia attempted a smile. "That would be nice, Jeannie, although I'm not very hungry."

Jean pulled whole wheat bagels, soy jalapeno cheese, mustard, soy mayonnaise, tomatos and sprouts from the refrigerator and bumped the door shut with her hip. She sliced each bagel, arranged narrow slices of cheese on them, and popped them in the broiler. When the cheese was melted, she spread on the mayonnaise and mustard and topped them with tomatos and sprouts.

She carried the two plates to the table. "That's a lot of food," Sonia said, eyeing her plate doubtfully. "I really can't imagine eating it all."

Jean pointed to the three dogs forming a semi-circle around them. "Don't worry about it. It won't go to waste." She bit into her bagel. "Wish I'd had avocado to put on this." She rose and wrote 'avocado' on the grocery list.

"Tell me about your walk."

"It was okay. But I was so anxious to talk to you about what happened to me yesterday that I couldn't really relax and enjoy it."

"Fire away."

"I ran into Vivian in town."

Sonia's brow furrowed.

"I was in a relationship with her for a couple of years back in the mid-eighties," Jean explained. "When we broke up, she moved to St. Louis, so I was surprised to meet her in the Las Palomas co-op. Although we exchange birthday cards, I haven't seen her since she left. Anyway, we decided to have lunch and catch up on each other's lives."

Jean put her elbows on the table and leaned toward Sonia earnestly. "Soni, I couldn't believe my ears. I thought she was such a sensible woman, but she's got herself mixed up with this group that believes in the ascension of the body after death or something like that. Their guru is a man who offers classes on how to resurrect your body when you die. She's living in the mixed community he heads. All the men are deacons and the women do the washing, cleaning, and cooking during the day and I'd bet you anything they're required to spread their legs for the men at night.

"I was horrified by what she told me, but even worse by the realization that I'd lived with this woman for over two years and had had *no* idea she was interested in this kind of stuff. None. But then thinking back on it, I remembered that before we began seeing each other regularly she showed me a book some guy had written about spiritual journeys and I immediately launched into my usual discourse on how men have nothing to teach women. She mumbled something about how someone had given it to her and never mentioned it again. I can see now that this sort of thing always meant a lot to her. How could I not have known?"

"Because that's what we do in relationships, Jeannie. Vivian could tell you weren't just disinterested but downright antagonistic about such stuff, so she kept quiet. And probably read it in secret."

"She went to town once a week for a meditation group," Jean remembered. "I assumed it was a women's group, because there were several other women going at the time. I never asked her about it because I wasn't interested. She told me that she enjoyed the socializing afterwards." Jean shook her head, still not quite believing her discoveries.

"Another thing became very clear to me during lunch. Even though we haven't seen each other for six years, we almost immediately slipped back into our old relationship mode. My voice became different, my language changed, I was more authoritative—the way I had been when we were together. No matter how hard I tried to be my real self, I couldn't stop being the Jean she'd known. It was bizarre! I felt as though I had stepped out of my body and was watching a stranger. Only the stranger was me, a me that died six years ago and then resurrected the second I caught sight of her in the store.

"You've said all along that you didn't think we could be friends once we've had a relationship with someone, that the old patterns are permanent, and that we can't get out of them. You're absolutely right, Soni. I saw it in action yesterday. Before then, I would have sworn that after six years those patterns would have died, or at least diminished. But it was as though we'd never broken up, never stopped being with one another."

"How was Vivian's behavior?"

"The same as I remember it. She was always very dependent on me, waiting for me to make the first moves, all the decisions. She never did a thing without asking me first. And yet obviously she's done just fine for six years without me."

"Maybe she has someone else to be dependent on."

"That's possible. But she made the trip out here alone, made plans while she was here without asking anyone else, so it's clear to me that she's capable of taking care of herself. And yet, as soon as we got together, the old roles surfaced and there she was, leaning on me as if her life depended on it."

Sonia pushed her half-eaten bagel aside. "I've noticed it with my mother and brothers and sister. Also every time I've had to see Vince over the last twelve years. Now I'm in a position to check it out again." She was quiet a moment. "I broke up with Clare last night. And I'm a mass of mixed emotions: relieved, desolate, glad, wretched. Desolate and wretched are ridiculous because when I look at her, I realize that though I'm fond of her, there's no great feeling there, to say nothing of love. I don't think I ever really loved her. She was easy and pleasant to be with and we enjoyed sex. But not 'love'—you know what I think about that.

"Like you saw so clearly with Vivian yesterday, in relationships we're too busy building facades to even get to know each other," she went on disconsolately. "I've watched Marcy. She's like a chameleon, taking on whatever beliefs and interests the person she's with wants her to take on. Becoming who they need her to be. I'm not criticizing. This is just what she does, and she does it well, but it means that I've never really known her. So I can't understand why I want to crawl into a hole somewhere and die."

"A pretty normal reaction I'd say. Shoot, I'd expect a whole lot worse even."

"No, I know it's not 'normal', that it's a conditioned response. It kept me thinking in circles all night. All I could come up with is that I'm grieving because my heart's still holding the illusions my head's given up. That Marcy represents all relationship nonsense, so my innards are having a hard time relinquishing *her* because they can't bring themselves yet to relinquish *it*. They're mourning as if I've given up something genuinely and incredibly sweet, something necessary for my existence, and my head can't talk them out of it. Every cell in my body seems to have taken on the lie of relationship happiness. I don't know what it will take to get them to celebrate the end of their captivity."

She closed her eyes and rubbed her temples with her finger-tips. "I've got a sad heart—and a terrible headache."

Jean gently pried her hands away from her face and raised her to her feet. "Let's go up to your room. I'll rub your head and you can rest. I doubt that you've had much sleep. That could be part of the headache." Arms around each other, they started for the stairs.

Sonia nodded. "That and bawling my head off. I've been in bed since eight last night, but most of the time I've been doing this insane sniveling . . ." she groped for a tissue in her pocket as the tears poured down her face. "I hate that I'm reacting like this. I hate that men's lies have so much power over me. I hate it!"

"Hey, don't be so hard on yourself, okay? This is legitimately a rough time and even though you've tried to prepare yourself for it, you're right when you say that we really can't prepare ourselves to give up the only happiness patriarchy promises. And regardless of how much illusion there was in your relationship with Marcy, there was sweetness there."

"But there wasn't, Jean. It seems as if there was, but I know there couldn't have been. That's part of the damned illusion. There was no sweetness there. Someday I'll see that, but right now I don't seem to have a choice but to mourn for what it appeared to be."

"Okay, but it felt that way, and regardless of whether it was illusion or reality, it still hurts like hell." In her room now, Sonia flopped on the bed and closed her eyes.

Jean positioned herself on a cushion on the floor and began massaging Sonia's head, neck, and face. "Jeannie," she murmured, "that's the best thing there is, your hands on my head. I feel like it's trying to break apart and you're holding it together."

A few more minutes of rubbing and talking and Jean asked, "Do you think you can sleep now?"

"I don't think so," she answered, sitting up and twisting around to look at Jean. "I just remembered something important. I've told you that I couldn't see the dishonesty in my relationship with Marcy. Well, last night I did see some of it." She lay back down and Jean continued stroking her head.

"There have been clues all along that Marcy didn't really agree with me about relationships. But I wanted her to so much, I ignored them. What made me realize that we don't see eye to eye is that she's not taking this seriously."

"You mean she doesn't believe that it's over?"

"Oh, absolutely not. Not for a second. Or that I *can't* do relationships any longer, or even that I don't *want to.* I'm almost
totally sure that she thinks I'm just upping the sadomasochistic
ante between us—withdrawing from her to see if she'll come after
me, checking out whether she really does love me, really wants
me. I don't think she herself can even imagine not having
relationships in her life."

Here she paused to consider. "Since she can't imagine not
wanting them herself, I think she projects her feelings onto me
and believes I must want them, too; that my saying I don't is just
part of some interesting s/m game. I think that's all she can even
begin to fathom."

"But Marcy is very bright, Sonia. Surely, after years of hearing
you talk about this, she must have some idea."

"There's no doubt about her intelligence," Sonia agreed. "But
there's a couple of things going on here. One of them is that
regardless of what she understands, she's still playing relationship games and thinks I am, too. But the essential difference
between us is that we don't want the same things at all. I
passionately want out of mensworld. Marcy enjoys its challenges
and has learned to live in it comfortably."

They were silent for a minute, each thinking her own thoughts,
while Jean continued her massage.

Then Jean said, "I'm not totally able to understand how you feel
now because once I decided not to do relationships anymore, I
didn't care if it meant being alone for the rest of my life, untouched
and untouching. You may not care, Jean, but I do. I want to be
touched. I want to touch. And if the only way out of patriarchy, out
of sadomasochism, is not to touch or be touched, then, frankly, I
don't want to live any longer.

"The only thing that holds me to life right now is the belief that
somehow there's a way out of this nightmare, that there's a way
to have closeness that isn't sex, that isn't sadomasochism."

"Do you think I'm doing sex with you now, rubbing your head
like this?"

"No, of course not. But don't you see, this is only okay because
you have a document giving you official permission. A document
that proclaims that this is not sex. It says: Jean Tait has a license to
touch from The New England School of Massage Therapy."

Jean laughed at the combined truth and foolishness of this.
"That license may proclaim that this isn't sex, and for me that's
true, but I know that for men who do massage, it is sex. In class

I heard them talk about how they almost always had erections while they massaged, that apparently this was the natural reaction. You'd better believe I never let any of them touch me. The thought of it made me sick."

"The erection business doesn't surprise me at all," Sonia said. "All touch is sex to men—physical sex if they're touching someone of the gender they like to do it with, but sadomasochism regardless and always. Watch them shaking hands with each other—you never saw such jockeying for position. Men even have erections when they're holding their children.

"But though women don't usually have a sexual response to giving massages," she continued, "let's say you're giving me one and right in the middle of it I reach up and touch you. Warning sirens would go off inside you: 'oh, oh, watch out! Inappropriate behavior! Sex!' The only reason you can touch me and not have it be sex is because it's been labelled professional by the authority of the massage school.

"This means that because you personally don't have a physical sexual response, you think what you're doing isn't sex. Not like when I touch you in return. That's instantly recognizable as sex because I don't have a paper saying it isn't.

"What I'm trying to say is that massage may be legitimate sex, but it's still sex. Often physical sex, but also always sex by definition because it's hierarchical. You're on top," she said, holding one hand above the other, "literally and figuratively, and I'm down here. That's sex, that's control, that's sadomasochism.

"I want this," she held her hands level with each other, "and in mensystem this is impossible. Somebody is always on top, somebody on the bottom."

Jean shook her head. "That's too fatalistic for me. There has to be a way for us to be equals. It can't be all that hard."

"Hard!" Sonia snorted. "Try impossible! Or so close it doesn't make any difference. Jean, I've been trying for six long years to figure out how to get out of sadomasochism, even for a minute. I've become expert on recognizing where I am—top or bottom— in every human contact I make, and where others are, all the time. There have been moments when the gap narrowed so much that there was almost no space between. But even then, I could discern the hierarchy. Try as I might, I've never been able to have peerness with anyone, and scrutinize as I might, I've never witnessed it between or among others.

"And that's because peerness isn't possible in mensworld. Patriarchy *is* sadomasochism, is hierarchy. It's all we know, all we've known for thousands of years. All our thinking, all our behavior is saturated with it. At the moment, there's no other possibility in our individual brains or in the communal human mind.

"Nevertheless, I'm sure there's something else, another way of being, totally different from anything we can yet imagine. Or at least I've held onto this belief until now. Now, I feel such despair. If I'm right, if there is another way, women's way, I'll tell you it's the world's best-kept secret. You won't find it described or depicted in books, there are no songs that tell you about it, no greeting cards complete with instructions, no movies portraying it. So with no map, no recognition that it even exists, I lose hope sometimes that I can ever find it in myself."

She lay in silence for a moment. Jean could feel her sadness. It filled the room.

"I do know a thing or two about it, though," Sonia roused herself to say. "I know, for instance, that it has to do with the body, it has to do with touch. Beyond that . . . well, I have to trust that somehow I'll stumble upon it. Because, Jeannie—I know this sounds melodramatic but I'm going to say it anyway—that's what I was born to do."

Jean nodded. "Of course. Why not? You know, what you're saying about touch brings back some memories that I haven't known what to do with.

"It's about my Hopi friend, Chenoa. She was a toucher, and she touched all the time, either herself or the woman she was next to. At first I felt uneasy with it because I thought . . . well, I don't know if I actually thought it but I'm ashamed to say that sometimes I wondered if she was coming on to me. That sounds terrible, I know, but I felt it at times."

"No it doesn't," Sonia interrupted. "This is what I'm talking about. In the menstream, anything more than a little hug or peck on the cheek is sex. Men have appropriated essentially all touching and proclaimed it sex. And touch and sex *are* synonyms to them. But this didn't become true for women until long after men came."

"Anyhow," Jean took up her story, "I finally figured out that she wasn't thinking about sex at all. I remember one time we were sitting on the ground and she was holding my hand, running her fingers over it. We were actually talking about sex and she was saying that men and women were totally different. Then she took hold of the first finger on my hand and said to me, 'This finger. If someone told you that this finger was a sexual organ, like you've been told your clitoris is, then you'd learn to respond to it the same as you do when your clitoris is touched.' At the time, I thought she was crazy, but now I know she's right."

"Of course," Sonia agreed. "She was saying that with women, sexual response is learned, not inborn. I'm interested to know if you touched her a lot, too."

"No, not much. And that's strange for me because I'm usually the one doing the touching."

"Why do you think you didn't touch her when she was touching you so much?"

"I don't know," Jean answered slowly. "I had a lot of respect for her and somehow it seemed that if I touched her in return it would, well, cheapen it." She winced. "Listen to my language. Cheapen it. If that doesn't tell you what I think about sex! Anyway, I don't know how to explain it. I loved her a lot, Sonia. I really did love her. But I wasn't drawn to her like that . . . Oh, I don't know what I'm trying to say." She gave an embarrassed little laugh.

"You're saying you weren't sexually attracted to her."

"I wasn't, that's true. Even though I thought of it, I just wasn't interested in her in that way. I felt that if I touched her when she was touching me it would give her the message that I wanted sex."

Sonia nodded. "And since that would have been deliberately deceptive, it would have 'cheapened' your wonderful bond."

"Yes, but I think it's also because sex is somehow intrinsically cheapening."

"I agree. By its very nature it smallens and narrows and contracts and finally destroys."

"Well, even though I didn't want it, it certainly came between Chenoa and me, lots more than I like to remember."

"Surprise, surprise! You were responding to male sex conditioning—that all touch, except for a few very specific exceptions, is sex. You were operating on the universal male model, the sex mind, and apparently she wasn't. I'd give anything to know how she escaped it."

"I have no idea. I didn't understand any of this at the time." She paused to shift to a more comfortable position.

"One day we were in her house," she went on. "It was a cold day and we were sitting in front of the fire, her in the chair and me at her feet. While we talked, she rubbed my shoulders. After she'd been doing this for a long time, I began to feel uneasy, and asked her if she was getting tired. She told me that if she got tired, she'd stop, that she wasn't doing it for me, she was doing it for herself."

It was as if lightning struck the bed.

"Jean! That's it!" Sonia shrieked, flipping over onto her stomach. The sunken, defeated look was gone and her eyes blazed into Jean's as she shouted again, "That's it! We've got it! Oh, I can't believe it! I'm going to die of joy!" Laughing and crying, she was nearly unintelligible.

At Jean's puzzled look, she reached down in a frenzy of excitement and began stroking Jean's leg. "Look at this—I'm touching your leg, right? I'm touching it *only* because at this moment I really want to, because it feels good to my hand, because right now it satisfies *me*. I have no ulterior motive, nothing that I'm trying surreptitiously to convey. It's not a way to communicate that I find you attractive and therefore hope you'll start thinking of going to bed with me. I'm not using it to say that I'd like you to touch me, too. I'm not trying to make you feel better. It isn't a means to some end. It's exactly, openly, genuinely only what it seems to be—me wanting to enjoy the touch at this moment.

"Because you can absolutely trust that, you can simply relax and feel it—no strings attached, no obligation to respond in any way. I don't want anything from you. I have no expectations, no hopes, nothing. There is total honesty, the touch is exactly what it seems to be. I am touching you for my own, immediate, pleasure."

Her face full of light, her body electrified, she leapt off the bed, opened her arms to the room, and shouted joyously, "Jean! Patriarchy is over! Do you realize what we've done? We've found the escape route out of sadomasochism! We're free!"

She swooped down upon Jean, wrapping her arms around her and pulling her up to dance dizzyingly around and around the room, happy tears streaming down her face.

"Sonia," Jean gasped, as they fell laughing onto the bed. "Sonia, please, let's keep talking about this. I'm afraid it's going to slither away. It's so slippery in my mind."

Sonia, between gasps and giggles, managed to say that her face was going to split open if she didn't stop grinning. "My cheek muscles ache, my jaw aches, the tendons in my neck ache," she moaned in delight. "I'm euphoric, I'm jubilant, I'm ecstatic, I'm . . . . what else am I?"

"Elated, enraptured, transported!"

"Yeah, you thesaurus you, not to mention totally blissed out!" She leapt off the bed again and began pacing around the room. "I'm so beside myself with happiness, I can't sit still." She spun and faced the bed where Jean was sitting, hugging her knees and beaming. "It's so simple, Jeannie! It's so incredibly simple! And it's been right in front of my face all this time. I've been looking past it, through it, around it."

She walked over to the window and looked out, but she didn't see the view; her eyes were filled with visions.

"Women are gift givers, and we always have been—unconditionality is our essence. Male essence is exchange and totally conditional: 'I'll give you this *if* you'll give me that.' Touching for a male is always conditional: 'I'll stay with you tonight if you let me have sex with you. I'll kiss you if you'll get excited. I'll stroke your breasts if you get even more excited. I'll caress your vulva if you'll let me fuck you. I'll marry you if you promise to be mine'. And so on, ad nauseum. Every touch has its price. It's never free."

"Exactly," Jean agreed, ideas flooding her mind. "Exchange is sadomasochistic because it's a form of control. Control in turn is dependent upon expectations: if we're good lovers, we expect her to have a relationship with us, we expect her to try to please us, we expect her to care about the relationship above all else."

Sonia nodded vigorously. "You've got it. The reason peerness is possible with gift-giving is that there are no expectations, therefore no control, therefore no sadomasochism. We do nothing to get a response, nothing for anyone else, everything for ourselves—purely, cleanly, simply for our own delight.

"In men's world, if we refuse to barter, if we don't make rafts of tacit promises, we won't ever get touched. But in women's world, touch is a gift, it's free. We touch because we genuinely want to at that very moment, not because it will buy us anything from another person then or anywhere down the line." She paused, thinking hard, face shining.

Sitting crosslegged with her back to the headboard, Jean leaned forward, animated, her hands shaping her thoughts as she spoke. "So means-to-ends and conditionality are the same thing. We could say that the definition of sex is using touch as a means to some end other than the touch itself. It's no wonder so many of us are dissatisfied with sex—it exploits touch . . ."

Sonia pounced on the word. "That's it!" she whooped. "Touch in men's world is exploitive and dishonest. So of course we can't find real intimacy through it. Intimacy requires integrity, and there is no integrity in sex because it's conditional, because it's never honest, because it means everything *but* itself."

She sat down on the bed. Looking directly into Jean's eyes, she said intently, "To me the most wonderful part of what we're figuring out right now is that it means I don't have to go the rest of my life untouched and untouching. There's a way, Jean. There's a way that has nothing whatever to do with sex, that's as different from it as it's possible to be. And it's simple, simple, simple!"

Jean's eyes glowed back into hers. "It's touching with honesty. It's touching as a gift, no strings attached, either in the moment or later on. It's touching for the touch itself and absolutely nothing else. You can always know that if I touch you it's because I want that actual touch. Period. I require no response from you, no payment or promise, nothing in return. It's exactly what it seems to be and nothing else. You know, Sonia, I feel like I'm coming home to myself at last."

Sonia nodded. "Me too. I've longed for this all my life. All my lives."

She stood and took up her pacing again, thinking as she moved. "I think that touch is how women communicated with one another before men came, and is still the only way we can really know other women. Something tells me that before men, we didn't have what we now think of as language. Most feminists recognize that the language is male and separates women from one another. But we have thought it was because of its structure, because of its vocabulary, its incredible limitations.

"So we've talked about inventing a women's language. But I've just realized that all verbal language is brain-born and male, that, in touch, we already have a full, totally expressive women's language, one that matches both our immensity and our intensity. That's why men took touch away from us and cordoned it off as taboo. As long as we couldn't communicate with one another— and we can really communicate with other women only in the way women communicate, through unconditional touch—we could never remember ourselves, never return to our power, never be free."

Jean jumped in. "It's clear that language is satisfactory for men. They're so limited, so definable, so eminently expressible. But I've never known a woman who didn't despair at the profound incapacity of words to capture her feelings and her ultimate meaning."

At the window, standing still for a moment, Sonia went on exploring the implications of the afternoon's discovery. "Archaic women, wild women, women before the advent of men, were totally integrated. Their bodies hadn't been separated from their minds and spirits, as ours have, so they had to have expressed themselves with their whole Selves: bodies, minds, spirits, all at once, all the time. I was right that what I was looking for so desperately had to do with the body, that women's power resided somehow in our despised bodies, not as reproductive units, not as sexers, but as something else altogether. As something we'd totally lost knowledge of."

With a radiant face, she exulted, "We're going to find it again, Jean. Our intuition is going to lead us back to femaleness. Shoot, woman, we're on the track of the greatest treasure in the world!"

Jean leapt up and put her arms around her. "All I know is that I keep feeling I've come home. As if I've been wandering a long time, lost, trying first one thing, then another, to see if it stirred a memory, if it was what I'd once been, what I'd lost. It never was, of course. But now at last something feels familiar. Something is reverberating inside me, shouting yes, yes, yes . . ."

She was cut off by the ringing of the alarm clock. Startled, they looked at each other, then giggled.

"Now if that isn't a sign, nothing ever was," Sonia grinned, turning the clock off. "I don't know about you, but I'm absolutely ravenous!"

"Voracious!"

"Insatiable!"

"Avid!"

"Wild!"

"Ready for anything!"

Hand in hand, they ran laughing down the stairs.

6

In the kitchen, Sonia began heating the dogs' food while Jean rummaged in the refrigerator for dinner ideas. "We've got some leftover Spanish rice," she called to Sonia. "I could heat that up with some black beans . . . oh damn! Hellsy damn, Sonia!" She stood quickly, hitting her head on the freezer compartment handle. "Tell me it isn't Wednesday, please tell me it isn't!"

"Okay. It isn't Wednesday," Sonia complied amiably.

"Murder Maids meets here tonight! They'll be here in an hour. How did I forget? What can I fix?"

"Hey, relax. You'll think of something."

Jean shot Sonia a murderous look. Sonia did not cook. Ever. Unless you counted peanut butter sandwiches, and that was no help now. Jean was a gourmet vegan cook and loved any opportunity to prepare food, especially for a crowd, so this mattered to her.

"I know. I'll fix artichoke spaghetti. We've got that homemade sauce in the root cellar, and the French bread I bought yesterday. And a salad. I'll make a salad." Calm now and satisfied, she set to work. "Fart-beetles," she muttered. "I forgot to get bubbly water. Soni, would you call Barb and ask her to bring a few bottles? We only have two left."

Jean, Sonia, Barb, Dana, Harper, and Lauren called themselves the Murder Maids because they were all avid mystery readers. They met twice a month at one of their homes for dinner and a mystery. The mysteries discussed, however, were not always of the murder variety.

"Barb's on her way over," Sonia announced, breezing back into the kitchen. "She'll trade the water for use of our copy machine and FAX. I'm going to run out and water the flowers before everyone gets here." Jean nodded distractedly and went on with her salad preparations. "And don't set the table!" Sonia hollered from the deck. "I'll do it when I get back."

The salad was done by the time Barb and Ashley arrived. After kissing Jean, Barb tucked the bottles of water in the freezer to cool quickly. The dogs and pig, who adored one another, were beside themselves with joy at this reunion. They immediately began a game of chase that threatened the integrity of the decor. Laughing in spite of herself at the absurdity of the big red pig chasing the three small dogs, Jean yelled at them to settle down.

Ashley was one of the most affectionate animals she had ever known. This often posed a problem. At five hundred pounds and growing, her affection could be deadly. There was no way she could understand why the dogs were allowed in laps and she was not. An intelligent animal, she was scrupulously clean and housebroken. Once over the shock of her genre and size, Jean and Sonia had loved having her visit.

Jean remembered an incident early on in their friendship with Barb. She and Ashley had come for dinner, and while the women ate, the dogs and pig lay together on the kitchen floor, making one anothers' acquaintance. But in mid-meal, the dogs heard something outside and tore through their dog door. Ashley followed. Or at least tried to. The dog door was made for 'beagle-sized and smaller'. She managed to get her head and neck through, and that was it. Hopelessly stuck, she cried for help. It took all three women a couple of hours to free her. They did it finally by removing the door from its hinges and leading Ashley *and* door outside to the hose. Barb sprayed her with water while Sonia squirted liquid soap around her neck and Jean coaxed and pulled from the rear. The next day Jean went to town and bought a dog door designed for Great Danes and St. Bernards, and now Ashley came and went safely.

Jean's musings were interrupted by hysterical barking and grunting, and a few minutes later the other three Murder Maids came through the kitchen door. Before they could even say hello, they had to pet and adore the four animals that were jumping on them and nuzzling their feet.

"Smells good in here," Dana said, stumbling over Ashley on her way to Jean. Giving the pig a dismissive pat on the jowls, she began taking plates down off the open shelves and setting them on the table. They were all familiar with one anothers' homes and at ease in them.

Harper joined Dana, taking flatware out of the drawer and glasses off the shelf.

Lauren came up behind Jean at the stove and hugged her. They were very fond of each other and openly demonstrative in spite of the fact that Harper was a jealous lover. But Harper, who normally kept a sharp eye on Lauren, didn't think that Sonia and Jean were a threat to their relationship. Years of living with Lauren had made her realize that Lauren was a woman who needed to touch. Since Harper did not particularly enjoy being touched—except in bed—she was glad Lauren had a safe outlet.

Fifteen minutes later they were all seated around the table. As they ate, they talked about what had happened in their lives since they were last together. Jean remembered the phone message from Pauline Running Wolf and hurried to the office. She disconnected the machine and brought it back to the kitchen.

"What's that for?" Barb asked, eyeing the machine as she wound spaghetti around her fork. "A group recording? You want us to chant something profound in unison?"

Jean hit the PLAY button and let them listen to the message. As soon as Sonia heard 'Pauline Running Wolf', she grimaced and shook her head.

"Never heard of her," Harper commented, sopping up spaghetti sauce with her bread. When the message ended, she said, "Howling Coyote sounds a little overdone, if you want my opinion. I'm leery of inexhaustibly cheery types like her."

"I attended a workshop she gave at one of the festivals," Dana offered. "Frankly, I didn't like her. She was bossy and condescending. A lot of women claim she isn't Native American at all but just uses that to get ahead. She looks Irish to me."

"I don't know her," Lauren said, "But her tone puts me off. That, and her assumption that, *of course* you'll want to build a sweat lodge for her."

Barb nodded emphatically. "I agree. And I automatically distrust women who include men in their ritual circles."

"*I* automatically distrust women who have ritual circles," Sonia said, helping herself to more spaghetti. "And particularly those who put their faith in Native American tradition, as if there were any more femaleness in it than in any other of men's institutions."

"Chenoa would have agreed with you there," Jean said. "She was disgusted by what she called the 'silly romanticism about Indians'. Since she had lived before the real influx of Christian missionaries into Hopi civilization, she knew as well as any living person how female her culture had been before that, and how drastically it had been changed by men. She often told me there was nothing female left in any Indian tradition, that it had all been hopelessly male-ified."

Sonia shook her head. "Native American stuff is as patriarchal as Catholicism and Protestantism, as cultish as Children of the Lamb of God, Scientology, or Mormonism. Totally antithetical to and destructive of freedom and femaleness."

"And look who's falling for it hardest, as usual: women," Dana said. "Not just New Age women but those who call themselves feminists and lesbian feminists. It makes me want to whack their heads together and yell, 'Wake up, you fools! They're tricking you again!'"

"Well, I'll call Running Wolf and tell her we aren't interested," Jean said, picking up the message machine. "I won't bother with reasons. As Nancy Reagan suggested, I'll just say no."

"What if she wants to know why?" Lauren asked.

"There are no rules that say you have to give reasons," Dana put in. "There's real power in not explaining yourself."

"A point I wish I could remember," Sonia said wistfully. "I'm always feeling that I have to explain. And though you may not have noticed, my explanations all too often turn into dramatic monologues."

"You don't say!" Barb commented wryly. "A quiet, mousy little thing like you?"

Returning to the subject, Lauren said, "Obviously, women are looking for alternatives to the traditional religious model. You have to admit that worshipping the sun or the moon or a tree is better than worshipping some male god."

"No, it isn't," Jean disagreed. "It's exactly the same thing. Worship is hierarchical is sadomasochism is patriarchy regardless of who or what's on the pedestal. I feel the same way about goddess worship. Goddess worship didn't exist before patriarchy. It couldn't, because before mensgame began, worship wasn't even a concept. Women never worshipped anything, we never placed anything higher than ourselves, we couldn't even think in those terms. We were, each of us and all together, everything that existed. We were the trees and the sun and the moon . . . "

"Native Americans say the sun is male," Lauren interjected. "And the moon female; the sky male and the earth female."

Over the moans around the table, Jean said, "The sexism of that is so blatant it almost knocks you over—the male being whatever is bigger, brighter, more, and 'above'. The truth, of course, is that everything creative and life-giving and life-enhancing in any way is actually female. Maleness destroys, its *essence* is destruction."

"But the sun can destroy," Harper pointed out.

"Only if she's out of balance with everything around her," Sonia countered. "In her natural state she can't and doesn't."

Dana turned to Lauren. "I think you're right, though, that women are longing and looking for something different, something that triggers their archaic memories. But they aren't going to find it in any ritual or existing tradition, regardless of what the focus or who's doing it. They've forgotten to look in the only important place, and that's right here," she thumped her chest. "We've got it all right here. We don't have to look outside ourselves for any of it."

"Chenoa would like that," Jean recalled. "I said something to her once about how I'd been looking for a teacher for a long time.

She became as close to angry as I ever saw her. 'Anything you have to *learn*,' she told me, 'isn't necessary or good for you.' She said that women already know everything, that we *are* knowledge. All we need to do is believe this and set about remembering.

"She said men have to have schools because they don't know anything of themselves, have nothing inside to remember. Everything has to come from somewhere outside them."

Harper frowned. "I find that hard to accept. I mean, I had to go to school in order to understand economics and finance, in order to do the work I do. I don't think that's in me."

"Exactly," Sonia said. "It isn't in you because economics is a male structure for controlling exchange. Women are genuinely, at our cores, not exchangers. We're gift givers. Jean and I were just talking about that today. We don't, on our own and without men's conditioning, do exchange. In order to do it, we have to be taught and retaught and overtaught. And more than that, we have to be terrorized out of our minds about scarcity. Even then we don't generally do it well."

"I take issue with that," Harper bristled. "I'm considered tops in my field and have been for years. I'm as good as any man out there."

An awkward silence followed this. Then Dana said quietly, "I'm not sure that's something I'd want to brag about."

"It pays the bills," Harper shot back.

"So does my photography," Dana responded. "But it occurred to me this morning while I was videotaping the birth of my friend Ginny's baby, that cameras are definitely not natural. Why do we have to have records? Why do we value memories? Is it because our lives at this very moment are so unsatisfying and empty?

"The camera lies, anyhow," she went on. "Maybe not in storing factual data, like how a birth looks, but deeply, in portraying the mood, the feeling, the emotional significance of the event. I suddenly knew that Ginny and everyone else would have had had very different feelings and responses if the camera hadn't been in that room. This happens all the time. Even when people feel like dying, they 'smile for the camera'.

"This doesn't mean I'm going to stop doing it. As you say, Harper, it pays the bills. But I'm trying to see it for what it is: evidence of another patriarchally-induced deficiency in us."

"Women can be made to believe in anything, even the military," Barb said. "I know I did. Towards the end of my service there, I could see it for what it was and hated it, which is why I opted for early retirement. But that realization was a long time coming."

She was thoughtful for a moment, smoothing her unruly grey cap of curls. "The thing that scares me is that I really thought the military was necessary and was proud to be part of it. I was even angry at the women under me who came in for other reasons. You know, because it was a good career choice, or for educational opportunities, or to escape bad home situations, or as a good place to find a husband—or a wife! I couldn't forgive them for having no patriotism, for not giving a damn about their country and not being proud to be serving it.

"It took a lot to get me to realize that it was just the Good Ole Boys Club all over again. Like you say everything is, Sonia, including all existing cultures and traditions. Put simply, my best friend was dishonorably discharged for lesbianism and it ruined her life. Having to watch that close up, not being able to detach as I had all the other times, having to face her suicide . . . ."

No one said anything for a moment, understanding all that Barb had left unspoken.

Jean broke the silence. "The military is a good example of a relationship. In relationships we blind ourselves to what's really going on because we couldn't do them otherwise. We're willing to do anything for them, especially early on, and we're oblivious to all their shortcomings, even to the fact that they may be and probably are devastating to our Selves."

I need to tell them about Marcy, Sonia thought, and for a moment felt guilty that in the incredible arousal of that afternoon with Jean, she had totally forgotten her.

"Speaking of relationships," she began carefully, "I ended mine with Marcy last night."

Everyone waited expectantly.

"I told her I couldn't do it anymore."

Noticing the looks of concern around the table, she hurried on before anyone could commiserate.

"I cried my heart out from eight last night until noon today. Then Jean and I sat down and talked for the entire afternoon and we figured out . . . I don't know how to describe it. But I've swung from feeling like death warmed over to raging ecstasy."

"Then I don't know whether to say I'm sorry or congratulations," Harper laughed. "Sounds as though both are appropriate."

"Just the congratulations, thanks," Sonia told her. "This break-up with Marcy is something I had to do eventually and I'm glad it's over. So I can't understand why I've been so miserable about it. I really thought I was going to die of sadness during the night."

"Nothing in a relationship is real except the pain," Dana said. "I've come so close to ending my life over a broken relationship it isn't funny."

"I think we can all identify with that," Harper said.

Barb nodded. "It's clearer and clearer to me why you refer to them as sadomasochistic, Sonia. I have to admit that at first I thought you were overstating a bit there."

"Me? Overstate? Come on, Barb, let's get real here."

The burst of laughter that followed this cleared the heaviness from the air.

"Seriously, though," Dana said, "what's going to happen with Marcy? Last time I saw her she was planning to move here."

Sonia shrugged. "I can't imagine she'll even consider it now, but we didn't talk about that."

As everyone began to clear the table, an explosive POP from the other side of the room froze them for a moment.

"Oh, shit!" Barb shouted, racing for the refrigerator and whipping open the freezer door.

"Damn, oh, damn, oh Barb, you stupid idiot! I hate myself, I hate myself! Stupid idiot, you stupid idiot!"

"What's going on, Barb?" Sonia came up behind her. The others crowded around them.

"I put the bubbly water in the freezer before dinner because I didn't think it was cold enough. I forgot it—and look!"

She made a sweeping gesture with her hand. "Glass and water all over the damn place! I'm really sorry. Damn, I'm so sick of myself, I can't stand me anymore! I'm a disgusting low-life fuck-up, a total *jerkinpoop!*"

Lauren raised her eyebrows. "Jerkinpoop?"

Dana collapsed on the counter, howling with laughter. "Jerkinpoop!" she gasped.

"You know, jerkinpoop!" Jean roared.

"Oh, jerkinpoop! Isn't that the rank just below Corporal? Or is it just below General?"

"It *is* General," Harper whooped, holding her sides.

"It isn't funny," Barb protested, bursting into tears. "I hate that I do these old-lady things. How can you stand me?"

Barb's tears had a sobering effect on the group.

"What I can't stand is the way you beat yourself up whenever you do something you think's wrong," Sonia said.

"Yeah, what's with this self-flagellation?" Dana demanded. "You just told Sonia you were recognizing sadomasochism. What do you think this is?"

"It isn't the same," Barb hiccoughed. "I really *am* an incompetent slob."

Harper was becoming impatient. "No. You're Ms. Perfect who can't tolerate mistakes. How do you think that makes me feel? What'll happen if I slip up? Will you ship me straight off to boot camp?"

"Don't be silly," Barb sniffled.

Jean pounced. "Right! You wouldn't do to any of us what you've just done to yourself."

"Of course not. This is different."

"I know what you mean," Lauren said. "I punish myself when I screw up, too, and I also feel justified. But when others do it, I can see how totally irrational and self-hating it is, and it upsets me. And I know from my own experience that it just makes me hate myself more. So maybe instead of doing sadomasochism with myself when I screw up, I'll say something nice to myself."

"Like what?"

"Oh, I don't know. Maybe something like, 'Oh, Lauren, you're so adorable!'"

Even Barb laughed at this.

"Hey, that's not a bad idea," Sonia said. "We all come down hard on ourselves. When we make mistakes, it would do us good to tell ourselves, 'You're so adorable!' instead of flogging ourselves to death."

Talking about this experiment, everyone pitched in to clean up the kitchen. Dana scraped the leftover spaghetti into the three dog dishes and the extra pan kept around for Ashley. A moment later, Jean moaned when the dogs looked up at her with orange faces. "Yeah, they're cute, you rat!" She flipped the dishtowel at Dana, who was laughing at them. "But *you* don't have to bathe them!"

Sonia lifted the whistling tea kettle off the burner and poured water into the teapot, while Dana set the tray with mugs. Then they retired to the library to discuss their latest mystery find, *Death Under the Deck*.

○ ○ ○ ○ ○ ○

"I'm so aroused by our discovery this afternoon I feel like I'm flying," Sonia turned to Jean, after waving goodbye to the last woman and locking the kitchen door. "But I know the minute I start thinking about Marcy, I'm going to crash to the ground like an avalanche. Guess the message is clear: think about what gives pleasure, not pain."

"You know you have to deal with what hurts, too, Sonia. Not just because it's part of getting over it but because you're the way you are." Jean yawned and stretched. "I'm exhilarated and exhausted. And so to sleep. Perchance to dream."

"Aye, there's the rub," Sonia agreed solemnly.

They turned out the downstairs lights and headed for the stairs. "I'm worn out, too," Sonia said, "but my mind is churning with ideas. Who knows how docile it will be about going to sleep? I'll remind it that we have the rest of the world to think and talk about this."

"Starting tomorrow, I hope," Jean added. "Let's take a walk in the morning."

"Sounds good to me." They stopped at Sonia's door. "I really enjoyed myself tonight. This group gets better and better with time, especially Lauren. There's something so dear about her."

They put their arms around each other for a long, gentle, rocking hug. "Good night, sweet woman." Sonia kissed Jean's forehead.

In her own room, Jean undressed quickly and left her clothes where they dropped. Her bed welcomed her, enveloping her in its softness and warmth, and again she was grateful that she had invested in a feather topper for her mattress. It was pure heaven to sink into.

But despite her fatigue and the bed's comfort, she couldn't sleep. Something beyond extraordinary had happened that afternoon, something that surpassed anything she had words for. Her body knew it, too; and though she was tired to the bone, she had to fight the urge to leap out of bed and cavort around the room.

Tossing restlessly, she tried to bring her turbulent thoughts into some kind of order, and found herself thinking about Elise, the woman with whom she had had the longest friendship of her life. She knew at once why Elise had come into her mind: when they were together, she touched Elise a lot.

It had started out with massage. Then as their friendship deepened and they spent more time together, there had been a fair amount of casual touching. They would be talking on the couch, for instance, with Elise's head in her lap and her rubbing Elise's back, shoulders and neck. She had never felt anything sexual during these times, and yet there had always been something vaguely disquieting about them.

As she thought about it now, she realized that what had disturbed her was that she had always wanted *more* than they had. She had wanted to connect with Elise in a way that wasn't possible through their limited touching. But in her mind, and surely in Elise's, going any farther would have meant sex. And neither of them had wanted that. But she remembered feeling an urgency she couldn't define and therefore had no idea how to resolve. Actually, she had believed it couldn't be resolved, that since they didn't want sex, she had to accept what they had and be happy with it.

She remembered a night she had given Elise a backrub to help her go to sleep. She had often done that; it was a way for them to be together and unwind at the same time. After rubbing her back for a half hour or so, she had begun to feel an ache, a longing so deep it was almost unbearable. In that moment, she had desperately wanted something more. At the time, she thought it must be sex she wanted—what else was there?—and had been disgusted with herself.

And that's the key, she thought. In mensworld there is nothing else. She and Elise had been treading on thin ice in their friendship—touching like that when they weren't a couple, when they hadn't made a decision to be sexual.

Della popped into her mind. She and Della had been friends for years, and though they had decided early on not to be sexual, the tension was always there, just under the surface. She frequently stayed with Della and slept with her in the same bed. After they had talked themselves out, she would rub Della's back until they both fell asleep.

She remembered one night in particular. She was half asleep, rubbing away, when her hand inadvertently brushed Della's breast. Instantly, she was wide awake and alert. Had Della felt it? Did she think she was coming on to her, trying to excite her? Did she want her to continue or was she upset by the touch? She had been glad they had stuck to their agreement not to be sexual. But, she thought, I must talk to Sonia about this, because it seems that by defining our relationship as nonsexual, Della and I were actually still in our male minds, accepting sex as the standard and defining everything in relation to it. So no matter what we thought, we were actually being sexual. She shook her head, trying to free her mind of the cobwebs.

She wished Chenoa were here. She had told Sonia about the night Chenoa's friend, Anita, had lost her daughter in a motorcycle accident and was about to die of it. How Chenoa had held her and rocked her and restored her by giving her her breast to suck. How she, Jean, had confessed to Chenoa that she had been horrified at first, thinking as she watched, "This is sex!"

Chenoa had been quiet for a long time then, Jean remembered, making designs in the sun-baked earth with a stick. Finally she had looked up and demanded, pointing to her breast, "Who said this is sex?"

She had unbuttoned her blouse and opened it to reveal her two brown, sagging breasts. "This is my body, Jean. This is me. This is not sex. My body is just me." She moved her hand to her vulva, cupping it through the cloth of her long skirt. "And who said this is sex? This is where I empty my body of wastes, this is where my bloods flow, this is where babies come if I choose to have them. This is my place of power. Nothing about my body is sexual. Men have lied about it, they have reduced and cheapened it by defining it as they are, not as I am."

Tears burned her eyes as she remembered Chenoa's words. She understood. Finally she understood. She flung the blankets aside and went to the window. It was so dark that the stars pulsing across unfathomable miles of black space were like signals between women throughout the galaxy. In that moment, she understood power. Without words for any of it, not in her head but in her soul, in her blood as it pounded through her veins, she knew, she remembered. It was about women's bodies, their whole bodies, not bits and pieces, not the parts men had claimed for their own to do sex with.

Sonia had said it years ago: "Women don't have to reclaim our power. It never left us, never changed. It can't. It isn't a separate entity, it isn't something we *have*. Power is what we *are*, through and through."

In touching one another, Jean thought, we mingle our power, pool it, creating more, and ever more. Power is the positive, generative stuff of life, the joy, the goodness, the sweetness, the passion, as well as the ability to be every living thing, and all living things at once. To be the universe, encompassing all experience.

Breathing deeply, she leaned against the window ledge, her eyes on the stars as they moved to make way for the moon. She wasn't watching the sky, she *was* the sky—infinite, infinite. She was the dark shapes of the ponderosas. She was the owl swinging effortlessly into a shaft of wind that swept it spiraling into the darkness. She was the tangy smell of the great slumbering mountains. Tears coursed unnoticed down her face.

She was everything, everywhere.

7

Sonia touched the 'full document' option and sat back while her laserjet printed out the new last chapter. Her eyes felt grainy and her head ached. She hadn't slept a second last night. Instead of getting into bed, she had gone straight to her computer and begun to put down the ideas that had flown so wildly about that afternoon.

It will have to do, she thought as she read it through. She hadn't captured their exhilaration, their absolute ecstatic frenzy. But at least she wasn't going to leave her readers completely baffled and hopeless as she had feared.

She read it over several times, watching for errors, checking for clarity and smoothness. Then she rose from her desk, looked at the clock, and went to Jean's door. She listened a moment, then quietly turned the knob. Seeing the bed neatly made up and no Jean, she ran quickly downstairs looking for her. The absence of the dogs told her Jean was out walking.

"Nuts," she muttered to herself. She wanted Jean to read the chapter, but she couldn't wait. She needed to get it to Federal Express as quickly as possible. She dashed back upstairs, threw cold water on her face, ran a brush through her hair, and dashed back down. In the kitchen she grabbed a handful of almonds and a banana and tore out the door.

Driving with the carefully-wrapped disk lying on the seat beside her, she felt better than she had for a long time. No longer a hypocrite, she thought to herself—relationshipping like mad while talking and writing about not doing it. I'm living what I know. Now the book has integrity. Now it can go out into the world with power. She sighed with pleasure, slipped Suzanne Ciani's "Velocity of Love" into the tape deck, and settled comfortably into the drive.

She knew that somewhere beneath her feeling of well-being, however, an enormous and fearful sorrow lurked: leaving Marcy, saying good-bye to relationships forever—there was still a universe of pain to get through. But not today, she promised herself. Today I'm going to rejoice. A new world of freedom and love opened before me yesterday afternoon, women's world began to flower in me. So celebration today, mourning tomorrow.

When she got home, she checked the refrigerator and found a container of already cooked oatmeal, resplendent with sweet, plump raisins. She hummed a tune as she heated it—Grieg's Triumphal March—and grinned as she recognized it. Triumphant. That's how I feel, she thought. Triumphant over my thousands of years of brainwashing to renounce my true essence and be, instead, a slave to sex.

She carried her oatmeal and soy milk to the table and ate absentmindedly, her thoughts far away. After their jubilant greeting when she came home—as if she'd been gone for a month instead of a few hours—the three dogs lay stretched out on the floor, uninterested in her late breakfast. They must have had their bickies. Briefly she wondered where Jean was.

It was all falling into place, she thought as she ate. Now that she knew the next step, she was impatient to take it. It was time to experiment, to try out the theory. There was so much she needed to know—was *avid* to know—and experience told her that living a concept was the only way to find out all it had to tell her.

But she couldn't do this experiment alone, although Jean had told her yesterday that Chenoa had constantly touched herself. I can do that, I can touch myself and I will, she thought, but it's touching other women in this new unconditional way that I have to try. She glanced at the clock and wondered again where Jean might be. She was eager to start.

Her thoughts were interrupted by Lauren's knocking lightly on the kitchen door. Motioning her to come in, Sonia noticed that she had a couple of books in her hand.

"I forgot to leave these last night," Lauren said apologetically. "They're the books we're going to discuss at our next meeting." Laying them on the table, she looked at Sonia's cereal. "Hope I'm not interrupting your breakfast."

"I rewrote the last chapter of the book during the night and had to get it to Federal Express immediately. So I zipped in and zipped back and am only now snatching time for sustenance." Slapping the back of her hand against her forehead, she rolled her eyes to heaven, and sighed, "The sacrifices we artists make."

"Poor baby," Lauren said, hugging her. Sonia put her arms around Lauren's waist and leaned into her soft body. "I've got water on for tea," she said, as Lauren released her. She went to the shelves that held their dishes. "Which mug?"

"Anything's fine," Lauren answered, kneeling to pet the dogs. As she prepared the tea, Sonia watched her. At five-foot-three, Lauren was almost her height, but that's where their resemblance ended. Lauren's round face and body contrasted with Sonia's leanness, and although she was three years younger than Sonia, her pretty wavy hair showed much more gray.

Sonia realized that she knew little about Lauren except that she had come to New Mexico with Harper from Boston, that she had earned her living there as a graphologist, that she had been widowed for almost six years, and that she had two grown sons. Aside from that, the only bit of knowledge Sonia had of her was that she and Harper lived now in a small but well-to-do community in the country, twenty minutes from Wildfire, and that she still did an occasional handwriting analysis. Sonia was about to ask her to analyze hers when Jean came in the door.

"There you are," Sonia greeted her with a hug and kiss.

"There *you* are," Jean echoed, returning them. "When I came back from my walk, I saw that your car was gone. I couldn't imagine where you might be at that hour, except maybe the hardware store."

"Try Fed Ex. I rewrote the last chapter and sent it off to the typesetter. Then I called the printer and arranged with them to hold the presses for another week. I wanted you to read it, but I couldn't wait, so it's flapping merrily across the continent as we speak."

"That's good news!" Jean hugged her again before she went to greet Lauren. Lauren, busy on the floor with the dogs, leaned back into Jean's embrace.

"The dogs adore you," Jean said.

"I think they adore anyone who'll rub their tummies and play with them. They're sweet, though. They make me wish I had a dog."

"Why don't you get one?" Sonia asked, bringing over the tea and mugs.

"Harper doesn't like animals, and would never allow one in the house. You know our house." Lauren made a little moue. "All that beige shag carpeting and white furniture. She brought me an outdoor cat a few months ago but she's so wild I can barely get near her. I just feed her and watch her flee from me in terror."

"Well, you're welcome here anytime you need a dog fix," Jean said, joining Sonia at the table. "They love to go for walks and would go with you just as gleefully as they go with us."

"I'd like that. We don't have many places to walk in our neighborhood. Too many houses and private property signs all over the place. It's wonderful up here, with all the trees and privacy. I'd enjoy coming over and walking with them." As if on cue, Nikki, who was lying in Lauren's arms, stretched up and began swiping at her face with her tongue.

"She can't hold her licker," Jean laughed, as Lauren tried unsuccessfully to dodge the persistant little tongue. "Want your tea down there?"

Lauren struggled to her feet and sat down at the table next to Sonia.

"How's the graphology business?" Sonia asked, laying her hand on Lauren's knee.

"Sporadic. I have a few clients now and then, mostly referrals but some from the ad in *Metaphysical Mind*. Not nearly as many as I had in Boston, though."

"I wonder why that is. You'd think the opposite would be true in this Land of Alternatives," Jean mused.

"That's part of the problem. There're so many things to choose from here. In Boston, graphology was much more of a novelty. Here, it's just lumped in with the rest of them." She played with her teabag. "And besides, Harper doesn't really want me to do it."

"Why?" Sonia asked, surprised.

"Well, it's sort of like it's beneath her. She's a serious business-woman, you know, and views all this stuff as unprofessional hocus-pocus. I mean, she doesn't come right out and say so, but I think she's embarrassed by my work and is afraid people will think I'm a quack."

"A quack?"

"Well, a charlatan, then. A fraud."

"I've known a few of those, and it's clear to me that you're not one." Jean was adamant. "Did I ever tell you that my mother was a graphologist? She was very gifted—and so are you."

Lauren blushed. "My teacher back in Boston keeps telling me I should advertise as a Career Counselor, because that's one of the things you can do with handwriting analysis. It would bring me clients regularly, and she thinks I'd be successful at it."

"Are you going to?"

Lauren squirmed. "Harper sure hopes not. She says it's a waste of time and effort when she makes more than enough money for both of us."

She caught Sonia's disapproving look. "It's not what you think, Sonia. There isn't much of a market here, and even if there was, the commute takes almost two hours."

"Harper makes that commute every day. Why couldn't you ride in together? Or you could work part-time. It sounds like you're not doing what you really want to do."

Lauren sighed. "I guess I'll never learn to run my own life entirely." At their questioning looks, she explained. "I feel like I've never really had a chance. When I graduated from high school, I wanted to get a summer job, but Daddy pooh-poohed the idea. The family didn't need my earnings, he said. But I insisted, so he humored me and made a job for me in his business.

"When I was nineteen Daddy called me and Mom into the study and told us that Lawrence, a man I'd been dating for a few months, wanted to marry me. Lawrence worked for Daddy and Daddy liked him, so he approved of the marriage. Mom went over to the desk, pulled out a legal pad, and started making up the guest list. No one bothered to ask me how I felt, if I even wanted to get married, and particularly if I wanted to marry Lawrence."

"But you did it."

"Sure. What else could I do? It wasn't like now. In those days it was very hard for a young woman to make it on her own; so unusual and so hard that it simply never entered my mind.

"Mine's the classic story of women who married in the fifties. Lawrence wouldn't hear of my working outside the home, even when the boys were away at college. I knew how to clean and cook and shop, but I had no idea how our finances operated, didn't know how to keep a checkbook, didn't understand about insurance or furnace repairs or any of that. Lawrence did it all.

"So when he was killed, I went to pieces. I had no idea how to even begin making decisions, and suddenly I was faced with thousands of them. When the boys came home, I turned it all over to them. They took care of the funeral, everything. I told them I couldn't live alone, that they'd have to help me. Then I saw the look that passed between them, and knew they didn't want me. They had their own lives. I honestly didn't know what to do.

"It was right at that time that I met Harper. A friend gave me her name as someone who could help me straighten out my finances. The idea was that she would show me, but I was still such a wreck that she just took it all over. Told me to leave it to her, and I did. I still don't know how to balance a checkbook." She sipped her tea thoughtfully.

Thinking that that was the most she had ever heard Lauren say at one time, Sonia said, "I'm glad you came over this morning. Every other time I've been with you, there've been others around and it's hard to find a quiet moment when we can just get to know each other."

"I'm not much of a talker," Lauren admitted. "Not articulate like the rest of you. And I'm slow. By the time I think of something to say, the subject has changed. You're all quick and witty and clever with words. I feel so outclassed. As you may have noticed, sometimes it's easier to let Harper talk for me."

"I have noticed," Jean said. "And I've always wished you'd say what you think, or what you want, so I could get to know you."

Lauren shook her head slowly. "Most of the time I don't know what I think or want. Especially when I'm with the five of you. My mind sort of fogs over. I hear what you're saying, but it's as though I'm far away. I just can't keep up." She smeared the wet circle on the table left by her tea mug.

Sonia put her arm around Lauren's shoulders and gave her a little squeeze. "Well, then I hope we have plenty of opportunities to be with you alone like this."

"Ditto," Jean agreed.

Lauren glanced at them, reddened, and looked down at the table. "I'd like that," she said quietly.

o o o o o o

"Okay, I'm ready for our experiment—at least as ready as I'll ever be," Jean announced as Sonia came back into the kitchen after walking Lauren to her car.

"Same here. Your room or mine? Or somewhere else? My bed isn't made yet."

"Horrors! Then we certainly can't go the*re*," Jean teased, grabbing Sonia's hands. "Being perfect, I made my bed, so my room is safe."

As they moved to go, the dogs crowded up the stairs ahead of them. "If you'd rather, I can keep the dogs out," Jean offered.

Sonia grinned. "I think they're old enough for this."

By the time they reached Jean's room, the dogs were comfortably settled on the bed, surveying their dogmain from the full windows at the foot of it. From there they had an unobstructed view of the back of the property before it disappeared over the hill and into the trees.

Sonia sat on the bed and began stroking Nikki. Looking down at her, she marvelled at how tiny she was, how fluffy and undoglike, with her shiny black nose and watermelon-seed eyes, her funny tail that curled up over her body. A Bichon Frise, Jean had told her, the name as foreign to Sonia as the dog herself. Still, she loved the little creature, loved her ways, her guileless heart, her intelligence and sensitivity. Picking Nik up and putting her in her lap, she continued to stroke her soft fur.

She looked up at Jean. "A perfect example of unconditional touch going on here," she said. "I love petting this dog. I could do it for hours and hours, almost indefinitely. Because it's safe. Because I know she doesn't think I'm coming on to her. Because I know she isn't going to try to do sex with me. There's infinite freedom in that knowledge."

Jean sat down next to her. "I know a woman—Ethyl—she's in her late eighties. She lived alone for a long time. Although I don't know her well, I never thought she was happy because she's very unpleasant and difficult, often rude to the point of cruelty.

"Anyhow, one day she called me in a panic. She had just inherited her sister's ten-year-old dog, Atta Boy, and was frantic to get rid of him. She insisted that I find him a home instantly.

"I asked around and put up a notice on the bulletin board in the office, but no one was interested in an old dog. When I told Ethyl this, she decided to take him to the pound. I felt bad about it, but I'd done all I could.

"A few months later I ran into her walking a dog. You guessed it: Atta Boy! Remembering her desperation to get rid of him, I was astonished. Turns out that before she'd been able to get him to the pound she got hooked on petting him. She became crazy about him. The whole time we talked she stroked that dog's head and ears. Atta Boy changed her life."

"Some living creature she could touch freely," Sonia said. "That was one of the things I loved most about my babies. They were marvelous to hold and touch, with their satiny skin and firm little muscles. It was pure pleasure for me. I think a lot of women have babies just so they can touch as much as they want without having to do sex. Animals and children are the only place in mensworld where we can do that."

She lifted Nikki out of her lap and set her on the bed, then kicked off her shoes. She stood and started to unbutton her jeans, paused, and headed for the bathroom. Jean took off her shoes and lay down on the bed, her face buried in Maggi's fur.

Holding up her unbuttoned jeans with both hands, Sonia came back into the room, talking as if she'd never been gone. "I want to remember what it was like before maleness struck the world. I want to touch again the way we touched then. I'm so glad you want the same thing."

She pulled off her jeans.

Seeing this, Jean rolled over on her back and wriggled out of her shorts. "I remember your saying once in a speech that a feminist life is an experimental life."

Tossing her shorts on a chair, "Part of me is scared that this experiment will turn out to be more of the usual relationship garbage. But another part of me knows it won't. Like you, I want to figure out how I was before mensmachine deformed me, I want to remember and live that way again, every second of my life. So I have to start somewhere. I'm afraid to try, but I'm more afraid of the consequences of not trying."

"I know," Sonia nodded. "It's like I always say, the most dangerous risk is not to risk at all."

She stood at the side of the bed in her T-shirt and underpants, waiting for Jean's next move. Out of the corner of her eye, Jean noticed that Sonia was standing there looking at her. *What's she doing?* she thought. *Is she just going to stand there? Should we take all our clothes off, or what?* Nervously, she reached over and played with Maggi's ears.

What's going on? Sonia wondered. *Is she just going to lie there playing with the dog? Should we take all our clothes off, or what?* As if on cue, Jean's eyes met hers and she burst out laughing. Smiling, Sonia sat down beside her. "Well, here we are with all our education."

"A lot of good that's going to do us. I feel kind of silly. I really don't know what to do."

"Me either. In the sex dance we had a goal, a destination, we more or less knew the steps, and we had excitation to grease the way. Not having any of that makes this feel pretty awkward. I guess there's nothing to do but start and see what happens."

Jean crawled over to the other side of the bed and lay on her side, facing Sonia. They moved closer and reached out tentatively to touch each other. Stroking shoulders, necks, and backs first, becoming more daring and touching buttocks, legs, and stomachs. Both realizing with surprise that they felt fine—tension gone, no more anxiety or embarrassment. It seemed absurd to them that they had been so uncertain with each other at first.

After twenty minutes or so, Jean noticed that Sonia had fallen asleep, but she kept on rubbing her back, loving the feel of smooth skin against her hand. This was for her, her own gift to herself. She stroked and petted, basking in the tremendous relief she felt. Not one twinge of sexual excitation had come between them.

Not surprisingly, Chenoa came to her mind. She remembered one of their walks up in the mountains near the pueblo. They were on their way to the raspberry meadow. As always, they held hands as they walked.

The plump, sun-ripened berries were better than any she had ever tasted. Removing their bandanas from around their necks, they folded them to hold their berries, and settled under some ponderosas to eat and talk.

"No woman fears touch," Chenoa said. "She fears what it might mean: sex, abuse, pain, manipulation. But touch itself is pure, it's what women are. Women can never really fear what we are."

"But I do fear what I am," Jean said. "Sometimes when I'm in deep despair, I catch a glimpse of a part of myself, a dark place, that terrifies me."

"That isn't you. That's what you've been told is you, what you've been told is *in* you. But what you *are* is what all women are: pure love.

"Men consider darkness evil because they are evil. They fear it because, like themselves, they can't see into it, can't understand it. So they project their evil upon it. They can't see or understand women, either, so they identify them with darkness and evil.

"But women are not evil. It is not part of our essence. We may behave in ways that are evil, but this is not inherent in us. We have learned evil at men's feet. Maleness is evil, which is why everything men touch sours, everything they do destroys.

"My husband drank. And when he drank he beat me. And when he wasn't drunk anymore, he forced me to have sex with him, because this was his love, his way of showing me. He could not understand why I so often refused him. He could not understand why I flinched when he raised his hand. I never knew if that hand was going to caress me or break my bones. Love cannot hurt, cannot cause pain. What men do causes pain and suffering. So we know that what men call love, is not.

"Men cannot love. Only women can. But we cannot if we go on believing in men's love. We have to remember our ways again. We have to go back to that time when we touched for the joy of it and nothing else, when we touched because that was what we were.

"When women are fully ourselves again, we will never have anything to fear from one another."

8

The smell of fresh-baked bread filled the house. Squeezing the water out of her hair, Jean stepped out of the shower, reached for her towel, and sniffed appreciatively. Clare had promised cinnamon-pecan bread for breakfast. Jean wondered if Barb and Lauren had arrived yet.

Bringing an old friend named Lise with her, Clare had pulled in just after supper the night before. She and Lise had met twenty years before at Goldcreek Ranch, a mixed-gender community. It had been love at first sight, and they had moved into the same cabin.

But the community's feeling about their relationship had become increasingly tense until, after a year, they had decided they would be more comfortable with women like themselves and moved to Hawthorn Hill, a women's community.

And they had been happier there—for awhile. But eight months later, Lise had informed Clare that she no longer wanted to be sexually exclusive, that she wanted to have an 'open relationship'. Clare had refused and, never believing that Lise would leave her, had insisted that she choose between her and non-monogamy. She had lost the gamble and had been nearly destroyed by Lise's leaving.

It had hit the community hard, too, because the woman Lise had fallen for was already in a relationship with another woman there. Everyone had taken sides, feelings had run high, and resolution had seemed remote. Clare had endured almost four months of agony before she left Hawthorn Hill for San Francisco. But change of place hadn't changed her pain, and two weeks after her arrival, she had tried to kill herself. She had ended up in a psychiatric ward with bandages on her wrists. Though her therapist had helped her express her anger, her depression had hung on.

Then Lise had called her. She had broken up with the other woman and wanted Clare back. She didn't tell Clare that the other woman had fallen for someone else in the community. Clare had been overjoyed to have her back, and for awhile things went smoothly. They both had well-paying jobs, a nice apartment, and a full social life. But neither of them was city-bred, and the longing for the country had finally become so strong that they had joined with a group of women and purchased an old farmhouse and eighty acres near the California-Arizona border. They had named it The Virginia House.

It didn't last. The conditions were harsh, water was scarce, the farmhouse in deplorable condition. While they were there, though, Lise bought a small travel trailer and parked it in a remote area of the ranch, claiming that she needed privacy and quiet. That roughly translated into her having an affair with another woman while maintaining her relationship with Clare.

Clare suffered in silence, hopeful that this too would pass. When the Virginia House women, exhausted and discouraged, decided to give up the ranch and move back to the Bay Area, Lise told Clare she wanted to live with both her and her new lover. Clare refused, and headed east, where she found No Man's Land, a well-established women's community.

"I didn't try to stay in touch with Lise," Clare told them as they ate their bread. "She tracked me down and wrote me dozens of letters. I ignored them."

"Until . . . ?" Sonia said.

"Until she showed up at No Man's one day. We went for a walk and had a long talk. I told her I wasn't interested in getting involved with her again, and she agreed, which surprised me." Clare grinned at Lise. "We decided to be friends, and that's where we are today."

"Is No Man's Land the community that makes the salad dressing?" Barb asked Clare.

"It is," Lise answered for her, cutting another slice of bread. "I think it's the best you can buy."

"If you can find it," Barb complained. "I wish regular grocery stores carried it, not just health food stores."

Sonia looked at Barb in horror. "Surely you don't still shop at sickness food stores!"

Barb punched her affectionately. "Smart ass."

"I forgot why you left No Man's Land," Lauren said to Clare.

Lise snorted. "Because all they do there is work! I've never seen anything like it. Eleven women trying to do the work of two dozen. It's insane."

Sonia was noticing with curiosity the pattern of Clare and Lise's relationship, still intact.

"Well, that was part of it," Clare said. "But there was the sex stuff and my wanting to be celibate. I'd lived there for almost five years, anyhow—longer than anyone else. I was ready for a change."

She looked at Sonia. "I know your community disbanded some time ago. But I'm so excited by your philosophy that I keep hoping you'll try again."

Before Sonia could respond, Lauren said, very decisively, "I've never had any desire to live in community. I like privacy too much. Having so little of it was the hardest part of being a mother. The only thing that made it bearable was that the kids finally went to school and I got back some of my life."

Lise raised her eyebrows. "Then I'm surprised you're not living alone."

"I just mean I wouldn't be comfortable living with a large group."

"I wouldn't either," Barb offered. "Thirty years in the military was enough for me, always having to fight for a space at the sink. Although it would be nice to have a sweetie with me now, I don't mind living alone."

Jean chuckled and pointed at Ashley asleep at Barb's feet, "If you can call *that* living alone,"

"She doesn't fight me for the sink," Barb laughed. "That's all I ask."

"Where do you live now?" Jean asked Lise.

"The Bay Area. I'm through with women's communities. They aren't stable enough for me, at least the ones I'm familiar with. Women come and go so fast you never get a chance to know them before they're gone. Weekly group meetings, emergency meetings, internecine politics—I'm too old for that."

She looked around her. "I'd love to live in a place like this, though. For me, the ideal would be to have my own house on a few acres of land with all my friends in their own houses on their own few acres around me."

"That's what our friend Dana talks about," Barb said. "Her dream is for us all to live next door to each other, like you say. We enjoy one anothers' company, and right now we're too scattered to get enough of it."

"Well, Clare, you seem to be the only one who's not ready to give up the idea of community," Jean teased their visitor gently.

"Always did say she never had much sense," Lise joked. "She's been bitten by the community bug and that's that. She's going to keep looking until she finds Shangrila."

So that's the pattern they established twenty years ago, and are still caught in, Sonia thought, looking at Lise. *Lise is in charge; she answers for Clare. Funny how Jean and I were just talking about this sort of thing. I wonder if she's noticed their little relationship dance.*

Jean had. Although Clare had only come into their lives three weeks ago, she had never seen Clare act so passive and uncertain as she was that night. She knew she was witnessing another aspect of Clare's personality, one that emerged only in Lise's presence. In this relationship, Clare was obviously much better acquainted with 'bottom' than 'top'.

Jean shivered slightly, experiencing an eerie sense of deja vu. Remembering their conversation about her chance meeting with Vivian, she wondered if Sonia was picking up on it. That meeting with Vivian was serving to make these dynamics very clear to her. It was true: once a relationship, always a relationship. But she would have bet her life that Lise and Clare weren't even remotely aware of what they were doing, that they honestly thought they had left their relationship behind and were 'just friends'.

"Okay, Lise, so what if I do want to live in community," Clare said defensively. "At least I know a whole lot more than I did when I so naively set out to find Utopia twenty years ago. Specifically, that I have to find women who want what I want, who are in the same place emotionally and philosophically."

"But you thought you'd found that before," Lise argued. "You were dead certain that No Man's Land was it. And now look. You're burned out, discouraged, frustrated. Why don't you try living alone for awhile? What are you so scared of?"

"Look, I know how to be alone, and I'm not afraid of it. And I know that living in community is no guarantee that I'll be free of loneliness. The worst times of my life occurred when I was surrounded by women. I'm not just looking for numbers, I'm looking for quality. That's why I'm here. I like what Sonia and Jean are doing and I'm drawn to it. Whether they'll feel the same about

me is another thing, but this is the closest I've found to being what
I'm looking for."

Lise shrugged. "You've always set yourself up for disappointment, Clare. I suppose it was too much to hope that you'd have
learned from experience."

There was nothing Lauren hated more than this sort of bicker-
ing. Always the peacemaker, the one to pour oil on troubled
waters, she searched for a way to change the subject.

"What happened to Hawthorn Hill?" she asked. "Is it still in
existence?"

Clare glanced at Lise. "Ask her," she said. "She's the gossip
columnist for the entire lesbian nation."

"Hey, that's not true!" Lise protested. "What's with you,
Clare?"

"It is *too* true. Everybody knows it. You make it your business
to know everybody else's. Anytime I need information about
anyone, you've got it."

And now Clare finds a way to get on top for a minute, Sonia
silently commentatored the game.

"Ever since you decided to be celibate, you think you're better than everybody else," Lise said angrily.

*Using whatever comes to hand, however irrelevant, Lise
struggles to win back top position,* Sonia continued the play-by-
play.

Clare stood and picked up her cup. She was glad Lise couldn't
spend the night, glad she hadn't tried to persuade her to change
her plans. But the thought of spending the rest of the day with her
was suddenly intolerable. She wanted her to leave now, but since
that wasn't a possibility . . .

"I'm going up to my room and lie down," she said, rinsing her
cup. "I think I may have picked up a virus at Carlsbad. I feel achy
and sick."

*Rather than risk bottom again, she resorts to a little passive
aggression to control the situation. Will it work, Folks? Stay tuned.*

"Well, maybe I'd better go, then?" Lise half stated, half asked
Clare. As if she weren't aware that she was meant to answer, Clare
turned away to hang her cup on its hook.

Lise got the message. Rising, she shook hands around the
table. "It's been great meeting you all, and I appreciate the
invitation to visit." Her chair scraped across the tiles. "If I'm back
in New Mexico again, I'll give you a call." She followed Clare out
of the room.

She pulled it off. But she doesn't have a firm hold on 'sado' when Lise's around, so she'll have to get Lise out of here quick if she wants to end this episode while she's still in that position.

Barb yawned and stretched. "I was up early this morning, phone call from my sister. Her idiot husband locked her out of the house again. I keep telling her to save her money for a divorce, not waste it calling me, but it's hopeless. She'll never leave him." She shook her head. "I'm going home, do a few things, then take a nap."

"Want a ride?" Lauren asked, standing.

"Thanks, but Ashley needs the exercise after all the bread I ate."

Jean threw a napkin at her. "Poor Ashley didn't get a crumb."

"If you'd seen her breakfast, you wouldn't throw things at her poor old servant. I'm going to have to take out a loan just to feed her." She kissed Jean and Sonia, hugged Lauren, then hustled Ashley, grunting and snorting, out the front door.

Lauren had cleared the rest of the table and was washing dishes. "Would it be all right if I walked the dogs? I have an appointment in town, but not until this afternoon."

"Sure, anytime." Jean started for the office door. "We've got orders to get ready before UPS gets here or I'd come with you. Enjoy yourselves, you lucky dogs."

○ ○ ○ ○ ○ ○

Sonia debated whether to turn her light on and try to read herself to sleep, or just resign herself to sleeplessness and get up and do something. This always happened if she slept during the day. She and Jean had worked hard that afternoon, putting out over a hundred orders, and after lunch she had gone to her room to 'rest her eyes'. The dinner bell had awakened her.

Two a.m. She sighed, turned onto her back, then kicked the blanket off. Hot flash. She leaned over to slide the window open. As she did, a movement caught her eye, then she saw something white leap onto the deck. Maggi, followed by Nikki and Tamale. Although she could not see Jean yet, she knew she was right behind them. Jean could not stay indoors on nights like this. Darkness and wind aroused such passion in her that, unable to sleep, she would sometimes roam the hills until morning.

Lying back, she rested her hands on her stomach, feeling its roundness, indicative of the good supper they'd had. It was just a little rounder than she liked, however, and she felt a qualm at this. Then she remembered Jean's telling her how Chenoa couldn't understand why women wanted to diet themselves nearly out of existence. "Our bellies are our power," she had told Jean, rubbing her own gently. "They're the place where we remember, where we know everything. Why do you think men are so eager to take our wombs? They want to take our power from us. They don't like round bellies because it means more power."

In the darkness, she smiled and pulled her T-shirt up so that her hands could rest directly on her powerful belly. She wanted to be more like Chenoa, wanted to have more contact with her body. Impulsively, she stripped off her shirt and proceeded to touch herself with both hands. First her arms and shoulders, then breasts and belly, neck, face, and head. She let her fingers trail lightly through her pubic hair, touching the outer labia briefly.

Then she realized she was avoiding her vulva. Well, well, she thought, look what's going on here! And she immediately covered her entire vulva with her hand. "Here's a hug for you, poor neglected thing," she whispered. "I avoid touching you because to me you still represent sex. I know I'm wrong. I know there's nothing sexual about you at all. But it may take me awhile to get rid of that ridiculous idea."

The rising wind, now cold through her window, interrupted her. "We'll talk about this later," she promised her vulva, and sat up shivering. She shut the window and pulled the blanket back up. Lying down again, her hands reached up to stroke her breasts. Though they were long dead to feeling, she knew it was important to touch them, to let them know she cared for them.

And then it hit her.

"I'll be shittly damned!" she whistled, sitting up in bed and groping over its surface for her T-shirt. "I can't believe I didn't get it yesterday. I can't believe it went right by me." Abandoning her search for the T-shirt, she leapt out of bed and dashed into the bathroom, knocked on Jean's door, and without waiting for an answer, charged in.

Sitting on the floor, going through her mail, Jean was momentarily shocked at the naked apparition that suddenly appeared above her.

"Genius, I was in bed touching myself just now, the way you said Chenoa did, and I realized something: we did sex yesterday!"

"We did?" Jean got up from the floor. "How do you mean?"

"Think about it."

Baffled, Jean sat down on her bed. In just a moment, though, her face cleared. "I get it. By avoiding breasts and vulvas, right?" "Right. We were both still in our male minds, both still believing the lie that our breasts and vulvas are sex parts." "You know why, don't you? It's because baby girls are born with SEX tatooed across their chests and vulvas."

They giggled. Then Sonia got serious again. "We obviously need to redo this experiment. We need to prove to ourselves that breasts and vulvas aren't sexual, that we can touch them without excitation."

Jean felt suddenly chilled and sick to her stomach. But the nausea was accompanied by a rush that was both familiar and heady.

Sonia was already on the bed, looking at her expectantly. Pulling back the covers on her side, Jean remembered with dismay that Sonia was naked. *Oh, great,* she thought, *that means I've got to take all my clothes off, too. I wish I hadn't eaten so much tonight.* Slowly she undid the buttons of her jeans, and pushed them down to her ankles. Her underwear followed, and she stepped out of it. She knew she probably looked foolish in her socks, but something stubborn in her wanted to leave them on. In a moment her T-shirt joined the clothes on the floor, then she capitulated about the socks and tossed them onto the pile. She got quickly into bed, shivering.

"I'm scared," she admitted. "Really scared. It's everything I can do not to bolt and run out of here."

Sonia frowned with the effort to understand why Jean felt so threatened.

"Part of it is that I'm afraid we won't be able to avoid doing sex this time, no matter how hard we try. What if we find out that men are right? If we do, we're sunk. At least I am."

"Me, too, friend," Sonia reminded her. "I've told you: if I can't get out of patriarchy—meaning sex in its myriad forms—then I'm going to get out of this body and out of this realm. I'm a little nervous about this too, but mostly just eager to try. If the theory's right—and here I am staking my life on it—we'll be fine."

"I'm up for it, Sonia. I hope you know I am, and that when I say I'm scared it doesn't mean I'm not going to do it. More than anything in the world I want out of the lies that rule my life."

Sonia nodded, and for a moment they looked at each other. "Well," Sonia smiled, "to borrow a phrase from somewhere or another, it's now or never!"

Jean giggled, but her insides were in knots. *Loosen up,* she ordered herself. "I don't know, Sonia. I've got ice-cold hands. I'm afraid if I touch you, you'll leap out the window."

"Give me that paw, woman." Sonia grabbed Jean's hand and stuck it under her arm.

Jean screeched. "How can you do that to yourself!"

"Hot flash," Sonia confided. "I'm having a doozy and this feels heavenly."

"I should have known. Your face and shoulders are blushing."

"Heat!" Sonia cried and, shoving the blankets to the bottom of the bed, revealed her glowing pink body.

"Oh hell, Soni, you're so cute in the flush!"

"You mean in the flash, silly."

Laughing, Jean grabbed her and pulled her down on top of her.

"Watch it, or we'll both go up in flames!" Sonia rolled off, fanning herself with both hands. "Actually, this isn't a hot flash; it's a power surge."

"That'd make a good bumper sticker."

"Yeah, that's where I got it," she said, reaching for Jean. "Come here, you."

Jean slipped her arm around Sonia, pulled her close, and began stroking her back with the long, slow strokes that came so easily to her.

"Find any sex back there?"

Startled, Jean stopped for a moment. Then smiling, she got up onto her elbow to peer at Sonia's back. "Not yet. But you never know where that varmint might be lurking. Don't you worry. If I find it, I'll ship it to Madonna."

She continued to run her hand down Sonia's back and over her firm buttocks, enjoying both the softness of her skin and tightness of her muscles. After a moment, Sonia turned over onto her back. Jean shifted her weight and gently stroked Sonia's pubic hair.

Sonia stopped Jean's hand. "Before you go any farther, there's something I have to tell you." She paused dramatically. "I have a prize hair."

"A what?" Jean asked, envisioning a large rabbit.

"Look." Sonia searched through her pubic hair, carefully retracted one, and stretched it out as far as it would go. "I think she's about seven-and-a-half inches long now. Another half inch and I enter her in the State Fair."

Solemnly, Jean said, "My, I had no idea I was in the presence of such greatness."

"Indeed, and don't you forget it," Sonia admonished her as she ran her hand softly over Jean's left breast, making sure to brush the nipple on the way. She'd be damned if she was going to let nipples be sex.

"This is your vulva, Sonia," Jean said wonderingly. "She's very sweet—and very furry. All this thick, soft hair."

She knelt beside Sonia so she could touch all of her vulva. This position allowed her breasts some freedom, and Sonia reached out to cup one of them in her hands. "You have lovely breasts, Jean. Really beautiful."

Jean laughed, a short, nervous laugh. "You obviously can't see very well. They sag and they're covered with stretch marks."

Sonia poked her gently. "Who said sag was ugly? Who said stretch marks were bad?"

"Just everybody, that's who. I haven't noticed that they're listed among the top ten desirable traits."

"The hell with the list! I'm looking at your breasts and they're beautiful."

Embarrassed, Jean changed the subject.

"I love knowing that I don't have to *do* anything to your vulva, that I don't have to display any technique or make her feel anything. I love that I can just be with her for the pleasure of her company. I hadn't realized until now that when I touched in sex I was always aware of my partner's response, always trying to get her excited, hoping I could touch her well enough to give her an orgasm.

"In contrast, I'm *feeling* you," she went on, still stroking. "This is the first time I've ever really touched a vulva, the first time I've been with one outside of sex. She feels wonderful. Even though I can't see her in this position, I can tell how she looks. Through my fingertips I can see that she's truly like a flower, with many petals, soft and sweet."

"It feels nice, Jeannie. Different, but nice. Especially that I don't have to *try* to feel anything. I'm not the only woman who's had to flip on her sex switch, try to tune into her sex channel, to even begin to get into the mood for sex. And I think a lot of women aren't able to get that channel anymore."

"I'm one of them," Jean admitted, lying back down. Sonia began drawing circles on her belly, and after a moment Jean grabbed her hand.

"Ticklish?"

"A little, but mostly uncomfortable with having my belly touched. She's covered with stretch marks, too, and looks hideous—so fat and lumpy."

Sonia snorted. "Fat! I'm having to keep a sharp eye out to avoid getting stabbed to death by your hip bones—and your shoulder blades, and your ribs. If you think you're fat, you're a prime testament to the truth that women don't have the foggiest idea what their bodies really look like. The next thing you're going to tell me is that you have stretch marks on your big toe, for crying out loud."

Jean shrieked and jumped several inches off the bed. "Don't do that!" she yelped.

"Don't do what? What did I do?"

"Your foot touched mine!"

Sonia collapsed back onto the bed. "Damnsy hell, Jean, I thought I'd murdered you!"

"Well, *that's* where I'm ticklish. Not just ticklish—torturish."

"I swear never to torture you again." She made a show of moving her guilty feet far over to the other side of the bed.

"No, don't go away," Jean laughed. "It's just that if I'm touched lightly on the bottom of my feet without warning, I get a little hysterical."

Wondering if one can get a 'little' hysterical, Sonia simply said, "So I noticed."

Tentatively, Jean touched Sonia's breast. Though it was unnaturally firm and upright, the skin was soft and the nipple small and delicate. Remembering that Sonia had said there were a few painful spots in the numbness, she touched the left one very gently, hoping not to hurt her. Tears filled her eyes.

"She's lovely, this breast of yours. It makes me sad that she's been so abused."

Jean began to talk to Sonia's breasts as she stroked them, promising never to hurt them, only to love and respect them. Sonia rubbed Jean's buttocks and thighs, moving into a calming, relaxing rhythm.

They were both nearly asleep when Jean's legs suddenly parted. They were both surprised, Jean because she knew they had parted on their own without any prompting from her, and Sonia because the movement seemed so fluid and natural. When Sonia smoothed the pubic hair back and began to touch Jean's vulva, Jean was incredulous.

"I can hardly believe it, Sonia, but I can *feel* that. I've never felt anything when I've been touched there before." She started to cry.

"I'm not upset, you know," she sobbed. "But I've been on the verge of tears ever since we began this experiment. They're tears of relief—and of hope. When I first became a lesbian, I thought it would be different with women. Sex, I mean. I thought I would finally be able to feel what I couldn't feel with men. But it wasn't different. There may have been less genital sex and more touching and cuddling, but I was as numb to it as I'd ever been. Even the women I thought I trusted and loved threw my numb switch as soon as they moved into sex."

Sonia wrapped her arms around her and held her close. Jean struggled for words, then gave up, realizing that she couldn't articulate her tumultuous feelings. She couldn't even begin to put into words what Sonia's touch had felt like to her, how it felt to be really touched for the first time.

She had never wanted to be touched before. She hadn't minded sex too much so long as she was the only one doing the touching, as long as she was the 'sexer'. But in her last relationship she had finally tried to be the 'sexee'—had, at least part of the time, tried to let her lover touch her—and it had been excrutiating, almost impossible to bear, let alone enjoy. She had had to leave her body in order to tolerate it. Withdraw and numb out. But Sonia's touch, so clean and so loving, had reverberated throughout her body and spirit.

Smiling damply, she reached up and touched Sonia's face, feeling the delicate strength of her bones, the softness of her cheeks. Her fingers traced the patterns made by her deep wrinkles.

"You have a fine face, Sonia. And a wonderful body. Muscular, tight, compact. Round muscles, not prone to atrophy, firm and yet not hard." Sonia burst out laughing and Jean gave her a light pinch on the hip. "I know, I sound like some kind of body-building ad. What I'm trying to say is that you're beautiful." She kissed Sonia's breast gently, amazed at the sweetness of the act, the pure beauty of it.

They both laughed as Sonia's stomach made a series of high-pitched squawks.

"Hungry?" Jean asked, stroking the demanding belly.

"I can't think how, after that enormous dinner."

"Then she must want attention," Jean decided, and leaned over to kiss and caress the soft skin.

"Delicious," Sonia murmured, smoothing Jean's hair. "Pleasant and easy and nothing like sex. I could easily fall asleep while you're touching me, even when you're visiting my vulva. And that's because your touch is exactly that and no more—no expectation, no goal, no hidden meanings. It's so nonlinear and simple it's almost not experiencable. I mean, it's like nothing else in this world.

"But it confirms my hypothesis, that sex is a conditioned response in women. This one experiment isn't going to prove it to anyone else, of course, but I knew before we began that it was true, as if I remembered it. I just needed to test it. And now that we've got past sex, we can discover what women's bodies are really capable of, what kind of beings we truly are, all our powers."

Jean murmured assent. "It reminds me of all the women I've dealt with in my practice over the years who came in because they were concerned about their 'sexual dysfunctioning'. Some who were able to be candid admitted that many times during sex they had to fight the desire to fall asleep, that rather than exciting them, the stroking of their vulvas calmed and soothed them."

"Falling asleep would have been the ultimate insult to their partners," Sonia said.

"Exactly," Jean said. "So they managed to stay awake or at least to wake up in time for the final hallelujah. Thinking about this now, I'm reminded of something Chenoa told me years ago. She said that when a woman was in deep distress, very agitated and unable to relax, another woman's gently stroking her vulva could calm her faster and more effectively than any tranquilizer."

"I think it's true, that when the vulva's being touched unconditionally, she can relax enough to lead us into sleep," Sonia said. "And I know, too, that she can experience arousal beyond anything we've ever dreamed of in sex. But when I've heard women say they had to fight drowsiness during sex, I've known this was about escape as much as anything."

This reminded Jean of her student days. "I was newly married and hated the sex. Not that I was conscious that I did; I managed to do a halfway decent hype job on myself, as women do, convincing myself that sex was fun and good. I even found myself joking with the other women at work about how hot and steamy our love lives were. But in reality, I didn't feel anything.

"Then as time went on, I began to resent Brad's sexual needs. Not that he was as demanding or insensitive as a lot of men. He simply assumed I felt the same way he did without bothering to find out. Of course, I was faking everything so even if he had been willing to try to improve the situation, how could he have when I had almost no idea what was wrong or what I wanted?

"About all I knew I wanted was to hold someone and be held, and that there wasn't nearly enough of that in our relationship. On the few occasions I suggested to Brad that we just cuddle, it turned into sex. Even when he swore beforehand that he didn't want it, his penis had a different agenda. After orgasm he usually sank into a coma, so so much for any plain old affection or genuine closeness."

"Then for some unexplained reason, the marriage began to deteriorate."

Jean laughed. "Pretty good. I'd say you were psychic, except I know it's a classic story."

"Yep. There's really only one story about men and women—with very minor variations."

"Anyway," Jean went on, "I saw a therapist who thought I needed to address my sexual problems directly, so she referred me to a clinic that specialized in female sexual dysfunction. Ridiculously enough, it was headed by a man and mostly staffed by men."

"Makes sense, doesn't it," Sonia said, "just like male obstetricians and pediatricians. What I love most about patriarchy is its logic."

"You'd better watch it," Jean warned her, "or you'll grow up to be a feminist!"

Smiling, she continued. "On the second visit, my therapist outlined a program for me that he thought would help me overcome my inability to enjoy sexual intercourse. I took one look at it, walked out of the office, and never returned. The suggestions were all horrible. I knew I couldn't and wouldn't follow them, so there wasn't any point in even thinking about it.

"Of course, the clinic blamed my problems on my childhood sexual abuse. What they didn't bother to tell me is that all women suffer from some form of sexual dysfunction. And yet, in the same breath, they claim sex is natural. For whom?"

"Alas, we know 'whom' only too well," Sonia sniffed. "My sexual experiences were different. With Vince, I liked the touching and found the sex tolerable, even pleasurable at times. But I also knew that if we never did it again I wouldn't miss it. Frankly, it was too much work for too little satisfaction.

"Sex with women wasn't a whole lot different, as you said. It was sweeter, there was more holding and touching, but ultimately it was the same: we had a goal, and the goal was orgasm. No matter how much women deny that orgasm is important, the truth is that it looms. Much of how we feel about ourselves is based on how good we are as lovers and lovees. If we or our partners don't have orgasm—or rarely do—we know the Ship's in trouble and that it's our inadequacy that's got it there.

"Everywhere I've been, it's the same thing: sex and relationships at the core of most women's misery. Then several years ago I began to wonder, if they're so natural, why can't we do them? Why are women reading every self-help book they can get their hands on and seeing therapists? Why can't we just do them without thinking, like we breathe and eat?

"It scared me, thinking this. Relationships are so basic to mensgame, the center of most women's lives. What would we do without them—not just romantic ones, but relationships with parents and siblings and children as well? Since the whole social organization of planet earth is based on relationships, I realized that the world as we have come to know it would totally disappear. And though I wanted patriarchy gone, I wasn't at all sure that if it went, there would be anything left. Pretty frightening stuff, especially when you're the only one you know who's thinking it."

Jean shivered and snuggled closer. "Lots of women say they want out of patriarchy, but if it came right down to it—well, as you say, the risks seem monumental. We've been taught to fear and avoid the unknown, even when the known is intolerable. We're like that frog you wrote about, the one that started out in the can of cool water on the fire, and kept adjusting to the rising temperature until it boiled to death."

"Patriarchy's heating up out there, Jeannie. Soon it's going to burst into flames and self-destruct. Yesterday we leapt out of its way. When it's gone—and that will be sooner than we believe possible—the female world will remain. In you and in me and in any other women willing to make the same leap."

Then she grinned. "Don't I always sound so portentous, though? So oracular?" They both laughed.

Jean buried her face in Sonia's neck and nuzzled her warm skin. She realized after a few moments that they were breathing in sync, and that it was very soothing. She pulled away, wanting to say more before she fell asleep.

"I had a disturbing reaction earlier when you came in and told me we had done sex and needed to redo the experiment. I've told you about my eating disorders, how I'd been in treatment programs and had all kinds of therapy and intervention. Well, no one really knew what caused them. Their theories centered mostly around childhood sexual abuse. But I never really bought that."

"How do they explain eating disorders in women who've never been sexually abused?"

"Oh, they claim they have been and have just blocked it." She paused, trying to put her thoughts into words. Her mouth felt terribly dry but she didn't want to interrupt this.

"I know it's taking me a long time to say this, but I'm figuring things out as I talk. Three years ago this past Halloween I managed to stop."

"What exactly did you stop?"

"Starving, bingeing and purging, laxative abuse. Before that Halloween, for instance, on the days I ate, I easily vomited ten times or oftener, and it wasn't uncommon for me to take 250 to 300 laxatives in addition. I was totally out of control and headed for a cemetary when my therapist got mad and told me not to come back, she didn't want to watch me die in her office. At first, I was furious at her for firing me, then I decided the hell with her, I didn't need her anyhow, good riddance.

"I went home—this was October 30—binged on rice cakes and avocado, threw up, binged on granola with soy milk, threw up again, then cooked up a pan of instant mashed potatoes, ate that, threw up. By then I was vomiting blood, so I quit and went to bed. I woke up sick in my soul—sick of myself, of my life—and feeling totally hopeless. It was Halloween, my favorite day of the year, and I didn't care. I wanted to die.

"I lay there in bed thinking about what food I had in the house that I could binge on. I'd learned long before to avoid certain foods because they're hard to throw up. I considered making a banana pudding, but was too tired to bother. I'd been invited to several Halloween parties that night—I looked so much like a corpse I wouldn't even have needed a costume—but I felt too depressed to go to any of them. When I finally got up, I discovered there was almost nothing in the house to binge on. I panicked. I had to get some food so I could throw up. I got dressed and was reaching for my jacket when I stopped. I just stopped. And knew I wasn't going to throw up again. That was three and a half years ago.

"But though I stopped vomiting and starving and taking laxatives, it didn't mean I stopped feeling the compulsion to do it. I was able to stop the behaviors, but I constantly had to fight the almost overwhelming urge to do them. There were times when the craving was so strong, in fact, that I would have to get all the food out of my house, and ask someone to keep it for me and mete out whatever I needed for survival until I could get past it.

"I was deeply addicted, especially to the vomiting. It's impossible to explain to someone who's never felt it, but I experienced a tremendous sense of euphoria from a good binge and purge. I felt cleaned out, light and empty and happy, especially when I took the laxatives along with the vomiting. I loved running my hands down my belly and not only feeling it flat but concave, the pelvic bones jutting out. I loved getting on the scale and seeing it register 95 or 90.

"Even now, when I think about weighing 90 pounds I feel a rush of power, knowing I can do it, knowing I can control my body absolutely."

"What was it all about?" Sonia asked. "What do you think was going on?"

"That's where this story is headed. When my last relationship ended, I vowed never to do another one. But then I had a brief, almost purely sexual, relationship with a woman and when it was over I knew I was through with sex, too. You see, prior to that I thought I could have sex without doing a relationship. That was before I met you and realized that sex and relationships are the same thing, that even if I just had a one-night stand, it was a one-night relationship.

"I didn't notice immediately, but about a month after I gave up sex, I realized that that whole month I hadn't thought about bingeing or purging. Not once. Two months later it was the same thing. I've been totally free of the urge since then. Until tonight."

Sonia raised her eyebrows questioningly.

"Tonight when you said we needed to redo the experiment, it hit me as strong as ever—that compulsion to binge and purge. I wanted to so much I didn't think I'd be able to stay in this room. I can't tell you how desperate I felt for a few minutes."

"Do you realize what you're saying?"

"Yes, I do. I'm saying that anorexia and bulimia and all eating disorders are caused by sex. Not just what's termed 'sexual abuse', because all sex is abusive, sex *is* abuse. Eating disorders are caused by sex, period.

"The connections were always there, right in front of my nose. I just couldn't see them. For instance, although I never had orgasms during sex, what I experienced after vomiting was just as good, just as exciting and exhilarating. It was as though I had taken some kind of sexual uppers. It made me sexually high. Sex and bingeing and purging were so interlinked, in fact, that I often masturbated to orgasm immediately after vomiting. And after sex, I often ate something so I could throw up."

Despite the lateness of the hour, both of them were very wide awake, sitting up in bed with a blanket thrown around their shoulders, facing each other. Jean was talking with growing awareness of the implications of what she was saying and Sonia was listening with such arousal she could hardly sit still.

"Wait, there's more. What I know from this is that sex and addictions are the same thing, they're synonymous."

Sonia nodded. "It fits my formula: patriarchy = men's world = relationships = sex = sadomasochism = control, abuse, addiction, violence, and destruction."

"Sex isn't *an* addiction, as the current fad has it. It *is* addiction, pure and simple. All addictions are sex."

"Yep, patriarchy, sex, sadomasochism, addiction—they're all the same thing."

Jean ran her hands through her hair distractedly, standing it even more on end than usual. "There's a piece to this addiction thing that I want to get clearer. A few years ago I talked at length to an endocrinologist. She said that during sexual excitation, the body releases hormones that we know as pleasure hormones; they've also been talked about in relation to running.

"This woman hypothesized that in women the release of this hormone is in reponse to a chemical imbalance within the body, that it is not a natural phenomenon at all but an aberration. That like many drugs, it causes a feeling of pleasure and well-being that is artificial and forced.

"She believes that it's the release of these hormones that hooks women into sex, just like heroin or cocaine. That this chemical imbalance causes many of us to become physiologically addicted. This, coupled with our emotional conditioning to want sex, makes a lot of women believe they like it and need it. I know

now that I released the same hormones and got the same high by bingeing and purging."

"But what causes this chemical imbalance in the first place?" Sonia asked.

"I asked her the same question, and she didn't have any answers. But I do. It's been coming to me while we've been talking. Sex causes it. Not just physical sex but sex in its widest, male context."

"Sadomasochism, you mean. Hierarchy, competition, comparison, exchange—all that."

"Yes, men's world."

"So sexuality in women is abnormal on every level—physically as well as emotionally. It fits everything I know, Jean. It's awesome the connections you've made tonight."

"And I know at least some of their implications," Jean said. "Breast, ovarian, and uterine cancer, Chronic Fatigue Syndrome—all women's diseases are caused by sex. Sex, that we know is sadomasochism, forces our bodies and spirits to do something totally uncharacteristic, totally antithetical to our female essences. It makes us sick. More than that, it kills us and it's killing the planet."

"I'm not going to let it kill me," Sonia said emphatically.

"That makes two of us."

9

"*Of course* you're having a relationship. You're just calling it something else," Della said to Jean and Sonia.

Jean sighed, frustrated by her inability to put into words what seemed so obvious to her. She had to fight the temptation to find some excuse to get away from the conversation she and her friends Della, Sonia, Barb, and Lauren were having around the kitchen table.

As she often did, Della had come up for the weekend, and though she was deeply and, Jean thought, irrevocably in relationship mode, she was always interested in what the women at Wildfire were thinking and doing. *What's the point in telling her,* Jean asked herself, *when she doesn't intend to change her life one iota? The point is,* she answered, *that I'm going to have to explain this again and again to all kinds of women. Might as well practice on Della.*

She and Sonia had been telling the other three about their discovery and experiments, and had been dismayed to find that, so far, their listeners were neither impressed nor very interested. When they had finished talking about the second experiment, Della had said flatly that it sounded like sex to her.

"But it isn't," Sonia insisted. "I agree that it looks like it, and I'm sure if you were to show up in the middle of a touching experiment, you'd think it was. What women did before men resembles sex, and men, being sexual, projected upon it the only interpretation possible to them. But women are touchers. Before men corrupted our consciousness, before sex contaminated our perception of touch, women's bodies were simply bodies— whole and fully integrated, not separated off into special sexual zones and non-sexual or safe zones. We touched freely, unconditionally, because that's how we were. And we can be that way again."

Jean explained about the lack of stimulus/response in her experience with Sonia, how she touched her even when Sonia was asleep. "When I touch her, I'm not trying to get a response, not monitoring her reactions because I want her to have an orgasm and need to know what move to make next. I have no ulterior motives, so there are no means to ends, no expectations or hidden messages. I'm touching because I love to touch."

"There's nothing new about that, as you should know, being a massage therapist," Della countered.

"Not true. Massage is totally goal oriented. If you come to me for massage, I'm going to ask you if there's anything in particular bothering you. If you tell me your lower back is aching, then my goal is to do whatever I can to relieve or eliminate that ache. I have a specific job to do and I'm going to do whatever I can to complete it."

"Okay, but what if I don't have any specific complaints? What if I just want a massage because it feels good?"

"I still have a goal, Dell—to make you feel good. As I go along, I'll be constantly alert for cues to what seems to please you most so that I can do more of that and less of things that you don't seem to enjoy as much.

"I'm in exchange mode, too, and that's more sadomasochism. Especially if I'm taking money for rubbing you. But even if I'm not, the exchange is there. When I give you pleasure, when I make you feel better, I feel competent, worthwhile, good about myself. That's my reward.

"Also, in assuming responsibility for making you feel better, I'm doing s/m—giving us both the message that you can't do this yourself, that you have to have me."

"I don't see anything wrong with that."

"What's wrong with it is that there's no peerness. I'm here," she held her right hand above her left, "and you're here," she indicated her left hand. "I'm in charge, I'm the expert, I'm taking care of you."

"I still don't see any harm in that," Della said stubbornly.

"Okay, you don't have to. I do, and it bothers me. Right now I don't know how I can continue to practice massage. Maybe I'll figure something out down the line but at this moment I can't think what."

"Getting back to non-massage touching," Della said. "I could decide just to touch you and not have sex with you. We've all done that," she looked at Barb for confirmation and Barb nodded her assent. "If the woman I'm involved with doesn't want sex on a particular night, I can just touch her and be close without having sex in mind."

"But you can't, Dell," Sonia plowed in. "Once you're in a sexual relationship, it's sexual all the time. The desire for it, or the lack of desire for it, or the absence of it at any particular moment, or the worry about it for one reason or another—something manages to keep sex central, even when we're not aware of it.

"But, of course, we don't just do sex in bed. Sadomasochism—sex—is the foundation of all relationships. Ships can't stay afloat without the non-physical sex of hierarchy and control, too. So no, we can't do unconditional touching with someone we're in a relationship with. It's impossible to separate sadomasochism, sex, control, and relationships. They're all the same thing."

Della waved her hand in impatience. "We're bogging down in semantics here. Call it what you like but anytime you touch the genitals, you've got sex. Only you're calling it 'strawberries' or," her eyes scanned the kitchen, 'begonias'.

"I had an uncle who was an alcoholic," she swept on, "only he denied it. He claimed he'd been told by some doctor that a little brandy every day would help prevent a heart attack. For Uncle Edward, a little brandy meant two quarts. But he called it medicine even when he was so smashed he couldn't move.

"But it's okay," she concluded, smiling at Jean and Sonia. "I love you and I can let you call your sexual behavior anything you want."

Barely controlling her anger, Jean rose abruptly from the table.

"I'm going to start dinner," she muttered, though no one paid any attention. Pulling a pot out from under the stovetop, she slammed it onto the burner with such force that the canary burst into hysterical song. Glancing at Sonia, Jean saw that she seemed willing to continue the conversation. *Then give it to her,* Jean thought, *really give it to her, Sonia.*

In the face of Della's blatant condescension, Sonia was also having difficulty keeping her temper, but she decided to make one last attempt.

"You're a dentist, Dell," she began steadily. "You're an expert in your chosen field. When I go to you for dental work, I trust that you know what you're doing, that when you tell me something, it's more likely to be accurate than something Mr. Chang at the nursery tells me about teeth. Even though he has teeth of his own, he is not an expert on them. You are. This is what you know.

"This doesn't mean that I think you will never change your mind about some things, that when new information comes in about some aspect of your work, you won't revise your opinion somewhat. It means that I trust that what you tell me is basically correct, that it's what, after long, careful, continuous study and experience, you know to be true.

"I respect you and the work you do. I don't understand it well and I'm not interested in understanding it. I'm glad there are people who want to be dentists because I most fervently don't want to have to figure it out for myself. I'm happy to accept you as an authority."

"I appreciate that, but what's it got to do with this?"

"All right. I've made it my profession to know and understand relationships and sex. They're what I've been studying, thinking about, researching, observing, experimenting with—concentrating my full attention upon—day and night, for years. I live and breathe, sleep and dream them. I've come to understand what they are, and why and how they function in our lives. This is what I've chosen to do, and like you, what I choose to do, I do thoroughly and well.

"So when I tell you that Jean and I are not having sex, I'm giving you a fact. I'm not playing semantic games. I'm an expert on sex, I know what I'm talking about, and I expect you to respect my expertise in this area as I respect yours in dentistry.

"I'm not saying that you should do what Jean and I are doing. I'm not saying that any woman should. I'm simply telling you why we're doing it and what we've discovered so far."

Della relaxed and sat back, her defensiveness gone. "I accept that," she said. "I'm not saying I understand it—the difference between touching and sex, that is. But I believe you know what you're talking about when you say they're different."

She shrugged. "But I like doing sex and I like having relationships. I agree with you that they can both be the pits and I agree that most relationships, especially among women, break up. I agree that there's something wrong with them because my own experience in life tells me that if something keeps breaking down, there's a serious problem somewhere. But I'm willing to take the bad with the good and I'm not willing to embark on the journey the two of you have. I'm glad you're doing it because you're right, there are women out there who are in despair and want something different. I'm not the one to look to for alternatives."

Jean breathed a sigh of relief. *That was perfect, Sonia,* she thought. *She could understand your being an expert because she's one. And she could let her defenses down when she realized that you weren't trying to change her, that you weren't judging her, that you were simply informing her.*

She emptied four cups of long-grain brown rice into the boiling, seasoned water and replaced the lid. Ratatouille was on the menu tonight, with tossed salad and Italian bread. She pulled the vegetables out of the crisper drawer and, washing them, tuned back into the conversation.

Barb's voice. " . . . but I couldn't believe I'd find a recipe like that in an architectural magazine. When no one was looking, I tore it out and now I'm dying to make it. I love Indian food, so what better combination than curry with cauliflower and broccoli—my two favorite vegetables."

Della made a face. "It's okay, if you like cauliflower and broccoli," she said, "but I can't stand them. Indian food, fine, but hold those two vegetables, please."

Jean's mouth fell open. She had known Della for years, had prepared countless meals for her, and, until this very moment, had not been aware of this aversion. In fact, she had always had the impression that Della *liked* cauliflower and broccoli, so had made it a habit, whenever she came for dinner, to prepare some dish with one or both of them.

I can't believe this, Jean thought. *Why didn't she tell me? Why did she force herself, meal after meal, to eat something she didn't like?*

She felt ill as she recognized the answer. *She did it to please me. She didn't want to hurt my feelings. I hate it!* Wiping her hands on a towel, she walked around the island and sat at the table.

When there was a lull in the conversation, she said, "I've been listening to the two of you talk about the things closest to my heart—food and cooking. And frankly, Dell, I'm shocked to hear you say that you hate cauliflower and broccoli."

Della looked sheepish.

"I realize that, as long as I've known you and as many meals as we've had together, I've almost consistently served cauliflower and broccoli because I thought you liked them."

Della blushed. "I know. I haven't wanted to say anything. And it's not as if I find them intolerable. I can eat them. Let's just say they're not among my favorite foods. Besides, I knew you liked them and that they were part of your diet."

"But Dell, how can we be close if we aren't honest with each other? Maybe this seems like a small thing, but how many small things do we believe about each other that aren't true? How many small things are there between us? If we've got broccoli and cauliflower, then we've got other things, too. I can't say firmly enough how much I want you not to do things you wouldn't normally do just to please me or because you're afraid you'll hurt my feelings."

Seeing Della's obstinate look, she plunged on.

"It's because I want to know you. What's the sense of being with you if I don't know and have no way of discovering who I'm with? Who am I calling friend when I call you friend?"

"I think you're overreacting, Jean," Barb said. "I think there's a time and a place for discretion, and I'd just call what Della did good etiquette. Now if she had served you broccoli and cauliflower in her own home, I'd say that was going too far. But we have to compromise, we have to have give and take in all our interactions with one another."

"No!" Jean shouted. "Don't you hear what you're saying? How can I know you, how can we be close, if I can't trust you to be honest, if you're pretending to be something you're not in order to please me? You're right, Barb. This *is* what we do in relationships. Because we have to, because the relationship demands it. That's how in relationships we lose ourselves totally—we lie, we pretend, we compromise, we even do things we hate and would never do if we were alone or with someone else. And we do most of this without even knowing it. I don't want any of you to do things to please me. And I don't want to do things to please you."

Turning back to Della, she said, "I have in the past, you know, and I regret it. I gave you a false impression of me. I let you believe I was someone I wasn't."

"How so?" Della asked, surprised.

For a second, Jean panicked. *Shoot,* she thought, *what have I gotten myself into?* But recognizing the fear as just more conditioning, she confessed.

"Okay, I've never told you this before, so it will probably shock you as much as the vegetables shocked me. But remember all those concerts I attended with you, Desert Chorale and the Gay Men's Choir?"

Della nodded.

"Well, I hate concerts, especially the Gay Men's—I have nothing in common with gay men. I went to please you. Totally. I went because you wanted to and I wanted to make you happy."

"You could have fooled me!" Della sputtered. "I thought you loved going!"

"I know you did. And there was no way for you to know otherwise because I wasn't honest about it. I thought I had to compromise to have a friendship with you."

"But we didn't have to go to those concerts together," Della protested. "I could have gone with someone else, and you and I could have done something else, something we both liked."

"Exactly! This is what I'm trying to say. We could have done something else that would have pleased us both, just as we could be eating something that we both like. Do you see what I mean?

"Up until this moment you've been going around believing that I love concerts. Now you find out I don't and have only being going to make you happy. How does that make you feel?"

"Lousy," Della admitted. "Foolish, condescended to, used."

"So let's not do it anymore," Jean pleaded. "Really, I want to be told. I want to know you. I want things between us to be clean and unrelationshipful. I can't stand this crap anymore."

"You've got a good point," Barb said, "a very good point. I'm guilty of it, too."

They looked at her expectantly.

"Well, I know Sonia loves Suzanne Ciani's music. I don't. In fact, I dislike it and would never listen to it if I were here alone. But when Sonia's in the room, I put it on. The other day Sonia told me she was glad I liked it as much as she did."

"Did you say anything?" Lauren asked.

Barb shook her head. "I guess I wanted to please her. I didn't think there was any harm in it and I still have a hard time taking it seriously. It's not like it's a major problem."

"But it is, Barb. All these things build up and we get into a habit of not being ourselves that's incredibly dangerous and hard to break. Sonia believes you love Ciani, believes you're a woman who appreciates that kind of music. Therefore, she doesn't really know you. If that matters to you."

"It does," Barb said, standing up. "Where is she? I need to talk to her."

Jean had seen Sonia start up the stairs to her room during the vegetable discussion. So pointing Barb in that direction, she turned back to the conversation.

"It seems so complicated," Lauren was complaining. "Sometimes I think that everything I feel, say, or do comes out of patriarchy and is wrong."

"You're right," Jean said. "We're so deeply conditioned to believe men's lies about women and the world that we have no idea who we really are or what's possible for us. The only way I know to change that is to question and throw out everything I've learned and believed."

She went back over to the stove. "Need some help?" Lauren asked.

"The table needs to be set."

While Lauren was taking down the plates, Sonia and Barb came back in. Sonia began rummaging around in the utensil drawer, and Barb put glasses and water on the table. Jean handed Della the loaf of Italian bread. Della put it on the breadboard and placed them both in the center of the table.

At the stove, Jean heated olive oil in the wok for the ratatouille. As the oil warmed, she stirred the sauce that she would pour over the vegetables at the end. In a few minutes, the mouth-watering smell of cooking vegetables filled the air.

"Lauren, how about ringing the bell for Clare?" Jean asked. As Lauren started toward the door, Sonia laid a restraining hand on her arm. "Clare's on the phone. She just wrote me a frantic note saying not to expect her for dinner. She's handling somebody's crisis."

"Where's Harper?" Della asked Lauren as they all took their places at the table.

"One of her co-workers is having a whoop-de-doo 30th birth-day party at Luciano's tonight."

"Weren't you invited?"

"Sure, but we'd been invited here first, and since I hate restau-rants and Jean's food is better anyway, it wasn't hard to choose between them."

"Maybe the food's better here, but the atmosphere at Luciano's . . . !"

Lauren smiled shyly at Sonia and Jean across the table. "I like the atmosphere here."

"Of course you do," Barb concurred. Reaching down by the side of her chair, she scratched Ashley's head affectionately. "Luciano's may have a strolling musician, but we have a drooling pig."

"Silly me," Della grinned. "Whatever was I thinking?"

They ate steadily and with gusto for awhile, making only desultory conversation. Between helpings, Della sighed, "Won-derful as usual, Jean. I don't know why I'm living all alone in Las Palomas when I could be here, eating healthy food and breathing healthy air."

The phone rang in the next room and Jean went to answer it. Returning, she said, "That was Pauline Running Wolf."

Sonia raised her eyebrows. "And?"

"And she was sure we'd changed our minds. She tried to get me to give her the directions to Wildfire right then, 'so we won't have to fuss with them later,' she said. She was determined to come, but I told her there wasn't a chance that we'd reconsider. She's a very unpleasant character."

"Which is exactly why I'm always surprised that she has such a following," Sonia mused.

Jean helped herself to salad. "That's another thing. She's some-thing of a feminist as well as a spiritual leader, yet she encourages women to be disciples. That doesn't make sense to me."

"Whether we like it or not," Sonia reminded her, "this is what women's spirituality is about: worship, hierarchy, looking outside oneself for direction and strength. I've said time and again that goddess worship is just another religion, and like all religions, it's male, hostile, and ruinous to women."

"True, just Mormonism or Catholicism or Protestantism with the pronouns changed. Every time I hear the words, 'women's spirituality', I cringe," Jean shuddered. "There's nothing womanly about spirituality. It's a totally male construct."

"I don't blame Pauline, though," Della said. "If women are determined to have a leader, someone or something to worship, then why shouldn't it be her? Sounds to me like she's just a good businesswoman, an entrepreneur, cashing in like the rest of them on a very viable movement, making money off women's gullibility . . . Hey, I'll do those," she yelled to Sonia, who was running hot water into the dishpan. "It's the least I can do. In fact, when you make this an old dykes' home, Jean, like you used to threaten to do someday, I'll move here and do the dishes every night in exchange for this wonderful food and conversation."

"You wouldn't like it here for long," Sonia called across to her. "No eggs, no dairy products, no refined sugar, and of course, no meat."

"No Haagen-Dazs," Jean reminded her.

At this Della clutched her throat and thrust her tongue out. After she had died a violent death by deprivation, she said, resuscitating, "I can always get a fix in town."

"You miss the point." Sonia was exasperated. "The point is to eat healthfully all the time. The point is to respect our bodies by putting only good things into them. The point is to remind ourselves constantly how important they are, how precious, and how much we love them. You wouldn't pull into a gas station and put diesel fuel in your car. You wouldn't pour alcohol into it instead of oil. Why wouldn't you give your body at least equal consideration?"

Della shrugged. "I know I could do better, but who's to say meat and dairy products are bad for you? Certainly not nutritionists."

"They're changing their tune, though, and fast," Jean cut in. "Guess who's been touting milk and meat to them madly for years? The dairy industry and the cattlemen's association, that's who. Real trustworthy sources."

They were interrupted by Clare's coming into the kitchen. "Sorry I missed dinner, but that was a freak-out call from my friend Luna at No Man's Land." Jean handed her a covered plate of food. "Thanks," she smiled gratefully.

"What's she freaking out about?" Lauren asked.

"Trouble on the home front, a couple of women wreaking havoc." At their expressions of interest, she went on. "Well, a new woman, Marti, took community money without asking, bought twenty-five bare-root fruit trees, and planted them on the west boundary of the property. Everyone was aghast. This was a really blatant disregard of rules, but it was a fait accompli. What could they do?

"Where she planted them, there's no water source. She soon started complaining about hauling water and tried to guilt-trip the rest into helping her—the trees were dying, etc. When no one volunteered, she got angry. Hell, what did she expect? We were already desperately overworked, months behind in our orders, and couldn't have taken on the care of a canary."

"What happened?" Lauren asked, wide-eyed as a child.

"She quit watering them and they died and she blamed every-body else."

Barb snorted. "Hey, she bought 'em. They were her babies, no one else's. In the army, I knew enough blamers to last me several lifetimes."

Clare shrugged. "I still felt terrible about it. Anyway, that's not the worst. A friend of Marti's came to live with her, and right away there were problems. Jill's an active alcoholic, openly drinking, and No Man's Land has a strict no-alcohol rule—six of the women living there now are in AA.

"Marti argued that because she and Jill lived in one of the outbuildings, not the main house, the rules didn't apply to them. But Jill would show up at the shop drunk out of her mind, or come to dinner and pass out at the table. It got more and more upsetting, until now three of the dedicated residents have left and others are threatening to. That's what the freak-out call was about."

"Unfortunately, an all-too-common plot," Jean sighed. "One or two women disrupt the community and drive everyone else out."

Della scowled. "I don't get it, why a dozen grown-up women would rather lose everything than stand up for themselves and tell those two to get lost. That's why you'll never see me moving in with a bunch of folks." She looked at Sonia. "Speaking of moving, when's Marcy moving here?"

A swift pain seared Sonia's heart. "She isn't, Dell. We broke up a few days ago. You'll see her, though. She's coming tomorrow to get the few things she left here." Her eyes misted. "And to say good-bye, I guess. Looks like it's going to be just Jean and me at Wildfire for a long, long time."

"My condolences about Marcy," Della murmured, reaching over and giving Sonia's shoulder a quick squeeze. Turning back to the group, she said, "I brought a wonderful video on Virginia Woolf. Let's live it up!"

"Great," Barb said sarcastically. "Really nifty. Seeing as how no television or VCR has crossed this threshold in lo, these many years."

Della grinned. "Brought my own. That is, if it's all right. They've been vaccinated and fumigated."

Everyone but Sonia and Jean headed for Della's car to bring in her TV and VCR.

"I'm going to walk," Jean said, "and I'd love your company." They took the dogs and walked down the driveway towards the road. There was never much traffic, and at this hour they were totally alone.

"I'm disappointed about the reaction to our experiments," Jean said. "As we were talking about them, I felt so aroused I could hardly stay in my skin. I expected everyone else to feel . . . well, delighted or pleased or something, and no one even seemed interested. Lauren got embarrassed. Della wanted to fight. That was about it." She paused. "I'm glad you got through to Della, anyhow."

"Don't be so sure I did, Jean. I got her to quit arguing with me, that's all. I don't think for a moment that she ever really understood what we were talking about. I don't think any of them got the significance of it. And I don't think many women are going to. It just mustn't matter if we're the only ones who get it."

Jean stopped and put her arms around her, emotion welling up inside until she could scarcely breathe. It was incomprehensible and painful to think that no one might care, might not even try to understand this incredible discovery of theirs. It made her feel like shutting herself off from the rest of the world, doing what she needed to do with Sonia to get free, and forgetting everyone else. She wanted to cry, but no tears would come.

"Sonia," she pulled away to look at her. "I don't want to be alone tonight. If it's all right, I'd like to sleep with you."

10

At first she didn't know what had awakened her. Something warm, bright. A single beam of sunshine was playing across her face. She squinted her eyes shut, then opened them with a start.

Sunshine? She sat up.

Sonia's room. Sonia's bed. And Sonia beside her, beginning to stir. She lay back down and watched the sun slowly fill the eastern sky. The events of the last two days jostled each other in her head, and what had seemed so clear and reasonable yesterday cluttered her mind this morning. Though the conflict between what she knew and what she had been taught had barely begun, it was already a melee.

"I don't want to get up," Sonia said, putting her arms around Jean's waist and nuzzling her side. "Let's just stay here all day and talk and experiment and forget the rest of the world."

Jean gently tousled her hair. "Suits me just fine."

"That reminds me," Sonia said, sitting up beside her. "Something important occurred to me last night just as I was falling asleep. I want to sleep with you every night; I want that to be the norm, not the other way around, and that we bring it up only if we *don't* want to. Somehow I don't think that's going to happen with me, though. I think I'm always going to want to. I can't imagine ever *not* wanting to, and I've become pretty expert at knowing my feelings on this subject.

"The truth is that it's so much more than sleeping with you. I love the way we touch, the way we talk ourselves to sleep, the way we dream together, the way we wake up in the night and laugh ourselves silly.

"I've been fighting this feeling because I really believed what I wrote in *The Ship*, that sleeping together every night is part and parcel of relationshipness. And I still believe it. But I know now that it can be something else, that it can be done without a Ship. I'm sure that in women's world, because there was no sex, no sadomasochism of any kind, we all slept together all the time, that we always wanted to be near one another. That's what I want— always to be near you."

Jean squeezed her hand. "Me too you, Soni. And you're right. Since we're not relationshipping, sleeping together is simply sleeping together. It's not an indicator of the success of coupling, not a reassurer that all is well, not a method of control."

"For me, it's a source of delight and pleasure. And that's all," Sonia said.

"For me, too. And that surprises me a lot. When I ended my last relationship, I almost got rid of my double bed so I wouldn't have to sleep with anyone again. But this is different. I know that if I don't want to sleep with you on a particular night, I can simply make that decision and not have to announce or discuss it. That either of us can, anytime. There's real freedom between us in that."

She looked out the window. Sunshine was splashing across the deck now, and the three dogs were soaking it up. The flowers Sonia had planted in beds were beginning to bloom, and the cosmos, sown as a wildflower beyond the yard and already well over a foot high, seemed to be growing as she watched.

Turning back to Sonia, she patted her knee through the blanket. "I just thought of why we can't just lounge around here all day, philosophizing and playing. Marcy's coming."

"Alas, alack, and rats." Sonia crawled reluctantly out of bed and headed for the closet. "I have a million things to do before she gets here."

"What if I run down and get us some breakfast and bring it back up?" Jean called to her.

"I could live with that."

Jean started down the stairs, wondering if Della and Clare were up. Neither was an early riser if she could help it. In the kitchen she took juice and English muffins out of the refrigerator, then filled the kettle and put it on to boil. Deftly she split the muffins and popped them into their four-slice toaster (extra wide slots for bagels). She peeled two oranges and broke them into slices, spread margarine on the muffins, poured boiling water into the tea pot, placed everything on a tray, and carried it back upstairs, detouring through the bathroom for a beach towel.

Spreading the towel on Sonia's bed, she lowered the tray carefully onto it.

"Perfection as usual, Genius." Sonia, sitting crosslegged in the middle of the bed, stuck an orange slice in her mouth and rolled her eyes heavenward with pleasure. She reached for a muffin half and bit into it. As she chewed, a curious expression came over her face. She held the muffin up and examined it.

"Something wrong?" Jean asked.

"It tastes odd. Not spoiled; just odd. And there are little green things in it."

Jean took the muffin from Sonia and looked at it closely. Sonia was right. There were little green things in it. What the . . .? "Oh, shoot," Jean squealed. "Oh, no!" She rolled onto the bed, shaking with laughter. "Oh, please, I can't bear it!"

"Can't bear what? Come on, tell me." Sonia grabbed her and began tickling her. "Don't you dare die of hysterics without telling me what I've just eaten!"

Hiccoughing and gulping for air, Jean managed to sit up. She reached for a tissue and blew her nose. "Oh, hell, Sonia, I'm so sorry." This brought another wave of uncontrolled laughter.

"Jean, for crying out loud, tell me! How long do I have to live?"

Jean sat up again. "Bay leaves," she choked.

"Bay leaves? In the muffins? That's *it?*"

"I put them in the wheat berries to deter insects," she explained, gasping. "I guess I missed one or two when I ground them."

"Well, only a cook could find that so funny. Bay leaves are harmless enough."

"Yeah, but I don't usually season English muffins with them. Maybe I should put a note on the rest of them renaming them 'Italian Breakfast Breads'."

She wiped her eyes, then held her arms open, an invitation for Sonia to rest her head on her shoulder.

"I hope things go easily for you and Marcy today. Knowing both of you, I'm sure it'll be friendly and civil, not like a few partings I've been through."

"I'm not worried about that. Neither of us is angry or at the stage where we can't bear the sight of each other. I just have to remind myself not to hammer away at her with the expectation that if I keep trying I can force her to understand. I just want to let her be and get on with my life."

She glanced at the clock. "Do you think it's too early to call Lauren?"

"She's an early riser, so I'd say no. Although I don't know what time she left last night."

Sonia reached for the phone. "I meant to get the name of her hairdresser. I love her haircut." She dialed. "Got the machine," she said, hanging up. "I'll call later."

o   o   o   o   o   o

But they were home. When the phone rang, Harper stopped Lauren from answering it. "Let the machine get it." She took a sip of coffee, watching Lauren carefully over the rim of her cup. "Okay, you were telling me why you were you sleeping on the couch when I woke up in the middle of the night."

Lauren sighed. "When I got home, you were sound asleep and I didn't want to wake you. Nothing more than that."

"You know I don't like to sleep alone."

"I know you don't like to *go* to sleep alone. I knew if I got in bed, you'd wake up. I was only trying to be considerate."

"I couldn't believe you weren't here when I got home. It scared me, Lauren. I didn't know what had happened. I thought you might have had an accident, especially on that narrow mountain road."

The night before, Harper had called Jean the second she walked into their house and found Lauren missing. She hadn't cared that she had awakened her. She wanted to know where Lauren was. Jean had put her on hold and looked out the window. In the dim light she could make out Lauren's car parked next to Barb's. "They're watching a Virginia Woolf video," she had told Harper.

"Harper, you said it was only nine o'clock when you got home. We didn't finish dinner at Wildfire until eight. And besides, you told me you wouldn't be home until late and not to worry. So I didn't."

"That's right." Harper slammed her cup down. "You'd rather be with that bunch than with me. I asked you to come last night, as a favor. Everyone except me was going to be there with her partner. But no, you couldn't bear to disappoint Jean. As if she'd care!"

Lauren lowered her eyes, not daring to meet Harper's. "You know I don't like restaurants," she said nervously. "We'd accepted Jean and Sonia's invitation and I didn't want to change it. I like going there; there's nothing sinister about that. I enjoy them and their friends, and they like and accept me."

"Oh, I get it. You're saying my friends don't accept you. That's a bunch of bullshit, Lauren."

"It isn't that, exactly. They just don't notice me. And I'm not blaming them, because I don't say anything. You know it's hard for me, Harper." She willed herself to meet Harper's eyes and to try to inject a little defiance into her next statement: "I had a good time last night."

"Well, I didn't, thanks. 'Where's Lauren? Is she all right?'" Harper mimicked in a falsetto voice.

"What did you answer?"

"You had a migraine. The truth wouldn't have been very kind, now, would it: 'Lauren didn't come because she can't stand any of you'."

"That isn't true, Harper." Lauren tugged at her hair. Then something inside her collapsed. "Never mind," she said wearily. "Let's not argue. I'm sorry my behavior upset you. I'm sorry you were worried when you came home; I thought I'd get home before you. I'm sorry. Really."

Harper's voice softened. "That's okay, Babe. It just scared me, that's all." She stood and went over to Lauren. Pulling her to her feet, she kissed her, a long, hard kiss. Lauren tried gently to deflect her. "Let's go for a walk."

But Harper pulled her even closer and kissed her again, this time with urgency.

"Harper," Lauren giggled uncomfortably. "It's 9 o'clock in the morning. What if someone comes by? Let's take a walk."

"Right," Harper murmured, her mouth on Lauren's neck. "To the bedroom." She put her arm around Lauren's waist and led her out of the room.

In their bedroom, Harper kissed her again, running her hands up and down her back, whispering into her hair. She pulled away just enough to undo the buttons of Lauren's shirt and slide if off her shoulders. Then she gently but authoritatively pushed Lauren back onto the bed, lowering her own body until it covered hers.

"Harper," Lauren protested feebly, then gave up.

○ ○ ○ ○ ○ ○

"It's a beautiful room," Clare announced, paintbrush in hand. "I've never seen anything like it."

Clare, Della, Barb, Sonia, and Jean had just finished painting the solarium/bathhouse. Sonia stepped back to survey their work. *Yes, it's magnificent,* she thought. The floor was pink cement with a pattern cut into it to resemble 12"x12" saltillo tile and the back wall was stuccoed in rose pink to match it. The remaining walls were painted a rich teal blue, the enormous beam and its supporting posts a high gloss black. Two shiny black sinks with gold-colored fixtures stood against a half wall, out of which the shower head pointed to a drain in the center of the floor.

Against the wall across from the sinks and shower, wicker shelves flanked a full-length mirror whose wooden frame had been painted glossy black. The shelves to the left held bath towels in an array of bright colors, the shelves to the right, bars of soap and bottles of shampoos, lotions, and bath oils. Sonia was a soap and lotion afficianado, which explained the sprinkling of exotic soaps and lotions among the more common varieties. It was a beautifully bright, warm, inviting room.

"You've really done it this time, friends," Barb said.

"You mean *we've* done it this time," Sonia corrected her. "I'm really grateful for everybody's help."

"When do the toilets arrive?" Clare asked, looking at the two side-by-side holes on the east side of the room.

"Soon, I hope. The first ones they sent weren't water savers, so we had to reorder."

"I love it," Della said. "Hers and hers toilets."

Jean looked around the room. The bathhouse *was* gorgeous, but it was going to be a challenge for her. She was not comfortable with the way her body looked or with its functions. At 112 pounds she still felt fat, even though she knew such a feeling was absurd. She often longed for the ease that Sonia and Barb had with their bodies, totally unselfconscious and, in Barb's case, proud of the way she looked. Though Sonia still struggled with accepting her breasts, she seemed on friendly terms with the rest of herself.

She glanced at the two toilet drain holes. Sonia had insisted on the side-by-side toilets. One day in a brainstorming session about the bathhouse, Sonia had referred to bathrooms as 'rooms of shame'. She had always wanted a totally open bathroom, she had said—windows everywhere and no curtains, walls, or doors—and finally she lived in a place where she could have it. Jean had agreed with her at the time.

But that was then. Faced with the almost-completed bathhouse, Jean found she wasn't looking forward to the day when the toilets were in. In theory, they were all well and good, but she had a feeling that in reality, living with such a public approach to bodily functions wasn't going to be easy for her. She couldn't even urinate in hers and Sonia's shared bathroom without shutting the door, and even then she got nervous when she thought Sonia might hear the splash. She didn't know how she was ever going to use the toilets out here.

Actually, it was worse than that, she admitted to herself. What Sonia didn't know—and no one else either—was that even with the bathroom door locked, it was impossible for her to have a bowel movement if there was anyone else *anywhere* in the house. Whenever she had to have one, she left the house and went to an outhouse on the property. But this was not something she was ready to deal with yet herself, let alone talk to anyone else about.

"Can I take a shower in here tomorrow?" Della's voice cut through her thoughts.

Jean thought it over. "I think to be safe we'd better wait a couple of days. Enamel dries slowly and I'd hate to pockmark this stuff."

"Drat. I wanted to be the first, but looks like I'll have to come back next week."

"The outside shower's hooked up, though." Sonia pointed out the window. "I'm heading for it as soon as I clean the paint off my hands."

They all gathered at the utility sink with a gallon of paint remover. Ten minutes later Sonia and Della were under the shower where first Della soaped Sonia's back, then Sonia soaped hers. Watching them, Jean felt such a surge of love that tears filled her eyes. She wanted women to be this way with one another all the time. She watched as Barb went through the sliding glass doors, naked, towel in hand, and joined them under the shower. Jean turned and hurried upstairs to the bathroom, turning on the shower as she undressed. Chastising herself for being a coward, she pulled the curtain and stepped under the water. She longed for the freedom those three women felt with their bodies.

She selected light khaki-colored jeans and a fuchsia T-shirt, gave her hair a few sweeps with the hair dryer, and hurried down to the kitchen. They'd invited Harper and Lauren and Barb to have lunch with them and Della in just thirty minutes.

Actually, she had started lunch preparations the day before, soaking pinto and anasazi beans until bedtime, then cooking them in the crockpot until they were soft. Right after breakfast this morning, she'd added seasoned tempeh, spices, and sauteed mushrooms, onions, sweet peppers, green chile, and tomatos, creating one of her favorite dishes, vegetarian chili. Now all that was left was to make the guacamole.

While Jean blended avocado, Della came in and set the table. Jean thought for the thousandth time how much she liked Della. Their friendship went back many years, and although they had very different opinions and ideas, they enjoyed each other.

"How do you feel about Marcy's coming?" Della asked her with studied casualness.

Jean looked at her in surprise. "Marcy?"

"You know, Sonia's ex."

"I know who you mean, silly. I just don't understand the question."

"I thought it might be a little awkward for you, since you've sort of taken her place in Sonia's life."

Jean sagged. "No, I haven't taken Marcy's place. She and Sonia were in a relationship. They had sex. They were a couple. They had ownership rights to each other. Sonia and I aren't in a relationship."

She stopped, unwilling to go any further. Sonia had been right; Della hadn't gotten it.

As if reading her mind, Della said, "I know what you and Sonia said yesterday, Jean. I'm not stupid. But I can also see that you care for each other a lot. Marcy's bound to have some effect on you."

"But I care a lot for you, too, Dell. Do I get out of joint when Phyllis comes to see you? Or when you talk about her? No. Because you and I aren't in a relationship. We don't hold invisible but powerful title papers on each other. What you do with your life is your business. That's how it is with Sonia and me. You say you heard us yesterday, but it doesn't sound like it."

"I understand that you're not having a relationship. But it doesn't mean you don't have feelings."

"You're talking about jealousy, and no, you don't feel jealous if you're not in a relationship. Look, I know it's hard. Relationships are deeply entrenched in us. We know their rules and regulations to a T. And one of those rules is that it's fine to have friends, but you can't do more than give them a brief hug. So what Sonia and I are doing immediately gets filed in the relationship folder because there's no other place for it. Mensmind says if you engage in any appreciable amount of touching, you're in a relationship and that's sex.

"Remember what happened to us a few months ago when Phyllis was on that business trip in Denver, and her friend called her and told her she had seen you and me in Consuela's having breakfast? She told Phyllis that we were doing a lot of messing around over our meal, and that when we were out in the parking lot, we kissed."

"She was an idiot," Della growled.

"Maybe so. But she saw us there, sitting next to one another, touching, laughing, obviously enjoying each other. Then when we said good-bye, she saw us kiss on the mouth. To her that meant we were having sex. And it meant the same to Phyllis. You two almost broke up over that."

"Phyllis understands our friendship now. She's been around you enough to see that you touch everybody a lot, that it's just the way you are. It's one of the things I love most about you, Jeannie."

Jean was not going to be either mollified or sidetracked. "I don't think Phyllis does understand, Dell. Since the two of you got together, I haven't stayed at your house with you once. If I decided to, if I called you next week and asked if I could stay over, could I sleep with you in your bed, the way we used to?"

Della frowned. "I don't know," she admitted reluctantly. "I guess if you did, I'd have to hope Phyllis wouldn't ask me where you'd slept. Or that she wouldn't even know you'd stayed over."

"See what I mean?" Jean said adamantly. "See how damaging mensmind is? See how it keeps us apart, keeps us from having closeness? How it rules our very existence? You're staying here tonight, Dell. I'd love to sleep with you. I miss you. I don't give a damn what the rules say. I'm giving them the middle finger and figuring out just what women are, sans our grotesque, misogynist socialization."

Della didn't say anything. She had been missing the closeness she and Jean had had before Phyllis came along. It wasn't anything Jean had done, for she had gone on being as affectionate as always. But the relationship with Phyllis had changed things, and she no longer felt the old ease with Jean. She deeply regretted that. But in order to appease Phyllis that hysteria-filled afternoon, she had promised not to be alone with Jean again, or at least not for long. Phyllis had wanted her to stop seeing Jean altogether. Della had refused. Hence, the compromise. She wanted to sleep with Jean too, wanted the cuddling and closeness. But she didn't dare.

○ ○ ○ ○ ○ ○

Marcy pulled Sonia aside after lunch. "Can we go someplace and talk?" Sonia nodded, and gestured toward the deck.

"I was thinking of someplace more private," Marcy said, disappointed.

"No one will bother us out there. Everybody's got other things to do. We'll be alone." She wanted to keep things as cool and impersonal as possible.

"This is a marvelous place," Marcy said out on the deck, taking deep breaths. "I can hardly believe the transformation it's undergone—everything, the house, the grounds. It was worth all the work. And your flowers are spectacular."

They sat on deck chairs, Marcy moving hers closer to Sonia's and Sonia, taking note of this, sliding hers back a little as she sat down.

Watching them from the kitchen window, Lauren could see Sonia gesturing, her face passionate, obviously trying to get Marcy to understand or agree with something.

Their breakup frightened Lauren. They had seemed to close, so happy. And now this. She liked Marcy a lot, her kindness, how easy she was to talk to, her predictably cheerful ways. Lauren had found their slight relationship comforting.

In contrast, there was Harper, she sighed. She was unhappy about her, though she could scarcely admit this even to herself. Harper's mood swings were disruptive to her life, more so because Harper confided in her and turned to her for comfort but also vented her anger and frustrations on her. Lauren was torn between feeling gratified at Harper's trust and overwhelmed by the burden of her emotional demands.

No one fully understood the magnitude of their relationship. Since they had moved to New Mexico, the problems that had seemed minor in Boston had intensified into major. Lauren attributed this to the fact that in Boston she had had many outside interests, had been busy with her practice, with her friends, with a multitude of diversions. Here, isolated, she was far more accessible to Harper's control. It was like living in a pressure cooker.

Six months before they left Boston, Harper and Lauren had agreed that they would try to end the sexual part of their relationship. This had been Lauren's idea, although after months of fighting about it, Harper had become suddenly and surprisingly amenable. Lauren soon learned why: she was seeing someone else on the side.

Although miserable in this knowledge, Lauren accepted it just as she did everything else in her life. Besides, it wasn't the first time. As usual, Lauren had hung on to Harper's reassurances that she still loved her the best and would never leave her.

But now, away from Boston, Harper had changed her mind about not wanting sex. She felt that they were both mature enough to transcend the sexual garbage most women get into in relationships. Although she didn't ask for sex often, once would have been too much for Lauren. But she couldn't tell Harper that. The couple of times she had tried, Harper had threatened to find someone else for sex again.

This threat, as Harper well knew, instantly destroyed whatever shaky confidence Lauren had, and kept her tractable. Lauren was terrified of losing Harper, terrified that Harper might find another woman and kick her out, and then what would she do? She had never been alone in her life.

She looked out the window. Marcy was standing now talking to Sonia, and Sonia was shaking her head. Marcy shrugged and walked across the deck, disappearing around the corner of the

house. Sonia did not follow her, but instead called Maggi into her
lap and held her close. A few minutes later Lauren saw Marcy's car
disappearing down the driveway. She had a feeling she would
never see her again.

o o o o o o

Once out on the highway, Marcy set the cruise control for 65
and leaned back against the headrest. She had felt miserable when
she left Wildfire twenty minutes before, but she loved to drive and
as the miles flew by, she relaxed, feeling better by the minute.

At the Las Palomas junction, she slowed to take the turn, then
quickly accelerated to 65 again. She glanced at her watch. Only
3:15. Too early to go home. She thought about calling her friend
Ruth and inviting her to dinner and a movie. But she erased that
from her mind. Ruth would probably insist on fixing dinner—
something very healthy—and then picking up a Doris Day video.
She liked Ruth, but an evening with her would be dullsville.

Searching through her mental rolodex for the name of some
woman she could call on the spur of the moment, she lit on Hillary.
For a moment she wasn't sure, though. Hillary was a Canadian
woman she had met at a party a few weeks earlier. She had made
it clear at once that she was available and interested in Marcy. Too
interested. It had put Marcy off, and besides, she had still been
with Sonia.

She had been doubly put off when Hillary came to see her as
a patient a few days later, ostensibly about a groin injury incurred
in a racquetball game. When Marcy had asked her nurse to be
present for the exam, Hillary had been piqued. She didn't need a
witness in the examining room, she'd said. Marcy had replied that
it was standard procedure and ignored her protests. When Hillary
hadn't even bothered to say goodbye, Marcy had been relieved.

But that had been nearly three weeks ago and today Marcy felt
different. Now, she remembered Hillary's gorgeous body. And
how much Hillary had wanted her. She felt a surge of warmth.

I'll call her, she decided, reaching for her bag. Hillary had given
her a business card and Marcy had dumped it in a side pocket
along with a dozen others. Finding the card, she punched the
number into her car phone.

She was surprised when someone answered, and even more
surprised when it was a man. I must have dialed the wrong
number, she thought. But when she asked for Hillary, he told her
to hold.

"Hillary, this is Marcy Sarendon," she said when Hillary came on. "I'm free tonight, and I'd love you to have dinner with me."

Marcy's directness excited Hillary, and she forgot her annoyance. "Marcy! This *is* a surprise! Tonight? Hold on, I have to check something."

Marcy could hear a conversation going on, but it was too muffled to make out. Hillary's voice came back over the phone. "Tonight's fine," she said. "My brother's visiting and I didn't want to dash off and leave him alone. But he's actually relieved. He turned down a dinner invitation so as not to leave me in the lurch, and he's delighted now that he can call and accept." Her voice and laugh thrilled Marcy. She loved British accents.

"Tell me where, Marcy, and when. Et cetera, et cetera."

"Las Hermanas. I'm a personal friend of the owner's and can always get a table there. I'll pick you up at 6:30, Baby Doll."

She hung up feeling great. She hadn't lost the old Sarendon touch. It might not be a wasted day after all. She'd go home, change, and head for the spa where she'd work out with the weight machines and swim. Pleased with herself, she switched on the radio and hummed along.

She was back behind the wheel, back in the driver's seat.

11

Sonia sat despondently at her desk, frustrated and depressed from her afternoon's conversation with Marcy. Though by this time she was well aware that Marcy hadn't agreed with most of what she'd been talking about for the past few years, she hadn't realized until today how very determinedly Marcy had put her own interpretation on it.

She still wants to think I'm talking about nonmonogamy, Sonia thought, defeated. Two minutes after agreeing that sex prevented intimacy, that there could be another way of being together that was so powerful and arousing that any woman discovering it would never want to do sex again, Marcy had said, "But what if you meet a really sweet woman, and you want to hold her and kiss her and make love to her? What do you do if you've taken a vow of celibacy?"

At that point Sonia had given up forever. I've pushed you, Marcy, she thought, pushed you well beyond your limits. I'm sorry I didn't realize it sooner. I guess I wanted so much to believe that you were a friend of my heart that I refused to see the truth. The whole thing was so painful she could hardly bear it. Her eyes ached with unshed tears. Closing them, she whispered, "Marcy, dearest Marcy," and for a moment let the tears burn hot furrows down her cheeks.

Stop this! she ordered herself impatiently. Stop wallowing in this sick fantasy! Looking at her hands before her on the desk, she began concentrating on the gold ring on the fourth finger of her right hand, the ring she had given herself, the ring inscribed in French: You and no other.

Suddenly, she yanked a side drawer open, pulled out a yellow legal pad and scrawled I'M THE ONE across the top. Under it she furiously began making a list:

I'm the one I miss when I think I miss someone else.

I'm the one who loves me unconditionally.

I'm the one who will never leave me.

I'm the one who will always take care of me.

I'm the one at the center of my life.

I'm the one whose total focus is me.

I'm the one I can count on absolutely.

I'm the one I can trust completely.

I'm the one who loves my company more than anyone else.

I'm the one who thinks I'm madly intelligent, delightful, and beautiful.

I'm the one who never criticizes me.

I'm the one who forgives me everything.

I'm the one who comforts and nurtures me.

I'm the one who makes me feel secure and safe.

I'm the one who loves my body as it ages and changes.

I'm the one who touches me all over lovingly and joyously.

I'm the one who makes me unafraid.

I'm the one who wants me to be free more than anything in the world.

I'm my best and dearest friend.

She laid the pen down, for the moment purged of relationshipness, remembering who she was, centered and at peace. Swiveling in her chair, she glanced out the window. Where was everybody? She could see Harper and Lauren's car, and Barb's, but the place seemed strangely quiet. No women, no dogs, no pigs in sight.

A cloud of dust down by the gate caught her attention. As it moved up the hill, she recognized Dana's van and started down to the kitchen to put the kettle on for tea.

A few minutes later, Dana burst in, flushed, her hair sticking out in several directions. "Sonia!" she yelped, swooping down upon her and enveloping her in a strong one-armed embrace. The other arm was laden with flowers.

"I know I should have called first, but I wanted to tell you in person. I just came from shooting a wedding." Carefully laying the bouquet on the counter, she began searching for a vase.

"I got this frantic call from a woman whose daughter was getting married today. The photographer they'd lined up was sick and they needed a substitute, quick. I hate weddings but these people were so desperate that they offered me a $200 bonus if I'd agree. So of course I did."

As she arranged the flowers, she effused on.

"Rich, Sonia. I mean this family has big bucks and a daughter who's an absolute princess. I'm sure she was shocked when I showed up looking like the un-fashion model I so quintessentially am. But she'll feel better when she sees the pictures."

She took the cup Sonia offered and poured tea from the pot. "Where is everybody?" she asked. "I see cars, but no bodies."

"I don't know. Marcy came for lunch and then she and I talked afterwards. She wanted to say goodbye to everyone, but there was no one to say goodbye to. Except me."

Dana saw the flicker of pain cross Sonia's face as she said this. Deciding to put off telling her own news for awhile, she asked gently, "How did it go?"

"I don't know, Dana. She can't understand why I need to keep my distance now. She really believes we can carry on as before, minus the sex—although, frankly, I think she believes she could win me back to sex pretty soon, too. I don't think she buys the idea that once you establish a relationship with someone, you can never escape it."

Dana shook her head. "I don't understand Marcy. I mean, I don't know her very well, but it's obvious that she's an intelligent woman. So how can she deny that it's impossible to have peerness with anyone you've been in a relationship with? Lover, parent, child, teacher, or boss, sadomasochism prevails between you forever more."

Sonia was thoughtful. "You're right, you know; Marcy is very intelligent. And she understands perfectly well what I'm saying about relationships. She just doesn't want to do what I'm doing. But instead of coming out and saying so, she says what she thinks she has to say to keep my good will. It's not even that she's dishonest. It's just that relationshipping is second nature to her, and she likes doing it. I'm sure she sees no reason whatever to stop. So she's walking a delicate line—saying one thing and doing another.

"Something happened that makes me sure I'm right," Sonia explained. "I just realized what it meant. Sitting out there on the deck looking at Marcy, I was almost overcome by my desire to have her with me in this . . ." she spread her arms, indicating everything. "So I gave it all the eloquence I had, painting for her my vision of women's world: joy always, touching, everything desirable in abundance; no jealousy, no illness, no unhappiness; the power to fly with the hawks, run with the panthers, to *be* them, and to be one another. I talked about intimacy such as we've never dreamed of in patriarchy, not only with all other women, but with everything that lives all through this universe and others. I talked about timelessness and spacelessness—the ecstasy of women's power to be anywhere we wish at any moment. I talked about not needing machines of any kind, being able to do everything effortlessly.

"At the end of this monologue, I was in tears of rapture, imagining, remembering, longing, knowing that I was going to live to experience everything I'd described and more."

"And Marcy?"

Sonia sighed. "She was in tears, too, but not for the same reason. I didn't get it then, but I think now that she was crying because she saw how totally and eternally we were separated. She said something I know is very significant, though I don't understand all the reasons why. She said, 'I can't do it, Sonia. I can't do it'.

"Maybe all she meant was that she didn't want to do it. In the world I described, there was absolutely no excitation, not a shred of sadomasochism. To her, it sounded boring. And she's not alone; lots of women have told me they think the Utopia I describe would be boring. Before I understood how thoroughly saturated with sadomasochism both our inner and outer worlds are, how profound our need for continual excitation, I never understood how they could think that. But now, of course, I understand only too well.

"It reminds me of a place in the Mormon temple ritual where one of the officials describes men's reality, men's truth, men's world. He says that in this world, everything has its opposite—joy and sorrow, pleasure and pain; that the bad is necessary so that we can appreciate the good. In other words, men's only pleasure in life comes through comparison, through the excitation of hierarchy: 'I bash my head against the wall because it feels so good when I stop.'

"And having been coached in bitter ways how to be men, sadomasochism is reality for women, too, until we renounce it. So I'm sure that Marcy finds such a world as I describe incredibly lackluster."

Dana nodded and poured herself more tea. "Well, at least you're a free woman now. It seems to me that that's all that matters. You. And Marcy being free to do her life in whatever way she chooses. I only know that my decision not to do relationships has been wonderfully freeing. And if I experience even a twinge of regret, I look at Harper and Lauren, and it's gone instantly."

"I hadn't known much about the dynamics of their relationship until Lauren stopped by the other morning to walk the dogs and talked to Jean and me. She said more in that short hour than I think she's ever said in all the times we've been together as a group. Jean pointed out that Harper speaks for both of them."

"I'm amazed she talked to you without Harper present to translate," Dana said trenchantly.

Sonia looked surprised. "I thought you were friends."

"I've known them since they came to New Mexico, and Harper's been great about sending work my way. I like them individually—although I don't know Lauren all that well. But together . . ." She shook her head. "I can't understand why Lauren stays with her, Sonia. I really can't. Harper is so condescending and domineering. And Lauren just takes it."

"She could get out if she wanted to. She's made a choice to stay with Harper. And that's her prerogative."

"Do you really think she has a choice? For all we know she may be one of those women who has been so destroyed—by incest, brutality, poverty, drugs, terror—that she really can't be said to have a choice, just goes from one abuser to another."

"No," Sonia said firmly. "This is not true. No matter how badly a woman's been damaged by mensmachine, she always has choices, and every single second of her life she can choose among an infinite number of them. Look at her life and you have a record of those millions, billions of daily choices."

Dana shook her head. "I can't see it. I think of my sister, Reba. She's been in and out of mental hospitals all her life, has a despicable, tyrannical brute of a husband, a raft of kids—most grown now, thanks goodness—and deteriorating health. She's so depressed she can hardly get out of bed. Can you honestly say this is her choice?"

"Without a doubt," Sonia maintained unwaveringly. Seeing Dana's continued skepticism, she explained. "I've thought a lot about this in connection with change. Can all women change or are there some who really can't? What I've realized is that it's the difference between possibility and probability. By this I mean that though the *possibility* for change is always present for every woman regardless of her circumstances or condition, the *probability* is not. That is, the option to change is always there but not the likelihood that she'll have the gumption to choose it. Out of fear, she will probably make some other choice. But the point is that she could if she would.

"Women are extraordinary beings, every one of us, Dana," she went on, "far more powerful, far more everything than we can begin to believe or give ourselves credit for. Given this, and that we're constantly making choices—we can't help it, that's what it is to live—any one of us could opt to change *if we wanted to badly enough.*"

Though Dana had nodded in agreement during this explanation, she looked doubtful at this conclusion.

"But haven't I heard you say that at any given moment every woman is doing the best she can?"

Sonia laughed. "Maybe. I know I've said that every woman was doing what she needed to do. But I don't believe that any longer. What I think now is that at any given moment every woman is doing what she *wants* to do."

"So you make a distinction between 'need' and 'want'."

"I don't; manunkind does. In women's world, needs and wants are identical. We want what's good for us, what we really need for happiness. We never want anything that isn't in our best interests. In patriarchy, we want what we're been conditioned to believe we need, not what we really need, and this is almost never good for us.

"So going back a few minutes to where I said that what was happening in Lauren's life was her choice, I could just as well have gone on to say, 'She's doing what she *wants* to do, but I don't think it's what she *needs* to do'."

"Well, I can agree with you there, and it makes me sad. I'd like to know Lauren in some context other than in relation to Harper. But as you say, it's her choice and ultimately none of my business."

She took Sonia's arm and pulled her gently up from her chair. "Let's sit out on the deck," she urged. "I came racing here straight from the wedding because I have something I'm dying to tell you."

They walked arm-in-arm out onto the deck, now in shade, and sat in the chairs so recently vacated by Sonia and Marcy. Dana leaned toward Sonia eagerly.

"I've been waiting all day to talk to you about this. Something wonderful happened at the wedding." Her eyes shone and her voice was strong and sure.

"As I told you, these people were totally out of my class. I'm sure there isn't one subject we could have talked comfortably about. Anyway, the mother was trying to explain to me what kinds of photos they wanted and I wasn't getting it. I was just about to throw in the towel and tell her to call someone else when something clicked inside me."

She pulled her chair closer to Sonia's and took her hand.

"I stopped trying to listen *to* her, and tried instead to *be* her."

Sonia felt something leap in her chest, but she waited quietly for Dana to go on.

"You know how when you're listening to someone, you respond to them by nodding, or saying, 'uh huh' or 'hmmm', and that if you try not to do this—like in your 'hearing into being'—you still respond in your head?"

Not waiting for an answer, she raced on.

"Well, while you're responding, aloud or in your head, you miss some of what the person's saying, the connections and the nuances, the feeling-tone. What I did, Sonia, was stop responding, even in my head. I got out of the stimulus/response mode."

"Which is sadomasochism."

"Right. I did it by pretending that her words were coming from my mouth. That it was really me who was speaking. And—this is the magical part—the instant I did that, it was as if it *were* me speaking. As if I *were* her. Inside her. And so of course I understood exactly and at once what she wanted."

She let go of Sonia's hand and sat back in her chair, momentarily overcome by the memory of that experience.

"It's what we've talked about so often," she went on after
awhile. "Men are externally oriented and motivated, totally,
which means that their world is organized this way. Women see
and experience everything from the inside. Which is why I
couldn't understand Camille. Her external world and my external
world were too different. But when I stopped viewing her from
outside and got inside her, *became* her, I knew perfectly well what
she meant. It was as clear to me as it was to her.

"I didn't have any time to process this because we were
moving so fast, but on the way home I thought about it and
realized how incredible it is. I know this is how we were in
women's world, Sonia. This is how we communicated. I don't
think we used words at all. I think we communicated by *being* one
another."

"What a wonderful story! And it's true that in women's world
we are one another. I've known that, but I didn't have any
particulars about how we did it. I can see exactly how this 'being
into intimacy', or whatever you call it, works. And I know you're
right about our having communicated this way before patriarchy.
With this, and with touch, and maybe in other ways. But as you
say, not with words."

She leaned back and closed her eyes for a moment. "While you
were talking, I started listening to you as if I were saying your
words, and I had an experience like you describe with Camille."

Dana glowed. "You know, if we do that with every woman we
meet, it's going to transform our lives."

They stood and began walking down the driveway.

"You see," Dana went on eagerly, "part of the problem today
was that Camille was talking about something I had no personal
interest or experience in, largely because of the class difference
between us. She was speaking a language that meant little to me,
about concerns that have never entered my life. There was no way
we were going to be able to communicate effectively in the usual
way. By listening to her as though her words were my own, I
understood. It doesn't mean I'll ever adopt her way of viewing the
world; her values, her ideas of what is important even make me
angry. It just means that I was able, effortlessly, to break through
the male communication barriers between us."

"This 'being into understanding'—what *are* we going to call
it?—would have been useful for me with Marcy today." Sonia

slipped her arm around Dana's waist. "But I wonder if I could have done it with her, given the tension between us and the fact that I haven't a shred of objectivity about her yet."

"It seems to me," Dana argued, "that it can work regardless of the circumstances. But," she relented a little, "it could be that a situation like yours with Marcy would be difficult to begin on. Maybe after lots of practice you could do it in such fraught circumstances."

They came to the bridge and stopped, leaning with their elbows on the railings and delighting in the profusion of wild roses blooming along the creek banks; the air was filled with their heavenly aroma.

Sonia felt a wave of gratitude for Dana's friendship and for her understanding of women's world. Her appearance in their lives had been totally serendipitous. Sonia had been referred to her for publicity photos, and during the course of their session they had started to talk. When Dana's next appointment hadn't shown, they kept on talking. Sonia had invited her to meet Jean and Barb, she in turn had invited them to meet Harper and Lauren, they had all discovered their passion for mysteries, and thus was Murder Maids born.

But except for Jean, it was Dana Sonia felt closest to, Dana who seemed to inhabit most similar intellectual territory.

Dana interrupted her thoughts. "How's the bathhouse coming along?"

"We finished the painting this morning," Sonia said, turning away from the bridge. "It's wildly beautiful, Dana. We're just waiting for the toilets to arrive, and then it's complete. I don't know what's on the agenda for supper tonight, but why don't you stay, and I'll show you our mistresspiece."

"Thanks, but I've got to fly home and get my film developed. They've promised me an extra $100 if I have the pictures ready by Wednesday. Besides, I ate a ton of food at the reception. Bad food, I'm afraid, but I was starving and it tasted wonderful. I'll come up soon and critique the bathhouse." They stopped at her van and hugged long and close before she drove off.

When Sonia got back to the kitchen, there was still no sign of life. She wasn't really hungry but the restlessness she had felt earlier was returning full force, so she opened the refrigerator and investigated the contents. There're enough leftovers here to feed an army, she thought. Taking out a loaf of whole wheat French bread, she cut several pieces and took them and a glass of soy milk up to her room.

She was eager to get on with the experiment, but afraid Jean might be too tired when she got back. It was already after seven. Settling herself on her bed, she began reading. Almost an hour later, she heard a soft knock on her door.

Jean came in, looking radiant. "I tried to call you several times, but no answer," she told Sonia. "We all took a long hike, then ended up at Barb's. She wanted to show us her latest painting. Since Dell and Clare had never seen her place, we got the grand tour. Then Barb persuaded us to stay for dinner." She looked closely at Sonia's face for signs of suffering. "What's been going on here?"

"After Marcy left, Dana came by and she and I talked for awhile about—guess what?—relationships. Then we walked down to the bridge and talked some more. Sounds like you had a good time."

"The walk was good. Barb's concerned that Ashley is getting a bit chunky, so she wanted to do a long one."

"Chunky! How could she possibly tell?"

"She's started scraping her belly on Barb's back steps when she tries to get up them."

Sonia laughed. "Where're Dell and Clare?"

"They're all still over at Barb's playing Monopoly. I didn't feel like it. What's wrong with your legs?"

They both looked down at Sonia's legs that appeared to be leaping about the bed on their own.

"I don't know what gets into them," Sonia confessed. "Periodically they do this 'jump-leg' number. I've been meaning to ask if you have any idea why, and what, if anything, I can do about it."

"Usually varicose veins."

Sonia shook her head. "I don't have any." She held her leg up in the air for Jean to see.

"Here, let me take a look." Jean took her leg and examined it carefully, then reached for the bottle of lotion Sonia kept on the bedside table. Squeezing a liberal amount into her hands, she massaged it quickly into the right leg. Then, holding onto Sonia's ankle with one hand, she began to run the fingers of her other hand up the inside of the leg, applying pressure with her thumb. Sonia shrieked and nearly leapt through the ceiling.

"I can't believe it hurts that much!"

"Varicose veins. They may not show all the time, but they can lie hidden deep inside the leg." She did the same with the left leg. This time Sonia almost fainted.

"How can I get rid of them?" she asked, face ashen.

Jean shook her head. "You can't. But massage helps. I'm pretty sure that with it and herbs, I can prevent them from getting worse. Maybe I can even improve things somewhat. But once they're that well-established, surgery is the only thing I know of that can 'cure' them. I'll do my best, but don't expect them to go away. They're not going to."

Even though Jean took great care with both legs, applying firm but gentle pressure, the pain was excruciating. When she finished, however, 'jump-leg' had subsided for the moment. "Probably terrorized," Jean joked. She leaned back into the pillows.

"I'll massage them every night before you sleep, if you'd like. That should stop the restless jumpiness."

Sonia laid her head in Jean's lap and gave herself over to the exquisite sensation of having her face and head rubbed.

"You know what I was thinking earlier?" she said sleepily. "Looking at Marcy, I was thinking how, now that I'm never going to do another relationship, I'm going to miss kissing. Kissing was my favorite thing. I could do it for hours. And Marcy had a sweet kiss, although for her, kissing mostly meant the beginning of the sex dance. I think I like kissing so much because I grew up in the fifties when it was all a good girl could do besides grope around a little. So we good girls developed a whole repertoire of kisses.

"But you kids that came after us, you didn't even bother with kissing as far as I could see. It seemed to me you by-passed the preliminaries completely and just jumped right into the act."

Jean laughed. "You're right. I never kissed much, either men or women. It was a prelude to sex, and we didn't do much foreplay in any of my relationships."

"I miss it," Sonia sighed. "Even back before I decided I didn't want to do sex anymore, I could have kissed forever."

"Well, ask your usual question, 'Who says kissing is sex?'" Jean said. "And give your usual answer: 'men, and they're always wrong'. Here you are accepting that kissing is sex without even examining your assumptions."

As if she were on springs, Sonia bounced into sitting position. "Okay, kiddo, pucker up!"

Though she felt anxious, Jean went along. She'd never done much kissing and hadn't liked the little she'd done. But as soon as their lips touched, her uneasiness vanished. It was indescribably sweet. Sonia had either had lots of practice or was born to kiss.

"Both," Sonia grinned when Jean asked.

"Whatever, it was really wonderful." They were sitting back, smiling at each other. "And didn't feel at all like sex. As soon as we began, my whole body relaxed."

"Mine, too. It felt different to me, though, like our touching. It'll take time for me to get used to not using it for excitation—as a means to that end—and to let its authentic sensations emerge. In the meantime, it's bound to be a little dull, I suppose. I hope you know that that hasn't anything to do with your expertise."

Jean shrugged. "I wouldn't be surprised, though—or hurt—if it did. I'm not exactly a gold-medal kisser."

"But I think you have a real advantage over me. You rarely felt excitation with any kind of physical contact. I felt it all the time—when it was called for, that is; I knew how to flip the sex switch and feel all the required feelings. So my body is well trained in excitation and at a loss without it."

Jean nodded. "Whereas mine is on the verge of total ecstasy simply because she's not numbed out anymore. You're right. I rarely felt anything during sex, especially if I was being touched. So I'm not sitting here thinking 'that feels good but not as good as before', or 'that feels nice but it's kind of boring in comparison to . . .'"

"Exactly," Sonia said. "This is what I'm going through right now. For me, both the touching and now this feel good but, without the sex/excitation zing, a little ho hum."

Jean said thoughtfully, "It reminds me of the very rigid diet I went on when I had cancer. No salt and virtually no seasonings at all on any of my food, which consisted mainly of steamed vegetables and well-cooked rice. At first I couldn't taste anything. Cauliflower and broccoli and carrots all tasted the same and, without the flavor the salt gave them, that meant almost tasteless.

"But gradually my body grew accustomed to not having salt and seasonings, and for the first time in my life I began to taste the vegetables. I discovered that they were full of flavor, all very different. Flavor far more subtle and delicate and wonderful than before. And also longer lasting."

Sonia sat up. Pulling Jean gently toward her, she kissed her again. They settled into it and kissed for a long while. But after a few minutes, Jean noticed that something bizarre was happening. She was not an experienced kisser so she didn't feel sure of her judgment. All she knew was that Sonia was holding her head tighter and tighter, and beginning to grab her lower lip between her teeth so that she could scarcely move.

Though she didn't know it, that was exactly the point: Sonia didn't want her to move. She had never kissed anyone like Jean before, who bounced all over the place, not content simply to hold a kiss, to savor it. Kissing Jean was a lesson in pecking—now here, now there, back here, now over there; a game of 'catch me if you can'.

So Sonia was on the verge of giving up, of deciding that kissing wasn't as important to her as she thought, and Jean was wondering why anyone would miss this absurd behavior, when Sonia finally realized she was doing passive aggression, and said right out what she wanted.

"Jean, I like kisses that are slow, barely moving, deep and long."

"Oh. I didn't know."

They kissed again, but this time Jean held still and Sonia, no longer trying to chase her all over the room, felt her body slide into that marvelous combination of relaxation and arousal where her thoughts slipped away, leaving her with nothing but the sensation of sweetness and warmth on her mouth and across her body.

When the kiss was over, Jean smiled at her, the smile threatening to turn into laughter. "That was lovely," she said, "absolutely lovely there at the end. But I have to admit that for awhile, I was really beginning to wonder."

Sonia waited for her to go on.

"I know I'm not an expert, but after the first few minutes, our kissing moved into odd and beyond, with you gripping my head so hard I'll have permanent indentations and grabbing my lip so I didn't dare move for fear I'd leave it clenched in your teeth."

Sonia laughed. "Genius," she said, "I was trying to get you to hold still long enough that I *could* kiss you! That last kiss was our first real kiss."

Feeling a little foolish, Jean said, "Well, I thought I was doing it right."

"Haven't you watched any movies? Surely you never saw any pecking around all over the place like that."

"Frankly, I never watched those scenes," Jean confessed. "I don't know why, but they either bored me or made me uncomfortable."

"Well, I'm glad we figured it out. I can't imagine women's world without kisses, kisses, and more kisses."

They kissed again and this time Jean felt herself move in and out of awareness, first awareness of the feel of Sonia's mouth on hers, firm and soft at the same time, gentle, yielding, then assertive, kissing so deep she thought she'd never return, then light, butterfly touches that played across her lips. She felt her body going deeper and deeper into the place of no-thought, into pure feeling.

Startled, she opened her eyes and found herself looking directly into Sonia's blue ones. Deep blue today, like the sky.

"I fell asleep," Jean said wonderingly. "We were kissing and I fell asleep."

"You did. I could feel you drifting away and could have wept from the dearness of it."

Isn't this strange, Jean thought. *If I'd been in a relationship and done this, I'd have been in big trouble.*

She tried to imagine it, and shook her head. Maybe once would have been forgiven, but regularly—it would have been a disaster. Because of course kissing like this would have been part of the sex, and to fall asleep would have been an insult, an admission that her lover's touch hadn't excited her. Looking at Sonia's peaceful, happy expression, she knew she was in another context altogether, the oldest tradition there was and yet seemingly a brand new one.

"I don't think many women are going to understand this, Sonia. Every word that comes to my mind to describe it is going to be construed as sexual. But I know what sex feels like and this isn't it, not remotely. How do we explain it?"

"Beats me, Genius. It's clear as a spring morning to me, yet I know you're right. Most women are going to see it as sex and think we're just calling it something else—you know the story. We don't have the language to describe what we're experiencing in any of our experiments. We're stuck with men's only language: the sex language, the sadomasochistic tongue. They breathe in s/m, think in s/m, talk in s/m, write in s/m. They sleep it and dream it and live it every second of their lives. It's their total reality. And we've adopted it."

Jean sighed and stroked Sonia's face, once again marveling at the fineness of it, the sweetness of her soft skin as it played over her bones. *She has a beautiful neck,* Jean thought as she touched it on her way to her shoulders. Sonia pulled her T-shirt over her head, wincing as she did.

"Something hurt?"

"This right breast," Sonia touched it and winced again. "I have to be careful how I touch it."

Jean placed her hand gently over Sonia's breast. It felt hot in her hand, an angry, unforgiving heat. She touched it carefully, discovering by the heat exactly where the painful area was. "No one will ever hurt you again," she whispered to the breast. "No one. You're safe now. I know it's hard to trust when you've been so badly treated, but it won't happen again."

She bent her head and oh, so gently, began to kiss and lick the area around the nipple. As she did, she lost awareness of time and space. Her mind stopped and she gave herself over to her body's wisdom, to the ancient wisdom of women who knew how to be with their bodies and the bodies of the women around them. She knew what it was to be Sonia's breast, knew the pain and sorrow and terror it had experienced and was still holding. Tears filled her eyes, but she kept on licking and stroking and loving it.

When she finished, she moved to the left breast. This one had no hot places, but instead felt totally numb. Still, she loved her as she had the other one, talked to her, told her it was safe to come back, safe to feel again.

Then on their own accord, without instruction from her, her hands began touching Sonia's sides and belly. They had no goal, no purpose, no plan in mind. They simply wanted to touch, wanted to feel another's skin against their own, wanted to mingle energies. She was aware that Sonia was rubbing her back and shoulders, but the awareness was far away, as though her mind was almost completely out of it and the two bodies oblivious of everything but each other.

She felt herself spiraling slowly towards sleep, a delicious, lazy loss of consciousness. But even in sleep her hands kept moving. They weren't ready to stop.

12

"My sister's are coming," Lauren announced, returning to the backyard after hanging up the phone. She and Harper were having a spur-of-the-moment cookout, and had invited the Murder Maids plus Clare and Della to meet their old friend, Star, from Boston. Star was on a business trip and had only one evening to spend with them.

Frowning, Harper sat up in the hammock. "When?"

"Next week, actually. They both have time off over the 4th of July. They've been wanting to come for a long time . . ." she finished lamely. She knew Harper disliked both her sisters, but particularly Priscilla, the outspoken one.

"Where are they from?" Sonia asked, taking another tempeh burger from the grill.

"Boston," Lauren answered. "I'm the only one who strayed far from the Atlantic. They've never been to New Mexico, so it'll be fun to show them around. Any suggestions about where to take them?"

"How about the State Pen?" Harper suggested. "They'd love it."

An awkward silence followed, all the Murder Maids remembering the night Harper had ranted on about what idiots Lauren's two sisters were, how Lauren had suffered through it silently, and how embarrassed they'd all been.

"You'd better make reservations for them at The Belle Starr," Harper said. The Belle Starr was an old hotel about fifteen minutes from their door.

"i was thinking of putting them in the study on the hide-a-bed, and borrowing a foldup bed from Wildfire." She looked inquiringly at Jean, who nodded.

Harper tried another tack. "But they'd be so much more comfortable at the hotel. The study's small, and they wouldn't have much privacy."

The thought of Lauren's sisters in the house was almost unendurable to her, but she didn't say this, hoping that Lauren would comply without her having to.

"I suppose so." Lauren's brow knitted. "But I so rarely see them that I thought it would be nice to have them close by. So we can just talk ourselves to sleep and no one has to drive anywhere if it's late and we're tired. I'd have to transport them back and forth, too, since neither of them drives anymore."

"It's not that far," Harper argued. "And besides, if you're together all day, you won't need to be up talking into the night. I can't imagine what you have to talk about, anyhow."

"Maybe you should get two rooms at The Belle Starr, Lauren," Barb suggested. "Then you could stay there at night and wouldn't have to drive back to the house."

Harper shot Barb a poisonous look.

"I don't know," Lauren said miserably. "I'll figure it out later."

Harper pushed her advantage. "I just think for their sakes they'd be better off in a hotel."

Why don't you just say you don't want them in the house, instead of being so damned passive aggressive, Sonia thought. *We all know you can't stand them, so just say it instead of pretending to be concerned for them.*

"Speaking of visitors, my daughter's coming for two weeks in August," Della said, helping herself to more potato salad. "I'm taking ten days off while she's here. If any of you can think of how to entertain an eighteen-year-old, I'm desperate to know."

"When in August?" Jean asked.

"The eighth to the twenty-second."

"We're leaving for the Michigan Womyn's Music Festival on the tenth. We'll need a dog and housesitter for that week. How does that sound?"

Della almost clapped her hands. "Perfect. Angie wanted to go camping—definitely not my thing, as you know. I think staying at your place would suffice for her and for me it'd be far superior."

"I'll have you over for dinner at least once," Barb promised, "And if she wants to, I can borrow the Blair horses so we can ride."

"She'd love it. I accept all offers gratefully."

"Do you have a picture of her?" Lauren asked.

Della rummaged through her bag and extracted a wallet-sized photo. "This is Angie," she said, handing it to Sonia.

Sonia smiled when she saw the picture. "She looks very lively and mischievous." She passed it to Clare.

"Yes she does," Clare agreed.

Della grinned. "She's a spunky one, all right." Then her face grew serious. "But I'm afraid she's got a major weight problem." Retrieving the snapshot from Barb, she returned it to her wallet. "Takes after her dad's family, unfortunately."

No one responded to this for a moment. Then Jean blurted out, "What does that matter, Dell? Why should her weight even be a topic of conversation?"

Della shrugged. "I guess it's because I've battled it with her most of her life and so it always comes to my mind when I think of her. I wish we could do something about it."

"Why not let her be?" Sonia suggested. "It's her body. It's interesting to me that you felt you had to mention it to us."

"Well, she's a fine, intelligent girl, and I just wanted to warn you about her weight before you saw her so you wouldn't judge her by it right off."

At this, Jean became angry. "Hey, what kind of neanderthals do you take us for, Dell? And who says fat's ugly? Frankly, your fat phobia pisses me off."

"Now hold on a minute, Jean. I don't hate the way Angie looks. I just know she'd be healthier and happier with some of that weight off. And I refuse to be one of those mothers who's blind to her children's flaws."

"So your daughter's body's a flaw. Good grief, Dell, what kind of attitude is that? She must know how you feel. What men do to us about our bodies is already horrific, we don't need to add to it."

"I don't hassle her about it," Della said defensively. "But at the same time she needs to know that I'm available and willing to help her with it."

"With her flaw," Jean said in disgust.

"You don't get it," Della said impatiently. "I'm being a concerned mother. She's miserable about it. The boys tormented her at school, her father and brother torment her at at home. I'm just trying to help make life easier for her."

As a therapist, Star felt she could not longer stay out of the conversation. "But of course that's not the message you're giving her. Your message to her is that you agree with society that her body's gross. Focusing on it *has* to increase her self-consciousness and self-hatred."

"No, you're wrong. My message to her is that I love her enough to do what I can to help her be happy."

"We're all fat phobic, Dell," Sonia said, "all girthist, every last one of us."

"Not you, surely," Lauren said to Jean. "I've heard you say you like fat women, women who look like The Venus of Willendorf or Gaia."

"I do, very much. I like fat on other women. The rounder a woman's body is, the more I love it, love the way it looks, the way it feels. But the thought of that same fat on my own body is unbearable, even terrifying."

"In other words, 'I love your fat but don't give it to me'," Harper said.

"Exactly. It's very conditional. As long as it's somewhere else, it's beautiful."

"The issue of body size looms in every woman's mind," said Star. "If not in her conscious mind, then certainly somewhere in there."

Sonia nodded. "Looms is a good word. We're tyrannized by it, totally controlled by our fear of it. I didn't think I was fat phobic until one day I tried to imagine gaining twenty pounds and nearly had a stroke. I'm fine as long as my body stays the way she is. As you said Jean, my loving her is very conditional."

"My Hopi friend Chenoa once accused me of having 'fat eyes'," Jean said. "At least where my own body was concerned. I'd look in the mirror and see a fat woman, even when I weighed less than a hundred pounds."

"I do that all the time," Clare admitted. "Especially if I'm around a woman who is very thin, or who in mensworld has an extraordinary figure. Right before my eyes my body expands to immense proportions."

They all laughed. All except Della, that is.

"I'm feeling pretty upset about this," she said stiffly, "and attacked. I didn't ask for any of your opinions about my behavior." She looked pointedly at Jean. "You've never been a mother, Jean. It's damned hard, but I've always been as open and honest with my kids as I knew how to be. I've never pretended to feel what I don't feel, even if it might have been kinder. And I'm not going to start now."

Star intervened. "If you don't want to change, Della, that's your right. But it might be useful to Angie if you confess your fear and hatred of fat, and leave her alone to take care of herself."

When Della refused to respond, Star rapidly changed the subject. Looking around at all of them, she said, "I think it's great that you're all friends."

"It is," Dana agreed. "I was feeling pretty isolated out here until I met these two." She nodded at Harper and Lauren. "Then I met Sonia and Jean, and they introduced me to Barb, and here we are. My only regret is that we don't live even closer together. We're still pretty scattered, except for you three up on the mountain."

"I like it this way," Harper contended. "I have zero faith in communal living. I don't think it can work."

"I'm not talking about communal living; I'm talking about living as neighbors, real neighbors. Think how much easier it would be if we didn't have to get into our respective vehicles to visit one another, especially in the winter."

Sonia smiled at her. "I'm waiting for the day when there are so many women in our mountains and this valley, Dana, that we can finally do our gift economy in earnest. I'm tired of being terrorized by men's exchange system."

"I don't understand what you mean by gift economy," Star said, perplexed.

"It's simple. We'd each offer whatever goods or services we produced freely to the community at large. Let's say, for instance, that Jean made twelve loaves of bread. She'd take the bread to the community center and leave it on a table for anyone to take. Neither she nor anyone else would keep track of who took how much of it, because no comparative value would be assigned to anything. Let's say that while she was there, Jean looked for zucchini among the vegetables that had been donated because she wanted to make a zucchini casserole. When she found it, she'd simply take what she needed. No one would notice or care how much."

"It requires a spiritual, emotional, and intellectual sophistication light years beyond exchange," Dana put in.

"But what about barter?" Star asked.

Dana shook her head. "Barter may not require money, but it's exchange all the same, because comparative value is assigned to every item and every service and someone still has to keep track and try to trade value for value as much as possible."

"Still pretty tedious and stressful, still based on the fear of scarcity. Still men's pitiful exchange system," Jean interjected.

"I don't know why you're knocking our economic system," Harper said crossly. "It's obviously worked for a long time."

Sonia groaned. "Only because it's always relied on women's economy, Harper, on our unconditional giving of time, energy, goods, and services. If women's economic system of unconditional giving were to end, men's would be gone in the same instant. Theirs functions *because* of ours; ours functions *despite* theirs. In our essence women are egalitarian, unlinear. Unconditional giving, giving gifts with no expectation of return, is outside men's hierarchical/sadomasochistic world.

"Being totally linear, totally dependent on time, totally hierarchical, men can't do a gift economy. In their essences, they are not gift givers, not unconditional. Maleness *is* hierarchy, *is* sadomasochism, *is* conditionality. Men are by nature exchangers—an eye for an eye. That's why we can't make a new world that includes them. 'New' means no sadomasochism, means total peerness. Only women can achieve and live in that metaphysical state."

Then she added slyly, "I know that would traumatize most of you, having to give up men."

Barb snorted.

"Anyhow, Star, this is why I long for enough women to come to this area to do a gift economy—women with no attachment to any man: husband, lover, father, son, brother, or friend."

"That's a pretty stiff requirement," Star murmured.

"I'm not totally discounting the idea, Sonia." Harper tucked her hair behind her ear. "I think it's interesting. But I think it's like most women's ideas—not practical in the real world."

"Save us from the real world," Jean intoned, her eyes raised skyward.

"All very dear and sweet, Jean," Harper said acidly, "but let's face it: you depend on that world as much as I do for your food, your car, your home." Then, pointing her finger at Sonia, "And so do you. Your books wouldn't mean a thing without that world you so scorn."

"Sure they would," Jean interceded. "In women's world, if Sonia wanted to write, she would, and then she'd take her books to some community center and leave them there for women to take."

"All right, already!" Harper threw up her hands in surrender. "I won't ask where she's going to get the raw materials for the book—paper, ink, a printing press, a binding machine, etc. etc.,— because you'll just say something like, 'Oh ye of little faith. Surely ye know they will simply appear like magic!'"

They all laughed. Even Harper couldn't help but smile.

"No, really," she protested over their chuckles. "If it's possible, obviously its time hasn't come, and I'm not willing to put energy into an idea that isn't practical right now. It may be a hundred years before the valley and mountains here overflow with women."

"Do you really believe that day will come, Sonia?" Star asked.

"I do. And that when it does, we'll have again what we had in women's world, what I call the cauldron. The cauldron was a magical, never-ending source of power among us. It represented eternal abundance, freedom, nurturance, and joy. It was sharing and loving, fearlessness and passion, the very stuff of women's essence. And its basis was peerness. It worked because women communicated freely with one another. We had no secrets, no hidden agendas, no need for privacy. We *were* one another, totally open and totally available to one another all the time because there were no users among us, no exploiters, no sexers in the total sense of the word. Just the safety and freedom and intimacy of genuine lovers.

"Our abundance, our cauldron, had nothing to do with how much labor or time or materials any particular woman contributed to the community. Being was the important thing. Not doing or having, but who we were inside, the quality of our spirits and minds.

"I long for this world. I ache to have women like this around me more than I can tell you. I want it with all the power of my soul, all the passion of my life."

This was followed by silence, each woman deep in her own thoughts.

Star broke the silence. "You say that men can't do what you call 'women's world'. I'm not saying I'd ever want to do it with them, but I'm not sure why you think they can't."

"Maleness is sadomasochism, which is sex," Sonia explained. "Because of this, men are inherently unable to have peerness. And peerness is women's essence. In our authentic, uncorrupted state, it is fundamental to our existence."

"That's a crazy thing to say—men are sex," Star countered crossly. "Sexuality is just an aspect of human nature."

Sonia shook her head. "No, not true of women, Star. We've just tried to be what men said we should be, but at our cores, we're really not sexual beings. That men and women are totally different in this has to be one of the most obvious, albeit most denied, facts of life."

Barb broke in. "That reminds me of the only time my mother ever mentioned sex to me; she was born just before the turn of the century, and was very Victorian in her attitudes. Anyhow, she told me that there were many times early in her marriage to my father when she'd feel such a great wave of tenderness for him that as she passed him sitting in his chair she'd stroke his hair or caress his shoulder as she passed by. But that she got over it fast, because every time she did it, he interpreted it as her saying she was ready for sex, and he'd want it either at that moment, or that night in bed.

"She told me that, even way back then, the women in her prayer group used to talk about this, everyone of them complaining that any show of affection toward their husbands got them into sex. And all of them mourning the lack of simple, spontaneous tenderness in their marriages."

"My sister, in a very rare moment of sharing, told me something along those lines," Dana mused. "She said she absolutely refused to go to the movies or see videos with her husband anymore because every time she did, he'd point to the panting, sex-crazed woman on the screen and demand why she wasn't like that. She'd tell him that what they were seeing was simply another male fantasy, and that if he should marry that woman on the screen, in six months or a year at the most, she wouldn't be interested in sex, either. That women were only like that in men's wet dreams."

Della cut through the laughter. "I had the same thing with my husband. He'd take me to hot, steamy movies hoping that some of it would rub off on me. Finally I told him to find somebody else. He did, thank goodness."

"My husband and I played bridge with a couple," Lauren said. "One night when we arrived at their house they were in the middle of an argument. Lawrence and I were about to leave when Ron asked us if he and Fiona could talk to us about a problem they were having. It was sex. He wanted it all the time and she never did. They battled it out right there in front of us. She told him that there had to be something wrong with him to want it so often.

"I know you don't believe in exceptional men," she added, looking at Sonia and Jean, "and neither do I, anymore. But Ron was pretty special in some ways. I used to fantasize being married to him instead of Lawrence. I mean, he was so understanding, so liberal. He encouraged Fiona to do whatever she wanted.

"Anyhow, I've never forgotten what he said that night. He told us—Fiona and me, not Lawrence—that all men want sex all the time. He told us that this is the way men are, that they acknowledge it among themselves, that he wasn't a freak or aberration. He said that as a man goes through the day, regardless of what's happening, somewhere close to the front of his brain, if not in mid-center, he's trying to figure out where he can next put his," she blushed, "his, you know, penis. Lawrence backed him up.

"Then he went on to say that if Fiona didn't give it to him, he'd get it somewhere else, that all men do. That he had to have it, that that was the way he was made—he must have said that a dozen times that night—and that he wasn't ashamed of it. He said he was tired of Fiona's trying to make him feel like there was something wrong with him, and that he wished women would simply accept men for what they were and stop trying to make them into women."

"He was telling the truth about men, Lauren—a very rare thing for a man to do," Sonia said. "In a speech not long ago, I said that men could not be intimate because they couldn't touch without sex. Afterward, an angry woman accosted me. I was wrong about men, she insisted. She had a wonderful man friend she cuddled with and kissed and hugged a lot without sex. I told her that he could only do that with her because he was getting sufficient sex from someone else. This infuriated her.

"In the group of people around us, a young man spoke up. 'You're right,' he informed me. 'Just recently I told my girlfriend that I'd have to find someone to have sex with, that cuddling and kissing were not enough for any man.' He turned to the young woman who was so angry at me and told her that she could be absolutely certain that her boyfriend was getting sex somewhere. I saw her face change. She didn't want to believe it but she knew it was true."

"Can you imagine being obsessed with something like that all the time?" Della demanded. "I like sex, but in moderation, for mercy sake. I don't go around thinking about it all the time, wondering when I'm going to get it next."

Lauren nodded. "My friend Fiona told Lawrence and me that night that when she and Ron were alone, he made so many references to his penis she finally called him on it. He got mad and told her it wasn't true. So one Saturday she kept track. By noon he had mentioned his penis nine times, and they hadn't even gotten up until ten." This drew a round of laughter.

"I see what you mean," Star said grudgingly. "It's true that in my practice sex is the number one problem among couples. He wants it, she doesn't. Even when we seem to arrive at a reasonable compromise, the woman is rarely happy. I can't even begin to tell you how many men admit to extramarital affairs for this very reason."

Jean shook her head incredulously. "It's clear that they're obsessed with getting their penises into something. I did sex because it was the only way I thought I could be close. But I didn't go around thinking about my vulva twenty-four hours a day."

"My brother married a wonderful woman," Harper said. "Smart, beautiful, successful. And yet within a few months he was running around with other women. She knew it but kept quiet. Everyone knew it. I couldn't understand why she put up with him. I thought he was a world-class jerk.

"So I talked to her about it. And you know what she told me? She said that while part of her was upset, she was mostly relieved because she didn't care if she never had sex again, that she should have been a nun. This from one of the most beautiful women you ever set eyes on!"

"When I was still at the clinic with Allison, a lot of men came to us about impotence," Jean said. "Almost without exception, their wives would take me aside and ask me fervently not to do anything to cure them. It was the first rest from sexual assault they'd had in all their years of marriage."

Sonia turned to Star. "This is what I mean when I say we can't create a world with men that honors and facilitates women. Women are intimacy. We're the affectionate, tender touchers, holders, cuddlers, lovers of the body. Men say that what they experience is 'human sexual response' or 'human sexuality', including us in it with them. But the truth is that men are in that category alone. They are the sexual ones. Women, in our essence, are intimate. And there's a world of difference between sex and intimacy—they can't exist in the same place at the same time. Men can't be intimate because they're sexual. Every time they touch, sex happens. This isn't a judgement or criticism, it's a fact. They can't help it and they can't change it, it's what they are. The problem is that they've got women convinced that we're the same and that when we don't perform, there's something wrong with us. What's wrong with us is that we believe them in the first place and try to do sex."

"And," Jean added, "that we project our feelings upon them and live in the illusion that we can be in harmony with them."

Barb glanced at her watch, then looked apologetically at the women she'd driven to the cookout. "I really have to get back," she said. "I've got a long day in town tomorrow and need to get my beauty sleep. If you three aren't ready to go, maybe someone could drive you later."

"I'm ready." Sonia stood, as did Jean and Clare, and all carried their plates to the garbage can.

"How long are you staying at Wildfire?" Star asked Clare.

"I'm leaving Tuesday to meet a friend up in Abiquiu."

"Are you coming back? To live, I mean."

Glancing sideways at Sonia and Jean, Clare said evasively, "I don't know yet. Time will tell." '

Later, after everyone had gone and Lauren had retired, Star and Harper sat together on the hide-a-bed in the study, Star rubbing Harper's shoulders.

"You've got nice friends, Harper."

"I enjoy them, especially as a group."

"What's with Clare?"

"You know about as much as I do. She's lived in some form of community all her adult life and wants to continue. Why, is beyond me. Actually, she wants to live with Sonia and Jean."

"Has she said that?"

"Not to me, but it's obvious, isn't it? She admires Sonia's ideas, she wants to live in community, and she loves New Mexico."

"Then what's stopping her? She seemed pretty non-committal when I asked her about her plans."

"Sonia and Jean. They're not interested in getting another community together. They're glad for their experience, but it made them very cautious. Smart, if you ask me."

"How are things with you and Lauren?"

"Okay. Some minor problems, but what's new?"

"She doesn't look good to me, Harp, so pale and withdrawn. I would've thought New Mexico would agree with her more than Boston, but it doesn't seem to."

"I know she's depressed, but she doesn't tell me much. Frankly, I think she hasn't come to grips with her sexuality yet. I made the mistake of mentioning that to Jean, and had to hear that women don't have any sexuality, and that it's our trying to come to grips with something we don't have that's causing so much trouble."

Star grimaced. "It's not that I disagree entirely with Sonia and Jean. As a therapist, I know that relationships and sex can be disastrous for women. But I also think they don't have to be. We just need to keep working on doing them better."

"It's a good thing Sonia can't hear you," Harper muttered. "She believes, and I mean *believes* that sex is the root of all evil, and there's no way she's going to tolerate any other opinion."

Star's eyebrows shot up. "Pretty rigid, is she? Well, she can only speak for herself. It's my opinion that we can each figure out ways to do relationships that work for us."

In full agreement, Harper smiled. "How's it going with you and Amy."

Star shrugged. "Okay, but definitely cooler. I'm not being sexually exclusive with her anymore. I'm checking out a couple of other cute gals and, who knows? One or both of them could turn into something hot."

Harper winked at her. "In your line of work, it shouldn't be too hard to get the love and affection you need—all that transference."

"True," Star laughed. "But I have to be careful, you know. It's become too dangerous. I usually date women on the clinic staff, not my clients, so I won't have to worry about getting taken to court. There's a young gal there now, just been hired as a secretary. She flirts with me shamelessly. And I mean heavy-duty flirts." She raised her eyebrows meaningfully, and they both grinned.

"When she gets through with me, my pants are wet and I feel racy for hours. The problem is, she's in a relationship. But from what she says, I think it's about to bite the dust, and I intend to be the owner of the shoulder she cries on, if you know what I mean."

Harper looked anxiously at the door as if afraid of being overheard, and relaxed when she realized that Lauren had probably been asleep for over an hour.

Lowering her voice anyway, she confessed, "Lauren doesn't want sex anymore. She keeps quoting Sonia and Jean to me. I'm fed up with it, Star. It isn't that I'm a sex maniac or anything, but I'm not a puritan, either. I see nothing wrong with pleasure and fun, or with the physical release sex gives me. And I want it. I feel . . . oh, I don't know, like I can take on the world when I've had good sex.

"I've been pressuring Lauren, and I know that isn't good. And the truth is, she really doesn't turn me on anymore. I have to fantasize like crazy to work up any heat, and you know what? Lauren's not in any of my fantasies. So I think it's time to find someone else, someone who isn't afraid of her sexuality, someone who can challenge me sexually, or at least match me."

"You've told me you've had affairs while you were with Lauren, so another one shouldn't make any difference."

Harper shook her head. "Not so. I found out later that those affairs upset her a lot more than she let on, so I've cooled it. After I stopped seeing Rita, I realized that Lauren had been really unhappy about the whole thing. Even though I'd told her a hundred times it was purely sexual and not emotional. So I decided to concentrate on our relationship, but there's not much closeness left. She doesn't even want to cuddle or snuggle anymore."

"Why not? What's that all about?"

Harper sighed. "All I can tell you is what she told me." She automatically lowered her voice again. "She claims that even when we just cuddle I'm thinking of sex. That even when I tell her

I don't feel sexy, my touching feels like sex to her. It's crazy, Star. I'm trying to be patient and understanding and helpful, but she's gotten so paranoid it's a drag.

"She keeps telling me she doesn't want sex, that she wants to experience what Sonia and Jean have been talking about—their hallowed 'unconditional touch' that frankly seems to me the same low-brow stuff they consider sex except they've slapped a snooty label on it.

"Anyway, I tell her fine, I'm willing to try it, but five minutes into the touching and she's cold as ice. She turns away, or goes into the bathroom and doesn't come out. When I check on her, she's in there crying, saying it's pointless, that I don't understand."

Harper pushed her hair back behind her ear. "She's right that there's one thing I don't understand. Why is it, when she'll hardly let me touch her, that when we go over to Wildfire for dinner or Murder Maids, she'll snuggle and love it up all night with Sonia and Jean?"

"Whew! What's she got going with them?"

Harper waved her hand impatiently. "I don't mean that, Star. There's nothing sexual there. They do it right in front of everybody, like kids. I'm not worried that there's anything dangerous going on, but it does hurt when I see her and Sonia with their arms around each other on the couch and Lauren looking happy."

Star frowned. "I had no idea things were so shaky between you two. I thought they were good and getting better."

"Oh, they are, really," Harper insisted unconvincingly. "I mean, we're working through a lot of old garbage."

"Sounds to me as though you may be creating more of it than you're throwing out. I wish I had the time to talk with Lauren alone. She gets up early, doesn't she? I could drag myself out of bed early, just this once. I'd like to help her."

Harper scowled. "*I'm* helping her, Star," she said coldly. "No one understands her like I do. Don't worry; we'll be all right. We really love each other, you know." She stood abruptly. "Well, guess I'll hit the sack."

Star stood up, too, and stretched. "I'll probably sleep until I just barely have time to catch my plane."

Harper gave her a quick A-frame hug. "I leave at eight, so I won't see you. But have a great trip and good luck with the cute little steno."

Alone, Star stretched out on the bed. After listening to Harper, she suspected that Lauren was in deep trouble and felt sure that

Harper wasn't the one to help her; not at all. She wished she could talk with Lauren, offer some assistance or comfort. She played with that scenario for a few minutes, enjoying holding and comforting Lauren in her imagination, relishing the feeling of competence and power it gave her. She wondered if she dared go against Harper's wishes and play the scenario out.

What the hell? she thought. The worst that can happen is that I'll lose Harper's friendship. And I can live with that. Smiling, she reached for her alarm clock and reset it for eight-fifteen.

13

The hot dishwater felt good on her cold hands, and she held them under the water for a moment even after she had washed the last dish. Briefly she contemplated climbing the stairs and taking a hot bath, but the thought made her droop with fatigue. She lifted her hands from the water and dried them, noting their rough, red appearance with indifference. Peasant hands, Harper called them, and urged her to keep them well-lotioned. She ignored the bottle of lotion next to the sink and wandered into the living room.

It was Monday, cleaning day, but the house didn't need it. In preparation for Star's visit, she and Harper had entered into a frenzy of cleaning yesterday morning. Still, she could wash the sheets on the hide-a-bed, and Star's towels. Instead, she sank to the floor in front of the couch and curled up, dragging the afghan over her. The scratchy carpet felt good against her cheek.

In the silence, the phone's sudden shrillness jerked her out of her reverie. She was going to ignore it but glancing at the clock on the television she realized it was probably Harper on her mid-morning break, and she knew Harper would persist until she got her, that she might even come home if she didn't answer.

"Hi, babe. Just wondering if Star got up and off."

"She left about half an hour ago."

"What time did she get up?"

"Oh, Harp, I don't know," Lauren lied. "She went tearing out of here with a piece of toast in one hand and a foam cup full of coffee in the other."

Harper chuckled. "Then she probably gave herself just enough time to throw her clothes on and fly. I don't know how she does it, always on the line. Listen, I've got a client, but I'll call you during lunch."

"No! I mean, I'm going over to Jean and Sonia's to walk the dogs."

There was a pause, then, "Surely the dogs get plenty of exercise without you having to do it, Laur."

Lauren felt her legs weaken. She held onto the edge of the desk with her free hand. It was too hard, too hard. "I like to walk, and I like to walk with them. They motivate me to go farther and stay out longer."

"Then for god's sake get your own dog. Get a big one that doesn't have to be in the house. It'd be better protection for you anyhow. I don't like you out alone in the mountains with those chickenshit little dogs."

"There's no good dog-walking area around here, Harper. If I had a dog, I'd have to walk it somewhere else anyway. I'm perfectly safe, really."

"I know. You hate our place. You never come out and say so, but I can tell. Let's sell it, for christ's sake, and get something that suits you."

"Never mind, Harper. This place is fine."

"I've got to go, Laur. I'll be home early tonight." The phone clicked in her ear.

She sank wearily into the swivel chair, wishing she had put on a sweater this morning. In spite of the rising temperature outside, the house felt cold. She wrapped her arms around herself.

Star had walked into the kitchen as Harper's car was bumping down their driveway. This in itself had been surprising since Star 'did not do mornings' as she put it; her work day started at eleven and ended at eight. But more surprising had been their conversation—or rather Star's. She had started out by asking, "Are you all right?" at which Lauren had burst into tears.

"Lauren," Star had murmured, kneeling beside her and putting her arms around her. Since Lauren had never had any physical contact with Star save a quick hug on arrival and departure, this had astonished her. She had tried to pull away, but Star had held tight. "Talk about it," Star had urged into her ear.

Feeling as though she were in a B-grade movie, Lauren had suppressed the urge to giggle. Talk about what? What did Star have in mind? Acutely uncomfortable but having no idea how to extract herself from Star's embrace, Lauren had said nothing. Star had taken her silence to mean she was too distraught to speak. So she had tried another approach.

"I talked with Harper last night and she admitted the two of you were having problems, especially around sex."

So that's what it was. Despite her deep distrust of therapy, Harper had decided to unload on Star. Lauren had kept quiet, wondering what Harper had said.

"Lauren, I work with intimacy issues all the time. And I know from what Harper told me that it's highly probable that you had some early physical or emotional abuse in your life that's causing problems now. I don't have time to go into it with you. I wish I did because I believe I could help you." She had held Lauren more tightly. "Unfortunately, we're separated by over two thousand miles. But I'm sure there are good therapists out here who can help you. For your sake and for the sake of your relationship, I urge you to try therapy." She had raised her arm and smoothed Lauren's hair.

Held then with only one arm, Lauren had been able to pull away gracefully and stand up. "I'll certainly consider it, Star. I'll ask around and see who's available." She had mumbled something about watering the garden and fled.

Star had gone back to the den, dressed hastily, and snapped her suitcase shut. In the empty kitchen, she had dropped two slices of bread in the toaster and filled a large styrofoam cup with the coffee warming in the pot. Then she had carried her suitcase to the car, tossed it in the back seat, and returned for her toast and coffee. She hadn't bothered to walk down to the garden to say goodbye; merely tooted her horn and waved as she drove out.

What a case, she had thought, as she pulled onto the highway. No wonder Harper's so unhappy. This is the original Ice Princess herself, a veritable mass of intimacy issues. Harper would be better off with someone else.

○ ○ ○ ○ ○ ○

Lauren stared in amazement at the large, red-brown birds. There were five of them, and they gave her and Nikki a long look before scurrying into the underbrush. It was only then, when she heard their distinct 'gobble', that she realized they were wild turkeys. Sonia and Jean had told her they had seen some, but she had not dared hope that she would. She was glad the bigger dogs had been so far ahead that they hadn't spotted them.

Back at the house, she let the dogs in the front door. They ran for the water dish, reminding her not to forget to carry water with her on future walks. A glance at the clock—2:15—told her she had been gone a little over two hours.

The house was quiet. She knew she should get back home, but at the thought an enormous wave of despair washed over her. She wasn't ready to go back yet. She thought of calling Barb and seeing if she could visit her for awhile. Heading for the phone, she caught sight of Sonia and Jean coming up the driveway and stopped to watch them.

They looked so happy, so content, so easy with each other. All the things she longed for and didn't have, had never had. Promises made and never kept. It had taken her years to realize that all those romance novels she had read—in a desperate attempt to understand what it was she was missing and how she could get it—were nothing but fantasies. She had decided years ago that only fictional characters had those wondrous, carefree, loved-filled lives. Until now. Watching them, she knew Sonia and Jean were living her dream.

She opened the door and stepped out onto the deck.

"I hope you wore the dogs out," Jean called to her. "Especially Maggi."

"I saw the turkeys, five of them. I didn't know what they were at first, but then they gobbled—just like in children's books."

They invited her to join them on the deck, cooler now, since the sun was moving west. She could not have said later what prompted her to talk about herself, and at such length, that afternoon. Maybe it was the warm hugs. Maybe she was tired of secrets, of living in fear, of never taking risks. Maybe it was nothing but the need for some closeness, for someone else to know her life.

Whatever, she told them about her childhood, how cold and distant her father had been. She talked about her mother, a nervous, anxious woman who suffered a break-down at Lauren's birth and never recovered enough to go back to her husband's bed. She talked about her uneventful marriage to Lawrence, their two sons, her housewife and mother years.

Then she talked about her illness.

When the boys were six and eight, Lauren got sick. At first she said nothing, simply kept going as women do. But finally she reached the point where she couldn't hide it, when even Lawrence realized something was wrong. It was the night she fell asleep in the soup.

He rushed her to the hospital. The diagnosis: severe mononucleosis. The prescription: bed rest. Lawrence made inquiries about live-in housekeepers, but he never hired one because his mother, Ellen, moved in, packed Lawrence off to his father, and took over the care of Lauren and the boys.

This behavior shocked them all. Ellen was a rich woman and a socialite, with a full-time housekeeper and cook, a life filled with charities, organizational work, and luncheons. To give that up for the drudgery of housework and nursing was totally out of character for her.

"I couldn't believe it when Lawrence told me Ellen was coming to take care of me and the kids," Lauren remembered. "She was immaculately groomed, beautiful, and perfect in every way. Before she moved in, I scarcely knew her. We'd gone on a few shopping excursions together, but I think she gave up on me because I had a 'difficult figure'—round in all the wrong places."

"Why do you think she did it?" Sonia asked at the very same moment that Jean asked, "How did it go?"

Lauren laughed. "I had such a high fever that I don't remember much about the first week or two. But Ellen was a wonderful nurse. I remember her laying cool washcloths on my forehead, one after another, for hours at a time." Her expression took on a faraway look. "One time I opened my eyes and there she was, stroking my hair and looking down at me with such love . . ." She looked away for a moment.

"It wasn't long before I was well enough to get out of bed for short periods. It was winter and very cold. Ellen would light a fire in the living room and settle me on the couch in front of it. She'd bring me tea and toast and sit with me. We talked about all kinds of things. She told me that what she had really wanted to do with her life was to be an anthropologist and study tribal peoples. She loved Margaret Mead, and read everything ever written by her. She told me that when Margaret died, a part of her died, too.

"I found it wondrous and amazing. I mean, here's this lovely, cultured, sophisticated woman telling me she'd rather be in the jungles studying primitive cultures. It made me feel very close, her confiding in me like that."

"It sounds as though you enjoyed each other a lot."

"She held me, Sonia." It came out as a cry. "She held me and I held her and it was so beautiful, so warm and sweet and right.

I told her everything, every secret, every thought. I can't even begin to describe the relief I felt at being able to have someone to talk to. And the touching.

"When you and Jean were talking the other day about your experiments, I could hardly stand it. I haven't consciously thought of Ellen in a long time. Your experiments brought it all back, except we weren't deliberately trying to touch in a different way."

Jean nodded. "It just happens sometimes."

"Why haven't you stayed in contact?" Sonia asked.

Lauren's face clouded. "I was doing much better, but I didn't want Ellen to go. She didn't want to go, either. She told Lawrence and Edward—her husband—that she couldn't leave me too soon for fear I'd have a relapse.

"Then one afternoon, Lawrence came home," she went on, her voice suddenly bitter, "and found us in front of the fire. We just had our arms around each other, I swear, but he obviously thought sex and romance were going on. I'll never forget the look on his face." She stared at a vacant deck chair, as though Lawrence were in it.

"He told his mother to pack her things and get out. Then he told me I was never to see her again, never to talk to her or think about her. And that was that."

"You never saw her again?"

"At family gatherings, the unavoidable things. But she was distant and cold and so was I. I was afraid of Lawrence. The last time I saw her was at Lawrence's funeral." Tears came into Lauren's eyes. "Probably for very different reasons, we were both in a lot of pain," she sobbed, "and I wanted so much to go to her, to hold her and comfort her and be comforted by her. And I couldn't. Even with him dead, I couldn't do it." She buried her face in her arms.

o o o o o o

"I thought it would be different with Harper."

They had left the deck and moved into the library, cool against the late afternoon heat.

"In what way?"

"Like it had been with Ellen. Like it never was with Lawrence."

"You mean you thought your relationship with Harper would be nonsexual?"

"No. I knew there'd be sex. Harper told me almost at the start that she was a lesbian and I knew lesbians had sex with other women. I wasn't totally naive."

"So in your mind what you had with Ellen wasn't a lesbian relationship."

"No. I never felt anything sexual with her. We cuddled and held each other while we talked. Sometimes she'd lie on the couch with her head in my lap and I'd stroke her face, or she'd hold and stroke me. But I never thought of sex with her."

"It never occurred to you that what you were doing might be seen as sexual?"

Lauren shook her head. "Not until the day Lawrence walked in. The way he looked at us. I felt sick, as though we were doing something evil."

"Men sexualize all touch," Jean said angrily. "They cheapen women's ways, project their ways on us. I hate that he saw you, Lauren."

"By the time Harper came into my life, the whole business about being a lesbian didn't seem so bad. I mean, we'd had gay pride rallies and marches in Boston for several years before. And my oldest son is gay."

At Jean and Sonia's surprise, she hurried on.

"I don't talk about it much, I know. But Kurt brought home all kinds of books and articles about it, and even tried to get me to join PFLAG, Parents and Friends of Lesbians and Gays."

"And did you?"

"No. I was afraid Lawrence would find out. Kurt hadn't told him and didn't intend to.

"Anyhow, I was willing to try being a lesbian. Before and during my marriage, I never met a man who interested me. Even Lawrence had never been sexually interesting to me, and that's the truth. And I'd never been attracted to any woman.

"I thought that being a lesbian would mean lots of touching and holding. And it did, sort of. I mean, Harper isn't much of a toucher, but we hold each other and cuddle. It's just that sex is always hanging over my head."

"You make it sound like a guillotine."

Lauren smiled wanly. "At first I tried to focus on how different it was from being with Lawrence. And in some ways it was, but in others it was just the same. Or it felt the same afterwards. I don't know how to explain it, but . . ."

"Sex is sex," Sonia finished for her.

"That's how it felt. And when I tried to talk to Harper about having less sex and more touching, she said that her way of showing love was through love-making, that for her sex was a sacred act."

Sonia shook her head in exasperation. "Sex is what men do. Sex is what men are. And women are so damned attached to men's ways that they'll defend and glamorize them to the end. But we aren't men, we aren't male, and men's ways don't fit us. No matter what we do to try to make them fit, they never do and never will. You found that out, Lauren."

"I think sex with women is even harder than sex with men," Lauren said, lifting Nikki into her lap. "Lawrence liked me to make noise and act interested, but even if I didn't, he got what he wanted. He'd try to get me excited, but if it didn't happen quickly, he'd give up and just take care of himself.

"But it's different with Harper. She tries all kinds of things to excite me; she works at it. It's as though my reaction is central to our sex lives. If I don't respond, she keeps at it, trying new things, until I do. At first I thought she might actually hit on something that felt good, but she never did. And every time, she'd get upset and depressed and ask me what I needed. I tried to tell her I didn't really need or want any of it, but that upset her even more.

"Now I just want to get it over with, so I fake it. The more noise I make, the happier she is, and the quicker we're through. With Lawrence I could have gone to sleep after a point and he wouldn't have cared. I wouldn't dare do that with Harper."

"I've had women tell me they like lesbian sex," Sonia said. "But what I know they're saying is that they like certain aspects of it. Some like the touching and holding and endure the genital stuff, and some like the excitation of controlling their lover's pleasure. No woman I've ever heard try to explain why she liked sex has ever made it sound like something I'd choose if there were some other way to get enough touching. Women believe men's lie that touch is sex, that if we want to get more touching than just a little pat, peck, and hug, we have to have sex. This is true for men, but it isn't true for women."

"Then why do we do sex at all?" Lauren asked. "What I had with Ellen was so much better than what I've got with Harper."

"What you had with Ellen was rare," Sonia said. "And yet, even though you didn't do sex with her, you were both in your sex minds."

"No we weren't," Lauren protested.

"During all of your touching and holding, did you ever touch Ellen's breasts? Or her vulva? Did she ever touch yours?"

"Of course not." Lauren turned crimson. "I told you we didn't have sex."

"This is what I'm talking about. You both avoided those areas because you believed men's bullshit that women's breasts and vulvas are sexual. You accepted their definition of your bodies, their sex mentality."

Lauren looked confused.

"Lauren, you've said yourself that you don't want to do sex, just touch and hold. What I'm hearing you say is that you aren't sexual."

Lauren nodded.

"Then why do you accept that parts of your body are? Why are you believing that part of the lie, while rejecting the rest?"

"I see what you're saying. I guess in that sense, Ellen and I were in our sex minds. But we never wanted sex. At least I didn't. And I don't think Ellen did either."

"I believe you. I'm just trying to help you see how deep that conditioning is in you. And not just in you. Now, at the end of patriarchy, nearly every living woman believes she's a sexual being and that certain parts of her body are sex parts. I've been trying to show you how damnably hard it is to get out of thinking that for even a second."

14

After Lauren left that afternoon, Sonia got on her bike and headed up the mountain road. While they had all been talking, an idea had kept pushing itself unbidden into her mind and she knew she needed to consider it seriously. But it was so frightening that she was sure she would find ways to avoid looking at it if she stayed around the house. So for a couple of hours she bumped over the rocky road, deep in thought.

Later, she and Jean sat together in the double papasan chair in the library, a plate of fresh-baked carob chip cookies on the coffee table in front of them, talking about Lauren and Harper.

Sonia bit into her cookie and munched gravely. "What I think is that those two are in trouble."

"Because Harper wants sex and Lauren can't stand it?"

"Yep. And somehow I don't think Harper's ever going to understand what Lauren's talking about. To her, sex and touching are synonymous."

"I used to believe that, that you couldn't have one without the other," Jean said, absentmindedly tracing circles on Sonia's arm with her cookie-free hand.

"Me, too. Now I can't imagine why." Jean's touch on the inside of her arm was sending goosebumps up and down her spine.

"Tired?" Sonia asked.

"Not really. I could probably sleep, but I'm wide awake at the moment."

Sonia couldn't help but smile. When Jean said she was wide awake, Sonia knew she was, at most, five minutes from sinking into a coma. But even with this time limit, Sonia began.

"I've had my kids on my mind all day, my relationship with them. Justin called Sunday. He was having a rough time and wanted to talk about it, but we didn't resolve his problem on the phone. So I've been worried, and finally called him last night. You know what he said? 'What problem?' He'd forgotten it as soon as we hung up. I'm the one who was weighed down by it."

Jean laughed. "I'm sure that's one of the commonest experiences of motherhood."

"Motherhood's the pits—the institution, not the children. I've said so for years. But it never occurred to me that I could be free of it. Until today. While Lauren was talking, I was thinking, 'Why doesn't she just get out of that relationship?' And suddenly, I heard my own voice in my head saying, 'Why don't you just get out of yours?' For a few minutes I didn't understand; after all, I had gotten out of mine. Then it hit me. My kids—that's the relationship I could 'just get out of'.

"That thought damned near scared me to death. My heart started to pound and for the last little while, I didn't hear a thing you and Lauren were saying. That's when I knew I had to get out of here and face it. So I did, and by the time I turned around to come back, I was telling myself that I could just step out of motherhood like the ill-fitting costume it is.

"Imagine, it's taken me nearly thirty years to let this outrageous thought enter my consciousness. Goes to show, doesn't it, that motherhood conditioning is the deepest and fiercest in menstream's whole sadistic repertoire for women. We've had 'once a mother, always a mother' pounded into us for millennia; that having given birth to someone, we're irrevocably attached to them for life."

"I've heard you say often that the mother/child relationship is completely wrong from start to finish."

"Yes, and I believe it. Completely and unavoidably hierarchical, slavery for everybody. Parents 'own' their children and in turn are 'owned' by them: my kids, my mom, my dad. Owning other human beings, being owned—this is physical, spiritual, ethical, emotional slavery. That's why I always maintain—to a chorus of jeers—that the definition of family is: it dysfunctions. Being units of control, all families are dysfunctional for women, all raw sadomasochism. Control may be an essential part of maleness, men may have to control and be controlled, but not women. Our essence is freedom and anarchy. So the family structure by its very nature is dysfunctional for us. It just never occurred to me until this afternoon that I could escape it. And not just that I could, but that I had to.

"I've written and said that all relationships are the same: sadomasochism/sex/patriarchy. But somehow it's taken this long to register that if I want to escape from patriarchy and find women's world, it's not enough to be free of romantic relationships; I have to get out of family relationships, too. I have to divorce my kids."

Jean was now really wide awake. "But your kids are all grown up."

Sonia waved that away. "You know that once we've done a relationship with someone, there's no way to stop doing it. Even though they don't need it, I'm still in 'taking care' mode with those four people, and if I stick in there, the albatross of motherhood will be hanging around my neck when I'm a tottering old woman and my kids are gray and paunchy. It's not my kids, it's me who thinks I still need to worry about them. I can see that for all our sakes, I've got to wrench that damned bird off my back."

Jean frowned. "But particularly for your own, I hope."

"That's hard, but yes, mostly." She paused, then shook her head. "No, not mostly, entirely for my own sake. Because even though freeing them—and I free them when I free myself—is the best gift I could ever give them, I know I'd have to renounce motherhood even if doing so were damaging to them."

For a moment, she sat quietly, thinking.

"They won't see it as a gift, of course," she said. "They won't understand. And they'll probably be angry and hurt. But I can't let that be a consideration in my decision. Those people I gave birth to, and myself . . . I have to release us all from dependence on and responsibility for each other."

"What're you going to do?"

"Call them first thing in the morning and tell them their mother's dead. Except for Jesse. I'll be his mother until he graduates from high school next May. But I have to let the others know that I've stopped being a mother."

"What exactly does that mean?"

"It means no more help, no more rescue, no more support. It means I don't ever want to see them or hear from them again—because the instant I do, I'll be back in the relationship. It means that every aspect of their lives is now irrelevant to my well-being. It means I don't worry anymore about whether they get jobs, have money, or a place to live. It means I don't allow their lives to determine the quality of mine.

"It means I'm handing them their lives back and taking mine back from them."

○ ○ ○ ○ ○ ○

Too spent to get up, she rested on the cool wood floor, marveling at how light she felt. Marveling that she had actually done it—lifted the crushing weight off her shoulders and heart that she had taken on 28 years ago. Yesterday at this time she would have sworn that she could never find the courage to walk away from motherhood. She would have insisted that to abrogate this deeply inculcated responsibility was too frightening, too guilt producing, too destructive of her identity and self-esteem.

But she had done it. Motherhood was over. Oh blessed, blessed relief!

She rolled onto her back and watched the clouds through the window, daring herself to allow the first delicate tendrils of joy to caress her heart. Such a long enslavement it had been, so seemingly eternal. At first, she had thought that when the children turned eighteen, she would be through with the aching worry about them. They would be on their own by then, out in the world doing their own lives, and her job would be finished. But though they had gone forth independently and done fine, she hadn't been able to pry menstream's rigid motherhood code out of herself: they were still her children, and always would be, it said; her life would always be inextricably interwoven with theirs;

if they were unhappy or ill, she could not be fully joyous; they were part of her. Deep, deadly indoctrination.

Touching her cheek, she felt the salt streaks left from a veritable torrent of tears. She had hung up the phone from the call to three of her kids, laid down on the floor, and howled in agony. Howled until her face and throat and jaws went numb and her vocal cords felt shredded and raw. Howled like the cornered animal she had been all those years, the rage and grief and terror thundering out of her like a tidal wave.

She had gone first to Carl, afraid he might leave for the day if she waited until after she called Oregon. As she pulled up to his place, he was just getting into his car, and she was glad she had hurried over there. They sat at his table and she went straight to the point. When she finished, he was confused, protesting that he didn't think of her as a mother anymore but as a friend. She asked him how many 55-year-old women friends he had.

She told him the same things she would tell his sister and brothers in a little while. That her repudiation wasn't of him but of motherhood. That she hoped he wouldn't interpret it as a punishment because it wasn't; as far as she was concerned he had done nothing wrong. She assured him that he had been a fine son, that he and the others had done childhood perfectly, that despite the institution of motherhood and family, she had mostly enjoyed their company and had no complaints. She said that though she sincerely wished the best for him in his life from here on out, she did not want to be involved in it in any way anymore or know anything more about it.

He asked her to tell him exactly what that meant. It meant, she said, that no matter what the situation, there would never be any financial help of any kind—jobs, school payments—or any emotional support. It meant that if he had a terrible accident or contracted a serious disease, or if he had wonderful success, or got married, or had children, he was not to inform her. She was no longer his mother or he her son. They were free of each other. Not owning him anymore, she was in no way, large or small, responsible for his happiness and well-being, or even any more interested in them than she would be a passing motorist's. The artificial ties were now broken. His mother was dead.

She stood and walked towards the door, then stopped, hand on the knob, and turned back to him. It was time, she said, for him to assemble his own support system, his own network of people he freely and consciously chose to have in his life—as he hadn't chosen those people he called "family".

Then, without emotion, she wished him well again, said good-bye, climbed into her car and drove off. All the way home she held herself carefully aloft, above the tumult in her soul, refusing to let herself think about or feel any of it until she had done it all. She parked the car behind the house and as if in a trance went directly to her room, closed the door, and called the other three.

Asking that they all listen in on the extension phones scattered throughout their house, she had gone straight to the point.

She informed Jesse, the 17-year-old, that she would be his mother until he graduated from high school. That meant he could call her with his problems, ask for money, get any help he needed, but that on graduation day, his mother would die.

Givonne didn't say a word, and the other two very little. It was soon over.

She rose from the floor, a little stiff from the hardwood and lightheaded from emotion purged. In the bathroom, she splashed water on her face, amazed that she was still alive. She had broken the profoundest taboo patriarchy had ever devised for women—and she hadn't been struck dead. She wished fervently that Jean were home, but she had gone to the airport to pick up her old friend Coral who was going to visit for awhile. Lauren, Harper, Barb, and Dana were coming for supper to meet her.

She walked aimlessly around her room, absentmindedly straightening a few things, trying to let the significance of what had happened this morning sink in.

She knew it wasn't entirely over yet. There was Jesse to mother for another year, and all the memories. She remembered wryly that constant vigilance was the price of liberty; she would have to move carefully through each day, refusing to let herself sink back into the illusion, refusing to let the sentimentality that in mensworld is cunningly termed 'motherlove' draw her back in and down.

Realizing that she hadn't eaten since early morning and that it was now mid-afternoon, she went downstairs and inventoried the refrigerator. But she couldn't get her mind on food. It was as if she were floating, as if, having wrenched the huge tumor of motherhood out of herself, she had freed every cell of her body of a deadly cancer. Disembodied, that's how I feel, she thought, and then corrected herself. No, not out of my body but very, very deeply in it. Finally embodied. Finally owning my body free and clear.

Taking a bag of carob almonds, she wandered out onto the deck. This is my body, she said wonderingly to herself, examining it from within and touching it gently with her free hand. My wonderful body, my own, totally my own, and whole. There are no pieces of it careening about the world. Those people who came out of it own nothing of it, have no claim upon it anymore. They have their own bodies, and that will do them just fine.

She had left the kitchen door open and the dogs, smelling the carob, soon joined her.

"You can't have any, kids. If you chewed properly I'd give you some, but you don't and that means that in two days you'll vomit almonds all over the rug. Whole. Bleached. And your mommy will hate me. So beat it."

They ignored her, giving her the big-brown-eyed-orphan-look they had all perfected. Then Tamale gave a sudden sharp bark and tore across the deck, followed by the other two. Harper, Lauren, and Dana stopped to pet them before continuing onto the deck.

"Catching a little sun?" Harper asked, reaching into the bag for an almond.

"Just being lazy," Sonia replied.

"Lazy! That'll be the day. We decided to take you up on your offer to come over early for some sunbathing." Harper pulled off her T-shirt and shorts to reveal an iridescent green bikini underneath. She spread a towel on the chaise lounge and settled on it. Lauren and Dana pulled up chairs close to Sonia and accepted the bag of almonds she offered them.

"What've you been up to today?" Dana asked.

Sonia told them about her morning.

"You disowned your kids?" Dana asked disbelievingly.

"That's the perfect word—disowned. What was I doing, owning them in the first place? Owning people is slavery. Today I emancipated us all. Just call me the Great Emancipator."

Lauren was visibly shocked. "You can call it emancipation, but the truth is that you've orphaned them."

"I think there must be an age limit on orphanhood." Sonia suppressed a smile. "Can one really be an orphan at 28, or 25, or 23? And can one really be an orphan so long as one has an an extant and perfectly serviceable father? Let them reactivate him."

Lauren was neither pacified or amused. "It seems so abrupt and heartless. Surely it would have been better to talk about it with them first and give them a chance to get used to it rather than drop a bomb on them."

Sonia shook her head. "I had to do it this way, Lauren. I could have talked with those kids for five years and they'd never have understood. Because they don't want to. No kid, no matter what age, wants to lose the titty and its endless supply of goodies: attention, care, help, the cushion of last resort."

"This may sound mean, but I don't know how else to say it," Lauren began, then blurted out, "You can't have loved them very much. I mean, I'm thinking that I love my sons too much ever to hurt them like that, or even want to be rid of them. I'm comparing you to me, I know, but I can't help it."

"You mean I can't have loved them as much as you love yours."

"I'm sorry if that's cruel, but that's how it feels to me."

"I'm not going to compare relative degrees of motherlove here," Sonia assured her. "I can only say that I thought I loved them more than life itself. That's what I would have told you yesterday morning. But I've learned a lot since then. About myself and illusion. About myself and brainwashing."

"I don't understand," Lauren said sullenly, obviously not really wanting to. But Sonia wanted to talk about it, and Harper and Dana seemed interested, so she plowed on. Besides, if Lauren didn't want to listen, she could leave.

"If you're willing, maybe I can show you at least a little of what I see," Sonia said to her. Though she wasn't happy about it, Lauren agreed.

"Okay, close your eyes and picture yourself in a large, old, beautiful house overlooking the ocean. Imagine that you and nine or ten others have been invited there for a week-long house party by the owner, and that, though she's a dear friend of yours and apparently of all the others, none of you knows any of the other guests. The guests, by the way, range in age from early twenties to late sixties, the average being about forty-five.

"Fill in that wonderful week with group activities of every sort you might enjoy: boating, swimming, skiing, picnics, costume parties, games, dances, story telling—everything and anything that would help you all get to know one another very well."

Lauren opened her eyes angrily. "I know what you're up to, but it won't work."

"But it may give you a little tolerance for me," Sonia said. Lauren reluctantly closed her eyes again.

"Now, imagine that your two sons are among the guests—21 and 25 years old and doing the best they can with all these old folks. Watch them go through the week, and ask yourself if, when the party is over, you will try to get together with them again or keep in touch with them in any way."

Lauren squirmed uncomfortably.

"You don't have to give me an answer, because I know it already. It doesn't mean that you don't find them delightful there at the party. But what in heaven's name would you have in common with two young men? Why on earth would you ever want to be with them again? And a more telling question—why would they want to be with you, unless you had money or were famous or had something else to offer them other than simply yourself?

"Well, they aren't strangers, they're my own children, so the whole exercise is ridiculous," Lauren said angrily.

"All right, you can play the same game with my ex-children, then, substituting them for yours. It will work just as well. You've met them—all good looking, a couple of them gorgeous, all charming, witty, smart, even a couple of brilliant ones, all attentive to others and lots of fun to be around. My unbiased assessment, of course," she laughed.

"Now insert them, ages 28, 26, 23, and 17, into the party instead of your boys. They're a riotous bunch, the lives of the party, and I'm sure you'll enjoy them a lot during the week. But would you honestly ever go out of your way to see them again? No, of course not, no more than I would to see your sons.

"Why, then, do we think that because we gave birth to someone that we have to want to be with them, that we have to want to be connected to them for the rest of our lives?"

Before Lauren could respond, she said quickly, "A rhetorical question only, of course, because the answer is obvious. Having so thoroughly internalized the voice of the Fathers, we would adjudge ourselves terrible people, horrible women if we didn't. Also, how can we face our true feelings? They're too dangerous. Our whole lives as mothers would suddenly become meaningless. Our conditioned belief that we love these people for themselves alone regardless of our relationship with them, and that we would choose to be with them even if they weren't our children, would seldom, almost never, match our genuine feelings."

"I still don't see why you can't be friends with your kids," Lauren argued. "I don't think of Kurt and Brandon as my children anymore. They're friends."

"Oh, please," Harper moaned. "Didn't you hear a word of what Sonia said? How many boys in their twenties have female friends in their fifties? Besides, the only time those two call you is when they need something."

"That's not true! When Lawrence died, I'd never have made it without them. They took care of everything."

"Okay, so once in their lives they did something for you. Once. Name one other occasion, Lauren."

Lauren bit her lip but said nothing.

"You can't think of any because there aren't any. Look, they're not bad kids. But do you remember what you said to me a few weeks ago when Kurt called and you weren't home? As soon as I gave you the message, you said, 'He must need money'. That's what you said. And you were right.

"Every damn time that phone rings you're afraid it's Kurt, calling to say he has AIDS, or Brandon, hurt or killed in a car wreck because he drives so fast. You lose sleep over them, Laur. They're always with you. God, I'm glad I don't have kids!"

"So am I," Lauren snapped.

Harper glared at her.

Dana looked thoughtful and troubled. "I don't have kids, but I seem to have the same kind of relationship with my parents. The phone rings and I wonder if it's the police, telling me my parents have wrapped themselves around a telephone pole, or that my mother's fallen and broken a hip. I mean, I love them but I live in constant dread."

"Maybe you should do what Sonia did," Harper suggested.

"You don't understand." Dana frowned. "They really are dependent on me. I make sure they get their taxes done, renew their driver's licenses, pay their bills. I can't tell you how many times a month I have to buy food for them because they forget."

"You don't have to do it, Dana," Sonia said. "If something happened to you, they'd figure out a way to survive."

"No. They'd die. They can't take care of themselves, Sonia."

"It's their choice," Harper said. "They've made a choice and you've made a choice. Either side could choose to do something different. You could choose to let them be responsible instead of running their lives."

"I know it's sick," Dana admitted. "You aren't the first to point it out. But they're in their seventies. They can't live a hell of a lot longer. I guess I'm just going to hang in there until the end."

"I'm glad I don't have parents," Harper muttered.

Sonia started to speak, then stopped when she heard Jean's car coming up the driveway. She was looking forward to meeting Coral, but right now she was more eager to talk to Jean. Though she suspected she'd have to wait until Coral went to bed, she wanted to celebrate her prison break with someone who would rejoice in it, too.

Unexpectedly, she got her wish. Coral was so tired from the long trip and from being up most of the previous night, that after introductions Jean took her up to the third-floor bedroom to rest. The four women on the deck watched them go into the house together.

"I didn't know she was black," Harper reflected.

"I didn't either," Sonia said. "At least if Jean mentioned it, I don't remember. She's certainly a beautiful woman."

"She is," Harper agreed. "Her skin looks like velvet, so soft and dark. I had the feeling her eyes would have danced out of her head if they hadn't been attached. And as tired as she is, too. Can you imagine her when she's rested?" Harper smiled at the image.

Sonia headed for the house, hoping to intercept Jean before she could get involved in something else, like cooking. Upstairs she could hear voices from the spare room. She hesitated a moment before knocking on the door and pushing it open.

Coral was stretched out on the bed, her hands behind her head, Jean sitting beside her, and it was obvious they had been laughing. Harper was right about Coral's eyes; bright, shiny, full of fun. She looked vibrant and alive and Sonia was suddenly very glad she was there.

"Jeannie, I'm going to be in my room for awhile and would sure like to talk to you when you get a chance."

Jean glanced at the clock. "I want to start dinner now. Come talk to me while I work."

Sonia nodded and turned towards the door. "Just stick your head in my place and let me know when you're going down."

"Now," Jean stood, giving Coral a pat on the knee. "This kid needs some sleep and I've promised to make baingan bharta for dinner."

"Bargain what?" Sonia asked.

Coral laughed, showing a crooked front tooth that added to her charm. "Baingan bharta," she repeated for Sonia. "Curried eggplant, my favorite dish. Next to about three dozen others."

"Coral and I are into food," Jean explained to Sonia, linking arms with her. "I'll throw the dogs on you when dinner is ready," she called to Coral as they left the room.

"You're right about her, Jean. She's lovely on the outside and I'll take your word for the inside."

Jean nodded. "I'm just glad that so far I haven't been in illusion about her, about who she is. She's very fair and honest and fun. I think you'll enjoy her. The nice thing, too, is that she can take care of herself."

At the stovetop, she bent down and picked up the large black pot she used for cooking rice. After measuring water into it, she added the rice, a teaspoon of saffron, and a tablespoon of canola oil. She set it on the burner, turned the flame up, and put the lid on. Then she reached down and hefted a large, cast iron skillet up onto another burner.

Sonia sat at the stool opposite the stove and leaned forward on her folded arms.

"I wanted to tell you about the phone call to my kids."

Jean nodded. "I've been thinking about you all day, wondering if you'd done it and how it went."

Sonia recounted every realization, every amazing act. She told her how she had hung up from talking to her ex-kids and laid on the floor, bellowing with pain. Not from the act itself but from all the illusion she had built up around these people—that they really loved her for herself and not for what she could give them. That she really loved them for themselves, not because they were her kids. She told her how she realized that she didn't even know how she felt about them.

"Motherhood is essentially a choiceless place," she said. "We question the role and its responsibilities very little, if at all. If we do change the scenario, we make only minor adjustments, such as those necessary for survival, emotional and econcomic—working outside the home, for instance. We have to be there for those kids, have to take care of them or see that someone does, all the time, even when we don't want to, even when we're too tired or sick to even take care of ourselves. We have to do it. And we don't dare admit even for a moment that we have allowed ourselves to be trapped, tricked into the same prison as millions of women before us. And—oh excruciating irony— all in the name of love."

Jean listened while she cooked. What Sonia had done made sense to her. It was true that the institution of the family, of which motherhood was the largest part, forced people together who otherwise would probably never in a thousand years choose each other's company. And then forced them to stay connected until parted by death—that, or feel guilty, lacking, and worthless.

Sonia had asked her children if, of their own accord, without having had their previous association with her, they would have chosen her for a friend. None of them had replied, but she had known the answer, especially her sons': no male under 30 would deliberately choose to associate with a 55-year-old woman 'for herself alone'. And probably no male of any age.

"Every minute of my life since my children were born I've been aware that I had four conduits to agony out there in the world," she said, then paused, thinking.

"But you know something peculiar? I'm sure that my misery about their unhappiness has always been greater than their unhappiness. I told you about Justin's calling, all upset. And how, because I did the worrying, he didn't need to; let Mom do the agonizing. I've dutifully done it for years. That's what mothers do, you know. We take on our kid's burdens, and by doing so, lower the quality of our own lives and make users of them.

"Without meaning to, of course. I'm not blaming anyone—us or them. It's the institution of motherhood that forces us into this behavior."

Jean put down the vegetable knife and came around the island to face Sonia. "What you've been telling me is just starting to sink in. I mean really sink in. Do you realize what you've done? Do you realize that you've just walked out of patriarchy's most sacred institution? Sonia!" Jean grabbed her in a rib-crushing hug.

"Chenoa wished over and over that women would wake up, for just half a day, really wake up and turn their backs on every male and every male institution, for just half a day. 'It would be the end of patriarchy,' she said. 'No more violence, no more pain and suffering.' You've done it. You've told patriarchy to take their dysfunctional family and stuff it. I trust you realize that this is more subversive than renouncing god!"

"No, it is renouncing god." Sonia sneaked a piece of celery and chewed on it for a few moments. "You know, nothing on earth could be more unnatural for women than motherhood."

Jean returned to her cutting board. "You mean motherhood in patriarchy."

Sonia shook her head. "No. Motherhood, period. Though you're almost right. Motherhood doesn't exist, can't exist, outside patriarchy."

"Surely there was motherhood in matriarchies," Jean argued. "Or are you simply saying that being a mother isn't an institutionalized experience except in patriarchy?"

Sonia shook her head again. "I said exactly what I meant. Matriarchies didn't even exist until after patriarchy struck. Men brought hierarchy with them, inside them, when they appeared among us. You and I keep saying that men aren't sadomasochistic, they are sadomasochism, that this is their essence, their name. Sadomasochism is hierarchy and sex. And what they add up to is a way of being in the world that is totally relational. Cleverly enough, they call it 'relating', 'having relationships', and tell us that there's no other way to connect with each other.

"In women's world, the world we were, the way we were for eons before maleness infected the universes, nothing was ever relational, ever dependent upon anything or anyone else, always only itself, having complete power and integrity in itself. Since we did not 'relate'—meaning, we were constitutionally unable even to conceive of sadomasochism/hierarchy/sex—an idea such as family would have been meaningless.

"Relationship roles were therefore impossible, as were words to describe them: mother, daughter, aunt, grandmother. To think of any other person as 'ours' would have been so alien that we couldn't have understood it. Children born to any of us—and they were all female—belonged to no one. They were absolutely free from birth."

"But they did need care, at least up to a certain age."

"Of course. But if women's world is what we strongly believe it is, then those children were only cared for by women who wanted to do it, and not exclusively by those women who had given birth to them.

"And I know that when we are finally living in a world where no one has to do anything, where she does only what she wants, those jobs that are now considered mundane and dreary won't be. When there is no coercion, no one 'in charge' telling us what we have to do, then at any given moment there will easily be dozens of women who want to care for a child. Because they have choices. And also because the children will be very different."

"I'm not sure I follow you there."

"Imagine being a baby born to women like these. There is no frazzled mother to make you feel as if you've done something wrong by needing her attention. No woman ever attending to you out of feelings of guilt or responsibility because, outside of relationships and sadomasochism, such concepts and feelings can't exist.

"That means that every woman who holds you, feeds you, plays with you, sings to you, tells you stories, bathes you, dresses you, rocks you to sleep, does it because she really loves doing it, really wants to, and freely chooses you over everything else she might have been doing. She is with you out of totally free choice!

"Imagine how easy it will be for you to love yourself in such circumstances. All you ever see in anyone's face is total approval, total joy in your existence and in your ways, total acceptance and genuine love."

"I like your emphasis on 'genuine'," Jean reflected. "We've talked about how what men call love, or rather, how they define it, is light years from women's definition. How for men, love is something you do; it's tangible and concrete. You beat your wife up and then you take her flowers the next day and that's love. Or you screw her every night and that's love. Women, on the other hand, are love. We don't do it, we simply are it, it's our essence. But since the coming of maleness, we've lost track of who we are."

"That's why I say 'genuine' love. Archaically, when women were actively love every moment, we were free and wild. Love as we knew it is possible for us only under those conditions—freedom and wildness. Love and freedom are inextricable. So we haven't loved anyone, including ourselves, during our 5,000 years of captivity. We've felt pity, need for approval, responsibility, kindness, caring, dependency, jealousy, fear of loss—all kinds of feelings patriarchy has taught us to call love. But never love, not since men came."

Jean sighed. "And we didn't have to 'work' at loving ourselves then, either. It was a given. No classes on how to do it, no books giving us steps in self-loving, no therapy sessions. And yet we keep buying the books, taking the classes, going to therapy, believing that someday we'll figure it out. The truth is that love and patriarchy can't exist in the same place at the same time. So in order to love ourselves, we have to get patriarchy out of our innards. Then love can remember herself and blossom again."

"And freedom and joy and power," Sonia added. "I have such a longing to be around women who are free, self-aware women doing only what they chose to do all the time, women fully in their power.

"No child born since patriarchy has seen a free woman—think of that! None of us has anything but remotest, vaguest, memories—not in our minds but in our feelings—of what a free woman might look like, let alone how she might act. Since we haven't seen or been one for so heart-breakingly long, we have no idea of who we really are or of the true magnificence and . . . glory of femaleness.

"You know my theory, that men patterned their male god upon what women were when men first knew them: omnipresent, omniscient, omnipowerful. Where they messed it up was trying to portray him as loving and understanding. Men simply can't be these things. Some of them give a pretty good imitation, but this is all it is—a mimicry of women. This is why they are so contradictory: one minute professing love, the next minute insanely jealous, destructive, and hateful.

"In the women's movement we prove how hopelessly lost we are from our original Selves when we equate women's power with being able to hold male offices and positions. I find painful beyond words our having allowed ourselves to be reduced to mere men."

They were interrupted by a high-pitched, shrill squeal slicing the air.

Sonia leapt off the stool. "What in the world was that?"

"Ashley," Jean said calmly, chopping eggplant. "She's happy to be here." Through the window, she watched Barb join the other women on the deck.

"Heaven help us on the day she's not happy." Sonia resettled herself and took up the dropped conversation.

"You know, today's experience reminded me of how deep in illusion women are about our sons. True, we can't know our daughters in patriarchy, either, but it's with our sons that the illusions run deepest."

Jean nodded her head emphatically. "I can't speak from personal experience, but I remember when the son of a woman I knew was picked up for armed robbery. He was caught in the act, holding a gun on the shop owner. Unfortunately for him there was a plainclothes cop in the store who nailed him as he tried to leave with a paper bag full of money. In spite of the fact that he was caught in front of a dozen or more witnesses and that he admitted to the crime, his mother denied over and over that he'd done it. 'Not my son, not my Dennis,' she'd tell anyone who'd listen."

"Naturally. What would it say about the worth of her life if she'd spent it raising a criminal?"

"I know that's an extreme example," Jean said.

Sonia considered that. "Well, maybe it is. But I know one that isn't, one illusion that nearly all women share, and that's that their sons are not like other men. They are not rapists, for example. However, since women are being raped by the millions, somebody's sons are obviously rapists. I wonder whose? Oh, I know it's not yours or mine. So it must be that other woman's. Ask that other woman and she says, oh, not mine. It must be yours and hers.

"The truth is that rape is inherent in maleness, part of the definition of it. And all men are one hundred percent male, no matter how gentle, how 'caring', how anything else society has construed as feminine they are. This means that every man is a rapist at heart, every single last one of them.

"Yet though the evidence for this is monumental, ubiquitous, and beyond argument, women blindly persist in believing that some men are different from others, particularly their sons and husbands.

"And feminists, too, many who are quick to understand the universality of rape, and even those few who understand the nature of maleness (from simply looking around the planet!), almost without exception exonerate their own sons. Isn't it extraordinary that they can believe that for some reason the children they gave birth to are different? They can believe that my sons rape, but they can't believe that theirs do.

"This is motherhood illusion, absolutely necessary to the continuation of male rule because it keeps women giving males the energy they need to survive."

Jean added, "But our illusion extends beyond the sons and husbands to all other males we think we like."

She went on to tell Sonia about the day she took her friend Joan to the airport, how during the drive, Joan had told her this story:

Years ago she had worked with a young man whom she came first to admire then almost adore. He was gentle, considerate, smart, funny, talented. An environmentalist, he often took to the streets to educate people. He had such an easy, warm manner that even hard-core industrialists were won over by him. Over the years that she knew him, they had many wonderful talks, and she felt very close to him. "I felt understood, cherished by him. I would have bet my life that he was different from other men."

Then one day, as she and his girlfriend and he sat at a booth at a street fair, a beautiful woman walked past them. Too sure of their affection for him, he got careless and let his facade slip. "Every time I see an attractive woman anywhere," he said, "in a store, on the street, I fantasize ripping her clothes off, throwing her to the ground, and fucking her."

"'I had to go home and throw up,' Joan told me, sadly. 'He was a rapist, pure and simple. None of the image he had so carefully built up for me was what he really was. I never spoke to him again, and left my job soon afterwards. I couldn't stand to look at him. But my disillusionment went farther than him. I knew that if he wasn't an exception, no man was.'"

"But didn't she just get married?" Sonia asked, surprised.

Jean shrugged. "You know the phenomenon. It's called 'slipping in and out of awareness'. One minute you see the whole ugly picture, the next minute you're prettifying it with swans and roses."

"True. But somehow I can't imagine slipping out of the awareness of what men are."

"You know we'd be called man-haters if anyone overheard us," Jean laughed.

Sonia sighed. "I know. That's why I say it only to you. To you I don't have to explain the difference between hatred and telling the truth."

"Facts," Jean suggested. "It's amazing to me how terrified women are of the facts, and how ready to cut off the head of the fact-finder."

"Well, you know why. Every man has at least one woman in his life who has dedicated her entire being to him, who has practically become him—remember Cathy's 'I am Heathcliff'? So she has to maintain her illusions about him, even in the face of cold, hard facts. I understand now what I had to do to believe that my sons were different, what all women have to do.

"We have to project the way we are upon the men in our lives and interpret their lives through the heavy scrim of our motivations, our values, our feelings and desires: 'If I acted like that,' we think to ourselves, 'it would be because I was lonely or hurt or frightened, so that must be why he's doing it. I'll love him so much he'll never feel lonely, hurt, or frightened again and then his behavior will change.' What a surprise we're in for, because their behavior doesn't change. It hasn't changed for thousands of years, except to get worse, because the acts that women would commit only out of the most terrible mental anguish and desperation are the acts that come most easily and naturally to men: killing, raping, rampaging, despoiling and destroying.

"So we project and then carefully, albeit unconsciously, edit out everything that doesn't fit that picture, that isn't essentially like us. And I'm serious when I say we have to do it, at least if we're going to continue to be mothers. If we didn't, not a one of us could live or associate with boys after maleness struck them down forever at puberty."

Jean looked up from her stirring. "In the early seventies, when I was a student, I heard of a study that a mixed group of feminists had done."

As she went on to recall it, the researchers had selected several large businesses and interviewed the women working at all levels in them; in those days, most of them were secretaries. They asked them to name the men in the office they considered "exceptions", men they believed really liked and respected women.

Then they hid microphones in the men's lavatories at each of the locations, and for several weeks taped the conversations that went on there. After editing out all the chaff, they got the women of each company alone together in a conference room and played the relevant tape for them.

The women simply could not believe their ears. They had to have the tape replayed several times before they could even begin to take it in. The "exceptional" men were as vile, raunchy, dehumanizing, and hateful about them as the others. Worse even, because they laughed at the women's gullibility, at how easily they were manipulated by flattery to do the men's work for them.

Several women became physically ill on the spot, some cried, some were furious, all were deeply hurt. Many consequently quit their jobs, and some had nervous breakdowns. Needless to say, the results of the study were firmly suppressed.

"But I'd bet my life," Jean concluded, "that as quickly as they could, the women blocked the experience out of their memories. Because if women saw their sons and fathers and brothers and male friends as they really are, it would kill most of them. And I mean it."

They were silent for a few moments, Jean staring unseeing at the food she was cooking, Sonia lost in thought.

Sonia spoke first. "If, as you say, the truth about men can equal death, then it's no surprise that denial and illusion dominate every woman's survival repertoire. Not accidental, the malestream making truth so perilous."

"It's also freedom," Jean added softly. "Ironic isn't is? Knowing the truth is the only way we can really be free and being free is the only way we can survive beyond patriarchy. Yet the truth can kill us. If we let it."

Laying down her wooden spoon, she went to Sonia, put her arms around her, and laid her cheek against hers. Then for a moment, she allowed herself to feel how deeply men's world has damaged women, how, in truth, it has irrevocably destroyed most of them.

Her tears wet both their faces.

15

The group gathered around the table that night was a rowdy one, with Coral at the center. From the outset, her open, friendly face had predisposed everyone to like her. And then she began so contagiously enjoying herself that the others caught the bug and joined in. Even Lauren seemed looser and more relaxed than she had for a long awhile. Coral had brought down her ukelele and was making up songs about each of them as she observed them and as they confided outrageous things to her about each other.

Every so often Harper would leave the group for a few minutes to work on her paratha bread—a flat, triangular-shaped bread that she insisted was essential to serve with baingan bharta. After kneading the dough for about ten minutes, she formed it into a ball, rubbed it with a little oil, and slipped it into a plastic bag to "rest". She then rejoined the group where Coral's impromptu revue was rapidly turning into a series of vaudeville acts as the women relaxed and began to ham it up.

Jean got up to check the enormous pot of simmering curried eggplant. It was done, so she turned if off. From the stove she watched the women gathered around Coral, singing and laughing, and she was again reminded of how hungry she was for this kind of intimacy with women.

She watched Harper reluctantly tear herself away from the fun and come over to see how her dough was doing. Apparently it was ready for the next step, because she oiled the cast-iron skillet and set it on a burner.

Then she quickly kneaded the bread again and formed 24 balls. Flattening one of them, she dusted it with flour and rolled it out to about six inches in diameter. She spread a small amount of oil over its surface and folded it in half. She spread more oil on the half and folded it again to form a triangle. Then she rolled it out to make it even larger, and slapped it into the hot skillet. A paratha was born.

She let it cook a minute, brushed oil on it and turned it over to cook on the other side for another minute or so. When both sides were golden brown, she transferred it to a tortilla-warming basket, and went on to the next one. Soon she had an impressive stack ready for dinner.

Jean scooped the rice into one large serving bowl and the baingan bharta into another, and placed them on the counter. Lauren carried the salad over and Harper, putting her parathas beside the rice and eggplant, announced that dinner was ready. Coral put down her ukelele and the troupe disbanded to fill their plates.

"What are those delicious-looking things?" Coral asked, pointing to the bread.

"They're called parathas and you're supposed to scoop up your food with it, instead of using a fork."

"Sounds as if you lived in India."

Harper shook her head. "Never even been there, but I'd like to go someday. I learned this from one of my ex-lovers. She was Indian and a fabulous cook. Ironically, she learned how to cook in this country. She grew up wealthy in India, with maids and cooks, and never had a chance to do any cooking on her own. Apparently, it was considered low class. But when she came here, she threw herself into it with the passion most of us save for love affairs. In fact, we broke up because she preferred the kitchen to the bedroom." This drew a round of laughter. "Now she runs a Punjabi restaurant in New York City."

"Sounds like my kind of woman!" Coral laughed. "I love food, love to cook it, eat it, talk about it, think about it, and play with it!"

"I love it too," Sonia said drily. "But just to eat. I wouldn't have a clue how to play with it, but I like the idea. Better than I like the idea of cooking it."

"Do you cook at all?" Coral asked politely.

Sonia clutched her head in mock horror. "What? Cook? Have you lost your mind, woman?" Then in her normal voice, "Actually, I don't if I can help it. I did it out of duty for twenty long years, hating every minute of it. I still find it hard to believe that women like you and Jean are real. Perhaps, I say to myself, they're really deceiving themselves."

"I find it hard to believe that women like you are real, too," Jean shot back. "For me cooking is a marvelous experience, both an adventure and something very familiar and dear. I'd be lost if I couldn't do it."

"I enjoy it sometimes but I certainly don't have the love for it that you do," Harper told Jean. "When I'm in the mood, I can throw myself into it. But I'm not in the mood very often."

"I hate it, but I'll do it rather than eat sandwiches three times a day," Dana said. "Maybe I wouldn't mind cooking if I got as much in return as you do, Jean. I guess I'm like Sonia. I think you can't really like to do it, that you just think you do—because it gets you so much attention and praise." Feeling the atmosphere chill, she affected a serious pose—leaning back in her chair and putting the tips of her fingers together, steeple-like in front of her chest—and said in a deep voice, "I think we need to look at that in one of our sessions, my dear."

Despite Dana's attempt at humor, Jean felt the slap of her criticism. She knew Dana wasn't joking, that under cover of teasing, she had said what she really thought. And she wanted Jean to know it. After all, what fun would it have been to do sadomasochism if Jean hadn't been put in her place?

"Oh, Sigmund! Any excuse to talk about food!"

Everyone laughed, relieved that the bad spot had been crossed without incident.

"I heard you were in Los Gatos today," Harper said a little too loudly to Dana. "Anything interesting going on?"

Dana shrugged, indicating her full mouth. She chewed quickly and swallowed. "I ran into Moya at the co-op. She told me about a meeting sponsored by the Women's Forum. It's on Wednesday, I think, and the topic is racism among feminists, or something like that. She gave me a flyer if anyone's interested."

"I take it Moya is a sister of color?" Coral asked.

Dana nodded, her mouth full again.

Coral shook her head. "When are they going to figure out that we can talk racism until we piss pennies and we aren't going to change one damned thing. It's an inside job."

Sonia looked at her, surprised. "I think so, too, and have for years. But since I'm white, you can imagine how delicately I treat the subject in public. I'm glad to hear it said by a black woman." Coral stopped smiling. "Do you think my black sisters take *me* to their bosoms when I say this? Actually," she temporized, "a very few of them do. But I'm talking heresy, and most women of color don't want to hear it. They want to be angry at you white girls because anger gives them a feeling of power."

Harper looked puzzled. "Are you saying you don't believe in fighting racism?"

"That, maybe, but a whole lot more. I'm saying that no matter how much we talk about racism to you palefaces, it's not going to change a thing, either for us or for you. I'm saying you can't love me unless you love yourself first. And I can't feel your love unless I love myself first. The change has to come from inside us both, and it comes from loving ourselves."

"But what about laws, at least to enforce some degree of fairness?" Lauren asked timidly.

"You women are going to starve me to death with your questions!" Coral laughed, wiping her mouth with her napkin. Then turning to Lauren, she said, "You can pass all kinds of laws to try to prevent racism, but the truth is that laws don't affect the way people feel. So in the end they don't make any difference in the way they act. No law is going to protect me from the hatred most people feel when they see me. Or see any woman, for that matter. Men hate women—really hate us—on every level, forget skin color. So why bother?" She paused to take a bite of bread.

Harper frowned. "But surely you care that they hate you. Surely you want to do something to try to stop it."

"Look—Harper, is it? If I'm loving myself, then what you or anyone else thinks of me can't affect me. And if I'm not, if I'm racist and sexist myself, then I'm going to think you're racist and sexist no matter what you say or do. Since it's inside me, my fighting something outside me—your bigotry—isn't going to make any difference in my feelings. Except that the harder I try to change you, the madder I'll get at you because I'll still be feeling shitty. To put it simply, I can't experience what isn't already me."

Sonia could barely contain herself. "That's true of every variety of oppression, large and small. If we don't wrench it out of ourselves first, if we constantly externalize it, it will go on forever. There's a metaphysical reason for it: trying to get others to change is sadomasochism, and being sadomasochistic is how sado-masochism is perpetuated. I always paraphrase Audre Lorde to make this point, where she says we can't tear down the master's house using the master's tools."

Coral nodded. "I've been fiercely attacked, fiercely. Women of color accuse me of having white racist politics and shun me. So do white women who are out there fighting for their black sisters. Why fight? I ask them. What good does it do? Let's get down to the real stuff, the self-hatred, the shit we're carrying around inside."

"By the way," Dana interjected, "this meeting on Wednesday is in reaction to a story written by a white women about the rape of her best friend. She was raped by a black man who also badly brutalized her in the process. It was published in a local women's paper and caused a furor."

"Why?" Coral demanded angrily. "Because he was black? So black men don't rape and attack and kill women? Since when?" Her eyes blazed.

"Maybe some of these idealistic women need to spend a few weeks in Detroit," she continued angrily, "in the downtown emergency rooms where I've worked, so they can see how many black women and children are admitted raped, beaten, cut, shat on, gang fucked, knife fucked, shot, burned, ripped open, starved, dehydrated, and killed by some black man—husband, boyfriend, brother, son, father, grandfather, uncle, neighbor."

Trembling, she pushed her chair back from the table and strode over to the counter to serve herself some salad, movement helping her regain her composure. Everyone sat very still.

"I worked as an emergency room reporter in a hospital in downtown Gary, Indiana," Jean remarked tentatively into the charged atmosphere. "The population in Gary was almost exclusively black, so the patient load at the hospital reflected that." She stopped for a moment and took a deep breath.

"Every day, women, young girls, *infant* girls were brought in to be treated for sexual-abuse-related injuries perpetrated by men. Tiny little girls and babies with their vulvas ripped to pieces . . ." She stopped for a moment as emotion silenced her. Glancing around the table, she saw Barb looking at her, her features soft with compassion.

"As you said, Coral, my saying this is not racist. It's simply a fact, evidence, if anything, of male nature. I know that the same thing occurs in predominantly white hospitals, too, but I guess I wanted to underscore your point about the difference between prejudice and fact."

Still at the counter, Coral nodded. "As you can tell, I'm a little miffed about the hullabaloo over this article." She walked back over to the table and sat down. "Here women are again, protecting a *man* because he's black, and attacking another woman for telling the truth. Sometimes I think we haven't made an inch of progress in this so-called movement of ours. When are we going to wake up and see how men have taught us to hate and distrust one another, to the point where we'll destroy one another to protect them. Really, it sickens me."

Then, to lift the heaviness a bit, she joked, "But not enough to take away my appetite," and dived into her salad.

"I'm sick of it, too," Sonia told her, then asked rhetorically, "You want to know what makes me sickest? The hard-ons women get by accusing each other of racism, sexism, ageism, ablebodyism. I'm sick of women getting their kicks like men do, lashing and cutting down and stomping on and tyrannizing and terrorizing and generally feeling so superior to other women who are not as politically correct as they are that they are in a constant state of emotional erection, ejaculating all over the place. I hate the blatant sadomasochism, the blatant *male sex* of it. I know absolutely that this is behavior women couldn't even have imagined before penises penetrated the world!"

Jean and Coral nodded at Sonia, while the rest of the women sat, silenced by Sonia's passionate outburst.

"You're both right about it's being self-hatred," Jean said. "Our conditioning to hate femaleness runs so deep I'm not sure there's much hope for the majority of women. Look at the lesbians out there taking care of their 'gay brother's' with AIDS . . ."

"Brothers!" Coral snorted. "Save us from all our brothers, blood or otherwise."

". . . and doing nothing at all for their lesbian sisters who are dying like flies from breast cancer," Jean finished her sentence. Then she leaned forward, her folded arms resting on the table.

"Sonia and I were talking about this as I made dinner. How women still, in the face of overwhelming evidence to the contrary, want to believe that there are some 'good' men out there instead of just men who know exactly how they have to act to get women's wonderful, juicy, necessary life stuff."

"It's not just that," Dana argued. "Men are considered important no matter how they act. I just read a book, a true story, about a man who manipulated his 14-year-old-daughter and his 17-year-old-sister-in-law into murdering his wife. It's a long, complex process but basically how he did it was by hitting them repeatedly with, 'If you really loved me, you'd do this for me'. He had been grossly abusive to everyone in his life—his daughter, his wife, her sister, his parents; sexually abusing his daughter and sister-in-law in horrific ways for years—and even made sure his daughter went to prison in his place, *after* he tried to kill her by forcing her to take an overdose.

"When he was finally found out and standing trial, his parents were so furious and outraged at their granddaughter for testifying against him that they refused to speak to her again. Because, though she had suffered terribly at his hands all her life, and though she had served nearly six years in prison for his crime, women don't matter and men, no matter how monstrous, do. It's that simple. And that sick."

"It's even that way for me," Harper admitted. "I mean, men have the money to invest. I make my living off them, and I really don't mind because I'd rather risk their money than women's. But every chance I get, I take advantage of them. Especially the pricks who constantly proposition me and drool all over me. They pay for it, believe me."

Coral laughed. "I worked for awhile in a restaurant in Detroit that was owned and run by three women. They wanted it to be a woman-only space but they got so much flack that they finally allowed men in. But they did it their way. They made every day in that restaurant 'Ladies' Day'—15 percent off every woman's bill. The men paid the higher prices all the time.

"The beauty of it was that the prices the women paid were normal prices, what the owners had to charge to make a profit. The men were paying 15 percent *above* that. When they complained, we told them there were plenty of other restaurants in town."

"Did it keep them out?" Lauren asked.

"Are you kidding? Men can't stand to let us have our own space. It's very threatening to them. Look at how they wormed their way into NOW, and all women's organizations."

"Why do you think that is?" Lauren asked.

Coral shrugged. "I don't give men much thought, but off the top of my head I'd say it's because they're afraid we'll talk about them, tell each other the truth about them. If they're not with us, they can't control us."

"That's why men take women studies classes, too," Sonia added.

"It's not just heterosexual men either," Jean agreed. "I was president of the Lesbian/Gay organization in Las Palomas for awhile. We'd had numerous mixed dances, and a lot of women wanted one of their own. So we organized a Cabaret, with live music, dancing, food, little round tables all over the room. The gay men were furious, called us separatists, told me I was going to split the organization. When I mentioned their gay-men-only video nights, they argued that that was different. But of course it wasn't. They just couldn't stand not being the center of attention. And also they couldn't understand why we would prefer to be only with women when we could be with wonderful *them*."

They all roared at this. When the laughter died down, Harper said, "I want to get back to the women's racism forum for a minute. For the record, I just want to say the obvious, that Moya and the other women are reacting against the stereotype of black men as rapists of white women. We know this originated with white men, maybe to keep white women from having sympathy with the slaves. Whatever, it's still alive and well in the minds of most Anglos, especially women."

"Oh, men too," Coral assured her firmly. "And you want to know something? Black men do rape white women. One of the oldest and most effective tactics of war is to rape the enemy's women; it's part of the definition of war. Well, there's war against blacks in this country, and like all men, black men understand rape as a weapon for humiliating the enemy. What better way to bring old whitey to his knees than to defile his most prized property? Of course, old whitey's busy retaliating in kind. So there's truth in that old stereotype, plenty of it."

She took her last forkful of salad, chewed a moment, then shook her head. "Just thinking about that forum makes me want to shout obscenities. All those feminists being led by red herring-isms smack dab into the killing nets. It makes me want to set the record straight once and for all. It makes me want to talk *facts*."

She held up one finger. "Fact number 1: Men hate, rape, humiliate, abuse, attack, maim, and kill women. This is true of all men, regardless of color, class, nationality, or religious beliefs, and no one group has greater proclivity in these directions than another. In this, all men are equal. This is not racism, classism, jingoism, or sexism. This is a fact.

"Fact number 2:" she announced, holding up the second finger. "Men in every race and class use prejudice on every level to control people, especially women, because it causes us to turn against one another instead of against them. This is what has allowed men and their institutions to survive so long."

"Just these two facts. My wish on that big brazen star out there," she pointed through the window at Arcturus, "is that every feminist of every color will take them to heart, that we'll pull our battleaxes out of each other's backs and get on with the vital work of learning to love ourselves. That we'll finally have a *movement*—a real going-forward."

"I hope you get your wish, Coral," Sonia said. "But I haven't much faith in it. Feminists are having too much satisfying, hardcore sex to want to stop."

"Yeah, I'm still back at something you said earlier, Sonia," Barb spoke up. "When you talked about women getting hard-ons. That's a new one for me. And later you mentioned 'emotional erections', again in reference to women."

"I define sex as sadomasochism, Barb," Sonia explained, "meaning that it occurs everywhere, not just in the bedroom between consenting adults. Sex is hierarchy, someone on top, someone on the bottom. This happens in business, in government, in education, in all relationships.

"Women in patriarchy have learned to get their jollies out of being on top, just as men do. And we get there in a variety of ways. One of the surest of these is to tear other women down, to criticize them, to point out how politically incorrect they are, or to gossip about them. It's the spiritual equivalent of men going around with hard-ons, raping everything in sight."

"I get it," Barb said. "It just struck me as so, well, graphic."

Coral choked on the water she was drinking, and it took her several minutes of coughing and gasping to calm down. "Knowing Sonia, as I do from her books," she laughed, tears running down her face, "I'd say being graphic isn't the half of it!"

"I have a friend," Jean said. "She's a well-known writer, and awhile ago she told me about the project she's been working on for years. She told me she had to abandon it because her research was taking her into territory that would leave her wide open to allegations of anti-semitism by the Jewish lesbian/feminist community. After almost three years of hard work, she opted not to be torn limb from limb for telling the truth about Judaism."

Harper frowned. "I can't understand why Jewish feminists cling so tenaciously to a heritage—to a racial/religious identity if you will—that's basically misogynist."

"All religions are," Dana reminded her. "They wouldn't be religions if they weren't. Jewish women are a good example of what we've just been looking at—women willing to fight other women in defense of their 'cultural heritage', i.e., patriarchy."

"I think theirs has a lot to do with group persecution," Coral said. "The more oppressed any group has been, the more safety they think they have in tradition. That just makes sense. Are you Jewish?" she asked Dana.

Dana flushed, looking down at her hands. "I used to be," she answered to everyone's surprise; none of them had had a clue.

"My mother was Jewish, but at my father's insistence, renounced it and became Presbyterian. When I found out, I was furious with my father and got back at him by taking instruction when I was 16. It lasted almost 20 years. Then one day I woke up and walked out and wouldn't associate with Judaism or any other religion for all the money in the world.

"But it's not just Jewish women that your theory of oppression applies to," she assured Coral. "Look at Native American women. Every place you go nowadays you see them fighting with other women to protect and elevate in status what they want to believe are 'their' traditions; traditions that don't reflect or include them at all, but are all men's ideas, all men's values, all male ways."

"That's true," Jean agreed. "Chenoa told me many times that none of the existing traditions of the native peoples originated with women. That what women had contributed to their societies had all been destroyed, and men's culture had taken its place."

Sonia shrugged. "That didn't just happen to native women, or women who were members of certain other persecuted groups. It's what happened to women all over the world, all over the universe, through all the universes, when maleness exploded onto them. Female culture was systematically and thoroughly stamped out. The only femaleness left anywhere is within us."

"Well, I just wish more women knew it," Dana sighed. "It seems to me that we'll do almost anything not to have to face the truth, not to have to give up our illusions and start the painful journey back to ourselves."

"I've noticed something else that women who choose to remain faithful to their 'cultural heritage' do," Sonia said. "In order to get comfortable enough to stay there, they ascribe meanings to certain concepts and rituals that were not only never intended but that can't possibly work within the overall framework. The reason their alterations can never be part of the tradition, the reason they can't work, is because they actually contradict and nullify its very essence, crumble it at its foundations."

"Give an example," Barb said.

"Jewish feminists. It's ironic that they get angry at us for not taking their heritage seriously when all the while they themselves are methodically and irrevocably destroying it. They've recreated ancient rituals with a feminist twist, and it goes against the very basis of Judaism, of all religions, to include women in any significant way."

"And more power to 'em, I say," Harper interjected.

Sonia waved impatiently. "Maybe. I just wish they'd realize that what they themselves are doing is so madly anti-semitic that it's ridiculous to come down on the rest of us.

"But I know that's not a realistic wish. As Coral says, the more oppressed women have been by maleness—and in that department, Judaism ranks right up there with Christianity, Islam, Confucianism, Buddhism, Hinduism, you name it—the firmer they bond with men and the harder it is for them to get free of men's worldview and paradigms. Like battered women who can't leave their husbands, like battered children who cling to their parents. Like Jewish women, Native American women, Mormon women, Catholic women, prostitutes, wives, daughters, mothers . . . who can't leave 'their' pimps and popes and husbands, who can't leave 'their' cultures. None of this is evidence of how women are. All of it is evidence of massive, spirit-breaking terrorism and final capitulation into the Stockholm Syndrome."

"That was something I'd never heard about until I read *Wildfire*," Lauren remembered. "How the oppressed bond so tightly with their oppressors that even when the jail door swings open, they choose to remain in subjugation to them."

"Then you'll be pleased with me," Coral smiled at Sonia. "Because I don't give a Friday damn about my African roots. It doesn't make the least difference to me where I came from or who my ancestors were. I already know all I need to know about my heritage. My father, an African diplomat here in the U.S. for a year, raped my mother on a date, only they didn't call it that. He couldn't marry her because he had a wife back in Nairobi.

"Anyhow, my heritage is like everyone else's on this planet: patriarchy, maleness, as you call it, a daily descent into hell for my foresisters for centuries. Revere it? I repudiate it. I spit on it and I will not sentimentalize it into something decent and noble. It never was."

Her voice was rich and vibrant with feeling. The others sat, mesmerized.

"I'm a woman!" she cried, half rising and smacking the table with the flat of her hand. "That's my heritage, that's my roots. It's irrelevant what color I am or what religion or how much I've suffered. I'm a woman. I care only about women, and I care about all women. Womanness is everything to me—tradition, culture, heritage, meaning. To me, it's life, absolutely all that matters!"

She leaned back in her chair, her upper lip glistening with sweat. The listening women all let out their pent-up breath at once, a long soft sigh that filled the kitchen. Then Dana leaned toward her.

"So what would you say to the woman who is so afraid of being caught being racist that she can hardly talk to you—that's me, actually," she confessed. "I've watched what happens to white women who try to dialogue with women of color about racism. It's not only a no-win situation, it's a massacre, and believe me, it's kept my mouth riveted for years."

"What I say to you, sister," Coral touched Dana's forehead with her finger and ran it down to the tip of her nose, "is for sweet sake stop being afraid! You can't oppress me unless I let you, and you won't live to see that day. If you're racist, it's your problem, not mine. I can choose what I'm affected by, and hear me now, I choose never to be affected by your racism. I choose never to be your victim. So stop matronizing me, stop worrying that you're going to make me feel any way at all under the sun. Because you can't. My feelings are never under your control. Regardless of anything you can possibly think, feel, wish, say, or do, I choose to feel exactly how I want to feel every minute of my life.

"Understand," she shook her finger around the table, "and never forget: you are all irrelevant to me."

Into the hush that followed this, Harper said, "I'm glad Sylvie isn't here tonight. She'd probably either throw the table and chairs at us or burn the house down over our heads."

Lauren nodded in agreement. "Sylvie is a Jewish lesbian," she explained to the others, "very outspoken on the issue of anti-semitism. I'm like you, Dana. I'm always afraid to open my mouth for fear I'll inadvertently say something that can be construed as anti-semitic; Sylvie's always on the lookout. One time I told her how much I loved bagels and she got angry and told me that bagels weren't the only food Jewish people ate. She was eating one at the time and it reminded me of how much I like them. Of course, because I'm so nervous around her, I tend to do exactly what I don't want to do, and that's talk about being Jewish or trying to find things that might interest her."

"She's also big on ritual," Harper said disparagingly. "She reminds me of what you were talking about, Sonia. I've been to several feminist Hanukkah feasts and Passover celebrations that she's rewritten to eliminate the sexism. And sure enough, what she has when she's finished is not Judaism."

"When there's no misogyny, there's no known tradition, no extant culture or religion," Sonia said. She had agreed with Harper's thought but not with the condescending tone in which she'd expressed it. So she added, "You know, Harper, I really mean it when I say that I want all women to do what they want to do. If they want to do sadomasochism, that's fine with me; I totally respect their right to choose anything. But I also have the right to choose not to be around them. Not in a judgmental way, just all of us doing what we want."

"Anyhow, rituals are what men do," Coral said, disregarding all the intervening stuff. "They have to, because they're so lacking in emotion, in spontaneity, in immediate personal creativity and power. I don't care how women do a ritual, or what women are involved—and I've been to a lot of them, done a lot myself—it's an embarrassment."

Heads nodded, some a little hesitantly, around the table.

"Why do you think that is?" Barb asked.

"It's obvious, isn't it?" Coral sounded impatient. "Women together are alive in the moment, aware of each others' and the earth's rhythms, energies, and desires, jubilant and ecstatic. And out of this way of being, spontaneously and effortlessly, comes a million combinations of motion and sound, a billion variations in intensity. Not once in a thousand lifetimes would they happen to repeat a single motion, a solitary sound. Because nothing about women is replicable, nor would we ever want it to be."

She paused, frowning a little. Then she looked up and smiled. "That is, if we were free, if we were ourselves again as we were before patriarchy."

Sonia's face was glowing. "I know, Coral. I remember and experience it often in dreams. You're right, as far as you go. But it's impossible to describe the joy of it. Maybe that's why rituals at women's events always seem weird to me," she concluded. "Contrived and wooden. Even silly. I never stick around for them anymore."

"Lord, no!" Coral agreed emphatically. Then, "Lord, yes!" she laughed as Barb set an enormous tofu cherry cheesecake in the middle of the table. "Really, Barb, you shouldn't have," she said, appropriating the whole thing.

Amid the chorus of protest, Lauren rose to get dessert plates. "Forget the plates," Barb called. "Grab a spoon and dive in!"

Harper sat back and watched the cheesecake frenzy. When the plate was almost empty, she said, "I met a woman at the bookstore yesterday. I normally wouldn't have given her the time of day—she wasn't my type—but I heard her talking about community and tuned in. She's on a research tour to gather information for a book. I told her about you two, and she was immediately interested. She's heard about you, Sonia. I gave her your number so she could call you. She asked me how far Antonia was, and I told her that was just your post office address, and that you were closer to Las Palomas than that."

"What's her name?" Jean asked.

"Pauline Rogers."

"Pauline Rogers," Jean repeated slowly. "Pauline Rogers. Oh, hell! That's Pauline Running Wolf, Harper! Remember, the woman who called here twice wanting to do a sweat lodge? That's her. Shoot. I'm glad you didn't tell her how to get here."

Harper blanched, but no one noticed; they were too busy telling Coral about Pauline. What no one knew was that Harper had told Pauline more or less where Wildfire was. While she hadn't given specific directions, once in the little village, Pauline could probably find someone to direct her. She had talked about coming out the next day, but Harper had reminded her to call first. Harper had also, in a show of importance, assured Pauline that Sonia and Jean would be happy to talk with her. Now Harper hoped fervently that Pauline would forget the whole thing. Taking several deep breaths to counter a panic attack, she assured herself that she would think of something, and kept quiet. She turned her attention back to the conversation.

"Oh, I get it," Coral was saying. "She rationalizes her male/female circles by saying that we've all been both male and female, and have both male and femaleness in us."

Harper rose and began picking up empty dishes. "I'd like to propose that we lighten up now and play a game of Clue."

"Ha!" Sonia pushed back her chair and started for the office. "I know just where it is."

"I'll clean up," Lauren shooed them out of the kitchen area. "I don't want to play." She picked a bag of onions up off the counter and headed for the pantry. Harper followed.

"Hey, I need to talk to you for a minute." She closed the pantry door. "I'm in a real fix, Lauren, and don't know what to do. I sort of gave Pauline directions here. She wanted to come tomorrow morning. I'm hoping she'll call first, but what if she doesn't?"

Lauren slumped against the wall. "You've got to call her and tell her not to come. You heard them in there."

"I can't call her. I don't know where she's staying."

"Then you'll have to drive over here in the morning and wait at the gate, in case she shows up."

"I've got to work tomorrow, Babe. Maybe you could meet her and tell her Jean and Sonia are sick, and there's no one who can talk to her."

Lauren shook her head. "I don't want to, Harp."

Harper jerked the door open, and followed the others into the library. Lauren dropped the onions into the bin, then returned to the kitchen and the sink full of dishes.

As she began to tackle them, Coral came back and set her empty glass on the counter. "I did most of the talking tonight and didn't give the rest of you much of a chance, especially you." She slipped her hands around Lauren's waist and hugged her. Lauren, momentarily startled, felt the warmth in Coral's touch and turned, hands soapy, to face her. She leaned into Coral's embrace, an act that triggered the tears she had been holding back for what seemed like years.

"I'm sorry," she sobbed. "I didn't mean to do this, I really didn't."

"Save sorry for someone else."

"It's so hard," she cried. "It's just so hard. I have two sons that I thought I loved, but after hearing Sonia today I don't know anymore. And then listening to all of you talking about men tonight. I'm confused and upset. You have no idea how hard it is to be a mother, especially of sons, and especially being around women who are so angry at men."

"I had six children," Coral said softly. "Four of them were sons."

"You?" Lauren pulled back, shocked. "You have six children?"

"Had," Coral repeated. "They're grown now and on their own. Actually Jean helped me with that when I lived with her and Allison. We were sitting out in front of my apartment, watching some kind of bird who'd built a nest under the roof of the porch. Allison had fashioned a little patio up in front of the nest so that the baby birds wouldn't fall down onto the porch into the waiting mouths of hungry cats.

"Anyhow, as Jean and I were watching them, the mother began trying to get her kids to fly. They weren't babies anymore. In fact, they were almost as big as her. And Jean said, 'Humans are the only creatures who maintain contact with their young after weaning. As soon as those four birds are able to fly, that's it. That mother bird will never see them again, never think about them or worry about them, and they'll do the same about her. They have their own lives to do and she has hers.'

"This impressed me deeply, Lauren, because I needed to do the very same thing and I knew it. So I did—wished my kids well with their lives and said goodbye. It had nothing to do with being angry at them or at men in general. I didn't hear any anger in the voices of the women tonight. They're simply stating facts, being strong and brave enough not to live in illusion about men and maleness. This is not hatred. It's the women who're still involved with men who hate them."

"Don't you miss your kids?"

"At first I missed the good moments, but I realized pretty soon that I didn't miss *them*. I sometimes thought I did, but it always turned out to be sentimentality. The relief at not having to think about them or worry about them was so phenomenal it soon outweighed memory, nostalgia, sentimentality—my whole social conditioning. When I said goodbye to my kids, my youngest daughter was involved with a violent man. It was almost breaking my heart. Now I don't care. It's her life and her business. Two of my sons were into alcohol and drugs and drove me to despair. No more. It's their choice."

She heard Sonia calling her.

"Do your life, Lauren," she said urgently. "Do it the way you want to, not how you think you should or think others want you to. If you want contact with your sons, then have it. Do what you want."

"I don't know what I want," Lauren answered simply.

16

It was 12:30 when the Clue game finally broke up. They were all shocked at the time—all except Coral, who often worked the midnight-to-8 a.m. shift at the hospital. It was early for her, and she teased them about their lack of stamina.

"Where's all that wonderful woman energy?" she boomed.

"Murdered by Colonel Mustard in the conservatory with the candlestick," Sonia groaned, staggering towards the stairs.

"Hey, keep it down, you wildgynes," Jean shushed them. "Lauren's asleep on the couch in the lounge."

Harper headed toward the kitchen. "I'll have to wake her."

"Why not let her sleep?" Sonia suggested. "One of us will run her home in the morning. She looked so worn-out tonight."

"I have to go for feed in the morning," Barb said, looking at Ashley. "I can swing by and pick her up on my way."

"No. She wouldn't like it," Harper said curtly, and hurried off.

"Well," Barb said. "It was a lovely evening, wasn't it, Ashley?" The pig snorted and wiggled when she heard her name. "See, she loved it, too."

"How can you tell?" Coral asked. She was highly amused by Ashley's presence in the house, by her good-natured attempts to emulate the dogs and crawl into any available lap.

"By the way she wiggles and snorts."

"She always wiggles and snorts," Jean laughed.

She and Coral saw the women to their cars, then headed back to the house, arms around each other.

"I'm so glad you came, Coral."

"It's good to see you again, looking so happy and healthy. And I've loved having this chance to meet Sonia. I have to admit that I envy your life."

"I have no complaints."

"You've got some interesting friends, too. Very different from one another."

"We share a passion for mysteries. Except for that, I don't think we'd all choose to be friends."

"Why not?"

They had reached the door. Calling the dogs, Jean herded them in. She and Coral sat at the table.

"They're nice women, Coral. But the truth is that I'm not interested in superficial friendships anymore, in having friends for the sake of having friends. For years I maintained friendships with women that I had almost nothing in common with, except we all called ourselves lesbians, or feminists.

"Sonia and I care about the same things, about the things that matter most to me: getting patriarchy out of ourselves, recognizing our conditioning, our illusions, our brainwashing, and refusing them. There isn't anyone else out there I can talk about this with, no one else who can accompany me to the depths—and heights—of myself.

"Thinking of what you said tonight, it occurs to me that I could probably do it with you. Or that if you didn't live thousands of miles away, it'd be worth a try. But about other friends, what I call 'friends of the road', I don't have the energy or desire to cultivate them any more. Even the Murder Maids. I'm not sure why I still go through the motions with them. If we never met again, I wouldn't miss them. And it's not that I dread the meetings." She laughed a little. "At least they give me an excuse to cook."

"What about Dana? She strikes me as being very bright."

"She is. And I like Dana, but . . . I don't know what to say, except that with Sonia I never have to explain myself, never have to worry about being misunderstood. We don't play games with each other; we're as honest and straightforward as we can be every moment. We regress sometimes, of course, but when we do, we talk about it. Every waking moment we're bent on getting out of mensmind and mensways and back to our Selves. That's all that matters to me anymore."

"Are you doing experiments other than the touching ones you told me about?"

"Dozens. One of the most important—and often funniest—is trapping and exposing our sadomasochistic thoughts. For instance, I'm the dog groomer around here; I grew up doing it, and made it my profession for years. Yesterday, I went into the grooming section of the bathhouse to find Sonia clipping Nikki's face, and my first thought was, 'She doesn't think I do it well enough.' My second was, 'I'm sure she'll do it better than I could.'"

"So?"

"So I plummeted headfirst into bottom position. I told her, we laughed at how crazy the whole thing was, and went on with our day. That's how it goes, all day long, every day: we catch ourselves figuring out ways to occupy either top or bottom—both places have their unique satisfactions, you know. At first, we sometimes didn't realize what we'd done until hours or even days later. Nowadays we're getting it during or even before it happens. We're easier on ourselves now than we were at first, because we're more aware how in mensworld sadomasochism is the only model we have. We both want more than anything to experience the incredible power and joy of peerness, as we did before maleness, long ago. We talk about how sadomasochism is inherent in maleness, but it's damned near become innate in women now, too."

"That dog grooming—it's a very small thing, really not important."

"But it is. These little things add up to be us. The only way we know to feel good about ourselves is in comparison with, at the expense of, someone else—relationally, in other words. Another example might help. Sonia likes to do the laundry, so she usually does it. Though I hate doing it, I certainly know how, having done it all my life.

"Anyway, a few weeks ago I wanted a certain pair of jeans, and since they were in the dirty clothes, I washed a batch of dark clothes. You can guess what happened. Sonia heard the washer going and assumed that I was making a statement about her: that she should have washed sooner, that she hadn't been doing a good enough job so I'd decided to take over. Sadomasochism absolutely rampages through our lives and thoughts—and through those of every living person. It's the only way we know how to *be*, how to feel. We're trying to stop its mayhem in our own lives by being scrupulously aware of its every manifestation."

"Man-infestation, you mean," Coral laughed. Then becoming thoughtful, "Now that you call attention to it, of course, I can see hierarchy and comparison everywhere. The education system's full of it: grades, gold stars, class rank."

Jean nodded. "It takes all kinds of forms, though, not just these obvious ones. One of the most common is passive aggression, and so of course, we're trying to purge that one from our lives, too."

"Got an example?"

"Oh, let's see. Well, okay. The laundry. When I realized that the blue jeans I wanted were in the dirty clothes basket, I went to Sonia and said, 'Are you planning to do a washing soon?' Saturday, she said. This was Wednesday, and I didn't want to wait until Saturday. So I said to her, 'Any chance you'll do it before then?' She shrugged and said she hadn't thought about it.

"You see, I was trying to get her to ask me if I needed it done sooner or to get her to offer to wash my jeans before Saturday, instead of just coming right out and saying, 'I'd like to have my jeans washed today.' That's passive aggression. She recognized what I was doing, and refused to be controlled, refused to respond as I was trying to set her up to. And I'm glad she did. I don't need any more encouragement to be afraid to ask for what I want."

"What if you'd said you wanted your jeans washed today and she said she didn't feel like doing it, then what?"

"Then I'd decide if I wanted them badly enough to wash them myself, or if I could wait until she did them."

"I do stuff like that all the time."

"Every person on the globe does, Coral. But Sonia and I don't want to any more. So we talk about it every time it happens."

"Harper could take some lessons from the two of you. She doesn't give Lauren a chance to say boo. I feel bad about Lauren; she's one unhappy woman. Miserable, in fact. She needs to do her own life." Coral stood and stretched. "Guess I'll call it a night. You look like you need toothpicks to prop your eyes open."

"I'll forego the toothpicks. Gravity's good enough for me."

○ ○ ○ ○ ○ ○

Moving carefully so as not to awaken Sonia, Jean sat up in time to see a magnificent goshawk sail across the deck. She had heard its call just moments before and had tried to incorporate it into her dream. She was glad that something within her had caused her to awaken in time to see it.

She lay back and thought about it, then shifted her thoughts to Sonia, who was stirring and making her wake-up sounds. Jean turned on her side and began stroking Sonia's long smooth back. Sometimes Sonia responded to this by going back to sleep, but at other times, like now, it speeded her waking process. She gave Jean a long kiss, then glanced at the clock and made a face.

"I know you're going to leave any second now because it's lots later than you usually get up. I know I should be grateful that you're still here, but I refuse." She feigned a sulk.

"It's your fault, you're corrupting me," Jean laughed, pulling her close. "In the past, the only thing that could get me to stay in bed beyond 5:30 was double pneumonia. And I only had that once. So you should be feeling *extremely* grateful." She jumped as Sonia pinched her lightly. The playful wrestling match that ensued came to an end when, sheet-entangled, they crashed to the floor.

A few minutes later as she stood under the shower, Jean marveled at how delightful Sonia was to be with. Never any unspoken tension between them, no uncomfortable silences, no second-guessing, no relationship games. And the touching! All her life she had fantasized being with such a person, a woman she could touch freely, without restraint, without the interference of sex.

As she stepped out of the shower, her thoughts were interrupted by a THUD that shook the bathhouse door, then a frantic scrambling sound, followed by a second THUD and door flying open. Ashley and the three dogs burst joyously into the room, nearly flattening her with their enthusiasm. A moment later an alarmed Barb appeared.

"Jesus, I'm sorry, Jean. I yelled at them but they ignored me. I hope they haven't wrecked the door."

"I shouldn't have closed it anyhow, but it felt drafty in here this morning. What brings you by so early?" Jean toweled her hair.

"Left my wallet here last night. I took it out of my back pocket because my hip was hurting, and forgot to put it back."

"You're going to hit the rush-hour traffic if you leave now."

"I was going to stop in Pajarita first and have breakfast so I'd miss it. But at Coral's invitation, I'm going to eat with you all instead."

Coral had made scrumptious burritos for breakfast, and although a loyal oatmeal fan, Jean couldn't resist trying just one. Four burritos later, she undid the top button of her shorts with a groan of relief.

"They're too good, Coral. I've made a pig of myself."

"Hey! Watch your mouth, you pigot!"

"Oh hell Barb, I'm sorry. Pigot," she giggled.

"Don't apologize to me . . ." She indicated Ashley, but Ashley was asleep.

"I'll watch myself next time," Jean promised. "No more pig-otry. Who's that?" She pointed down the driveway at a figure coming up the hill. At this distance, they couldn't tell if it was a man or a woman.

"I left the gate open," Barb moaned. "I thought I was just going to dash in and out."

Jean opened the door. They could now tell it was a woman, and although they couldn't make out her features, even at this distance they could hear her jingling, as if she were wearing a hundred dog tags. Jean hurried out to waylay her.

The woman called to her, raising her hand in greeting. As she came closer, Jean saw that the jingling came from hundreds of little bells sewn into her long flowing dress and onto the bracelets encircling her arms. She was wearing a beaded headband and deerskin moccasins, and Jean recognized with dismay that she was Pauline Running Wolf.

She felt a sudden desire to turn and run, but instead, as the woman approached, she asked, "Can I help you?"

"I'm Pauline Rogers," the woman answered, holding out her hand for a hearty handshake. Jean realized that Pauline did not remember her.

"What can I do for you?" she asked again.

Pauline frowned slightly. "I'm hoping someone up here has a four-wheel-drive vehicle. I had trouble getting up your hill. I backed up to try again, and landed in the ditch. You really should get that hill fixed."

"How did you get here?"

Pauline gave Jean an exasperated look. "I met a woman in town yesterday who knows you. Harper. She told me you'd be interested in talking to me about community and gave me directions. What's with the interrogation? I feel like I'm about to be searched and impounded."

"She gave you directions?"

"Well, not exactly. She said you were in these mountains and gave me the name of the town. I stopped and asked a forest ranger and he told me where you lived."

"Look, Pauline. Harper doesn't live here and had no business telling you we were interested in seeing you. She mentioned she'd run into you yesterday and had given you our phone number, but she said she told you to call first."

"I tried. Nobody answered."

"We were here all day yesterday, and this morning. And even if we weren't, the answering machine is always on." Pauline's blatant lie angered Jean even more.

"And besides, I talked with you twice last month and told you Sonia and I weren't having guests."

"But you didn't know about my book project then."

"We're still not interested. I have a 4x4 truck that can get your car out. Then I'm going to ask you to leave."

"Hey, I appreciate help with the car, but I was told you'd like to see me today. I don't have anywhere else to go. If I hadn't been told I could visit here, I'd have made other arrangements."

Before Jean could respond, she was joined on the deck by Coral, Barb, and Sonia.

"Hey, Sonia, hey sister!" Pauline cried, hurrying to embrace her. "Wonderful to see you again!"

"I didn't know you were coming, Pauline," Sonia said stiffly. "We aren't really having visitors right now. I thought you'd gotten that message."

"Right. But then I ran into Harper and she was so interested in my research project that she suggested I interview you. I can only stay until Tuesday, but that will give me plenty of time."

I will not be able to bear this woman until Tuesday, Sonia thought. Aloud she said, "When Harper told us about your book, neither Jean nor I was interested in being interviewed. I'm sorry you didn't call first. Then you wouldn't have wasted a trip out here."

Pauline sat in a deck chair and crossed her arms stubbornly in front of her. "As I told her," she indicated Jean, "I don't have anyplace to go right now. You can't just throw me out."

"How did you get here?" Barb asked.

"Her car's in our ditch, just beyond the bridge," Jean explained. Barb groaned.

Pauline was angry now. "Look, I'm feeling ripped off and I don't like it. I received a legitimate invitation and now I'm being told I can't stay. I cancelled two other engagements to be here, you know, women who were eager to talk to me."

"Then they'd probably be glad to have you back," Barb suggested hopefully.

Pauline ignored her, staring defiantly into Sonia's eyes.

"I'm interested in this book you're researching," Coral said conversationally, settling herself in a chair beside Pauline. "I hear it's on communities. Women's or mixed?"

Relieved at the change of focus, Pauline relaxed. "Women's, of course."

"I understand that most of your ritual circles include men, so I wasn't sure."

Pauline tensed again. With a tight smile she said, "I include men because they exist, because they're here. I figure every little bit helps the planet. My mixed circles have been very successful.

Although I don't want to live with men, I certainly don't hate them. And I can see their place on the tree of life."

"And just where is that?" Coral asked innocently.

The other women stared at her in amazement. What in the world was she doing? They wanted to get rid of this woman, not engage her in conversation. Jean tried unsuccessfully to get Coral's attention.

"Everything in nature has its opposite," Pauline said, warming to her subject. "Darkness and light, evil and good, male and female. Femaleness represents nature's nurturing, caring, giving aspects, while maleness represents power, energy, force. In the right combination they balance each other. Out of balance, they cause destruction, violence, and death. One of my jobs is to help women and men return to that place of balance. To help them walk in the beauty way."

Sonia moaned quietly and sank into a chair, knowing another lesson in futility was imminent.

"So you believe we all have male and female energy in us." Coral leaned forward in her chair.

"Of course we do. That's what it's all about. But you see, the balance of the two energies is critical. When it's askew, you have chaos and upheaval. Medicine women like myself know how to restore that balance."

"I used to believe that women had male energy and vice versa," Coral said. "Then one day I watched some male construction workers harassing women in the street, and I knew that no way those guys had any female in them and no way I had any male in me."

Pauline shrugged. "Of course there are ugly men out there. But I'll tell you something, most of the time it's worse being around women."

"It's just more obvious," Coral said. "For men to be condescending, cruel, or hateful is natural, we expect it, it seems right to us even though we may hate it. But for women, this kind of behavior is a perversion, pathological. Because it's so unnatural, it sticks out and makes us much more uncomfortable, makes us feel sick, as poisoned, diseased, gangrenous things do."

Sonia roused herself, "But it's true, too, that women are willing to be much more open about their hatred of women than men are. Men, desperately and continuously needing women's energy to survive, have to pretend civility. Women, even misogynist women, are their own power suppliers so they don't have this constraint.

Pauline was unconvinced. "Unkindness is just one of the unfortunate aspects of human nature. We each just have to learn to control it."

"The concept of 'human nature' has been a masterpiece of male doublespeak. Lumping men and women together in this way blurs and excuses male behavior. But the truth is that men are an entirely different species, not the same as women at all, and that ignoring this is dangerous business for women.

"I watch Nikki, our little dog," she said, pointing to the small fluffy ball of white fur at her feet. "Nikki loves to play with her toy squeaky mouse. I swear she looks like a cat sometimes, the way she tosses and bats that mouse around. But just because she exhibits cat-like characteristics doesn't mean she has any feline in her. She's all dog.

"Mensystem works hard at getting us to believe that maleness and femaleness are opposite ends of the same continuum. This isn't true. Maleness and femaleness are entirely unique and distinct categories, with no intersection or overlap, just like cats and dogs. When you talk about your male side, what you're saying is that you have some characteristics men have *called* male. But there's not a particle of you or me that's male, Pauline, and no man, living or dead, who has a particle of female in him. All evidence points to this: if men had ever been women or had any femaleness in them at all, they would be incapable of the atrocities against women and the planet and all living things that they continuously perpetrate."

Pauline gave a little shake of her head. "We all have our truths, Sonia. It doesn't mean that yours is right and mine is wrong, or vice versa. I believe that we're all in this together. I believe there's a place where we can achieve harmony and balance with one another and with every living thing on this planet. This is my goal."

"Then you'll never reach it," Jean said, "because men can't live in harmony and balance—a fact they've proved every second of the past thousands of years. I know that New Age men want women to believe what you believe—that all people are simply human, all united by a common bond of oppression and suffering. Though this is not true—since when have men ever told us the truth?—it's obvious why they want us to believe it. If women saw men as they really are, we'd instantly withdraw our energy from them. That would be the end of them and their hideous world."

"Men suffer just as much as women do in this system," Pauline countered crossly.

"You're right," Sonia agreed. "Men do suffer. We can tell, because miserable people create misery around them, and the world men have made is a wretched place. But there's a dangerous assumption under your statement, one I think most women make. And that is that patriarchy is somehow *external* to men. As if one day we all just woke up and found it lying all over the ground like dew. As if, like dew, it appeared seemingly out of nowhere.

"The truth is that patriarchy comes *out of* men, out of their feelings, their values, their beliefs. Out of their *maleness*. What men suffer from is from being male, from recreating their brutal natures with every breath, from not being able to escape maleness."

"You're so dogmatic, Sonia!" Pauline lost her patience. "Where do you get such ideas? You have absolutely no proof of any of this."

"Proof?" Coral snorted. "How much do you need, Pauline? All there is out there is proof. Who do you think make and perpetuate the horrific mess we see all around us? You and I both know. It's a fact. Not a feeling, not a judgement, not a criticism, not hatred. A fact. The fact is that maleness—violence, fear, scarcity, suffering, hatred, jealousy, greed—has nearly destroyed all life. It is as far removed from femaleness as it could possibly be.

"You ask for proof that this is true. I ask you for proof that it *isn't*. Show me one place under the sun where men don't rape and murder and start wars and lay waste, where they have made a world of equality, cooperation, plenty, health, peace, and love. Proof? That's all we've got."

"Let's just pretend you're right." Pauline held up her hand. "I'm not saying you are, but let's pretend. Is your solution to the problem simply to withdraw? To pretend that men don't exist? If so, it seems pretty counterproductive to me. I feel that as women, with women's values, it's up to us to educate men to be sensitive, to learn to love and value the things that we as women value. Let's face it, men are here to stay. I say let's do what we can to help them get back in touch with their gentle natures."

"What gentle natures?" Jean pulled her chair close to Pauline. "Coral asked you for proof that they exist and you can't come up with any. Nothing out there indicates that men have the slightest idea of what it means to be gentle. Nothing, Pauline."

Pauline shook her head. "I'm sorry none of you have had the privilege of knowing the wonderful new men I've met in my circles."

"What you're seeing in those men, Pauline, your wonderful new men, is not character change," Sonia said. "It's just a change in the way they know they have to act to get you to give them your titty to suck from."

Pauline winced, but Sonia galloped on.

"What women do, and have done for far too long, is project what we are—*our* feelings, *our* values, *our* way of being in the world—onto men. And of course men encourage this in every way they can—by appearing to be making serious changes, for instance.

"But every living woman knows somewhere inside that men are not like us and what they really are. We simply can't face it; the implications are too appalling. So we're easily led to believe the propaganda that they're just like us except conditioned to fill different roles in society. We forget that we can only create what we are, that we can't create something that's not inside us. We forget that the external reveals the internal. Men's world reflects them. They *are* society. Since they created it, every aspect of global society screams what they are: hunger, sadness, disease, violence, ugliness, desperation, despair."

Pauline glanced at her watch. "This has been fascinating, ladies, but I'd like to use your phone and see if I can connect with some women in San Pedro. And I'd appreciate your help in getting my car out," she said to Jean.

Forty-five minutes later, they all watched in relief as her car disappeared down the driveway.

"Do you think we offended her?" Barb asked.

17

The rustling sound was familiar, but it took her a few minutes to place it. A mouse. Listening more carefully, she realized that the beast was in the closet, either chewing paper or making a nest with the wastebasket contents. She leapt out of bed and looked around for something to apprehend it with. An empty flowerpot sat near the closet door. She grabbed it, crept to the doorway of the large, walk-in closet, and peered cautiously in.

Clad only in a magenta and orange T-shirt, Sonia sat on the floor, surrounded by stacks of photographs, large envelopes, and boxes. The clock above her read 5 a.m.

Sonia glanced at the raised pot. "All right, I surrender. It's all yours."

Jean sat down beside her, and picked up a photograph of a toddler standing in a bubble bath, pointing at the camera, an enormous grin on her face.

"Givonne, when she was two." Sonia picked up another photo, this one of a shaggy dog of indeterminate breed walking a child. "Justin. I think he had just turned three." She sighed.

"I got to thinking during the night that I wanted to send my ex-kids all the things I've been keeping for them: their birth certificates and other personal papers, all the pictures of them. I should never have been keeping that stuff anyway, especially since most of them haven't lived with me for so long.

"Looking at these pictures," she indicated the piles around her, "my heart started to ache and I felt weepy. I thought maybe I couldn't go through with this. Then suddenly I realized that this was exactly what men intended, that this was the purpose of nostalgia and sentimentality—to keep us hooked into people and institutions long after we should have left them behind.

"These sweet baby pictures—I had to remind myself that none of my ex-children is a little baby anymore. These pictures are of children who no longer exist, children from a time long ago who will never return. Feelings from that time, about those children, aren't appropriate now."

"It reminds me of your friend, Betsy," Jean reflected, sifting through the photos. "Remember how she talked to you about her marriage, how she knew her husband had been screwing around for a long time, how she knew he didn't care a damn about her, and how she had decided to divorce him? Then how just as she was getting up the courage to leave him, she pulled out their old photo albums and there they were—at their wedding, and during the early years of their marriage with their young children—and she got all soft and mushy inside and decided to stay with him in memory of the good times?"

Sonia grimaced.

"Focusing on the good times apparently removed her enough from the present to make the unbearable bearable," Jean concluded.

"Apparently." Sonia looked up from packing a large envelope stuffed with photos into one of the boxes. "I felt like shaking her and shouting, 'But what about *now*, Betsy? The *present* with Roy is definitely not good and never will be again. To avoid it you have to stay numb all the time. Is this they way you want to live? Is this living?' But I didn't, because she's too afraid to live without her illusions, terrified to be fully awake in this moment as it honestly is. It demands a kind of courage she doesn't have."

"I'm sure that's why she looked at those photographs in the first place—to prevent herself from having to face and overcome her fear."

Sonia nodded. "Yep. That's why I have to get rid of these memories. They mislead me, they seduce me out of the present—the only time I'm alive and can be in my power; that's why the malestream's so big on memories. The truth is that the past is irrelevant for women because it's nonexistent. The present is all there is. And in the present, unfortunately, three of the people I gave birth to are male, and therefore can mean nothing to me anyway.

"But my ex-daughter, oh my. She's truly remarkable—creative, alive, fearless. But she's too young, too interested in men, and, in our relationship, too willing to to hold the past over my head. Until patriarchy's over, our relationship is going to keep us apart. But when maleness is gone from the earth, she and I can be intimates, and I want that very much. I want to know her and to have her know me and for us to love each other they way I think we can.

"Anyway, that makes four birth people who can't be in my life right now, four people attaching me to the past, to linear time, to family illusion, to relationships—to all the things that are antithetical to power and joy."

She looked up again from her sorting and met a pair of steady green eyes. "I mean joy, Jean. You do know this, don't you? That it's not just a word I toss around because it sounds good? That it's what I intend for myself?"

"I understand very well," Jean replied soberly. "Everything you've just said and all it's implications."

Before she had moved to Wildfire she had assembled all the photos she had had that linked her to the past—photos of her parents, her brother and sister, other relatives, ex-lovers—and destroyed them. The past hadn't mattered to her anymore and she hadn't wanted or needed to be pulled back into it.

Once when she had mentioned her photo-burning experience, a friend had remarked that she had probably done it because she had had such a painful past. But this was not true. She had done it because in her viscera she had come to feel what she had first only hypothesized—that history is a male construct, necessary only to men.

What mattered to her was the present, what she felt and thought right this minute. She remembered an ex-lover's request for the photos of the two of them, saying she wanted reminders of the good times. In other words, she didn't want to face the reality that overall their relationship had been a nightmare, a regrettable mistake they had managed to hide from the eye of the camera. Those pictures of them together smiling and looking happy were a lie. Oh yes, she understood what Sonia was talking about.

She leaned down and kissed the top of her head, then headed for the bathroom. She loved this room, especially since Sonia had replaced the tiny, frosted "privacy" window with a three-by-six-foot triple thermal pane. The new window also opened, allowing fresh air into the room when they wanted it, and a clear view from the toilet of the forested north slope. Much more pleasant than staring at the wall.

By the time she had showered and dressed, Sonia was in the kitchen having breakfast with Coral. Jean was momentarily surprised to see Coral up so early, then tuned into the conversation to hear Sonia telling Coral about her decision to send her ex-kids their photos and personal items. When she reached the part about how the photos kept her emotionally tied to the past and not realistic about the present, Coral nodded.

"Absolutely. Even when my kids were adults, all I had to do was look at their baby pictures to forgive them anything. Never mind that just a few hours before one of my sons had called me a castrating bitch, or that my daughter had sworn she'd never speak to me again. I'd remember how cute they'd been when they were little, how utterly adorable, and reality would fly right out the window."

She finished her oatmeal and sat back. "I was always there for them, triple overtime. I felt guilty because they didn't have a father, so I had to make it up to them. And I did. By giving them damn near everything they wanted.

"When I told them my life was my own, that I wasn't going to be Mom anymore, they didn't believe me at first. Finally, after I'd said 'no' to all requests for nearly a year, they began to get the message. And they were furious. Not at losing *me* in their lives, but at losing *Mom*, the meal ticket, the old reliable. That's when I fully understood the term 'conditional love'."

"Everything in patriarchy is conditional," Sonia said. "'I'll love you if . . .', 'I'll give you this if you give me that'."

"A-women!" Coral agreed. She carried her dishes to the sink and washed them. She was meeting Dana in town for a photo session at eleven, and Dana had offered to show her Las Palomas and take her to lunch afterwards. She went back upstairs to dress.

Jean stood up and looked out over the deck. The feeders were abustle with grosbeaks and pine siskins. It was as she was cranking open the window to let in some air that she saw them, two tiny specks in the clear blue sky, growing larger and larger until their red tails shone in the sunlight. Sonia joined her at the window. Seeing the tears glistening in Jean's eyes, she looked out and finally spotted the hawks, soaring and gliding. She knew that Jean was not really at her side, but up there with the hawks, wild in the wind.

Jean's reverie was shattered by the dogs' noisy rush to the door. Soon Barb's red Dodge pickup appeared in the drive and backed up to the deck, Ashley enormous in the back. Barb jumped out of the cab and opened the tailgate. Then she pulled out a ramp and rested it on the edge of the deck, barely in time to catch the full brunt of Ashley's weight as she stampeded toward the house.

"Get the door before she does!" Jean yelled.

Sonia skidded to a stop and jerked the door open a split second before Ashley would have plowed into it.

"I should put a harness on her," Barb said, kissing Sonia before coming into the kitchen.

"You do that and you'll both smash through that door—you waving in the wind out behind," Jean laughed, returning her hug and kiss. "What are you doing up so early?"

"It's seven. I've been up for hours. Anyhow, I brought these for you to try," Barb waved a square pan at them. "I'm trying to get off chocolate and decided to make those good carob brownies of yours, Jean. Try one."

Jean broke off a piece and put it in her mouth. Chewing, she frowned. "These are carob brownies? They don't taste like it."

"Taste it," Barb urged Sonia. Sonia cautiously broke off a piece and sniffed it before popping it in her mouth. "Nope. Not Jean's brownies. They don't taste bad, though. Just strange."

"You bet they do," Barb said, tossing the pan on the bread-board. "They taste strange because I put a cup of cinnamon in them instead of carob!" She turned to Jean. "Remember? Last week I asked you if I could borrow some carob powder and you told me it was in the gallon jar in the pantry? Well, I went in there and found a gallon jar with dark brown powder in it and took some. Who else has a one gallon jar of cinnamon powder in their pantry!"

"Oh hell, Barb. I'm sorry. I forgot about the cinnamon. But couldn't you smell the difference?"

"I wasn't using my nose. It never occurred to me you'd have so damned much cinnamon."

Sonia tried another piece, but soon had to admit that it was too strange to eat. "In little bits, maybe," she told Barb, "but I don't think we're going to devour these in one sitting."

"I know," Barb answered, thoroughly disgusted. "Ashley won't even eat them. She took one bite and started sneezing and snorting all over the place. I'm going to have to dump them and start all over, damn it."

Jean broke off another bit, and rolled it around on her tongue. "Yeah, you've overdone the spices."

"Very funny, Jean. Ha ha. I'm off to the hardware store, then the post office. Need anything mailed?"

Ten minutes later she staggered out to the truck under the weight of a box of filled book orders. Dumping the box in the front seat, she whistled for Ashley. Jean noticed that the pig was much slower getting into the truck than out.

"How about a short walk?" Jean slipped her arm around Sonia's waist. They headed for the forest road that would take them as far into the mountains as they cared to go. The air was alive with swallows swooping down in front of them to pick up insects. Jean, pointing to a pygmy nuthatch, nearly tripped over Nikki sniffing something with great vigor in the middle of the path. Scooping her up in her arms, she squeezed her against her chest for a moment, then put her back down. Nik immediately resumed her sniffing. Looking ahead, they saw Maggi and Tamale dashing up the road, hoping to flush a rabbit. She watched them running, heads high, Maggi's tail a flamboyant plume over her back, both crazy with joy. They so loved their lives here: an infinite number of places to explore, more freedom than ever before, peace and plenty.

She knew exactly how they felt.

18

The dice rolled across the table, and when they stopped, Jean was dismayed.

"If I don't get more fours, I'm sunk."

"May the fours be with you, Genius," Sonia intoned.

Coral groaned from the kitchen door. "That's so bad I'm going to pretend I didn't hear it." She came over to the table.

Sonia let out a low whistle. In a flowing red and gold caftan, gold hoop earrings swinging from her ears, Coral was stunningly exotic. "Dana's going to love working with you," she smiled, handing Coral the truck keys. "I feel as though we ought to call a limousine service for you, instead of sending you off in Ruby Red."

Coral laughed and shook her head. "This is my all-purpose dress-up costume. I can wad it up in a ball and throw it in my suitcase, and it looks great when I put it on." She sat down and glanced at Sonia and Jean's Yahtzee score cards.

"I'm doing lousily," Jean complained, as Sonia rolled the dice. "I don't know why I keep on playing this stupid game."

Five sixes turned up. "Damn!" Jean yelled. "You're on a roll, Soni. You've really got six appeal today!"

Coral groaned again. "I can't take it." She got up and wandered over to the organ. "Somebody going camping?" she asked, lifting a sleeping bag off the bench.

"Me," Sonia answered. "I mean, no, not camping. I'm going to sleep in the mountains tonight."

"Is this a 'communing with nature' experiment?" Coral settled herself on the bench.

"No, it's a getting-over-my-fear-of-the-dark experiment. I'm tired of being afraid of things I know I once loved and was intimate with. I'm going to sleep out until my fear of the dark is gone."

"You couldn't get me to do that in a million years. I'll just have to take that fear with me to the grave."

"But don't you wonder why you're afraid? And why you aren't afraid of the day?"

"Well, sometimes I am afraid of the day," Coral admitted. "The truth is that there are always things out there to fear, but especially at night."

"No more than in broad daylight," Jean got into the discussion. "Everything that exists in the night exists in the day. The scary part is that we can't see as well at night. We used to, though. I know there was a time when women saw as well as owls and cats in the night. But we've grown so accustomed to artificial light that we've lost our night vision."

"Well, I've got to tell you one thing: it's so dark here at night it's been hard for me to sleep." Coral shuddered. "I haven't experienced anything like it since my brother used to lock me in the closet."

"And there began your fear of the dark," Sonia said. "At the hands of men, of course. Men are what we fear in the dark, and we have excellent reason to. But also, men have trained us to fear the things they fear, and they fear the dark—though few of them will admit it. They never have had night vision, so of course the dark has always frightened them. They feel powerless in her. If men had been able to see in the dark, they would have had no need to invent artificial light. Women certainly never needed it before patriarchy."

"When we first came here," Jean told Coral, "there were four big lights on the property that came on automatically at dusk. It nearly drove us to distraction. Our bedrooms were never completely dark. We'd go out at night and couldn't see the stars, couldn't experience the night. And it was very expensive. So we had the electric co-op come and turn them off."

Coral grimaced. "I like artificial lights, I'm afraid. I don't like shadows, things I can't make out. My imagination is too active. When I'm in the dark, I'm sure there's somebody behind me, somebody I can't see, somebody about to kill me."

"Me, too," Sonia said, "and I haven't any more patience with it. But I know that simply going out and sleeping alone on the mountainside at night isn't going to take that fear away. Because fear isn't specific. By that I mean that in patriarchy we've accumulated a hefty supply of generic fear. Every time our conditioning calls for some, we simply dig it out of the fear pit and attach it to whatever's relevant at that moment. So as I get rid of fear about anything, I reduce the amount of fear in that pit, making less that can attach to other things.

"All this is to say that we can't get over our fear of the dark if we're still afraid to take our eyes off the guys and their world: quit our jobs, divorce our husbands, take our energy out of politics, really examine and change our lives. As long as we fear anything, we'll still fear everything, at least somewhat. Even before I began walking at night, I was less afraid of the dark than before simply because I'd got rid of so much fear in other areas of my life."

"But," Jean countered, "actually facing the fear has to be useful, too."

"It all depends on what you mean by 'facing the fear'," Sonia said. "It's important to know what we're afraid of, I agree, and too few of us do. But I've known women who actually increased their fear of the dark by trying to be in it as much as they could."

"I was thinking of the story that woman in Virginia told us about Margaret Mead," Jean reminded her. Then seeing Coral's face light up with interest, she went on to explain.

"As the story goes, Margaret Mead was afraid of the dark most of her life. Toward the end, when she was very ill with cancer, she went somewhere out in the country to consult a woman psychic about a possible cure. One night after a session with this woman, she was walking back to her cabin, feeling her usual terror—that something unspeakably dreadful was stalking her and about to lunge at her from behind—and suddenly she was furious at her fear, sick of it. She stopped on the path, turned to face her nemesis and screamed at it, 'Get out of here! Leave me alone! I'm sick of you and want you out of my life. I refuse to be afraid of you any longer!' And she was never afraid again."

Coral grinned. "That's a wonderful story."

"There's more to it," Sonia remembered. "According to the story—which may be apocryphal, of course—not only was her fear of the dark gone, but she no longer feared death, either; death and darkness are entwined in our psyches. It was a major transformation. So I'm going to try it. I don't want to be afraid of the night. It's a beautiful, rich, natural rhythm of my life and I want to experience it that way again."

"Well, I admire your courage and I'm interested in hearing what happens," Coral said, glancing at her watch. "Time for me to spread my wings and fly!" With a hug and kiss to both, she was out the door.

○ ○ ○ ○ ○ ○

The city of Las Palomas is an intriguing mixture of old and new, tasteful and crass. Also known as The City Lost, tourists visiting for the first time discover a second, less romantic meaning for the name: they inevitably get lost. Rumor has it that, as in so many towns and cities of the American West, the entire street system was laid out on former cowpaths. Coral swore out loud as she made a right turn into a one-way street. Amid blaring horns and shouted oaths, she executed a quick U-turn and was back onto the Street of Great Distress, hopelessly lost. Only a miracle landed her finally in front of Dana's studio.

From there, Dana took her on a tour of the city. No longer having to navigate the city's mad maze, Coral relaxed and enjoyed the adobe buildings, the second oldest church in the United States, and the startling discovery that pigs and chickens and goats cohabitated with humans on tiny city lots. Dana explained that the old zoning laws were still in effect here even though the farms had long disappeared. Coral expected at any minute to see a cow lumbering down the middle of El Camino.

By one o'clock she was nearly faint with hunger. Dana had convinced her that the only restaurant worth eating in—if you were *forced* to choose—was Lupita's where they could either stand in line for a table or simply wait until the noon crowd was gone. Coral had opted for the latter.

But even at that time, the restaurant was nearly full, a testament to its good food and atmosphere. Before they were even seated, a young woman had descended upon their table with an enormous bowl of chips and a smaller bowl of salsa. Coral dug in with great pleasure.

But Dana warned her to go easy, to save her appetite for what was to come. "You order for me," she had said to Dana, scooping up more salsa. "I like to be surprised."

The plate that arrived more than surprised her—it overwhelmed her. Two crisp-fried corn tortillas stuffed with home-made guacamole, tomatos, and onions, flanked by heaping portions of papitas and pinto beans, all steaming in a thick, rich sauce. Coral eyed it a moment before turning to Dana.

"I can't possibly eat all this," she said.

"Try," Dana urged, her mouth full of burrito.

Twenty minutes later both plates were empty, and Coral sat back with a groan.

"What's this?" she asked, as the waitress placed a cloth-covered basket on the table in front of them.

"Sopapillas. You eat them with honey. They're the best things you're ever going to taste." She lifted the cloth, took one out, and poured honey on it from a plastic bottle.

"This is really too much," Coral protested.

"Then you can take yours with you, though they're best eaten hot, like this." Dana bit into hers and closed her eyes, savoring the warm sweetness.

"Well, maybe just a taste," Coral relented, lifting the cloth. A few minutes later she was signaling the waitress for another basket.

"I love to eat," she admitted. "I have a daughter—an ex-daughter—who's so thin it's scary. She wasn't always that way, though she was never what you'd call fat; she just had a nice, full figure. Then she hit high school and that was it. She quit eating. All she wanted was grapefruit juice. When I'd try to get her to eat, she'd scream that she didn't want to look like me and her grandma, and that I couldn't make her eat. That was true enough, although I kept battling with her." Coral bit into her sopapilla.

"What's happened to her?"

"You mean now? I don't know. I haven't talked to her or heard anything in over a year. I stopped caring. I stopped letting her fucked-up life mess mine up, too. The same with two of my sons. I figure they have a right to do whatever they want with their lives. I'm out of them."

"But you have three other children. Are you in touch with them?"

Coral shook her head. "I'm no one's mother anymore. And besides, they're men, and I've got nothing in common with men. Twenty-seven years of my life belonged to someone else. Now I'm claiming it for me." She finished her sopapilla.

Before Dana could formulate a response, her mobile phone rang. Coral rose and pointed to the restrooms, leaving Dana some privacy. But by the time she returned, Dana had paid the check and was waiting impatiently for her.

"I hate to do this to you, Coral, but I've got an emergency. That was my mother on the phone. The electric company has shut off their power again."

"Why?"

"Because my father forgets to mail the bill. I go over there the middle of each month and do all the bills. My father doesn't mind that, but he insists on mailing them. The exercise is good for him, he tells me. Then he doesn't do it and I have to go through this shit. Or call the telephone company to have their phone reconnected. It drives me nuts sometimes."

"Why don't they take care of it themselves?"

Dana cursed the slow-moving traffic, then accelerated around an RV. "They can't, Coral. If they could, I wouldn't be doing it for them."

"Alzheimer's"?

Dana hesitated, "Not really. They're just very dependent on me."

"I don't understand. If they're okay in the head and reasonably healthy, why can't they take care of themselves?"

"I haven't always taken care of them. Eleven years ago, my younger brother was killed in a car wreck. My parents never recovered. In fact, they fell apart. Somebody's got to look after them, and fate has pointed her fickle finger at me."

"I still don't get it. I mean, I can understand their needing some support and help right after your brother's death, but eleven years later?"

Dana shrugged. "It hit them pretty hard. He was the only son, the youngest, all that stuff."

"What's in it for you?"

"What do you mean?"

"Just that. You wouldn't do it if you weren't getting something out of it."

"Sure I'm getting something out of it," Dana snapped. "My whole life is on hold, ready to be disrupted at any moment, night or day. I never know what new disaster is going to strike. Last month it was the fire department, calling to tell me they'd received a call from my parents' neighbor that there was smoke billowing out the window. My mother had put a pot of potatoes on to boil and then gone back to her soap operas. The week before that the police called. They were holding my father at the station for shoplifting. He stole a lousy fifty-cent candy bar. I'm getting a lot out of it, all right." She clenched the steering wheel.

"I'm sorry, Dana. I had no right to interfere. But I'm interested because my cousin Leona is taking care of her abusive father and I'm trying to understand why women do these things."

"My parents aren't abusive," Dana said defensively. "Just pathetic."

Looking at Dana's face, Coral was sorry she had said anything.

Driving as fast as she dared, Dana fought back the anger that threatened to choke her. Just once she wished her friends would offer sympathetic ears, refrain from psychological analysis, and simply let her be. Because no one, including Dana, understood where the compunction to care for her parents came from.

She was the second of three children. Upon hearing that he had a second daughter, her father's first words, were, "For Christ's sake, Rebecca, we've got one already. I want a son." As if Rebecca could do a thing about it.

In retaliation he had named her Dana, an androgynous name but tending toward masculine. Unlike her older sister, Grace, who took after their beautiful mother, short, tom-boyish Dana looked like no one in the family. She had suffered far more from the teasing her mother received about the mailman than her mother had. Where Grace excelled in everything she tried, Dana only partially succeeded. A terribly shy child, she was always searching for the magic key to her parents' heart. The birth of a third child, this one the revered son, virtually finished her off. She was a nobody.

Grace and Daniel needed neither braces nor glasses. Dana was in glasses at age seven and braces at age nine. Grace was an excellent horsewoman, winning trophies and ribbons by the time she was twelve. Daniel excelled in polo, and later, semiprofessional golf. The second time Dana sat on a horse, it threw her, breaking her ankle and collarbone. In high school she went out for girl's softball. Three weeks into the season she was hit right between the eyes, breaking her glasses and her nose. Grace, and later Daniel, were both valedictorians of their high school graduation classes. Dana struggled to maintain a B average. While the other two were busy winning scholarships to prestigious colleges, Dana worked in a nursery near home.

At twenty-one, Grace married, and married well. Daniel held off, enjoying his playboy lifestyle until he finally met the girl of his dreams. Her father's connections sent him on a highly successful political career until his death at age thirty-four; he crashed through a bridge railing and fell three hundred feet into the Hudson River. His blood alcohol level was never revealed.

Dana had unconscious hopes that now she would be somebody in her parent's life. So although they had more than enough money to hire all the help they needed, she moved into their lives, took care of all their affairs, all their problems. When the family doctor recommended a move to the Southwest for her father's allergies and her mother's arthritis, Dana gave up a thriving career to move with them.

For the first time in her life, she felt as though she mattered.

That nothing had changed in her parents' feelings for her was irrelevant. She now had an important job to do, a job that had gained her some recognition—from Grace, from various relatives and close family friends. Often she would hear, "I don't know what your parents would do without you, Dana." These words were balm on her soul.

She was a good and worthy person, a self-sacrificing daughter.

○ ○ ○ ○ ○ ○

"Where did you go for lunch?" Barb asked.

Sonia, Jean, and Coral were having dinner at Barb's. It was the last day of Coral's visit, and Barb had prepared vegetarian chow mein.

"Lupita's."

"Well, then I know you didn't starve. I'm surprised you're eating tonight," Barb nodded at Coral's plate.

No wonder you're so fat, she added to herself.

Coral grinned. "To be honest, it's a struggle. I barely managed to clean my plate and then the waitress brought those puffy things you pour honey on. I ate three of those."

Barb waved that aside. "They're mostly air. Just be glad Dana didn't take you to that new Thai restaurant. Marcy and I went there a few weeks ago. The food was okay, but the servings! I left hungrier than when I went in. Tiny, tiny little portions, just a taste, really. And expensive! Might not be a bad place for a wealthy anorexic, though," she mused. "And a bulimic could eat there and not have to throw up." She laughed uproariously at her own joke.

Coral told them about the phone call from Dana's mother, how Dana had dropped everything to hurry over there, and how she had managed to upset her with her questioning.

"It was none of my business," Coral admitted. "But it was so awful I couldn't control myself. My cousin Leona's doing the same thing—taking care of her father. Dana says her parents aren't abusive, but what does she think their behavior toward her is—benevolent and loving?"

"Dana has never talked about it with me," Sonia said. "What I know came from Harper. But apparently it's pretty bad. Her parents lean on her totally, and then resent the decisions they force her to make."

"If she's so damned concerned about them, why doesn't she move in with them?"

"She did, originally. But according to Harper, her father asked her to move out because she 'cramped his style', meaning she kept nagging him about his health. Harper also said that her parents were afraid that Dana might bring some woman home and do something indecent in front of them, like hold her hand. They refused to accept her lesbianism."

Barb shook her head. "Why's she doing this to herself? They've got money and could afford a live-in housekeeper or two. Dana never wanted to move out here. That I know."

"In my opinion, the whole thing is about self-esteem and control," Coral said as she began stacking the dishes. "I mentioned my cousin Leona. Her father's a tyrant, and her brothers and sisters have done everything they can think of to try to get her to institutionalize him. But she refuses. Because in spite of his obnoxiousness, he's dependent on her, and that gives her a lot of control.

"She's been made executor of his estate and attorney-in-fact. She's completely in charge of all his money affairs, and this guy's got plenty. At a family gathering a few years ago one of his brothers complained that Leona was probably stashing some of that money away for herself, and I said I hoped she was. She should have it all, for staying with that creep all these years.

"And then I realized she'd made a choice. No one was holding a gun to her head, telling her she had to take care of him. In fact, the opposite was true. She insisted on doing it in the face of everyone's displeasure."

"I can see the control part of it," Sonia said. "And I'm assuming the self-esteem comes from her feeling that she's wonderful for caring and doing so much for him. Taking care of him probably also justifies her existence; she's useful and therefore has earned the right to live. I take it she doesn't have children."

Coral carried a stack of plates to the counter. "No. Never married either. I think she's a closet case myself, but her father's life has been her life. She hasn't had one of her own."

"What woman does in patriarchy?" Jean asked. "If she marries, she does her husband's and children's lives. If she gets into any kind of relationship, she does that life—the relationship's life. If she throws herself into a career, then she does the career's life; a job, the job's life. Women don't have the foggiest idea of what a life of their own might be.

"And besides, I think it's more than just control and self-esteem. Women *assume* that they'll take care of their parents if and when the time comes. I know I did. It never occurred to me not to take care of my mother when she was ill. It was a given.

"I had a teacher in high school, a brilliant woman, who had six kids. My mother asked her why she'd had so many children, and she said 'So I won't have to worry about being alone in my old age'. This is the prevailing attitude out there, whether it's verbalized or not. And there's an implicit exchange going on: if I take care of my parents, then my children will take care of me. So it's irrelevant what kind of people our parents are. It's irrelevant whether we get along or not, whether we even like each other. We simply do it. Because we're supposed to. Because we're not good if we don't. Because it matters to us what others think. Because we want to be taken care of in return."

"You're right, Jean," Coral sighed. "This afternoon I wanted to tell Dana to stop being a martyr and get a life. But I know it wouldn't have done any good."

"We can hope, but you're right, it's better not to expect it. Most women aren't willing to make really important changes, those that would give them back their own lives."

Sonia looked at Jean sharply, her interest suddenly piqued.

"That's intriguing, Genius, the distinction you just made between hope and expectation. I never thought of it like that. But now that I do, I realize that I've been using them interchangeably when they're not the same at all. In *Going Out of Our Minds*, I talk about my alarm at the T-shirt slogan, EXPECT NOTHING. No, I said, women should expect *everything*. But what I should have said was, Right. Expectations are dangerous and destructive. They set us up for disappointment and failure, and they encourage us to try to control others. So we should expect nothing. But we should hope everything. Hope is pure positive energy with no strings attached, no control. So if I hope for something that I don't get, there's no disillusionment, no disappointment, no blame, no misery. I can live in hope every moment and be happy. I can't live happily for a second with expectations. Expectations eat you up."

"In other words," Barb said, spearing a mushroom with a chop-stick, "it's okay to hope I'll win a millions dollars in the sweepstakes, but not to expect to."

"You got it," Sonia laughed.

"That's hard. I've been looking at a new truck with a hydraulic lift in the back for Ashley. Every time I think of that truck, I see Ashley in it. I even dream it."

"You deserve it, Barb," Coral chuckled. Alarmed at first by the sight of a pig in the house—especially one of Ashley's girth, Coral had not only grown accustomed to her but found her charming. Ashley was such a friendly, guileless soul, her worst habit backing up to a pair of legs and rubbing herself into a state of ecstasy—

if she was lucky enough to find someone willing to withstand the sudden onslaught of her five-hundred-pound affection.

"When do you leave for Michigan?" Coral asked, changing the subject.

"Too soon," Sonia answered. "August 10. Our friend Della and her daughter will dogsit at our place while we're there. When we get back, we only have a few days before we have to leave for the West Coast Women's Music Festival. Then a few days home before we leave for a three-week Canadian tour."

Coral whistled. "I don't envy your schedule. Who's staying the rest of the time?"

"A woman named Clare. She visited us this past spring and called a few weeks ago, asking if she could return as a paying guest. We told her we needed a house-sitter for the month of September, and since this fit her schedule, she was delighted."

"Is she the one who wants to live with you?" Coral asked.

Jean nodded.

"I liked her." Barb stood to get the dessert. "I wouldn't mind having her for a neighbor."

She set a plate of brownies on the table in front of them. "Carob this time, by god," she muttered.

"I like her, too, Barb," Sonia said. "But I'm not interested in making another stab at community right now, and maybe never. She's a very nice woman and I'm glad she's going to be at our place while we're gone. And I wouldn't mind having her visit every now and then. But that's all."

Jean nodded. "Ditto."

"Why doesn't she buy the land that's for sale next to you?" Barb suggested. "Then she could be close, but not part of your household."

Jean shook her head. "Despite numerous attempts and failures, she's determined to live in a women's community."

"And she's probably determined that Wildfire will be her next one," Barb predicted.

"Women aren't ready to live in community yet," Jean said flatly. "We've got to recreate ourselves before we can live that dream."

19

The Michigan Womyn's Music Festival is the largest annual gathering of women in the world. Held on the eastern shores of Lake Michigan, it attracts between 6,000 and 8,000 women every August. The setting is beautiful—acre upon acre of hardwoods and pines in a virtually unspoiled setting. Unspoiled by permanent structures, that is. By the first day of the festival, the place is packed with tents of every description, hundreds of booths, and many temporary structures—an enormous stage, for example, in a large clearing where women will listen to music late into the night.

Jean had been to the festival once thirteen years before, and while she was glad she had gone, she had never had a desire to return. Once had been enough. But for Sonia, women's festivals were an important way to meet women and circulate her books. Every time she had a new book out, she toured the major festivals.

So on the morning of August 10, Sonia and Jean hugged and kissed Barb and Della good-bye, climbed into the book-and-gear laden Honda station wagon, and headed out. Since they were carrying all their own food and planned to eat as they drove, they expected to make good time. They had each other for company and, without the distractions of home and business, were able to carry on long, uninterrupted conversations.

Jean, not a traveler, enjoyed the trip immensely—except for Indiana. Crossing that state seemed to her to take forever, maybe because she had lived much of her life there. She was relieved when they crossed the border into Niles, Michigan. She steered the car into a truck stop, pulled up to the gas pumps, shut off the engine, and turned to Sonia.

"Another hour or so and we'll be in Holland where we can stop for the night. If we leave early tomorrow morning, we should be at the festival before noon." She went to the office to prepay for the gas.

Getting out to go to the restroom, Sonia noticed three truck drivers lounging on the station steps, enjoying a late lunch or early dinner of cokes and microwaved sandwiches. At the sight of them, she stopped abruptly. She was in shorts, actually short shorts, in which her unshaven legs figured prominently. It had been—what?—ten years since she'd stopped shaving her legs? And still she had moments of anxiety like this. Unlike Jean, whose leg hair was so light you would have to press your nose to her kneecap to see it, hers was thick and dark. Speculatively eyeing the men again, she decided the hell with them, slammed the door, and started in their direction.

And then the strangest thing happened. As she was walking around the pumps, she suddenly felt *beautiful*, legs and all. It wasn't that she was just saying this to herself, repeating it like an affirmation or mantra. She actually *felt* it. And with the feeling came the sensation that her feet weren't touching the pavement but rather that she was floating a few inches above it. Knowing she was beautiful. Knowing she was perfect. A sense that stayed with her as she floated up the steps, past the coke-chugging men and into the restroom. A sense that did not desert her when she came out and walked back to the car. Or rather floated.

It was her turn to drive. She slid into the driver's seat, waited until Jean got in and buckled up, then pulled the car out of the truckstop. Heading down highway 31 toward Interstate 94, she told Jean her experience.

"I wonder what happened to you," Jean mused. "Something shifted, that's for sure. When I saw you walking back to the car I could tell you were different, but I didn't know why."

Sonia laughed happily. "Well, I don't know why either. It wasn't something I could have done on purpose. When I saw those guys sitting there, I didn't even try to pump up my courage. I just dismissed them from my mind, like I was finally past caring what they thought. Anyway, I started walking toward them and . . . well, . . . took off. I've never experienced anything like it."

Jean nodded. "I've had those moments occasionally. I was watching you walk back to the car and you looked taller, more self-assured, and radiant."

"It was a wonderful feeling, Jeannie. It still is. I've struggled with these legs for a long time, loving the idea of not shaving them but not loving the way they look. And not just around men. Anybody. Especially when there are women present with very attractive legs. You know the type: tanned, smooth, perfectly shaped, no varicose or spider veins, no cellulite dimples."

She fell silent, remembering one of her early experiments back in 1983. She had been in Florida, near a beach. Donning a bathing suit, she had taken a walk along the water's edge. The beach had been jammed with people, right down to the water. As she had approached each group, an obvious, sudden, and stunned silence had fallen. No one could believe Those Awful Legs. *Her legs.*

Strange what power those darkly hairy, middle-aged legs had over conversation. Never mind that there was a body attached to them, that they belonged to a woman who had a mind and a spirit and a life. For them, she had been Those Awful Legs.

Coming out of her reverie, she said to Jean, "That's one of the beauties of the festivals. Lots of unshaven body parts. Lots of body hair in evidence."

Jean nodded in agreement. "I know this sounds trite—everybody says it—but it's true that the biggest shock for me at Michigan was seeing all those women nonchalantly walking around naked. I knew it was going to happen, but somehow I wasn't prepared for it."

"I don't remember if you told me you took your clothes off there," Sonia said, taking the exit to I-94.

"I didn't," Jean admitted. "I wanted to, very much, but I just couldn't bring myself to do it. I did manage to shower—but only at night. I knew I was where many women felt free and safe enough to be publically naked, but I never quite reached that place."

"I'd have no trouble at all taking off my clothes . . . from the waist down," Sonia said. "None at all. But I could never, never take off my shirt. That much I know."

As soon as the words were out of her mouth, she paled and began to tremble. "No!" she cried. "Oh, no, I can't, I really can't." Shaking even more intensely, she began to sob. "Jean, I can't do it, I can't take off my shirt!"

Jean grabbed the wheel of the dangerously swerving car.

"Pull over, Sonia," she urged, struggling to keep them on the road. "Pull off right here and stop." Fortunately they were approaching an exit and Sonia got herself together enough to steer the car off the ramp and into a small cemetery. There, she rested her forehead on the center of the steering wheel, her arms circling it above her, and cried her heart out. Jean rested her hand on her trembling leg and waited for the tumult to subside.

Sonia raised her head. "I know I have to take my shirt off at the festival. I have to do it."

"I don't understand why you're determined to put yourself through the hell of exposing your breasts there. Just the thought is obviously agonizing for you."

Sonia pulled a wad of tissues from the box on the floor and swiped impatiently at her face. "Of course you understand why I have to. There can't be any doubt in your mind." She paused to blow her nose. "I want to stop feeling ashamed of my breasts, I want to learn to love them and myself, accept them and myself completely. So of course I have to. I have to stop talking about it and start doing something about it.

"Sure, I can tell my breasts a million times in private, 'You sweet things, you perfect, wonderful, adorable breasts, I love you just the way you are'. What good will that do if I qualify it by acting in a way that clearly says, 'This is only true as long as no one else sees you'? I can't betray them or myself that way any longer. So I have to take my shirt off and keep it off the whole time I'm there. Except maybe in our workshops. I need to think about that."

In her mind's eye, she watched herself moving bare-breasted through the throngs of women at the festival, sitting bare-breasted at her booth. Fear rose up in her throat like bile. She moaned aloud and began crying again, crying as if she could never stop, pounded by waves of feelings suppressed for twenty-three years.

The intensity of her anguish frightened Jean. She was afraid Sonia was going to die right there in her arms.

But slowly the convulsions lessened. When she could talk, Sonia turned to Jean and said through her tears and hiccoughs, "The worst part is that I can't explain to anyone. I can't carry a sign that says, 'Yes, I've had breast implants and yes I know how politically incorrect this is. But please try to understand. I did it when I didn't know any better, long before I was a feminist. And I've been so terribly sorry ever since. Please be kind. I've suffered enough already'. I can't say anything at all, just take my shirt off and stand there.

"Any explanation, any excuse, would mitigate the shame so I wouldn't get the full impact of it. If I don't experience it fully, I can't get rid of it. And that shame has tyrannized me for nearly a quarter of a century. I want it gone. So off with my shirt," she joked weakly, but immediately began her spasmodic, uncontrollable shivering. "I'm so sacred, Jean," she whispered through chattering teeth. "I'm so damnhell scared!"

Fifteen minutes later she was still shaking so hard that she and Jean traded places and Jean drove out of the cemetery, toward I-196 and Holland. They rode in silence, both drained from the experience. Numb with misery, Sonia stared unseeing at the trees whizzing past.

"The truth is," she said flatly, "that the women's movement is not a safe place for women, maybe less so for those of us who have made a name for ourselves, but really not for any of us. Women get massacred for crimes much less heinous than having breast implants—as you know."

Keeping her eyes on the road, Jean reached over and took her hand. "I do know, Sonia," she agreed sadly. "I've watched it again and again, like the re-run of a nightmare. But I don't believe it's going to be obvious to most women there that you've had implants."

"Almost any woman looking at my breasts will know they aren't real," Sonia replied dully. "They have that funny hump at the top. They're also too firm, not like breast tissue, especially at my age. I'm not saying that all women will realize it, but many will."

Jean nodded. She was accustomed to Sonia's breasts, to the way they looked and felt, and she thought they were very pretty and sweet.

She pondered what Sonia had said about the women's movement being an unsafe place for women. *That's an understatement,* she thought to herself. *It's not unsafe, it's murderous.* Her twenty years of feminist experience were fraught with examples of this, as was every feminist's.

The one most fresh in her mind had happened not long before at a lecture. She had been in the audience when the woman speaker was almost torn limb-from-limb for admitting that, although she no longer had any desire to be with men, she sometimes had sexual dreams about them. Instead of applauding her honesty and courage, the audience, composed mostly of lesbian feminists, were so angry at her that they shouted her right out of the room.

Sitting there beside Sonia, she felt depressed. *We're conditioned to hate ourselves, to hate our bodies, to hate everything that's female. So of course we hate one another, scapegoat one another, climb over one another's bleeding bodies to get just a little higher, feel a little superior. I'm better than she is because I have a master's degree, or because I dress better. Or, as is now the current fad, I'm better because I've suffered more: I'm a woman of color, or I've been incested, or raped, or I'm poor and don't have a college degree and wear second-hand clothes.*

Women can use anything at hand to put each other down, she thought dismally, remembering how Sonia always pointed out that slaves are trained to turn against one another so they'll never have any power.

It's too hideous, too sad for words, she thought. *We've almost totally forgotten how to come together in a cooperative, loving, powerful way, the way we did before men came, the way we did in women's world.*

Realizing with a start that Sonia was talking, she tuned in.

"I don't understand it," Sonia was saying. "I don't understand why I'm having such a ferocious reaction to this. What other people think about me has never been very important—thank goodness, or I'd have had a lot harder time moving through my stuff than I have. So why now? Or maybe this isn't what the terror is really about. If not, then I want to know what's really hurting."

She blew her nose again, winced, and dug in her purse for salve to coat the raw spots she had rubbed there.

Turning back to Jean, she said, "I'd like to know if you have any idea what might be behind it."

Jean thought for a minute, biting her lip in concentration. "I can't put my finger on anything definite. But maybe if I just think out loud, without editing, something will come up."

Sonia waited, listening.

"It's true that you aren't concerned about others' opinions of you. But that has always been about your ideas."

"Not so," Sonia interrupted. "I didn't care when I fought the church and was excommunicated. I didn't care when I got arrested a dozen or so times for actions around the ERA. I didn't care when I fasted. I didn't care when I became a lesbian."

"Okay, but none of those things was as, well, as *personal* as this."

"Religion isn't personal? Sexual preference isn't personal?"

"Sonia, this is your body. Women have deep, deep negativity and despair and grief about their bodies. More than about anything else. Our bodies are us. And we've all battered them, abused them, tried to kill them."

She became aware that she had been seeing tulip gardens and windmills for a little while, and realized they were in Holland. She drove slowly through the town until, on the north side, they spotted a small motel. The vacancy sign and the posted rates were all they needed. She turned the car into the driveway and pulled up to the entrance.

"If you don't mind doing this one, Jeannie, I'll wait here for you," Sonia said. She looked exhausted, wrung out. Half wishing the naked-at-Michigan discussion had never started, Jean entered the motel office and signed them in.

After a light supper of food they'd brought from home, they took up the conversation they'd been having in the car. Sonia wanted to know where Jean had meant to take her idea of their bodies being what women are most emotionally vulnerable about.

"I'm not sure what I was going to do with it. Maybe all I wanted to say was that since you already hate your body—particularly your breasts—and since you're already full of shame and anger and grief about what you allowed someone to do to them, perhaps you fear that other women will reinforce those feelings. That instead of getting rid of them, you'll just be made to feel them deeper."

Sonia considered that. "That makes sense," she admitted. "But I think there's something else as well; actually there are probably many factors at work here. But I picked up on something particularly interesting that you said: . . . 'what you allowed to be done to them,' and I felt a jolt."

Jean waited.

"I may have been feeling like a victim all these years," Sonia explained. "Menstream-in-general's victim, my husband's victim, the doctor's victim. I can't say I've been aware of it, but then victims mostly aren't. In fact, I've consciously blamed myself for all of it. But underneath—well, who knows?

"Anyway, let's suppose that, all unaware, I have been feeling like a victim. Being a victim is a very powerless, vulnerable position, a very fearful place. At any moment, someone could *do* something to you. You view yourself as always acted upon from the outside and not being able to stop it. And not as acting positively for yourself.

"That would explain why I'm so terrified. If I'm in victim mode about my breasts, then I'm expecting to be victimized about them, I'm expecting to be badly hurt, and I'm expecting not to be able to do anything about it."

Eyes shining with unshed tears, Jean moved next to Sonia, putting her arm around her waist, resting her cheek against Sonia's. "Soni, dear Soni," she spoke quietly. They rocked gently together until Sonia pulled reluctantly away.

"I need to sleep," she said matter-of-factly. "Tomorrow is going to be a long, l-o-n-g day."

20

"How many women are you expecting this year?" Sonia heard the festival-goer in front of her ask the worker in charge of the identification wristbands.

"Around 7,500, give or take a few hundred," the worker answered, snapping the bracelet onto the woman's arm and handing her a packet containing information on where to park, where to camp, where to eat, where to shower. Turning from the table, the now-officially-branded festival participant almost collided with Sonia. "Oh, it's you!" the woman cried, throwing her arms around her. "I came because of you. I can't wait for your workshops."

They talked a moment, then Sonia moved up to the table. The worker, whose name tag read "Jude", opened a second notebook to the section marked "Performers". Running her finger down the list of names, she found Sonia's, with Jean's underneath.

"Let's see, you both get two bracelets. One for performers and one for craftswomen. The best of both worlds." She snapped the bracelets on their wrists, handed them each a lavender packet and asked if they had any questions. Sonia shook her head; she'd been here enough to know her way around. She and Jean set out immediately for the crafts area.

On the way, Jean watched women's reactions to Sonia. Most appeared genuinely glad to see her, so much so, in fact, that a trip that would normally have taken fifteen minutes stretched into forty-five. Finally at their space, Jean took over organizing and setting up their booth. Sonia was totally involved with the small crowd of women that had already gathered around her.

The booth was soon ready and even though the festival wouldn't open officially until the next morning, both women were kept busy selling books and talking. A lot of craftswomen and workers wanted to take advantage of the comparatively small crowd to see what was available and have first chance at it. Toward late afternoon, as the crowd around Sonia's booth thinned out, Jean left to set up their tent and organize their gear at the campsite they had chosen in the craftwomen's area.

As she struggled with the center pole of the four-woman tent, Jean heard someone call her name and felt arms encircle her waist. She laid the pole down and turned.

"Cheryl!" she cried, returning the hug. "You're here already. Shoot, it's good to see you!" Cheryl had visited them very briefly the year before and both Jean and Sonia had liked her. Before she left, they had invited her back to visit any time she wished, and even suggested that she consider becoming a member of the community. Then the community dissolved, and although they still maintained contact with her, the question of her joining them was now moot.

While Cheryl helped her set up the tent, she filled Jean in on what had been happening in her life since her visit a year ago. She also told her all the festival gossip up to that point: who had already arrived, who was saying what about whom, who was already being trashed. From her flushed face and the fervor of her conversation, Jean could tell she was in a high state of excitement, and it became her.

They walked back to the booth together to find Sonia in the midst of women. She broke away to embrace Cheryl, genuinely glad to see her. Cheryl had offered several weeks before to be on hand to staff the booth whenever they were doing their workshops, so Jean quickly took her through the basics. Having owned and operated a woman's bookstore in the past, Cheryl was an old hand at selling books and she soon had a firm grasp on Wildfire Books' procedure. With a quick hug she told them she would be back later and left.

When the dinner bell rang, Sonia announced to the circle of women around the booth that she was starving and needed to close down and eat. Quickly, she and Jean returned the books to their boxes and stashed the necessary book-selling paraphernalia under the table. Waving goodbye to the still-lingering women, they followed the signs to the performers' dining area.

As they waited in line for food, Sonia introduced Jean to dozens of her friends and acquaintances. The tent was full of women that Jean was accustomed to seeing only on the stage, and she enjoyed seeing them up close in this casual setting.

The food was excellent and plentiful, as was the conversation. But during a lull at their table, Sonia leaned towards her and whispered that she was ready to go. "I just want to climb into my sleeping bag," she said as they made their way out of the dining tent. The next day was their six-hour workshop and she needed all the energy she could muster for it. They headed for the camping area and their tent. They found the camping area with no problem, but they had a harder time finding their tent. In the short time since Jean and Cheryl had set up the tent, multitudes of other tents had sprung up around it, like mushrooms after a good rain.

Inside the tent, Sonia threw herself down on her sleeping bag and groaned. "It feels so good to lie flat. Maybe I'll just sleep in my clothes so I won't have to get up." She had no sooner said that, though, than she leapt up. "Where's the pee pot?"

Jean rummaged through a Save-a-Tree bag and pulled out the plastic, lidded container that Sonia had very specifically designated the pee pot and handed it to her. Sonia carried it towards the entrance, placed it on the floor, and undid her pants. Jean curled up on her sleeping bag, a mild anxiety growing inside her. As they had been packing for this trip, Jean had asked if the porta-janes were going to be close enough to the campsite that she could go there in the night. Sonia had snorted. "Probably, but you really don't want to be out looking for them in the middle of the night. So we take a pee pot."

In all her many years of camping, Jean had never used a pee pot. She had either found the outhouse or squatted behind a bush. Here, this was impossible. They were almost on top of one another, the tents nearly touching. A woman who stepped outside to urinate would most likely soak someone else's tent. Besides, it was against the rules.

Rules or not, Jean did not think she could use the pot. Alone, in the tent, yes, but with someone there, even Sonia, she could not imagine squatting over it as Sonia was doing. It felt too exposed.

And yet, something in her was rebelling, was not going to let her have any peace with this. She was obviously ashamed—of being seen, of the act itself. Although she felt fine about Sonia's doing it, she felt as if there was something inherently evil about her peeing in that pot. This told her something: she had to do it. Now. Her bladder was full and instead of heading for the janes, she was going to get up and occupy the space Sonia had just vacated. Right.

Wrong. She was paralyzed, stuck to the sleeping bag as though it were coated with super glue. She couldn't move, let alone get herself to perform the simple act of peeing in the pot. *This is ridiculous*, she told herself. *Grow up, you wimp. At least talk about it*. But it all proved fruitless. *Okay then, sit here and die of euremic poisoning*.

As Sonia undressed, music began in the distance. Although the night stage was not officially open, women were gathering for informal music and song. Tomorrow night the air would throb with guitars, drums, bass, and women's voices. Tonight would be quiet by festival standards.

Sonia pulled her sleeping bag around her and looked at Jean curiously, wondering why she was curled up on top of her bag, fully dressed and looking miserable, but she said nothing. She knew that if Jean wanted to talk, she was going to have to take the initiative. Nevertheless, she was bursting with curiosity.

Jean stirred and allowed her eyes to meet Sonia's.

"I'm having a hard time," she finally said. "Actually, I'm in agony. I need to pee and I'm too ashamed to use the pee pot, I could go to the janes but I know I have to do it here if I want to be free of shame, but I don't think I can," she said in one long breath. "Can you believe that up until a couple of years ago, I'd never peed in a public restroom—including school restrooms—in my whole life?"

Sonia listened quietly.

"Of course, *you* could leave, but that wouldn't solve the problem. Since it's your presence in the tent that's causing my anxiety, you have to stay in order for this to work."

Then getting up off her sleeping bag, she said firmly, "I'm just going to stop talking about it and do it."

Slipping off her jeans, she folded them carefully and laid them at the foot of her bag. She hesitated a moment, then pulled her socks off and draped them over her shoes. Turning towards the pee pot, she lifted the lid and positioned the pot carefully in front of the door. "Where's the toilet paper?" she muttered merely to distract herself since it was sitting right in front of her. Slipping down her underwear, she positioned herself over the pot, willing her bladder to empty.

But nothing happened. It was the quiet that daunted her, the fear that Sonia would hear every little tinkle and splash. It was different from being in the bathroom at home when Sonia came in. Then they talked or Sonia brushed her teeth or washed or for some other reason turned on the water, drowning out the sound of her pee striking the water in the toilet. Now she wished that Sonia would hum, or that the music from the night stage would get louder.

She was really in a fix. She thought about getting up, pulling her jeans back on, and going to the janes. But she knew she wasn't going to do that. The other option was to just give it up and go to bed and die. *Or you could pee,* she suggested sarcastically. *That would be a novel solution.*

She felt tears threaten. *I can't do it,* she told herself. *I just can't do it and I hate myself for it. I'm such an idiot, such a spineless wonder, a total hypocrite, a wimped out acid-hole.*

"I sure think you're wonderful, Jeannie," Sonia's soft voice carried right to her heart, loosening the tears and letting them pour down her face. Suddenly Sonia was beside her, holding her, rocking her, murmuring sweet, reassuring sounds into her ear, so warm and loving and dear.

"Come back to bed and let me hold you," Sonia whispered. Jean nodded and pulled a piece of toilet paper off the roll to wipe her face. She followed Sonia back to the bed, and snuggled down in her arms.

"I don't know what it is, Sonia. I just freeze up. I know it's silly but I can't seem to get past it, can't talk myself out of it."

"I don't need to tell you this because I know you know, but there's obviously something going on here that's pretty deep. You've taken the most important step, and that is deciding that you don't want to be this way anymore. I think the rest will come when you're ready."

Jean nodded, but didn't feel reassured. She was afraid she might not be ready for a century or so. Nestling closer to Sonia, she felt herself drifting off to sleep despite her discomfort. She could not have counted the times in her life when she'd had to sleep with an almost bursting bladder because there were people around and she could not pee. They both slept soundly until the 7 a.m. bell announced breakfast.

Jean was first up. Grabbing her towel, shampoo, and soap she headed for the showers, stopping first at the janes. She felt a twinge of guilt as she sat down, but quickly dismissed it and continued to the performers' showers where there were short lines and always plenty of hot water. A few women were already there, washing the sleep off their bodies and enjoying the hot water in the cool morning air. Jean joined them, moving quickly because she could see more women approaching. She toweled off, brushed her teeth, and hurried back to the tent, where she hung her towel on one of the tent ropes. By this time, Sonia was up and ready for her shower.

Jean offered to bring breakfast for both of them, and Sonia accepted. "You know what I like to eat, and I'm glad to have you do it. It'll save time."

More women had arrived in the night, so the breakfast crowd was bigger than last night's dinner crowd. Although the menu featured omelets and fried potatoes, there was also oatmeal, fresh fruit, several different kinds of bread and bagels, margarine, butter, jams and jellies, and peanut butter. Jean spooned oatmeal into Sonia's bowl, filled another with potatoes, selected an orange and banana and returned with them to the tent.

As they ate, they put the finishing touches on their ideas for the workshop. After breakfast, they went to their booth to set things up for Cheryl, then set out with the throngs of other women for the workshop areas.

Their workshop site was already full to overflowing, and a steady stream of women was still coming. Though women squeezed closer together to make room for the new arrivals, it wasn't enough. Women continued to come, continued to fill every available space, until they were even crowded in among the trees and bushes. Sonia turned to Jean and told her they were going to have to shout—"And I mean *shout!*"—to be heard.

Sonia had been adamant that from here on Jean do all speeches and workshops with her. The nature of her work had changed when she and Jean began their experiments, and she knew the workshops would mean more if Jean were included. Jean's perspective and ideas would not only compliment hers but, she believed, Jean would lend credibility to her ideas.

"Women have a tendency to think that a well-known person is not like them," Sonia reminded her, "and that therefore how she lives isn't relevant to their lives. Most women who attend my workshops at the festival will know me or will have heard about me, how radical I am. Because I'll be perceived as different from ordinary women, they can easily dismiss what I say.

"But they're going to recognize you as one of them, someone they can identify with. So when you talk about the experiments we've done, they'll find it easier to imagine themselves doing them. We're talking about hard stuff, Genius. And while I have no desire to persuade women to believe what I say or to do as I do, I'd like them to be able to see the picture as clearly as possible. Then they can decide whether it's for them or not.

"Besides, it's exhausting work, and after all these years of doing it alone, I'm more than ready to have help. I'm tired. It'll be wonderful to have someone else help bear the burden. And it'll be fun to create something new together."

So Jean, who had been very reluctant in the beginning—"This is not what I do well. I'll just ruin everything"—gave in and agreed to give it a try.

As the women began to settle down, Jean moved carefully through them until she found a spot on the ground where she could sit. Sonia stood, her back to an enormous oak tree, and waited for them to get quiet. At a signal from her, Jean rose and began slowly to make her way to the front, saying as she walked, "I remember a time when women were together all the time."

Sonia answered back, "I remember a time when women touched each other constantly."

Jean responded, "I remember a time when women healed one another with touch."

At that point Sonia addressed the audience. "How about you? What do you remember?"

For about 15 minutes the air reverberated with women's memories, not only memories of the near past but also of women's world. One woman—"I remember a time when there were no men"—was roundly applauded. Another woman, totally naked, called out, "I remember a time when there were no bras." The crowd roared at this, especially since it was so difficult to imagine this woman wearing anything, let alone a bra. It was a good way to move into the gist of the workshop: before men, women were together in a way so powerful and satisfying that men's innovations—sex and relationships—looked paltry, boring, and silly in comparison. Women's world. How to restore it, how to recreate it, how to return to it.

After the lunch break, during which Sonia and Jean had hastily eaten peanut butter sandwiches, the talk shifted to women's hatred of their bodies and how we might begin to move out of it. Sonia told them how she had become more aware of her body by touching herself. Jean told how her Hopi friend, Chenoa, had touched herself all the time, how she was never *not* touching herself: stroking her arm, her leg, caressing a hand, or her face. Or how if she was not touching herself, she was touching the woman next to her.

"Let's try it," Sonia suggested, stroking her own arm. "Touch your body and focus on that touch, really feel what it's like, and be aware of how your body likes it." She continued stroking her arms, her shoulders, her neck, running her hands down her breasts, her belly, over her hips and down her legs. Jean did the same. But both of them were also watching the women in front of them.

What they saw was that though many women were able to touch themselves with relative ease, the majority were either having some difficulty or were totally unable or unwilling to do it. They watched several women, their hands poised above their arms, ready for the descent, rapidly change course to land quietly and sedately on a knee. It was obvious that something seemingly so simple was not simple for most women. After a few minutes of this—during which one woman in the group magically began to sing—Jean suggested they turn to a woman they did not know, and touch her.

Suddenly the air bristled with tension. While some women—the same ones who had jumped immediately into the first experiment—showed no hesitation at touching a stranger, others were very disturbed about it. One agitated woman stood and addressed Sonia and Jean.

"What you are suggesting is disrespectful and dangerous. Many women are incest victims and don't want to be touched. It seems to me that if we want to avoid serious trauma here, we should ask if it's all right before we do it."

Sonia shook her head. "Oh, no. There are no victims among us, only women who have been incested, who were once victims and are no more. So we must never think of any woman in that way. What we've been saying here today is that every woman is capable of taking responsibility for herself and that only she, never we, must do it. Our responsibility is to ourselves alone. We are each obligated to ourselves to do only and always exactly what we want to do. It is the responsibility of others around us, involved with us, to say—as you just did—how they feel about it.

"So if the woman you choose to touch here does not want to be touched, she must say so. The ultimate disrespect is to assume that a woman cannot take care of herself, that she is a victim, without volition, and that she needs us to anticipate her needs.

"Every woman here now knows that it is her prerogative and her privilege, and hers alone, to decide what she wants and to tell this to any interested party. If you get nothing else from this workshop, I hope you get this. There are no victims here, only powerful women."

So saying, Sonia knelt down by a woman near her and began to rub her shoulders and neck. Jean, looking around, spotted a woman sitting in a folding chair, a woman about as far from the stereotype of a Michigan Festie as she could imagine. Sixty-five and matronly, dressed in a polyester pantsuit of bright pink, she looked as though she would be more comfortable at a church bazaar. But something about her interested Jean so she squatted beside her and began to stroke her arm.

The woman didn't look at her. In fact, except for the reddening of her neck and face, an observer would have thought she didn't know Jean was there. Jean sensed that she was uncomfortable, but kept on because the woman didn't tell her to stop.

She continued to touch and stroke her, enjoying the feel of her soft skin, skin that had apparently suffered little exposure to either sun or wind. She closed her eyes and let her hands guide her, let her hands talk to this woman's body. What she heard was that in spite of the anxiety, her body wanted to be touched.

When Jean felt ready to stop, she opened her eyes and looked up. The woman was looking at her, tears spilling down her cheeks. Jean reached up and gently brushed one away, and the woman took her hand and held it against her face for a moment. They did not speak a word, and yet they said everything that needed to be said.

When the gong sounded announcing that dinner would be ready soon, the group began to break up. But Jean and Sonia found themselves spending at least another hour talking with women who were eager and ready to break out of their patriarchal mindset concerning sex and intimacy. At least that was what they said. But as Sonia and Jean were later to realize, many women were interpreting the workshop—and *The Ship*—in a very different way than intended.

They were not surprised.

21

Sonia stretched and yawned, flinging her arm onto Jean's sleeping bag. It was empty. Propping herself groggily up on her elbow, she squinted around the tent. Jean was gone. The watch hanging from the strap next to her announced digitally that it was 7:15.

Then she remembered. At nine this morning she would take off her shirt and not put it back on until the crafts area closed at five. At the thought, dread squeezed her chest, taking her breath away.

As she was trying to calm her racing heart, she heard feet crunching on dried leaves outside the tent. A moment later, balancing two bowls and a plate in her hands, Jean pulled back the flap, pushed her way in, and set the dishes carefully on the floor. Then she leaned over and kissed Sonia. "Good morning, Your Eminent Sleepiness," she said.

"Smells good," Sonia murmured into her neck. "Probably a combination of you and fried potatoes."

Jean picked up the cereal and held it out to her. "Not yet," Sonia grunted, struggling out of her bag. "I need to pee first." She picked up the container, and, squatting a little, held it against her in such a way that she would be sure to catch everything.

They sat together and ate, first the luscious amalgamation of hot, seven-grain cereal with raisins, almonds, and soy milk, and then the fried potatoes. When they were finished, Sonia sighed with satisfaction. And belched, a long, round, juicy belch. Too late, she clapped her hand over her mouth and blushed. "Woops," she muttered. "Excuse me."

"There's nothing to excuse," Jean assured her. "I didn't mind it at all. In fact, I enjoyed it." Seeing the disbelief on Sonia's face, she insisted, "Really. I think it has to do with my upbringing. My grandmother was a prize belcher and we all thought it was adorable. I don't belch because my body doesn't produce much gas, but I admire women who aren't uptight about it, who don't worry about its being unladylike. I say, let 'er rip!"

"You're joking," Sonia laughed, then stopped herself. "No, I think I know you well enough now to trust that you're not. You're just so unusual, Genius. I mean, so much conditioning bypassed you. Luckily for me, I might add."

Jean took her hand. "Dear Soni," she said softly. "You just burp and belch . . . "

"And fart?"

". . . and fart to your heart's content."

Sonia howled with laughter. "You may be sorry you said that," she choked. "I'm a real gasbag. It seems to me that I've spent half my life on hold."

"On hold?"

"Holding gas in until I can find a private place to expel it."

"Sounds pretty uncomfortable to me."

Sonia made a face. "It's dire. And not only that, but having to make up excuses to run off somewhere, especially when I'm in the midst of a conversation. I'm not yet at the place where I can announce that I need to go off into the bushes and pass gas. To say nothing of being able simply to let it fly."

She began gathering her clothes and bathing equipment together. Hesitating a moment, she glanced over at Jean, who was looking at her with such warmth and love that she sat back down.

"I've been fighting off massive anxiety since I woke up," Sonia admitted.

"I wondered about it this morning in the showers."

"I'm just trying not to think about it, that's all. I know I'll do it but for the life of me I don't know how."

"You'll probably just go on automatic pilot," Jean surmised thoughtfully, then added, "There are more shirts off than on around here. At least that's what it looks like."

"That doesn't help," Sonia sighed. "And it's not only that many women will recognize these breasts as implanted. That's the worst, of course, and bad enough. But there's also the problem of status."

Jean raised her eyebrows questioningly.

Sonia explained. "A common complaint about the festival is that it's so hierarchical. One example is that here were are, among the privileged, eating better food, showering with hot water, and rarely having to stand in line anywhere. High status.

"But in the fathers' 'archy', nakedness connotes low status—vulnerability and powerlessness. Witness the famous paintings you know where totally naked women are lying or standing among men dressed to the nines.

"What I'm getting at is that it's fine for the festival goers to take off their shirts or walk around naked. It's also fine for the workers and craftswomen. But it isn't fine—because it isn't appropriate—for performers. It breaks down status barriers, is too leveling, too diminishing to the star-worship that brings so many women here. So it's simply not done."

Jean shrugged. "Okay. But I don't know why that bothers you. It's not like you to care about that."

"I hate hierarchy, Jean; it's the essence of oppression. So you can bet your life that if I hadn't had implants, I would have taken my shirt off the very first time I came to this festival nearly ten years ago and every time since. What bothers me now about being a performer and taking off my shirt is that it will draw even more attention to these breasts."

She glanced at the robotic timepiece. "Shoot! Look at the time!" Leaping up, she pulled on her jeans, T-shirt, and sandals, flung her towel over her shoulder, carefully picked up the pee pot, and started out of the tent. As she held the flap open, she paused and turned back to Jean. "Actually," she said, "now that I think about it, that's a big plus. The more obvious I am, the faster I'll be able to dump my shame."

After she'd gone, Jean straightened things up a little and left for the crafts area to get the booth ready to open. On the way, she met Cheryl and they walked over together.

"A lot of women are talking about your workshop," she told Jean. "There are signs up all over announcing 'Intimacy without Sex' discussions."

"I'm not sure if that bodes well," Jean frowned as she pulled a box out from under the table.

"I don't know, either, since I haven't gone to any, but I think they're just groups of women from the workshop who want to talk more about your ideas. I think some of them even want to try some touching experiments. I'm thinking of going to one tomorrow afternoon."

She was interrupted by a woman who stopped to ask if Sonia was going to be available to sign books. "Is it nine o'clock already?" Cheryl asked. Jean told the woman to come back in 15 minutes or so, that Sonia was on her way. Just then, as if summoned, Sonia appeared. Jean shoved the book in front of her and Sonia spoke with its owner a moment while she signed it.

When the woman left, Sonia gave Jean a long look. Then, pulling her T-shirt over her head, she flung it on the back of her chair. As if on cue, a large group of women walked up to the booth, eager to talk with Sonia and to buy her new book. Jean watched the women's expressions. If any of them thought it odd that Sonia was shirtless, or if they found her breasts peculiar looking, they did not show it. As they wandered off to the next booth, Jean turned to Sonia with the intention of saying something about their reaction—or lack thereof.

But Sonia wasn't there.

Her body was, but Jean could tell by the look in her eyes that starkest terror had driven her spirit out. As two more women approached the booth holding out books to be signed, Jean put the pen in Sonia's hand, slowly and distinctly repeated the names she was to inscribe, and placed the books in front of her, again repeating the names. Sonia mechanically wrote in each book. This went on all morning.

When Cheryl showed up at noon with lunch for both of them, Jean was flooded with gratitude. She had not wanted—and in fact had not thought she could—leave Sonia alone at the booth in her nearly-catatonic state. Placing the food before her, Jean thought for a moment she would have to feed her. But fortunately when she was told it was time to eat, she dutifully ate—or at least went through the motions.

Later, Sonia could recall almost nothing about that day. She simply endured, sitting at the booth and signing books and managing somehow to make conversation while not really being there at all. She was aware, on occasion, that Jean was prompting her, repeating things to her that she had missed. Later she could remember taking her shirt off in the morning and putting it back on when the crafts area closed for the day, but she had absolutely no memory of the time in between.

The next day wasn't much easier and had its new stresses. Jean had managed to get her to drink more, and at a certain point, Sonia knew she would have to go to the porta-janes. For a fleeting moment, the thought of walking shirtless through the hundreds of women between her and the toilets tempted her to don her shirt for the trip. But she shook that panic off and set forth as she was.

After a few steps, she felt an almost uncontrollable urge to hunch over, wrap her arms around herself as protection, and run as fast as she could. To counteract this temptation, she threw her shoulders back, put her hands on her hips, held her head high, and sauntered casually—or so she hoped it look—through the throng, stopping to greet women, stopping to look at this craft or that, refusing to be hurried, receiving hugs along the way. And nearly in a coma of terror by the time she closed the porta-jane door.

On the way back, she whistled—albeit shakily—to make herself even more obvious. It was amazing how many women turned and waved to her or smiled. Several stopped her for a hug and a few minutes' conversation. Back at the booth, she slipped gratefully into her numbness, accepting the books Jean put before her and talking when prompted.

The third day she began to come out of her protective fog. To stand there in her man-made silicone mammaries was a little easier, a little less gut wrenching. She was aware of most of the women who came to the booth and was able to function more or less on her own, seeking refuge less often in fugue.

Then a woman about her age and also shirtless stopped by the booth. On each of her large, drooping breasts she had painted a cat's face. Taking one look at Sonia, she exclaimed, "Oh, you have such pretty breasts! Only one thing would make them prettier. Cats' faces!"

Sonia blanched, then stepped out from behind the table. "Go for it!" she told the cat woman.

The woman pulled non-toxic crayons from her bag and, under the gaze of a gathering crowd, carefully painted a face on each of Sonia's breasts. Nipples became noses—surrounded by long black whiskers and surmounted by large green eyes. If anyone had missed her breast exhibition before, Sonia thought wryly, there was no way they could avoid it now.

From beginning to end, Sonia's breast experiment affected Jean powerfully. She saw at close range and unmistakably how terrified Sonia was of revealing her breasts at this festival. She knew that ultimately it was irrelevant to Sonia what any other woman thought about them. It would have been irrelevant if not one single woman had figured out they were implants.

The point was that Sonia had been profoundly sexually abused 23 years before by the medical establishment. Sexual abuse is terrorism, and like all abused women, she had lived in terror half her life, terror centered in her breasts. She had been filled with such shame and guilt and anxiety about them that she had had to block it out in order to live. But that day in the cemetery it had all erupted into the open, like pus bursting from an infected wound. Now she was flushing that wound, doing something immensely courageous to heal it forever.

During that week-long experiment, Jean began, slowly, to look at herself, at her own fears and shames. And as she did she realized that if she really wanted freedom, if she craved it as she thought she did, she also had some very difficult times ahead.

The rest of the festival was largely anti-climactic for them. They did a couple more workshops, met a lot of wonderful women, and sold almost all the books and tapes they had brought with them. The week at Michigan was a good one, in all ways.

But mostly they were relieved that by its close, there had been none of the usual women-hating conflicts or confrontations, none of the attacks of women against women that were seemingly requisite at most festivals. All signs indicated that women would go home without killing one another this year.

But Sonia wasn't entirely convinced. "I don't trust this blessed state to last," she told Jean anxiously. "Let's get out of here before some woman or group decides to get their last-minute sado-masochistic fix by bashing some other female heads."

They packed up in record time and left, both sighing with relief as Jean drove the stationwagon out the gates. Whatever happened now at the festival site, they were out of it. Also, it had been a long, emotion-packed week and they would have less than a week back in New Mexico before they had to leave again, this time for the West Coast Women's Music Festival. They were more than ready to be home.

"How far do you think we should drive tonight?" Jean asked, as they turned from the dirt road onto the paved. Sonia unfolded the map and studied it a moment. "I don't know about you but I'm tired and could stop almost anytime. It's 5:30 now, but you're the driver and if you feel like going farther, it's fine with me."

"I'd like to get to Holland, at least," Jean replied. "Maybe even to Benton Harbor, if I feel all right. If we make it to Benton Harbor, we can be lazy in the morning and leave late enough to avoid rush-hour traffic."

Sonia put down the map, stretched and yawned. "I'm just looking forward to sleeping in a bed and to not having to talk to anyone except you for a few days. I like meeting and talking to women while I'm doing it, but I'm always glad when I'm through and can relax." Sonia put her seat back and closed her eyes. Within minutes she was asleep.

Jean concentrated on driving. When she reached Grand Haven, Lake Michigan spread splendidly out before her. She caught her breath with pleasure.

She had grown up very close to this lake, and had loved going with her family to the Indiana Dunes State Park to see the many species of birds and wildlife there. After she had gotten her own driver's license, she had frequently driven out to the dunes to walk along the lakeshore. Particularly in winter, when she could almost certainly count on being the only person on the beach.

She remembered one December when she was only 18 or 19. During a fierce snowstorm, she had sat high on a dune under a huge white pine, watching the waves of the lake pound against the sand. Then suddenly everything became very quiet. The lake calmed and the blizzard turned into lazy, fat, drifting snowflakes. Pulling her shawl closer around her and snuggling down against the tree trunk, she had fallen asleep and dreamed she was flying across the water, feeling the snow on her face. It had been a long time ago. A long, long time. But she still ached to fly.

The sign loomed large before her: Benton Harbor, one mile. And then a second, smaller sign: St. Joseph, four miles. She decided to go on to St. Joseph, and almost immediately found a motel there that looked both nice and inexpensive. Stopping the car at the office, she got out very quietly, careful not to disturb Sonia.

But when she returned to the car with their room key, Sonia was awake. "I really slept!" she announced. "I feel a lot better but I've forgotten what planet we're on."

"We're in the Pleiades, at the 'Gull's Inn' motel. The woman in there told me about a combination health food store and restaurant just around the corner. I'd like to go and get some supplies for the trip back. Maybe they'll have some decent soup or something for tonight, but if not, we can always fix ramen noodles." She steered the car into the space designated for room number seven.

The instant she stopped the car, Sonia grabbed the room key off the seat and darted into the room. The suddenness of it surprised Jean, and also that Sonia hadn't helped unload the car. But she shrugged it off, and opening the back of the wagon, began sorting through their suitcases and boxes, trying to decide what to take in. She had more or less figured it out when Sonia burst out of the room.

"Genius!" she shouted, dashing over to her. "I just discovered the damndest thing!" She grabbed a bag from the back of the car and followed Jean into the room, talking—a steady, rapid-fire stream of arousal.

"The reason I bolted so abruptly into the room was that I had to have a bowel movement. Not desperately. I could have waited a few more minutes and helped you unload the car. But instead I tore into that room, did it as quick as I could, then turned on the fan in the bathroom and frantically tried to open the window to let out the odor so you wouldn't know what I'd done—as if it were a crime, or something.

"Suddenly I saw myself, how crazed I was behaving. 'What kind of bizarre behavior is this?' I asked myself. Talk about shame!"

From the depths of the food box, Jean grunted. Sonia continued talking to her back. "So I've decided that from now on, whenever I need to have a bowel movement, you're invited. In fact, any woman who happens to be around at the time is invited to join me in the bathroom for a veritable sensory bonanza—sight, sound, and scent."

Feeling distinctly flustered, Jean was unable to suppress an embarrassed giggle. "That is," Sonia quickly qualified, "if you want to, of course."

Jean closed the box and turned around, her gaze automatically taking in the low-budget motel room complete with double bed, table and two chairs, and television set. Then her eyes fell upon the scene of the crime: the bathroom.

She felt odd, but managed to sound normal enough when she said, "I'd be glad to do that, Soni. I laughed because I was uncomfortable. That probably means I need to look at my own bathroom stuff." *Probably, nothing. You know you need to look at it. Like 30 years ago.* Quickly changing the subject, she went on, "But right now I'd like to get to that health food store before it closes, if it hasn't already."

"You go, Genius," Sonia said. "I'll take our dirty clothes to the laundromat across the street. I like doing laundry when I have something interesting to think about."

As Jean put her hand on the door knob, Sonia called her back. "I know you're in a hurry but I need to say something else before I conveniently forget it. When we talked a few days ago about my problem with gas, I was relieved that you weren't offended, but I didn't really take seriously your recommendation to keep 'burping, belching, and farting'. I've been thinking that it's one thing to say it—as you did—but another to really mean it, especially if I were just to let myself go.

"But I'm beginning to understand a lot about shame and how it affects me, so I know that regardless of how you feel about it, I'm going to have to do these things openly. Starting now, no more holding back!"

Jean hugged her hard. "Okay, folks. Let's give this little old lady in army boots a big fart . . . I mean, a big round of applause." Then she kissed her soundly.

"You're such a darling little old lady!" she laughed, opening the door for Sonia. "I mean, such a darling big womanly woman! Meet you back here for supper."

"Bring me something good, like mushroom stroganoff over toasted bread points with creamed baby onions and peas on the side!" Sonia called after her, and shifted the sack of dirty clothes into one arm so she could flip her vee for 'vulva power' to Jean as she drove off.

An hour and a half later, they were both back in their room eating hot soup and pita bread stuffed with hummus from the health food store. "Wonderful stroganoff!" Sonia murmured, swallowing a spoonful of minestrone soup. Between bites, Jean began telling Sonia what had happened to her at the health food store.

She had been wandering around the store, picking up this and that, browsing, reading labels, things she ordinarily did in an unfamiliar health food store. Suddenly she had noticed that the women behind the counter was looking at her intently, as though she might be a shoplifter.

So she stopped browsing and took her items to the checkout counter. The woman started to ring them through, then reached out and grabbed Jean's hand. Jean thought she had lost her marbles.

"Jean," the woman said urgently. "My name's Emily and I just got back last night from the festival up in Hart. That's where I saw you."

She went on to say that she'd never even heard of the festival until two weeks earlier, when one of her regular customers, Sage, came in to buy supplies to take there. She told Emily about it and then invited her to go. Emily thought she couldn't since she had to run the store, but Sage left her name and number, hoping she'd change her mind.

Emily didn't know what came over her but she found herself asking her two part-time helpers if they could manage the store for a week and they said yes. Then she called Sage and told her she wanted to go. Sage asked her if she had any camping equipment and Emily felt bad because she didn't; she'd never camped in her life. She assumed that that was the end of the discussion.

But Sage showed up the next day with a tent, sleeping bag, and other gear, and the next thing Emily knew, she was in Sage's truck headed for Hart.

When they got to the festival, Sage invited Emily to camp near her and her friends. They all helped her set up. But then they left and Emily felt very alone. She had no idea where to go, and besides, there were all these naked women all over the place and even though she was 55 years old, that scared her. At lunchtime Sage came and showed her where the food tents were, and it was there that she met a wonderful woman about her own age named Ruth. They liked each other right away and decided to do things together. Hang out, as Ruth said. She'd been to Michigan before and knew the ropes. Emily decided she wanted to camp near Ruth and her friends in an area designated for crones.

They attended Sonia and Jean's workshop, the one on sex and relationships. It changed Emily's life. She was married, had been since she was fifteen. Their workshop turned her head inside out. It made her realize that she didn't want to be married anymore, and that she didn't even like Sam, let alone love him. That was hard to admit because she knew she was supposed to love him through thick and thin.

When she told Ruth, Ruth introduced her to several women who had been married, and they talked for hours. Most of them had divorced later in life. Emily told them that she wanted to divorce but was afraid. Sam was a very powerful lawyer in St. Joe and she was sure he wouldn't let her go through with it. Ruth, who lived in Detroit, told her she could stay with her during the divorce proceedings, and Sally and Peg told her the same thing. Everyone was very helpful.

When she got home, she went straight to Sam and told him she wanted a divorce. He laughed at her, told her she was crazy, that she wouldn't last a minute out there alone, that she needed a psychiatrist, not a divorce. When she insisted that she was serious and that she was moving out, he got nasty and threatened to commit her. He scared the daylights out of her. Then, when she came out of the bathroom after her shower, he grabbed her and raped her.

As soon as he fell asleep, she got up, put a few things together, and went to the store. In the morning, she called her lawyer and began divorce proceedings. After talking with her lawyer, she called Rita, one of her part-time helpers, and asked if she still wanted to buy the store. She did. Then she called Ruth, who was delighted to hear from her and very supportive of her decision. She reminded Emily that there was a room for her in her home.

She told Jean, "I'm excited and scared and happy, and it's all because of you and Sonia."

Jean told her it wouldn't have mattered what she and Sonia had said if she hadn't been ready to hear it. She had done it because she was a courageous, powerful woman who finally realized she didn't have to take anymore abuse. Jean told her that her decision was going to make it easier for other women to leave abusive situations and have their own lives. When Jean pulled her wallet out to pay for the groceries, Emily told her no. She wanted the food to be a gift.

Sonia let out a long, low whistle. "That's quite a story, Genius. You're right, of course. Her escape does make it easier for all the rest of us. But that doesn't really matter. What matters is that she's doing it for *herself.*"

Then Sonia ran a hot bath and soaked in it while Jean consulted the map. "I think I'd like to take I-94 through Indiana and then pick up I-80 on the trip home," she called to Sonia.

"Sounds good to me. Jeannie, come join me in here. The water's still hot."

Jean folded the map and placed it in Sonia's bag. Then stripping off all her clothes except for her T-shirt, she went into the bathroom, stopping at the toilet to pee before taking off her shirt and joining Sonia in the tub.

"I didn't know you'd brought bubble bath," Jean said, sitting between Sonia's feet.

"I didn't. I just poured in some of the shampoo." She scooped up a handful of bubbles and rubbed them over Jean's shoulders and neck. The warm water and the sweet smell of shampoo made Jean suddenly aware of how tired she was, and she let herself relax against the back of the tub. She was almost asleep when Sonia got out, but roused herself enough to pull the plug and follow her. She barely made it to the bed, and thought she would be asleep before she got her light off.

But serious abdominal cramping kept her wakeful. Finally, she gave up and turned towards Sonia, who was propped up on pillows working a crossword puzzle.

She studied her a long moment, marveling at how dear she looked in her oversized glasses, and she felt flooded with deep, deep appreciation. That feeling was soon replaced by such a sharp pain that she was surprised into a small, involuntary cry.

Startled, Sonia looked up from her crossword.

"Just a little twinge," Jean explained quickly.

Sonia closed the puzzle book and lay it beside her. Jean *never* cried out, never even complained about anything, so she suspected that the 'little twinge' was a good deal more than that.

Neither spoke for a moment. "It's like the pee pot," Jean finally said. "The same thing. I'm sick of it and I'm sick of me."

Sonia looked perplexed but kept quiet.

"I know the first step. I know I have to talk about it, that silence just reinforces my feelings of shame and guilt and self-hatred."

She frowned. "But I don't want to. I really, really don't want to talk about it." Then with a sigh, she relented. "But I know I have to."

She was quiet again for a few moments. "Okay," she forced herself to say, not looking at Sonia. "I'm having abdominal pain and cramping, not unusual under the circumstances." She hesitated again, for a moment searching desperately for a way out of having to go on. She felt as if she couldn't say it, *couldn't*.

"I don't know how to begin," she protested. "It's so hard I don't think I can." Sonia, who was determined to stay out of it, was beginning to be afraid. She couldn't imagine what it was Jean was trying to tell her, but she was prepared for the worst. AIDS, a brain tumor . . .

"Jean," she said, "I'm sorry you're having such a hard time."

Jean nodded wearily. "I know, Soni. I'm so sick of myself, that's all. Before I started these experiments, before I came to Wildfire, I had no idea I had all this stuff in me. I know it's good to see it and even better to get rid of it, but I seem to have come up against a brick wall with a couple of these things. Like the pee pot. And now this.

"I know I'll never get free of the shame and guilt and fear if I don't first acknowledge and talk about it, but I'm feeling discouraged because I talked about the pee pot thing and that didn't do any good."

"That was only five days ago," Sonia reminded her. "And also that was a very unusual situation. You don't have any problems urinating when I'm in the bathroom with you at home now—an enormous step for someone who has been unable to use public restrooms at all."

"You're right," Jean admitted. "But I'm afraid of this other one, afraid to look at it and talk about it because I don't know if I'm ever going to be able to get over it."

"Try," Sonia urged softly. "Trust yourself."

Jean stared unseeing at the pattern on the bedspread, absentmindedly tracing it with a fingertip. Taking a deep breath, she started to speak, her voice oddly flat and emotionless.

"We've been gone for over a week now, and in that time I haven't had one bowel movement. I can't. When I travel something happens to me and I freeze up, or I should say, stop up. This is the main reason I don't like to travel, especially for more than a few days, because I end up bloated and miserable.

"But it's not just a problem when I'm travelling. I can hardly have a bowel movement if there's anyone else in the house with me. I wait until you're downstairs or outside, and hope you won't come up before I get through. Sometimes I've gone to the third floor bathroom. On days when there are other women around, I go down to the outhouse by the barn. Or I just don't go at all and then get painfully constipated. So you can see how serious it is."

She finally looked up and seeing the surprised look on Sonia's face, hurried on.

"It all came up tonight when you told me about your bowel movement experiment, and how you want me or anyone else who's around to come into the bathroom with you when you're having one. I tried to imagine doing that and nearly lost it." Sonia nodded but said nothing.

"I've been living with this forever. I've known there was something really wrong with my reactions and my fears, but I've thought that since this was the way I was, I'd just have to live with it. So somehow I've managed to cope."

"But now you're beginning to see that you may not have to live with it," Sonia prompted.

Jean nodded, and her eyes filled with tears she was determined not to shed. "I'm just afraid I won't be able to do it. I mean, terrified doesn't begin to cover the feelings I have about this. The thought of doing what you're going to do, Soni, makes me want to die on the spot." She picked up the glasses Sonia had discarded and began worrying at the frames.

"I had no idea, Jeannie."

Still looking at the bedspread and the glasses she held in her hands, Jean moved doggedly on. "Even when I was in a relationship, I couldn't have a bowel movement if my lover was in the house. I had to wait until she left, or use one of our motel bathrooms.

"I remember the winter I had pneumonia. I had a raging fever and was so weak I could barely get out of bed. One night I was awakened by excruciating cramps in my bowels and knew I had to get to a toilet, fast. But I was in bed with my partner, and although she was asleep, I knew I couldn't use my bathroom. I managed to pull some clothes on and leave the house to go over to the motel.

"When I stepped outside, I was almost blown back inside by an icy, snow-laden wind. We were having a blizzard so fierce I couldn't see more than two inches in front of me and could barely keep my balance. Nevertheless, somehow I made it to the motel in time, but was so weak I knew I couldn't fight the storm again to get back to my house. So I crawled into the bed in the motel and spent the rest of the night there, sick with worry that my partner would wake up, find me gone, and call the police or something. Just before dawn, I managed to get up and stagger back through the storm to the house. She was still asleep. It took me five weeks to recover."

"No wonder!" Sonia exclaimed. "Snowstorms aren't renowned as cures for pneumonia."

Jean looked at Sonia. "I know there's a truckload of shame here, but I think there's more than shame. I'd really like some suggestions if you have any."

"What if you just take one step at a time, beginning with not leaving the house to go to the outhouse? Close the door, lock it if you need to, but stay in the house, even if there are others in it. Then, when that seems comfortable, you might try not locking the door, or not waiting until I go downstairs. You may still want to close the door. I think you shouldn't push yourself beyond what you're capable of at the moment."

Jean nodded. "I know I'm not ready to do what you're about to do, Sonia. But I really hate waiting. Part of me says I've got to push or I'll never get anywhere, and yet, I'm afraid that if I push I'll only regress. Now that I've talked about this I want it to be over with. I want to be free of shame, easy and relaxed with my body and all its functions."

"I'm sure you know what's best for you and I'm glad to be involved in any capacity you'd like," Sonia told her. "I'll depend on you to let me know what I can do. I would like to say that if there's any way you can empty that poor, suffering bowel before we get home, I'd be ecstatic."

"That won't happen. If it did, I'd be ecstatic, too. But it's impossible at this point."

Jean sighed. She was too warm, so she sat up and took off her T-shirt. Sonia followed suit, and Jean waited for her to lie down with her back towards her so she could rub it until sleep overcame them both.

Jean was still more comfortable doing the touching than being touched, so Sonia bided her time. She knew that Jean was slowly relaxing her inner guard, and that when the day came that she was sure there would never be—*could* never be—sex between them, she'd find she loved to be touched every bit as much as she loved to touch.

Sonia shivered deliciously as Jean lightly stroked her back, then snuggled closer and went to sleep with a smile on her face.

They were going home.

22

The Michigan Womyn's Music Festival marked the end of summer, the West Coast Festival at Yosemite the beginning of autumn. The Yosemite Festival was a pleasant change from Michigan—smaller, more personal, less frantic.

Their workshop was scheduled for Thursday afternoon at two. At 1:30 a woman in her mid-forties, dressed only in a loincloth, rushed breathlessly up to their booth.

"I'm so excited about your workshop," she told Jean. She and her lover, she said, had wasted five hundred dollars on a lesbian couples' workshop a few weeks before.

"The strategies the presenters suggested for success were the same dreary, doomed, deadly ones that everyone already knows. They must have said 'compromise' a hundred times that weekend. They talked about fairness, about the necessity of checking out how the other was feeling, about keeping the sex hot, and about being willing to sit down and process problems. I could hardly wait to get out of there."

Jean's head spun with deja vu. The therapist she and one of her exes had seen for 18 months had said these same things to them, promising that if they would do them, their relationship would work. "Work" did not mean they would be happy, of course; it meant they would be able somehow not to break up. It seemed that happiness was not a therapeutic concept. In all their sessions, she had never heard it mentioned. Maybe it was because women did not remember any longer what happiness was, what it felt like. Maybe they mistook contentment for it and assumed that this was the most they could expect. Or maybe, despite the common brainwashing to the contrary, somewhere deep inside them women knew full well that relationships do not and cannot deliver happiness.

She thought about how often during those long months of therapy she had protested, "But I don't want to process; I just want to talk about things," and how neither her partner nor their therapist had been able to understand the difference. Over and over she had explained that because processing was goal-oriented, demanding resolution, participants manipulated and coerced each other into some sort of compromise, and that they most often did this through guilt. Talking about things was very different, she had insisted. Each person simply said her piece and the other just listened without taking any responsibility for the feelings expressed. Her partner and therapist thought that sounded futile.

Jean grimaced at the memory. She knew now why they had felt that way: processing is integral to relationshipping, and they were in therapy to try to make their relationship work. She also knew now that she had been right about talking things over. She and Sonia did it all the time and it worked like a dream.

Once when the Murder Maids group had been discussing this, Lauren had asked her to give examples of both processing and talking about things so she could see the difference.

"Okay," Jean had said. "Supposing that at one of our meetings, I complain that Murder Maids isn't what I expected it to be, that I thought we'd get to know each other better than we have.

"Your socialization would tell you to process this, to try to solve my problem. You might all try to think of ways to disclose more about yourselves, and to get to know me personally. You might decide to set aside time to visit me, or to call me on the phone more often. You would all try to take responsibility for alleviating my discomfort. This is processing.

"If we were just talking about it, on the other hand, you'd listen to me but you wouldn't feel guilty, or responsible for my feelings, and wouldn't think you had to do something about them. Since I'd know you weren't going to take my problem on, I'd take responsibility for solving it and talk only about what I myself could do to feel closer to you. Your treating me like a competent adult would help me be one."

Jean shook herself out of her reverie. Glancing at her watch, she gathered her things and hurried to their workshop site where she spoke first to the woman in charge of the sound equipment. Another woman, holding a large reel-to-reel tape recorder, waylaid her and asked for permission to tape the workshop. Excerpts of it, she explained, would be played over station KMUN in Los Angeles. Jean gave her permission, then turned to survey the crowd.

Most of the women who had attended the previous workshop had remained in their seats for this one. However, by the time two o'clock rolled around, many more had joined them. Jean watched Sonia maneuver her way through the crowd.

They had only two hours, not enough time to say all the things they wanted to say, so they condensed the Michigan workshop, picking out and concentrating on the key elements. But somehow, as it always did, the workshop took on a life of its own.

About halfway through Jean took the mike and told the audience about a woman sociologist who, over a twenty-year period, interviewed women about their sex lives. Sonia and Jean had both been boggled by the findings: of the thousands of respondents, 100 percent admitted to faking pleasure some of the time during sex, 95 percent admitted to faking orgasm at least part of the time, and 75 percent admitted to faking orgasm *all the time*.

It was the 75 percent that had made the greatest impact on both of them. Seventy-five percent of women were lying to their partners *all the time*. "How can we have intimacy," Sonia challenged the audience, "if we're lying to each other during what patriarchy tells us are our closest possible moments?

"I felt very smug after hearing those statistics," Sonia went on, "because I'd never faked an orgasm in my life. When I bragged about this to the woman who had done the study, she asked, 'But have you faked pleasure?' I thought a moment and then admitted I had. 'What's the difference?' she asked. She had me there, because of course there is no difference. Faking is faking. Lying is lying.

"You might be thinking, 'So, what's the big deal? Why does it matter?' Well, when I pretend to feel something I don't, I give the woman I'm with inaccurate data about me. If she has false data, she makes false assumptions about who I am. In this way I have prevented her from knowing me. She can't be close to someone she doesn't really know. That means that if we want intimacy, faking matters. Faking of any kind of enjoyment—of meals she prepares or movies we see together or each other's parents or children or friends or pets—destroys closeness.

"Relationships demand that we fake, all the time. Sex demands that we fake all the time. That's the only condition upon which we can have either of them. That's why I state unequivocally that sex and intimacy, relationships and intimacy, are antithetical, that they can't exist in the same place at the same time. Sex and relationships *destroy* intimacy."

She stopped to gather her thoughts and to let her words have a moment to sink in. "Let's take a look at what those statistics mean in real life," she went on. "They mean that the odds are very high that the woman you are sitting next to, the woman you are in a relationship with, is lying to you about what she feels in bed. She's probably faking orgasm, and she is almost certainly faking pleasure. And so are you. What the hell is going on with you two? What are you doing? Where's the joy in living this way? Why are you accepting men's lies about sex so willingly?

"I have no doubt that men are sexual, that they have to have sex. This is their nature. I also believe that men have no concept of truth, that they lie all the time because this is simply the way they are.

"But I don't believe women are like this. In fact, I know we aren't. So let's stop trying to be like men and figure out instead what we are as women, what it means to be female."

She stepped back and gave the microphone to Jean. Those statistics had caused her a great deal of distress, Jean told the audience, because she was one of that 75 percent who had never experienced orgasm with a partner and had always lied about it.

"It got to the place where I didn't even know I was faking," Jean admitted. "It was automatic, not even conscious anymore. It was just what I did at a certain place in the sex dance.

"And then I reached the place where I wasn't satisfied with faking just once. I faked multiple orgasms and pleased my partners even more, made them feel even better about their skills as lovers. Being a compulsive over-achiever and a please-aholic, it was not unusual for me to fake twelve or thirteen orgasms in fifteen minutes." The audience first gasped, then roared with laughter.

Sonia took the mike. "Some of you are very aware that you fake both orgasm and pleasure. But I'm sure there are others of you sitting here who think our statistics have nothing to do with you, like Jean did until a week ago— faking everything but really believing that you don't because you've denied it so long. Really believing that the writhing and moaning you turn on at the crucial point is an orgasm.

"I feel an incredible urgency for us all to wake up, as if there's not much time, knowing somehow and fiercely that remaining asleep is far more dangerous than we can imagine. The longer we live in illusion, the deeper we dig our own graves. I want us to be alive and free, totally and completely who we are, and not who we think we are."

She stepped back and Jean took the microphone.

"They say sex is natural, but nothing could have been less natural for me. I had to fantasize in order to feel anything at all," she said. "If I tried simply to experience what was actually happening, I felt nothing, or very little. Often I even felt turned off, and eager—almost desperate—for it to be over. So in order to work up any sexual excitation, I had to get out of my real feelings, out of the truth of the moment, and fantasize myself into some illusion. And even that wasn't always successful. Often I'd just give up and, as Queen Elizabeth suggested, close my eyes and think of England. And even this didn't always work."

Jean waited for the laughter to subside. "But one of the most sobering experiences I ever had occurred in a workshop on lesbian sexuality. On the last day, the participants were asked to write down what they did in order to enhance their sexual experiences with one another. This was done anonymously, so no one would feel awkward or exposed. In a group of more than forty women, at least a dozen who wrote that they watched videos of men fucking each other in order to be able to have sex."

The audience gasped, and one women yelled, "Gross!"

"You act shocked," Jean went on, "but I'm willing to bet there are women in this audience right now for whom this applies. This is *natural?*

"Obviously, I don't think sex is natural for women. What something like this tells me is that sex is basically a male thing, and that many women have to watch men's excitation in order to feel it themselves, have to get a vicarious turn-on because it's really not part of their natures. Have to imitate men."

"I may never have had to fantasize," Sonia told the crowd, taking her turn, "but I always had to work like mad to get my body to respond the way I thought it should. Let me tell you how it went.

"It's night and Marcy and I are lying in bed snuggling and kissing a little before we go to sleep. Suddenly, I get the message from her—perhaps some way she touches me, some unexpected urgency in her kiss—that she would like to have sex. I immediately examine my physical and emotional condition to see if there's any chance that I might want or even be able to go through with it. Let's say that this night I decide to do it.

"I let her know this by responding to her urgency with my own. I press my body harder against hers, I kiss her deeper, I let her know that the answer is yes. As she goes into action, the first thing I have to do is flip my sex switch. That is, I tell my body that it can't just lie there and do what it wants to do, it has to get to work and get excited as fast as it can.

"So let's say that in due course Marcy has, not without difficulty, managed as gracefully as she can to get her head between my legs and her mouth on my vulva.

"At this point my anxiety level soars. I know chances are pretty good that she's not totally comfortable down there. Beds and bedclothes aren't designed with this activity in mind, you know. So even though I'm as far up at the top of the bed as I can get, and even lying kitty-corner so she has more room, she's probably half off the bed, her legs tangled in the sheets and blankets, slowly going numb. If we haven't thought to elevate my bottom enough, her neck's certainly breaking, and may be anyway. There's not much air down there even when we've made air tunnels in the bedding, and she's also working, so she's probably about to expire from the heat. And to ease the pressure on her neck, she may be up on one elbow, rubbing it raw. She's also surely beginning to feel the need to pee. So all in all, I know I have only so long to get this show on the road before she regrets ever thinking of the idea."

She paused while the audience screamed with laughter.

"I also know that if it takes too long and she suffers too much too often, she's going to look around for someone who gives her more and quicker reward.

"So to save the relationship, I get seriously into my sex mode, gathering up all the feelings in my body and focusing them in my vulva. I close out all other thoughts, all other sensations, and focus. Focus now, Sonia. Focus. Focus. That's it, it's beginning to happen. Don't let your mind wander. Focus on that vulva, focus, focus, that's it, that's . . . Dammit, the telephone's ringing!

"We both wait, suspended, until the machine picks up the call. Having completely lost the hard-earned flickers of beginning excitement, I rise up on one elbow, search for her head among the jumble of blankets, and ask her if she is still interested in going on. She hesitates a moment, then says yes, but she has to pee first. After she struggles up out of her cocoon and goes to the bathroom, we assume the position and start all over again. This time, I am frantic with the need to hurry. This has been going on for centuries.

"Hurry, Sonia, focus, focus, hurry now. There, focus, don't think, just do it. Good, good, there's something happening now. Stay with it, don't let it go. Focus, focus, ah, here it comes, keep it coming, don't take your mind off it, don't stop, keep coming, now do it, do it, do it, DO IT! Oh, what a relief—here it is. I did it! Finally I did it. All is well. The relationship is saved!"

The audience was in hysterics of recognition.

"And so I have an orgasm, and I enjoy it. At least I think I do. What I'm sure I enjoy is the relief that I was able to do it, that I made it happen again, that in the nick of time I saved the day, again. Thank goodness."

She stopped abruptly and a look of shock passed over her face. "My god," she said to the audience. "I just heard what I said. I made my body have an orgasm. I *forced* her." Now oblivious of the audience, to herself she quickly re-ran the tape of what she had just said.

"Do you know something?" she continued aloud, wonderment in her voice. "I haven't the slightest idea what my body would do on her own, if I didn't tyrannize her to get excited. How could I know? I've never given her free rein. I've always made her exhibit sexually appropriate behavior. I've always dictated to her what she had to feel. I haven't the least idea if she even wants to have orgasm. It's just an assumption I've made based on the usual man-aical disinformation."

She shook her head in disbelief, tears rolling unnoticed down her face. "How could I have been so dense, so cruel? I came out of my mother's womb shouting 'Freedom!' and haven't stopped talking about it since, but all the time, I've kept my body in bondage. No more," she stated firmly. "I promise my body that I will never make her do anything, ever again."

The women in the audience leapt to their feet, applauding, screaming 'Go for it, Sonia!' It was a perfect ending, totally unrehearsed and unprepared for.

Later in the tent, the sound of music and women's voices in the distance, Sonia turned to Jean in the soft evening light. "You know, Genius, I've been lying here thinking about what happened in that workshop today, and I realize that one of the things I miss about sex is the feeling of a woman's warm mouth on my vulva. Not the excitation, stimulus/response aspect of it, just that warm mouth. Now I'm asking myself, 'Who said that was sex?'"

Jean sat up in her sleeping bag. "You're right. It never even occurred to me. Somehow I've just assumed it must be sex, but why? Nothing else we've done thus far has been—not kissing, not touching vulvas and breasts. Why would this be different?"

"You know what this means," she said, crawling out of her bag. "Out of our bags and into another experiment!"

Ten minutes later, Jean, propped up on pillows, was looking down at Sonia's head between her legs. She felt very strange and slightly foolish. She had never enjoyed this and now she felt awkward in addition. She had always liked having her mouth on a woman's vulva, but not the reverse. She tried taking deep, slow breaths to get herself to relax, to get her mind to stop interfering.

And then . . . a flood of warmth, indescribable feelings of love and joy and sorrow rolled into one, mixed with tears and trembling and salt spray. It was like nothing she had ever felt, ever known. Pulling Sonia tightly against her, she wept with relief and joy, her body vibrating with life and wildness.

As Sonia later described it in a speech: "At first I was nervous. I knew how to act in sex where my purpose was to give my partner an orgasm, to 'satisfy' her. This accomplished, I could assure myself that I was a good lover.

"But with Jean that night there was no goal. Before I began, I wasn't sure how I would feel when I was there with her vulva and not doing sex. Would I really want to lick and kiss her? I made up my mind that if it didn't feel good to me, I wouldn't continue.

"But fortunately it was delightful—and the first time I had ever *experienced* a woman's vulva. Because in sex we aren't experiencing one another at all; we're experiencing each other's *reactions*—a very, very different story. That night, in that tent, I knew what it was like to have my mouth on a woman's vulva: lovelier than anything I've ever known."

She smiled over at Jean. "Your vulva may have been numb in sex, but out of it, it's very vul-vacious and lots of fun."

Jean blushed. Her vulva's rowdiness embarrassed her.

"Also," she admitted to the assembled crowd, "I had a hard time understanding orgasm. Once I understood that sex was not normal for women, not what we ever did in freedom, I assumed that that was also true of orgasm; that orgasm was a conditioned sexual response. When I first had an orgasm with Sonia touching me, I was horrified. I thought I'd slipped back into my male mind and done sex. Even though it didn't feel like it, the fact that I'd experienced orgasm threw me. Now I know that if we don't force our bodies, if we just let them be and refuse to flip the sex switch, orgasm is a natural response.

"I don't always have orgasms when Sonia touches my vulva, or when I'm touching her myself for that matter. Sometimes I drift off to sleep, or come very close. Sometimes I feel as though orgasm is imminent, then the feeling dwindles away; my body has had all she wants. But whatever happens, it always feels lovely and sweet, and I don't have to worry about it."

When in the course of the experiment, Jean put her mouth on Sonia's vulva, Sonia's experience was different from Jean's. She *had* experienced orgasm from having her vulva kissed and licked in sex, so her body—and hence vulva—were trained to respond to that stimulus in a specific way. Now she had consciously to turn her mind off, and deliberately refrain from flipping the sex switch—a hard habit to break. Without excitation, the experience felt a little flat to her.

"In fact," she told Jean, "I almost fell asleep once I got past the familiar urge to flip sex on. Your kissing and licking felt good, very relaxing and very comforting—not at all what I'm accustomed to in sex. But I'm afraid that, without the switch, my vulva's going to be pretty numb for awhile. I'm hoping that once she realizes I'm not going to do sex with her anymore, she'll dare revert to her original wild self—and be as vul-canic as yours."

Like Sonia, when Jean had her mouth on Sonia's vulva, she felt as if it were the first time she had ever really *felt* what it was like to kiss and lick a vulva—indescribably sweet.

"What worries me," Sonia admitted to Jean that night, "but only a little, is that women will listen to us talking about our experiments and think we're doing sex. It makes me want to shut up forever. But I know that talking about it, telling the truth as I see it, is part of my purpose in this life. Part of me wants other women to understand—that what we're doing is as far from what men call sex as it's possible to get—and part of me doesn't give a hoot. The part that doesn't give a hoot is growing larger, thank goodness. I keep telling myself that all that's required of me is to say what I have to say, without making assumptions, without having expectations. What women do with it is none of my business."

She leaned over and kissed Jean lightly on the mouth before turning over in her bag and going to sleep.

Twenty minutes later, however, she woke up abruptly, and lying there trying to figure out what had awakened her, began wondering what was going on with Jean. She seemed uncharacteristically restless, changing positions every minute or two.

"Genius," she whispered. "Are you all right?"

Jean unzipped her bag and gingerly sat up. "My back aches a little," she admitted. "I helped Carrie load all those boxes into her van and I guess I overdid it."

Knowing how stoic Jean was, how fiercely reluctant ever to admit that she was ill or in pain, Sonia realized that she must be in terrific pain now, probably in need of an ambulance and emergency procedures.

"I've never told you this," Jean said, "but when I was sixteen, I broke my neck and was in a cast for a year. I qualified for disability after that because my entire back was affected by the accident. I was unable to turn my head to either side and was told I'd be on muscle relaxants and pain pills the rest of my life. Anyhow," she waved that aside, "I've managed to do well in spite of the prognosis, but sometimes, if I overdo it, it gives me some trouble."

While Jean had been talking, Sonia had been thinking about the varicose-vein experiment. Jean had kept her word and had massaged her legs every night in an attempt to prevent the varicosities from worsening. And although the massage had helped, Sonia had been resigned to living with them for the rest of her life.

Then one night, as Jean had begun her massage, she had suddenly stopped in mid-stroke, leaned down and begun kissing and licking Sonia's right leg along the varicose vein. As she had, she had spoken gently to the leg: "You are so perfect, so beautiful. You don't have to be sick for me to do this, you know. I'll stroke you and kiss you even if you're well." She had then repeated this with the second leg.

The next night, she had rubbed oil into the right leg, and, before beginning the massage, made her usual examination of the vein by running her thumb over the top of it, applying some pressure, to see what Sonia's reaction was. In the beginning, Sonia hadn't been able to tolerate any pressure. A month later, she could tolerate some, but not a great deal.

When Jean had made her examination that night, however, Sonia hadn't stirred. Jean had tried again, this time applying more pressure. Still no reaction. She had made a third attempt, applying even more pressure and getting no response. Not only that, but she had not even been able to find the vein that just the night before had been very obvious under her fingers—ropey, tough, and protruding. Ridiculous, she thought. It has to be here somewhere.

A quick examination of the left leg had showed the same thing—no pain, no vein. Unable to believe it, Jean had begun searching the leg all over, looking for that darned vein. It was gone. The varicose veins had simply vanished.

Although they had hardly been able to credit it, they had known that it had to be the result of unconditional touching and licking.

And now, in a tent in the Yosemite wilderness, Sonia was wondering if she could do the same thing for Jean's back. She argued with herself, pointing out that she wasn't a healer like Jean so she couldn't do it. *But why not?* her obstinate side argued back. *Just because Jean's done a lot of healing in her life and you haven't doesn't mean you can't start now. In our wild state all women healed, all the time.*

"Jean, I don't know how much I can do, but I'd like to try to help your back."

Willing to try anything, Jean took off her T-shirt and lay down on her stomach. All Sonia knew to do was what she had watched Jean do with her legs. So straddling her, she prepared to lick and kiss and talk love-talk to her back.

"Before I start," she whispered to Jean, "tell me where it hurts most so I can concentrate whatever little bit of healing stuff I have on the worst place. I'm sure there's not enough in me to spread over your whole back."

Jean laughed softly. "Sounds like you're buttering toast. Okay, the worst pain is high between my shoulder blades, right here." She crooked her arm around to point it out.

"Try to relax, if you can," Sonia told her, and, feeling very foolish, bent over and began.

Earlier, while Jean had been explaining why her back hurt, Sonia had been trying to imagine herself kissing and licking it. In imagination, it had seemed awkward and distasteful. Licking, for crying out loud! She hated having a wet face, and the thought of dragging her chin through her own saliva and having to kiss skin wet with it was disgusting.

But, as so often is the case, reality was quite different from fantasy. "This is easy," she thought with surprise, "and nice." It felt familiar, like something she had done a hundred times, knew how to do very well, and loved. Almost at once, she felt Jean relax and knew by her breathing that she was asleep. But she continued, and as she did, the familiarity and pleasure deepened, thinking stopped, and she became all body, body out of time and space, body melting into Jean and the night until she was encompassed by and encompassing everything. She had never before felt such power and well-being.

Finally, she brought herself back into time and space, and sat up. *I've been out of patriarchy*, she thought exultantly. *And I got out through my body. That's the key, somehow. The body. It all keeps coming back to the body.*

Then, knowing without thought what to do next, following her body's direction, she took off her shirt and lay down gently, covering as much of Jean's back with her own body as she could. Just as she had known to lie down, she knew when to get up. Jean was still asleep. Quietly, she put her shirt back on and crept into her own bag.

She was awakened by a series of small rustlings, stifled coughs, and muted blowings of nose. Prying one sleepy eye open, she looked directly into two wide-awake green eyes, very near her nose. Her own eyes forgot their reluctance to greet the day and flew open, accompanied by an involuntary shriek. "Jean, holy fartbeetles!"

Jean looked startled herself.

"You scared me, that's all, your eyes up so close and enormous. I didn't know what they were at first. What's up?"

"Soni, I still can't believe it. I woke up around four o'clock and knew something was different. For one thing, it was four o'clock and the first time I had wakened all night. This is *not* normal for me. And then I realized I couldn't feel my back." At Sonia's surprised look, she hastened to explain.

"I mean, I could feel my back, I knew I had one, but it didn't feel the way it usually does. So I sat up and moved around, and nothing happened. Then I tried stretching it, still nothing. You know how I can't sit with my legs straight out in front of me? Well look, I can do it now. And watch this." She crossed her legs. "I haven't been able to sit cross-legged since I was fifteen years old."

Her eyes were shining.

Sonia started to say something, but stopped when she realized Jean wasn't through.

"After I'd tried each of these positions and realized that I could do them and that I didn't have any pain at all, the only explanation I could come up with was that I was dead, that I'd died in the night and that my spirit hadn't left yet. Death was the only thing I could imagine that would take the pain so entirely away.

"Then when I heard some woman in a tent nearby get up to pee, and another one cough, I knew I wasn't dead, and that's when I remembered what you did last night. I'd forgotten until then, probably because I went to sleep almost immediately.

"You did it, Sonia. With your little teeny bit of healing stuff, you stopped the pain for the first time in two decades."

Sonia frowned uneasily. "Well, it probably won't last very long so better enjoy it while you can."

"Stop," Jean shushed her. "Ask yourself if your jump legs have come back and then ask yourself why this should be any different.

"Anyway," she went on quickly before Sonia could retort, "I was dying to tell you, but you were so sound asleep I couldn't bear to wake you. So I just lay here for a couple of hours until I couldn't stand it anymore and began making little noises . . ."

"Aha, you passive aggressor, you!"

". . . like clearing my throat, and zipping and unzipping my sleeping bag, and . . ."

"And coughing and blowing your nose."

"You got it."

"Yeah, I tried to integrate all those little sounds into my dreams, but finally there got to be too many to make room for and my frustration woke me up—to two big scary green eyes."

Speculating about how and why they had been able to heal each other, Sonia said, "I'll bet this is what women did before patriarchy. But maybe not quite. There was probably no illness in women's world because we so loved and cherished ourselves and one another, were so completely happy. And knew our bodies and one another's so intimately, knew the taste and smell of every healthy body—like Chenoa told you. If a liver even thought of having difficulty, for instance, one of us would taste or smell that thought and lick and kiss and love that liver until the impending illness was dispelled—a kiss or two, a lick, a word of love and appreciation. That's all it took. Women still have this instinct; you know, 'Let Mommy kiss it better'."

Jean smiled. "I love the thought of it, Soni. I want that again, more than I can say."

"We have it again."

Jean shook her head. "That's not enough. I want all women to have it."

"And they could, if they got out of their sex minds. But no one can heal as women once did—so quickly, so effortlessly—as long as they're doing sadomasochism with each other. That means women in relationships can't do this with each other."

"I'm sure you're right. No woman can do it until she's in her power again, and all things patriarchal strip her of that, particularly relationships and sex; as we know, these are the essence of maleness. I just wish other women would understand it."

She slipped out of her bag and crawled to the door of the tent. "Even when they're told what relationships are about," she went on, squatting over the pee pot, "they close their eyes and ears and keep on doing them, or rationalize by saying they're doing *something different*." Seeing the surprised look on Sonia's face, she realized what *she* was doing. "Good grief," was all she could say, looking down between her legs at the pot rapidly filling up. Looking back up at Sonia, she began to laugh.

All it had taken was for her to be out of her conditioned, fearful, shame-filled mind long enough for her body to take over and do what it wanted to do. Their experience and arousing conversation had given her body the break she had been waiting for, and she had gone for it, straight to the pee pot before Jean could realize what was going on and stop it with her fears. One more piece of shame biting the dust that Sunday morning.

Despite her hope that both her legs and Jean's back were permanently healed, Sonia found it hard to believe that her ministrations of that night would have any lasting effect. But as month after month went by and Jean had little or no back pain, she finally had to acknowledge that somehow she had permanently stopped it.

"It's just too good to be true," she'd say. "Things like this just don't happen." And Jean would say, "You're right. It didn't just 'happen', we did it. We did it with unconditional touch, the power we used—the power we *were*—for billions of years before men came."

23

On Sunday afternoon, they packed their gear and personal belongings and, leaving the spectacular Yosemite wilderness behind, headed for home. They had only a few days before their three-week tour of Canada, a few days in which to ship out the orders that had accumulated, make hundreds of phone calls, and pack for the unpredictable Canadian weather.

Clare was ecstatic when they pulled in the driveway, eager to hear about their trip and to have someone to talk to. Although she and Barb had gotten together almost every other night, Clare was a social woman who enjoyed lots of women around her. "I talked to the dogs almost non-stop," she confessed.

Jean wracked her brain trying to think of someone who might come and stay with Clare while they were gone. As it happened, the day before they left, Sonia's old friend Sandy called. A fugitive from patriarchy, she was living in Los Angeles and finally, joyfully, going out of her mind. She needed a place to do it and thought of the mountains, of Sonia's place. Sonia handed the phone to Clare, they hit it off well, and Sandy was on her way. Clare's spirits were high as she drove them to the airport.

On their first weekend in Canada, they did a three-day retreat that opened up whole new vistas for experimentation and led to some of their most important insights.

In this workshop, they talked for the first time about shame. A lot had happened between Sonia's moment of realization in that motel bathroom in Michigan and the Canadian tour. One afternoon, she told the group, between Michigan and California, she and Jean had been lying naked out on the deck, sunbathing. She had been very taken by the way the sunlight was glinting off Jean's pubic hair and had called her attention to it. When Jean had raised her head to look, Sonia had jumped up and run inside for a mirror. Although Jean had felt embarrassed and very exposed, she had tried hard to suppress it. Then she had realized what she was doing and had told Sonia how she really felt.

"I didn't intend to make you uncomfortable, Genius. It was just so pretty I wanted you to see it."

"I'm glad you did because I didn't know I still felt so ugly and self-conscious. It's ridiculous to feel this way, and I want to get over it. So if you want to, I'd like you to go even further and look at my vulva."

Jean had been lying on a blanket, with her knees up. Sonia had gently pushed them apart, but all she had been able to see was reddish-gold fur and the insides of her thighs. "I'm going to get a pillow so I can see better," she had told her, and had gone back into the house to get one.

The pillow had made a lot of difference. When Sonia had parted Jean's legs, she had gasped. "Oh, Jeannie, you are so beautiful. You look like an O'Keefe painting, like New Mexico, with the pink-red rocks, the arroyos, the faintest hint of purple. You are so beautiful." During this, Jean had lain perfectly still, her eyes closed, and when it was over, had told Sonia truthfully that it hadn't been as bad as she had feared.

"Now, I'd like you to do the same thing for me," Sonia had said.

They had switched places and Jean had had the same initial reaction as Sonia: "gorgeous!" She had then gone on to describe her vulva to her, but in mid-description Sonia had suddenly lifted her head and said, "I know what's wrong. I'm lying flat on my back, my eyes closed, while you're looking at me. You might as well be giving me a gynecological exam. There's too much hierarchy here. I'm being too passive. What I want is to look at you looking at me."

So half-sitting, half reclining on a pile of floor pillows from the house, Sonia had then been able to see Jean's face clearly. This had made the difference.

"I could tell from looking at Jean's face that she was telling me the truth," she told the women at the Canadian workshop. "I knew I looked beautiful to her. Not that I didn't believe her before, but the language is men's, not ours, and often we express ourselves inaccurately because there aren't words for our feelings. But looking at Jean's face as she looked at me, I knew what she was feeling. I read the truth in every muscle of it."

Then Jean told them, "I wanted to try this, too, so we traded places again. Even though Sonia had told me less than fifteen minutes before that she thought my vulva was lovely, the idea of watching her look at me still scared me. I thought 'What if, when she looked at me a few minutes ago, her *desire* to find vulvas beautiful stood in the way of her realizing that in reality she finds them repulsive. If this is her true feeling, I know I'll be able to see it on her face.' At the same time I knew that when I looked at her vulva I was also seeing my own, so the fear was short-lived. And then, watching her face soften and sweeten as she looked at me, seeing the tears glisten in her eyes as she told me that I was exquisite beyond words, I knew she was telling me the truth— both of how she felt and of the nature of my vulva. I've felt very different about that part of my body ever since."

Then they moved on to talk about the pee experiment. "Because we were both comfortable with having other women around when we peed," Sonia told them, "we thought we didn't have any shame to get rid of about urination. But as soon as we asked ourselves the crucial question, 'What would be harder than having someone in the room when I pee?', we recognized that there was still plenty of work to do."

"Peeing in a can in a tent," Jean laughed, and briefly told them about the Michigan experience, and how it ended at West Coast. She then went on to clarify and stress their process for getting rid of shame: thinking of something about the body that was difficult to do, doing it, and then asking themselves what would be harder, and doing that. Then, after they tried that, what would be even harder, and so on, until they were totally at ease with that particular part of the body or that bodily function.

"For instance," she explained, "having Sonia look at my vulva was hard for me, but watching her look at me was even harder. The same was true for her. So, wanting to be rid of every bit of our conditioned shame about urinating, we asked ourselves what would be harder than having someone in the bathroom with us while we peed "

Sonia spoke up. "We both thought that having the other actually watch the urine come out of our bodies would be harder. So the next time I had a full bladder, I took off my pants, climbed into the bathtub, parted my legs so that Jean could see my vulva and especially my urethra, and urinated. It was hard for just a minute or so, then it passed. The same thing happened with Jean.

"'Okay'," we said, "'what's even harder than that?'" and agreed that even harder would be to have someone touch our urine while we were urinating.

"Now this was a large hurdle for both of us. From the time we're infants, we're told that urine is dirty and dangerous, and we're strongly discouraged from touching it or getting it on ourselves. It's one of our society's strictest taboos. In order for us to break it, we had to remind ourselves that it came from the same source as all other lies, trickery, and evil—mensmind.

"This experiment was harder than the last but we persisted with it until we were both totally comfortable. Then we asked ourselves, 'What would be even harder?' and decided it would be to get into the shower together and urinate on each other. And we were right—it was hard, but not terribly, because by now we both realized that our urine wasn't going to destroy anyone it touched or cause some vague but terrible catastrophe."

"The hardest part for me with that particular experiment," Jean broke in, "was that I had read and heard how men, especially gay men, urinate on each other during sex to generate excitation. In that context, I found it disgusting. But, as with all the rest of our experiments, I needn't have worried. None of them ever turned into excitation, none of them ever became sexual, because neither of us was ever in reciprocal, relationship mode. And we weren't in that mode because, finding it genuinely repellent and spiritually destructive, we'd rejected it forever."

Sonia's description of her on-going bowel movement experiment, her 'multi-sensory performances', soon had everyone laughing and talking. When Jean admitted that she had not yet been able to do this one, it was amazing how many women in the group also admitted that they were deeply ashamed of their odors and noises during elimination, and how many were not able to empty their bowels in public restrooms.

Everyone seemed to have anusphobia—the conviction that their anuses were dirty, ugly, and bad. In fact, the reaction to the word 'anus' was so strongly negative, and so few women in the group could even say it, that Sonia and Jean led them in a rousing chorus of Anus! Anus! Anus! until the word lost most of its terror and everyone was saying it with little difficulty.

During the lunch break, one young woman stood up and announced that she was about to give a performance—Sonia's term for bowel movement—and would love to have an audience. At least half a dozen women followed her out of the room. Several others made the same or a pee announcement. Sonia and Jean were delighted with the response, and as a result of that particular session saw very few closed bathroom doors during the remainder of the weekend.

The shame workshop took place on Saturday morning. Lying in their bed that night, Jean told Sonia that watching how fast the workshop participants were moving through their bowel-movement conditioning was making her feel abnormal and depressed. After all, she had had almost a month's headstart on them and had made absolutely no progress. "I want to get through this," she insisted, "but I feel so stuck."

She had made several attempts at it, asking Sonia to accompany her to the bathroom when she felt she was going to 'stage a performance', but each time had resulted in a no-show; her body simply would not cooperate. They had both shrugged it off, agreeing that it would happen in its own good time. But now Jean wasn't so sure it would, and she was becoming impatient for some affirmative action.

"I'm going to do something about it tomorrow," she told Sonia firmly.

The workshop ended on Sunday afternoon and they spent that night at a woman's home near the site of their next speaking engagement. Early in that afternoon Jean had taken two herbs which were known for their laxative and purgative properties—cascara sagrada and cape aloes. Wanting to make sure that her body could not refuse to cooperate, she had swallowed at least three times the normal dosage. She reasoned that since they had been on the road for five days now and she was totally constipated, her body simply would not be able to resist. So much for reasoning.

It was close to midnight when they finally went to bed. Though they were exhausted, enough adrenaline was left over from the workshop to keep them awake for several more hours. So they lay in the darkness, talking.

"I was surprised at how inhibited the women in the workshop were," Jean said. "Look at how long it took them to join in the Anal Chorus."

Sonia laughed at her pun. "I think it's true that Canadian women, like the British, are more restrained on the whole than American women. I wonder if you've thought what would be harder than saying 'anus'."

In the dark, Jean blanched. "Oh, shoot, Sonia," she moaned.

"Well, I can think of some harder things, such as you . . ."

"Stop!" Jean shrieked. "You're tired. You're delirous. Don't say anything you can't take back!"

"Too late now," Sonia sighed. "I've thought it and it's as good as out. So, to continue, having you look at it . . ." she paused, swallowing audibly, "I mean, look at my anus, that would be harder. But even harder would be . . ."

With both hands she wrestled Jean's hand off her mouth. Holding it away from her face as Jean tried to clamp it back, she said quickly ". . . to have you touch it."

"Oh, nooooo," Jean groaned, flopping back limply on the bed. "I can't do this, folks. There's no way in hell I can go through with this one." She covered her eyes with her arm, then raised it, her eyes suddenly bright. "That's not true," she said, sitting up. "I could easily look at and touch your sweet anus, Soni, but . . ."

"Sweet!" Sonia choked. "Give me a break, please, Genius."

"No, it's true, and it wouldn't be any problem for me. But the thought of you looking at and touching mine . . . well, anyhow, never mind. I'm up for the first half, that's all."

"And *I'm* up for the second half," Sonia threw a pillow at her. "Which means, both halves are going to get covered in this experiment."

"You're so mean," Jean said, without conviction. "Okay, but I want to take a shower first. In fact, it's so cold in this place I wouldn't mind a bath to warm me up at the same time. We could have one together."

"Look at what you just said. I had the same thought—about the shower, that is. That I've got to wash myself before we do this experiment. My upbringing was pretty typical, I'm sure. I've always believed that our anuses are dirty and that our excrement will make us sick. Actually, I still think this."

Jean thought a moment. "I had a patient a few years ago who was a bacteriologist and had just completed a seven-year study. She had three groups of subjects: carnivores, lacto-ovo vegetarians (those who don't eat meat but do eat eggs and milk products) and vegans (those who ingest no animal products in any form). Her conclusion after seven years of testing the feces of people in these three groups was that whereas the feces of those in the first two groups always contained several forms of harmful bacteria, the feces of the vegans contained none. She concluded that any and all animal products are dangerous to human health."

"I suppose this means that I shouldn't worry about washing my bottom," Sonia said gloomily. "But you know, even if my feces are perfectly harmless—given that I'm a strict vegan—I'm not fond of the idea that some may be stuck on my anus. Or, heaven forfend," she winced, "that some toilet paper may be wedged in there."

"Aaagghh!" Jean choked, thinking of her own anus.

Sonia's shoulders straightened. "Well, damn the toilet paper, and damn the stuck feces. I refuse to be ashamed of any of it."

Jean sighed, sliding down the pillows until she nearly disappeared under the blankets. "Me, too," she muttered unconvincingly, as Sonia hopped out of bed and groped on the wall for the light switch. "We've got to have some light for this," she explained cheerfully. "In fact, I'm going to put this desk lamp on a chair at the end of the bed so we can see better. Like a spotlight. 'And now, the star of the show, Annie Anus!'" she held the imaginary microphone to her mouth. Jean groaned and pulled a pillow over her face.

"Okay," Sonia said, plugging the desk lamp in. "Come on, Genius. I'm ready for you."

"It would be better if I went first," Jean protested weakly. from under the pillow. "I mean, if I look at you first, then you me." Sonia shook her head firmly. "Oh, no you don't. Not this time. Somehow you almost always manage to go first. Now it's my turn."

Jean paled. "I don't think I can do it. I'm having terrible cramps from those herbs I took this afternoon."

"Then we'll wait for another time," Sonia replied.

Jean protested, "But I could look at your anus. I just don't think I can lie still while you're looking at mine." Sonia shook her head. She wanted to wait until they could do it together.

"Then, dammit, let's do it now!" Her jaw set firmly, Jean flung back the blanket and scooted to the end of the bed. It was a low bed, perfect for this experiment; the one who was looking could sit on a cushion on the floor and have full viewing ease. Sonia tossed a pillow on the floor.

Jean plumped up a couple of pillows and lay back on them in such a way that she could watch Sonia looking at her. Sonia moved the lamp closer and then placed her hands on Jean's knees and gently began to push them apart. They wouldn't yield. She tried again with no luck. "You know, Jean, we really don't have to do this tonight. I'm happy to wait for a better time."

"No!" Jean cried, her eyes screwed shut. "I'm ready now so let's get it over with!"

Again Sonia tried to push her knees apart, sighed, and sat back. "Jean, look at me." Jean opened her eyes. "I'm willing, but right now all I can see are your knees. You need to relax them so I can push them apart."

"Okay, okay," Jean said, parting them an inch. The tears were running down her face.

Sonia tried again to push them apart, but with no success.

"This isn't going to work," she told her. "No matter what you say, it's obvious that you don't want to do it. I feel like I'm forcing you, and I won't go on."

By this time, Jean was shaking as well as crying. "I really want to do it, Sonia," she insisted. "But I need to talk more about it first."

Sonia waited. When she didn't say anything, Sonia said, "Okay, so talk."

"I don't want you to see that thing!" Jean sobbed.

"That thing?" Sonia looked puzzled. "You mean your anus?"

Jean sat up. Wiping her face with the sheet, she said dully, "No. I mean the ugliest, grossest thing you've ever heard of. Technically, it's called a herniated rectum. I've had it almost all my life and no one seemed to know where it came from or why. It's a protrusion that looks like a blood blister—very dark and incredibly ugly and I hate it and I panic at the thought of your seeing it, especially now, because it's much more obvious when I'm constipated."

Sonia listened quietly.

"I said nobody knew where it came from, but that's not true. I do know. A few years ago I was reading about a young girl who had been sexually abused by her father when she was quite young. His frequent anal rape of her caused a rectal herniation, because little girls' rectums are small. I knew where mine came from as soon as I read that.

"Sonia," she wept, "you have no idea how awful it is. I can't even bring myself to touch it. When I have to examine it periodically, to make sure it hasn't changed—become cancerous or infected—I can barely make myself touch it with a tissue. It makes me sick just to see it."

"Jeannie, it's clear that this is grim stuff for you, and I'll say one last time that you can back out, temporarily or permanently. You know that.

"But whatever you choose to do, you have to believe me when I say that the thought of seeing 'that thing', even of touching it, doesn't bother me. Maybe because I don't have the same associations with it as you do. But also because nothing can scare or disgust or repel me more than the idea of staying trapped in men's world. I know that as long as I feel afraid or put off by anything about women's bodies, I'm in the male mind. This is what scares the hell out of me, and it's the kind of fear to which your herniated rectum can't hold a candle."

"I know," Jean said. "That's why I have to go on with this. Especially since I'm this close. I may never be able to get myself to this place again." She slid back down towards the bottom of the bed and parted her legs. By now the tears were falling steadily and she was shaking so hard the bed was rocking.

Sonia brought the lamp closer. With Jean's legs apart there were no obstructions to her view. What she saw brought tears to her own eyes.

"Oh Genius, you beautiful woman, you. Your anus is lovely. She looks like a sunset, all purple and blue and pink in perfect symmetry."

"But that thing's there!" Jean cried, her eyes still shut. "How can you say that!"

"I've got news for you, Beauty. There isn't any 'thing' here."

"Yes, there is," Jean insisted. "I checked it a few months ago and it was there. I don't know how, but you're missing it."

At this, Sonia's patience gave way. "Jean," she said firmly, "I'd never lie to you and I'm a little angry that even in extremis you could think so for a moment. Now, with that out of the way, let me go back and say it again. I have a very strong light here that is so brightly illuminating your anus and all surrounding areas that there are no shadows. And I'm telling you there is no blood blister and no sign that there's ever been one. You have a little skin tag, just like I have, but your anus is perfectly symmetrical, perfectly unblemished. You look normal . . . and exquisite."

Finding all this impossible to believe, Jean opened her eyes and cautiously reached her hand down to touch the spot where the hernia had lived for almost 36 years. She felt nothing but smooth tissue.

"I don't get it," she said slowly, trying to take in the implications. "They told me surgery was the only way to get rid of it. But for once they didn't recommend it because it could result in permanent damage to the sphincter muscle." She looked dazed. "I don't get it, Sonia," she repeated slowly.

Tears were running down Sonia's face. "Your body's healing herself, Jeannie. With the love and respect she's been getting from both of us."

Deep in thought, she stroked Jean's leg for a moment. "I'm telling you right now," she finally said, "that this anus of yours is so beautiful I can't believe I've gone through my entire life thinking anuses were ugly. Adult ones, that is. I always thought everything about my babies' bottoms was adorable."

And then she leaned forward and ever so gently stroked Jean's anus, again marveling at the beauty of it, at the absolute perfection of it. Part of her joy was in knowing that Jean was going to see the same thing in her. She stroked it until Jean relaxed and her shaking abated a little.

"Not so bad after all, is it," she said gently.

Jean shook her head. "I wanted to die when you first brought it up," she confessed, "but I also knew I had to do it or die. It was die or die," she laughed feebly.

Sonia crawled up onto the bed and put her arms around her, nuzzling her neck and soft face. Jean whispered into her ear, "Your turn, Madame."

So they switched places, and immediately Jean understood why Sonia had been so moved. It was gorgeous, just as Sonia had described, with various shades of purple, blue, and pink raying out from the center. When Jean reached out to stroke it, she was amazed to find how soft it was, how sweet and dear. "I told you it would be sweet," she said reprovingly.

"Nothing to it," Sonia announced with relief.

Elated and exhausted, they slept deeply.

For at least an hour.

24

That hour of sleep was the only one they were destined to get that night. Jean woke at four a.m. with such severe cramps that in order to get up she had to roll off the bed onto her knees. From there she was able to struggle to her feet, but in such a deeply bent-over position that she could hardly walk. Although she needed Sonia if she were going to carry this through, she hesitated to wake her. Fortunately Sonia had awakened on her own.

"Jeannie?" she whispered. "Where are you?"

"I'm here at the door. I have to get to the bathroom quick," she said urgently, fumbling for the doorknob. She fled down the hall, calling over her shoulder to Sonia, who was right behind her, "I'm not sure I can make it." Together they crowded into a bathroom so tiny Sonia could barely close the door. With great relief, Jean sank onto the toilet, biting her lip to keep from crying out at the nearly unbearable pain. She had a momentary vision of blowing the toilet apart with the force that had built up inside her.

But instead, nothing happened. After a few moments she looked down at Sonia sitting on the floor and said, "I can't believe it, but I don't feel a thing now. The cramping has quit."

"Maybe we just need to sit here awhile," Sonia suggested, shivering. Typical of so many underheated Canadian houses, this one was freezing at night. She pulled a towel off the rack and wrapped it around her.

They sat in expectant silence for a few minutes.

After awhile, Jean said disconsolately, "Nothing's happening. We may as well go back to bed and get warm." They made the return journey back down the dark, narrow hall to the bedroom and plunged gratefully into the warmth of the bed. But as soon as

Jean lay down, the cramping and griping resumed with a vengeance.

This time she waited until she was certain there would be no turning back. Then once again they negotiated the dark hallway to the bathroom only to have Jean tell Sonia again that the feeling had stopped, that there was no peristalsis, nothing.

"Jeannie, why don't I go back to bed and let you sit here alone? Really, we can do this another time."

Jean shook her head. "Give me a few more minutes," she begged. They shivered another ten minutes before she gave up and followed Sonia back to bed, where they replayed the whole thing: as soon as Jean lay down, the cramping and griping returned. For the third time, they burst out into the hallway and flew to the bathroom. And for the third time, everything stopped the minute Jean sat down.

Half a frigid hour later, she roused Sonia, who was drowsing against the door wrapped in a couple of towels. "Go back to bed, Soni," she said gently, stroking her hair. "I'll sit here until things let loose. Then I'll just wait until we get home and try again."

Disappointed and frustrated, she sat there for another half hour after Sonia left. She hadn't counted on her body's being so strong that it could withstand the powerful herbs she had given it. She knew these herbs and their properties well. If anyone else had said they had had this experience, she would have been sure they were lying. She would have thought it was impossible. Now she knew otherwise.

But she was in for a further surprise. Even with Sonia out of the bathroom and several rooms down the hall, her body remained numb and her bowels quiet. Not only that. Unable to urinate even so much as a drop, she realized her kidneys had also shut down. She felt the first tremor of fear. This was serious.

It was growing light outside when she finally crept back into bed beside Sonia, snuggling close to her to get warm. As she lay there, she waited expectantly for the cramping to resume. But nothing happened. *The whole damned establishment has shut down*, she thought ruefully.

All that day she waited, but to no avail. No urine, no peristalsis. By bedtime she was really frightened, feeling as though her entire excretory system was in danger of permanent paralysis. *I have to do something*, she thought desperately.

So lying in bed, she poured lotion into her hands to warm it and then gently rubbed it into her abdomen. As she caressed herself, she whispered, "I promise you I will never do this again—never try to force you, never terrorize you again to try to get you to do what I want you to do. From this moment you're free to do exactly what you please. I don't care if you ever get over this inability to function when you're traveling, or when someone's in the same house, or in the bathroom. I will not tyrannize you again, I promise with all my heart."

A few minutes later she went to the bathroom and urinated long and easily. Her bowels, however, were not so trusting and she went another three days before they moved. Relucantly so, she noted, but who was complaining.

The remainder of the tour was a whirlwind of speeches and workshops. They were eager to go home, but had one last commitment to keep, and that was a two-day visit to an established women's community several hours outside of Toronto. Sonia knew the founder personally, and was eager to visit her at Wiseroots.

Founded in the late sixties by an idealistic, twenty-one-year-old heiress named Linda Champlain, Wiseroots had originally been intended as both a refuge for draft dodgers and as an experiment in anarchy. It had not taken long, however, for Linda to conclude that anarchy was impossible with men, and to close the community down.

Nearly twenty years later, as Lindy, a radical lesbian separatist, she had reopened the community for women only. Those long years of living and thinking alone had taught her a lot, and she was confident of success this time. Sans men, she and other women would be able to create the utopia of her dreams.

Women arrived in droves, and in less than three months Wiseroots boasted thirty-three committed members. Then they hit their first major snag. One of them left for a week's visit to Toronto and returned with a three-year-old son she had previously neglected to mention.

"This is a lesbian separatist community," Lindy had reminded her. "No penises allowed." The woman argued with her. "There are no rules prohibiting boy children," she insisted. "There are no rules, period," Lindy had shot back. "We have trusted that women who come here know what separatist means." The woman eventually left, but not before inflicting painful wounds.

The remaining women met together shortly thereafter and decided they had to have enough rules to make clear what was and was not acceptable there. They spent three days drawing up a community statement and getting it in print. From then on, all visitors were asked to read and abide by the four-page statement. The second blowup also occurred around the issue of gender. Two young women, Cedar and Andi, had arrived within days after Lindy had announced her intentions to open Wiseroots up to all women. Lindy had been impressed by their passion for and commitment to women's land and women's ways, and they proved to be hard, uncomplaining workers. A month after their arrival, they announced at a community meeting that Cedar, the younger of the two, was pregnant. Hers was a turkey-baster pregnancy, done in the presence of seven other women during full moon to insure a girlchild. Since Wiseroots had no objection to girl children, the birth of this baby was eagerly awaited.

Only *she* turned out to be a *he*. Cedar could not believe it, and kept asking what they could possibly have done wrong. Andi went into shock, then managed to convince herself that Cedar's jealous ex-lover must have put a spell on them.But the reality of the situation demanded that they do something about their son. Resigned, they determined to raise him to be different, exceptional, to be a woman-like male. But to their great shock, they were nevertheless told that they would have to leave when the baby, Lake, was three months old.

Andi, who had been one of the strongest proponents of the 'no males allowed' rule, became furious. Lake was different, she argued. He'd been born here, for goddess's sake. It wasn't like bringing an already maleized boy onto the land. But the rule held, and the two women left—angry, hurt, and seething with resentment.

Then things seemed to settle down for awhile. Women continued to come and women continued to leave, more or less as expected. But recognizing the need for solidarity and stability if they were to succeed, Lindy emphasized over and over again the importance of commitment, of hanging in there and making it work. As time passed, the goals of the community became clearer, at least in Lindy's mind.

Number one was self-sufficiency, necessary if they were to break away from patriarchy and all its invidious ways. They grew as much of their own food as possible, put in windmills to pump water and generate electricity, bought solar panels to be used whenever there was enough sun, did all their own building and repairs.

Number two was to promote physical health and safety. No alcohol or recreational drugs, no meat, and no firearms or other male-type weapons were allowed on the land.

And so their community statement went for four full pages. Lindy felt good about it, figuring that it would prevent most arguments. If someone didn't agree with something, then either she didn't come or she left. It was that simple.

But what happened at Wiseroots is what happens in every women's community, because it isn't that simple. The women who came did agree on those things. Somehow, however, there was never harmony for long. Wiseroots never prospered, holding onto existence by its very teeth.

"It's because of women's perpetual, unconscious need to control," Sonia said, sitting crosslegged on the living room floor of the main community house. Lindy and the five remaining Wiserooters had asked their visitors for their thoughts on the subject of why women's communities were not flourishing. They sat in a circle before the fire.

"Even when we say we don't want to control anybody else, even when we believe we aren't doing it, we are. Control is root, core, and branch of mensgame. And mensgame has been the only game in town for so long it's become our game, too."

"I wouldn't say it was only about control," argued Wren, a four-year veteran. "It was also about interpretation. I can give you dozens of examples. For one, diversity. We all agreed that it was necessary, but we just couldn't get together on what it meant. A quota system? One woman of color, one differently abled, one old, one poor, one working class woman for every so many middle-class WASPs? Even if we could have agreed about quotas—in theory and in practice—where were we going to find such women who also wanted to be here? We were working fourteen-hour days that first year, falling into bed with our clothes on we were so exhausted. We had dozens of pressing survival problems, so somehow the political-correctness ones got put aside. Does that horrify you?"

"Of course not," Sonia laughed. "Political correctness is bullshit. In order for our communities to have even a breath of a chance, we have to choose women we know and like, who are as much like us as possible. We'll soon find out that even when we do this, the diversity is nearly overwhelming. We forget that each woman is a universe. You may be white, able-bodied, lesbian, middle-class, and reared protestant, and so may I, but men's categories don't even scratch the surface of who we are, of our rich, incredible, unique invividuality. Even with just the two of us, we can stop worrying about diversity; there're two universes right here. Those other categories you mentioned, the PC ones—race, age, health, class, wealth—these are patriarchal variations, very limited in scope, depth, and importance."

She grinned at Wren. "Does that horrify you?"

Everyone laughed, and someone clapped.

Wren looked nonplussed. "A little, frankly. But it fits in with what I was going to say. Let me go back and give you another example of misinterpretation—because of our marvelous diversity, of course." She smiled at Sonia.

"We all agreed that a garden was a necessity; there was no problem there. But everyone had different ideas about how to do it. Some said plant at full moon only, others said plant certain seeds at certain moon times, others said the dark of the moon. Planting stymied us because everyone wanted to do it her way."

Sonia shrugged. "What can I say? More control."

"Well, maybe, but surely other things, too. Audra wanted to do a French-intensive garden, with raised beds and double-dug soil. Lindy wanted to do what she'd read wild women did—simply cast the seeds into the wind and let them fall where they chose. Someone else said we had to have goat manure, others said no animal wastes. Another wanted to install a slow-drip irrigation system, and was argued down by a woman who claimed that that made plants water dependent. So what happened that first year was that no garden got planted because we couldn't agree on the details."

"Since you wanted anarchy, why didn't every woman just plant her own little garden the way she wanted to?" Jean asked.

Wren looked startled. "I don't know that anyone thought of that. But you're right. That would've solved the problem."

"No," Lindy shook her head. "Remember, there were women here who didn't want to garden, or who had disabilities that prevented them from gardening. We needed one large garden, a group effort, like we have now."

"It's still the source of endless arguments and tears," Wren reminded her. "The thing is, even those women who didn't want to do any actual gardening had their opinions about how it should be done."

"This is control, Wren," Sonia insisted. "You see, you were all in agreement about having a garden. Where you got into trouble was the need in every woman to be in control of some piece of it. Even the non-gardeners had to have their say. I'm sure there were women fighting about this who didn't know the first thing about gardening and weren't even interested. But they needed to control to feel good about themselves."

This exasperated Wren. "That's gross oversimplification, Sonia," she said irritably. "You know, there are hundreds of issues in the world besides control issues."

Sonia shook her head. "No, there aren't. There are just the endless variety of strategies men have devised to get on top and stay there, to control people, nature, and circumstances. Those strategies are what we call 'life' in patriarchy; they're all we know of how to think, what to do, how to be. They're our definition of ourselves: I am more intelligent than most people, a harder worker, a better mother, a kinder person, etc.

"Every day I see more clearly how sadomasochism governs all, is all, and how this manifests itself in me and my life. For instance, in our community, I honestly wanted every woman to do what she wanted to do. At the same time, I thought we were all dedicated to figuring out new ways of being, to creating women's world, and that we were in agreement about how to do this—getting out of our relationship minds, for example. In that last sentence alone I've mentioned two virulent forms of control: assumption and expectation. Making assumptions and having expectations were the subtle but formidable weapons I used to try to control what happened at Wildfire."

"Me, too," Jean said. "When I realized my part in it all, how deep and insidious it was, I almost despaired. How could I ever get out of it? But since then Sonia and I have been doing an experiment to keep as aware as we can of when we try to control each other, when we use sadomasochism to feel better than someone else, to be on top. The instant we recognize it, we go right to the other and tell her about it. We talk about it, and somehow that takes some of the 'oomph' out of it. We've also agreed to point it out if we see the other doing it without awareness, because recognizing it is absolutely necessary for ultimately getting rid of it. That and the desire not to keep doing it, the fervent, passionate, all-consuming desire for freedom."

Sonia turned to Lindy. "You're on the hotseat in this community, Lindy. Regardless of what you say or do, you're perceived as 'the leader', the one in charge. That means you're subject to all kinds of attempts at control. Women in patriarchy—and we're all in it, no matter what we like to think—maintain our self-esteem by being on top, by controlling people and situations. So what many women want at Wiseroots—without being aware of it, of course—is to be in charge, and that means being in control of *you.*"

"That has been a problem," Lindy admitted. "It took me a long time to figure out that that's what was going on. And the way you describe it makes it even clearer: they wanted to control me so that they could control Wiseroots. Why else kowtow to me, or attack me, or try to seduce me, or find a dozen ways to insinuate themselves into my favor . . ." she sighed. "You know all the ways."

"Too well. And, as I said, they're usually not conscious of why they're doing it because control—sadomasochism—is so basic to our being now after all these millennia of mensworld that it's as invisible as air . . . actually more invisible than air nowadays."

The blazing log snapped and popped in the fireplace, sending a shower of sparks up the chimney.

"That explains a lot to me," said Vera, a robust, grey-haired woman. "Remember when I wanted to put in the composting toilets and Violet had a fit?" she asked the community members, then turning to their two guests she explained, "Violet was paranoid about germs and sanitation. She had a fear of flies that was downright pathological. She was convinced that composting toilets in the house would attract flies and kill us all. Now, while no one felt as strongly as she, a number of women were concerned about the smell.

"But I'd lived with composters for years and knew how to deal with them. I told everyone that I'd be personally responsible for them, and would post clear directions in all the bathrooms, as well as give a short seminar. Everyone except Violet was pacified. She fought me tooth and nail.

"We finally agreed to have one flush toilet in the house for her. Even so, she complained about our composters, and everytime a fly got into the house, she'd point it out to me, claiming it was because of them."

"Remember when you discovered her pouring full-strength bleach into them?" Lindy reminded her.

"Remember! I almost murdered her, and that's the truth. She kept leaving pamphlets and articles around about dangerous germs in the homeplace, and the possibility of a tuberculosis, or typhus, or typhoid epidemic. She finally left, thank the goddess!"

"She had to," Sonia said, "because she couldn't control you. I'd bet my boots that control—going both and all directions—was at the root of every single woman's leaving Wiseroots. In fact, I'll go farther than that: that women's need and efforts to control each other is what has caused the dissolution of every women's community that's defunct, and what, after their first year or so, is paralyzing the others as we speak. Control destroys. And none of us is exempt from it. We all do it, or try to, all the time. It's the only way we know to live.

"In fact, it's so imbedded in our souls," Sonia mused, "that I'm afraid we're not going to be able to be out of control completely until mensworld's gone. All we can do now is be aware of it in ourselves and give it as little energy as possible."

"I understand what you're saying," Lindy said. "But if you're right—that we can't be totally free of sadomasochism and control until men are gone—how in the hell are we going to do communities? How are we going to survive? I mean, Wiseroots is still here, but the truth is we're mostly limping along, barely keeping afloat. And frankly I think the only reason we're still here at all is because the turnover rate is so high. We're surviving on newcomers' fresh, idealistic energy and oldtimers' pure, raw adrenalin."

Long pause. Finally, thoughtfully, she went on. "I want more than that. I want something solid and invincible, something men can't destroy—that connection with all women you talk and write about, Sonia. But it sounds like you're saying we can't have it yet. And that bums me, totally."

"Don't let it," Sonia said. "I know it's hard, but we have to keep hanging in there, not expecting anything and hoping everything, as out of control as possible, decent and kind, generous, forgiving, and gentle to ourselves and one another, for just a little longer. Mensmadness is almost over, Lindy. Love is on its way."

25

The Canadian tour had been good in many ways, but Sonia and Jean were eager to be home again, out of the never-ending drizzle and greyness, and into New Mexico's sunny blue skies. Ironically, they landed in Las Palomas in a torrential rainstorm.

As usual, Jean ignored "passengers must remain in their seats until the plane has come to a complete stop" and had their carry-on luggage from the overhead compartment in her arms seconds after the plane landed. As soon as the plane reached the gate, she was out of her seat, with Sonia close behind, the first in line.

Inside the terminal they paused, scanning the rain-coated crowd for Clare. Jean spotted her, leaning against a pole, dressed in a wild day-glo T-shirt and Sophia Loren sunglasses, affecting a pose of nonchalance and utter cool. As soon as she saw them, however, the pose slipped. Coming at them at a gallop, she flung her arms around Sonia with such force that the two of them nearly landed on the floor. Watching, Jean braced herself for the onslaught.

Clare loved Wildfire—the land, the house, the dogs, the women. She had missed Sonia and Jean hugely, and while her houseguest, Sandy, had been fun, she was given to frequent mood swings during which she disappeared for hours or even days. Clare found that unpredictability difficult. Barb's dinner invitations had helped, but had not filled the void.

She wanted to hear about the tour, and was eager for details, but the travelers were suffering from post-tour fatigue and total adrenaline depletion. Sonia immediately claimed the backseat, curled up, and was asleep before they hit the freeway. Jean listened to Clare's account of what had happened on the homefront while they were gone. Home at last, she and Sonia dragged their suitcases in, peed, and collapsed for a nap.

Jean was awakened by the smell of food cooking. Rolling over onto her back, she tried to guess by the odor what Clare had whipped up. Spicy and rich, it soon had her stomach growling. Middle Eastern, she guessed, but it didn't make sense. Clare didn't cook.

She edged quietly off the bed, trying not to waken Sonia. But she hadn't gone two feet when Sonia called, "Genius? Where're you?"

"I'm here, Soni." She sat down on the bed. "Having a starvation attack."

She waited while Sonia stretched, yawned, and rolled off the bed. Together they went downstairs.

The table was set for a feast, with candles and the best dishes. In a criss-cross pattern above the round table, Clare had hung colored crepe-paper streamers and a Welcome Home sign. She escorted them to their seats, and proceeded to set before them an elaborate Indian meal of saffron rice, curried eggplant, curried potatoes and peas, curried lentils, two kinds of chutney, chapatis, and cucumber salad.

"Where did you learn to fix this kind of food?" Jean asked.

"I didn't," Clare confessed. "Just before I picked you up, I stopped by the Delhi Connection and got take-out, except for the dessert." She set it on the table: sliced fresh mango and papaya, arranged tastefully in an old milk-glass bowl. "I know Indian food is your favorite."

For some reason, though at the moment she couldn't have said why, all this fuss made Sonia nervous. The candles, the dishes, the expensive meal, the party decorations . . . .

They told Clare a little about the trip, then pleaded fatigue and retired after the last dish had been put away.

The dogs got to the bed ahead of them and for once, Jean hadn't the heart to order them back down. They were sticking close to their two loves, seemingly determined never to let either of them out of their sight again. She would take them down just before she was ready to sleep.

Sonia stripped off her clothes, and headed for the bathroom and a hot bath. To her hollered, "Should I save the water?" Jean answered yes, then searched her bedside table for something to read, something inane and shallow, requiring no thought. She opened an old Agatha Christie. Lost in the mystery of why the dead man had a pocketful of rye, she was startled when the bathroom door opened and Sonia stuck her head out.

"Water's still warm," she said, then disappeared back inside.

Fifteen minutes later, Jean crawled back in bed, clean but cold. She could hear Sonia unpacking her suitcase, and watched with pleasure as she finally crossed the room to the bed.

"Okay, dogs," Sonia pointed toward the door. "Out!" Not an ear twitched, not an eyebrow raised. "Hey, come on you bums, beat it." They were all stone deaf. "Not a creature was stirring, not even a dog," Jean giggled.

Sonia ran to the door. "I've got a COOKIE over here!" That did it. Three furry forms spilled off the bed and raced towards her. Shrieking, "cookie, cookie, cookie!" Sonia tore down the stairs, the dogs in close pursuit.

Her interest in murder gone, Jean lit two red candles and turned off the light. She watched the flame patterns dance on the ceiling, and listened to the wind howling outside. Winter was not far away. The thought depressed her, and not for the first time she wondered what she was doing in a place that could have snow six months of the year. I'm just crazy, she told herself, shivering at the thought. When Sonia crawled under the blankets, Jean almost threw herself at her, so glad for her sweet warmth.

Happy to be together, they wrestled playfully for a few minutes, rolling back and forth across the bed until the blankets were a tangled mess and they were breathless with laughter. Finally, Sonia sat up and tried to sort and straighten the blankets. Then she reached over and turned on a light.

"Listen to this, Genius," she said, putting on her reading glasses. "I found it downstairs in the mail while the dogs were eating their cookies." She picked several sheets of paper up off the bedside table and began reading aloud a long letter from an old friend who had finally found the courage to leave a thirty-year marriage. Jean listened awhile, then pulled down the blankets and began massaging Sonia's legs. Although 'jump-leg' was a thing of the past, she had promised Sonia's legs that they didn't need to be sick or in pain for her to spend time with them. When she finished, she pulled the blankets over them, then pushed Sonia's sleepshirt out of the way and put her mouth over her vulva.

"You beauty, you dear, lovely, womanly vulva you," she whispered. "So perfect, so wondrously perfect." She carefully parted Sonia's thick fur and gently licked and kissed her, stopping now and then to murmur words of affection. She lost herself in the sweetness of it.

While this was going on under the blankets, Sonia continued to read aloud. Not that she was unaware of what Jean was doing; she just didn't have to do anything about it. She could go on reading and let her vulva feel and do whatever she chose. At first she had seemed happy simply to be touched, and like a contented cat, had settled down to enjoy the stroking and licking.

But then something shifted, and Sonia could feel a growing awareness in her vulva, a warmth that spread through her groin and down her legs. Still she kept reading, not wanting to interfere, not wanting to control her body in any way. But soon the page blurred before her eyes and, involuntarily, they closed. She was amazed at the sounds that came from her throat as the bud of pleasure between her legs blossomed into poppy-red lightning that zigzagged through her body. On and on it went, finally coming back to her vulva for a few moments before it waned.

"She's so dear, Soni, so totally lovely, so vul-icious," Jean said, smoothing down the wet fur as the pleasure contractions flowed away.

"How about vul-uptuous? I can hardly believe her. She never set off fireworks like that in sex," Sonia laughed, reaching for Jean. "Now that I'm just letting my body be, letting her do whatever she wants, orgasm is effortless. And only delicious, not all the other things it used to be—necessary, onerous, difficult, sometimes exhausting, a triumph or a disappointment. It's just itself, and getting more so every time. I wish we had another word for orgasm. What she's demonstrating for me these days is so all-encompassing, so sustained, so much *more* than that rush I used to call orgasm."

"I have to admit that that orgasm surprised me," Jean said, settling beside her. "One minute you're reading your letter, the next, you drop it on my head and your vulva explodes in my mouth." She looked inward at the memory.

"I still can hardly believe it, but it really is irrelevant to me now how you feel or if you react," she went on. "Being with your vulva tonight was exactly what I wanted to do, and I figured if you didn't want me to, you'd say something. I can also hardly believe how thoroughly my head isn't involved anymore, how I don't think at all, don't try to figure out what you need or want. Because I wasn't in my head tonight, I felt as if I weren't here in the usual sense. I was totally in my body, and my body and your body were singing up a storm. I didn't have to understand with my mind. They knew what to do and they did it."

Sonia nodded. "Every once in a while, though, I slip back into male/brain mode. Like tonight, it occurred to me, 'I really shouldn't be reading this letter while she's doing that,' but the thought was gone before I finished thinking it. I wanted to read the letter, so I did. And I wanted to let my body do her own thing without my fussing at her. Every time I let go of control, I realize more fully how incredible she is when she's wild." She reached over and turned off the light.

Jean watched the flickering candles catch the silver glints in Sonia's hair and highlight the planes of her face. She's so beautiful, she thought. Turning, Sonia saw her expression and leaned over and kissed her. Jean reached up and pulled her close. They kissed, their mouths almost frantic at first, then settling into a long, deep kiss that went on and on, a kiss that was out of this world . . . .

Until, lips still touching, they fell asleep in each other's arms.

26

Jean pulled the vacuum hose out of the outlet and wound it carefully around the caddy next to the refrigerator. Although the house had been spotlessly clean when they got home yesterday, by the time they had finished unloading the car, the floor had been littered with wet leaves and other outdoor debris.

She turned to look at the three dogs standing almost on her heels. Still anxious about being left, they were beginning to make nuisances of themselves, like static cling. She noticed that their paws were wet and, scooping Nikki up in her arms, she carried her to the grooming table. Twenty minutes later, Nik and Maggi had both had a thorough brushing and the fur around their paws trimmed.

Back in the kitchen, she set about preparing lunch. The lentil soup had been simmering all morning in the crockpot. All that was left was to make 'better than fried egg sandwiches'.

Clare was curled up in the rocker, knitting an afghan of multicolored yarns. It was still raining, a good day for indoor chores and simply relaxing. Sonia had thrown herself into doing their laundry.

"You were going to tell me about some of the experiments you did on your tour," Clare said, looking up at Jean. "You were too tired last night."

As Jean cooked, she told her about the workshop where women were very reluctant even to say the word anus, let alone talk about it. She told her how this reluctance had lead her and Sonia into their next experiment: looking at and touching each others' anuses.

Clare was not impressed. "I don't see why that was such a big deal," she said, then added hastily, "of course I can understand why it was for you, with your herniated rectum. It's a good thing you did it because otherwise who knows when you'd have discovered it was gone."

"It was a big deal for me in more ways than just that," Jean countered. "Seeing Sonia's anus was a revelation for me—so beautiful and sweet, not anything like I'd imagined. I mean, even though I knew I wouldn't find it distasteful, I wasn't prepared for how truly exquisite it was. Then having seen hers, it was easier for me to believe that mine wasn't as horrible as I'd thought, and to come away with very different feelings about it."

Clare squirmed. "I don't know about all this 'beautiful and exquisite' talk. I've seen anuses, and while I'm not repulsed by them, I can't get lyrical about them either. I've had several lovers who enjoyed anal sex—I don't mind it myself—but I never went into raptures over it. I can take it or leave it."

Something niggled at Jean's mind, but she couldn't get hold of it. Trying to, she asked Clare to tell her more. "Tell me what you experienced when you had anal sex."

Clare was visibly uncomfortable now but, having asked about the experiment, felt compelled to carry through.

"My first experience with it was with Rae. We were making love and suddenly she started touching it. At first I thought it was a mistake, you know, like you sometimes do if you aren't paying attention. But then she kept doing it and I realized it was on purpose. We hadn't been together very long and I didn't want to say anything to her."

"Did you like it?"

"Not at first. In fact, I kept wishing she'd stop, but she didn't. After awhile I got used to it and didn't mind. She was really into it, and wanted me to do it to her, too."

"Did you?"

Clare blushed. "Yeah. I didn't want to at first, but once I got used to the idea, it wasn't bad. She liked it a little rough, and said it didn't hurt as much as my fingers in her vagina."

"She liked you to be rough with her anus?"

Clare nodded. "She was post-menopausal and her vaginal walls had become fragile. If I wasn't careful, she'd bleed from having my fingers in her. But in her, you know, her anus," she blushed, "there were no problems."

"Was she rough with you?"

"A little, but not in a bad way, Jean. I didn't mind. She thought that women were uptight about their bodies and she wasn't going to let puritanism get in her way."

"What if you were with her now, Clare, both naked and getting ready to have sex, and suddenly she tells you she wants to look at your anus, just look at it. And while she looks at it, she gently touches it and tells you what she's seeing. How do you think that would make you feel?"

"I wouldn't like it," Clare said flatly.

"But why? If you didn't mind the sex, what would be the problem with having her just look at it and touch it?"

"It's hard for me to believe that you and Sonia found them beautiful," Clare admitted. "I mean, it's one thing to include them in sex, but to act as though they're Monet masterpieces is ridiculous. Besides, I don't know what you're getting at, Jean."

"What I'm getting at is something I've been trying to figure out since we started this conversation. I've known women who enjoyed anal sex, and yet, if you talk about it with them, many of them are uncomfortable, like you. They can do sex with anuses, but they don't want to talk about them. And I'd be willing to bet they wouldn't want to touch them the way Sonia and I've been doing—as though they're something to be cherished instead of scorned.

"It's telling me something about sex, and how women feel about it. In spite of your attempts to sound liberated, it's clear to me that you still view the anus as something dirty and unpleasant. You don't want to talk about it and you don't believe me when I say I think it's wonderful. But it's okay to talk about and touch it in sex. Why? Because somewhere in every woman's mind, sex is dirty and abusive. And since our anuses are dirty and bad, it's okay to subject them to it. The real taboo here is not anal sex, but anal love and appreciation."

Clare was quiet a moment. "You know, not long ago I would have argued from here to there with you on this. But something you said rings true to me. I used to think that sex was dirty, especially when I was with men. When I came out as a lesbian, I thought everything would change. Some things did, but that feeling—although less obtrusive—still lingered. I worked hard trying to convince myself that that feeling was puritanical and that sex was actually a beautiful, spiritual experience. Especially with the right person.

"It's true that I think my anus is dirty and unpleasant, and I understand and agree that I can tolerate the thought of having it sexed because it and sex are alike in this and therefore belong together. But it confuses me that suddenly I don't know how I feel about so many things."

"I find the whole subject fascinating," Jean said. "We're told from day one that our anuses and bowel movements are bad. This is very early, very basic conditioning. And so we grow up shunning them, being ashamed and embarrassed by them. So much so that in many women this becomes a pathology.

"Then some of us meet an 'enlightened' woman—or man— who tells us this is bullshit and introduces us to anal sex. And this is taboo, though that doesn't mean that men don't break it—as they do all taboos—and do it, anyway. For men, anal sex is exciting largely *because* it's taboo: it's daring, even courageous. In this round-about way, it has become the only legitimate anal contact—outside the doctor's office.

"What Sonia and I discovered is that—surprise!—men lied again. Anuses are not dirty, dangerous, or evil. Maybe men's are, but women's aren't. As I said before, the taboo we broke is not in touching them, but in touching them outside the pollution and abusiveness of the sex mind, touching them in reverence and admiration."

"I hear what you're saying, Jean. But it's still such a struggle to feel positive and loving toward my vulva, I can't imagine how I'm going to feel that way about *this*."

"Actually, the vulva's in the same predicament as the anus: it's only okay to touch it during sex, because it's a sex object, deserving of the disdainful, abusive treatment reserved for things men associate with sex. I see now that our vulva experiments—viewing them as gorgeous, powerful, delicious, and non-sexual—have been flaunting the same convention . . . ."

She was interrupted by Sonia bustling into the kitchen, unwrapping the vacuum cleaner hose from the caddy, and hauling it into the laundryroom/dog-grooming area of the bathhouse.

"Didn't you just vacuum in there?" Clare asked.

Jean nodded and dipped a slice of tofu in a mixture of nutritional yeast, sea salt, black pepper, and garlic powder. When she had assembled six slices, she took out her large skillet and heated a small amount of olive oil.

Sonia returned to the kitchen and, winding the hose back around the caddy, muttered, "Spilled some soap powder." Suddenly, in mid coil, she stopped and stood up, vacuum hose trailing forgotten from her hands. "Now why did I say that?" she asked aloud. And immediately answered herself, "Because I knew you'd just cleaned out there and I didn't want you to think you hadn't done a good enough job."

Jean turned the tofu to brown on the other side. "I didn't even think about it, Soni."

"That doesn't matter," Sonia said. "What matters is that I was relationshipping—worrying about your feelings, taking care of them. In fact, I've been doing nothing but relationshipping all morning."

Jean looked mystified.

"This morning I told you about the call from Sylvia, how I'd invited her for lunch on Saturday. I asked you if it was okay. Remember?"

"Right. I assumed you asked because I'm usually the one who makes lunch around here. But I only do it if I want to, you know. And though that tends to be all the time, I know you're perfectly able to do it." She lifted the browned tofu slices onto whole wheat bread that was coated with soy mayo and mustard. Sliced tomatos and sprouts waited on a separate plate. "If I don't want to fix lunch on Saturday, or don't want to see Sylvia, I won't."

"I know that, so it's all the more frustrating when I slip into permission-asking mode."

Jean smiled. "Then you also know that if I'm freaked out about anything, it's my problem and I'll take care of it."

"Old relationship habits die hard, the monsters!" Sonia stormed. Then sighed. "Godly hell but I'm sick of 'em, Genius."

"Wait a minute," Clare protested. "I don't get it. You were just being considerate, Sonia. You invited Sylvia for lunch without checking it out first with Jean, then you asked if it was okay. I don't see what that has to do with relationships. It's common courtesy. It's kindness."

"No," Sonia said. "It's pure relationShit. I can do whatever I want, Clare. I don't need Jean's approval or permission for anything. She's right. There was no reason even to tell her I'd invited Sylvia except simply to share the news—and I can't pretend that that was my motivation. Believe it or not, I can prepare a pretty decent lunch. So why check with her except to indulge in a gaggy old habit?"

"I don't agree. You two live together, you share the same house. If I were Jean, I'd be annoyed as all get out if you invited someone without at least warning me, so I could decide whether I wanted to be here or not."

"You can decide at the moment," Jean argued. "Just as I could. In relationships we have to 'check in' with each other, we have to get permission to do things, because we own each other. Since Sonia and I aren't bound by the Code of Possession, what she does is irrelevant to me. I can make choices freely, and so can she.

"When Sonia came in a few minutes ago and told me about spilling the laundry powder, that was one hundred percent relationshipfulness. She was trying to reassure me that she wasn't vacuuming because I'd done a lousy job. But I don't need or want to be reassured. I can't let it matter to me when or where she vacuums. But if I regress and allow myself to get bent out of shape about it, it's one hundred percent my responsibility to take care of those feelings. Sonia doesn't have to give them a thought."

"I still think you're confusing relationships with just being considerate and kind," Clare said, biting into her sandwich.

"It's a very fine line, Clare," Sonia said. "Men have to have a code of conduct, they have to be trained and retrained to be considerate, because it's not in their nature to be so. Their essence is harsh, barbaric, and brutal. Projecting their way of being upon us, they include us in 'human nature'. But what manunkind calls 'human nature' is exclusively male nature. In women's world, for example, a concept such as 'considerate' couldn't exist because women, untainted by mensmadness, are in their very essence considerate, kind, and loving.

"Of course there are women out there who have so absorbed the male way of being that they too have to be governed by men's code of conduct. They would see what Jean and I are doing as carte blanche to be rude and cruel. This experiment would be a disaster with women like that, women who get feelings of elation and power from putting others down or hurting them, from confronting them, from pointing out their errors and faults."

She quickly finished her soup.

"Let me try another example. Let's say there's a woman living here who's allergic to cats. I'd have known this before she came of course, and would have decided that it wouldn't cramp my style. Because I love this woman, I'd never bring a cat into this house now, even if I wanted one.

"However, let's suppose that there's no one here who has a cat allergy. I'm visiting a friend, she offers me a kitten, and I bring her home. If anyone has any objections, it's up to her to say so. It isn't my responsibility to try to figure out beforehand what the reactions of each woman will be. To do so would be sadomasochism—assuming that they can't take care of themselves, that they're fragile, and that in my greater strength, I need to protect them and make decisions for them."

Clare fiddled impatiently with her spoon. "But what if one of those women hates cats and you know this? Would you still bring that cat home?"

"Frankly, I can't imagine living with someone who hates cats, so I'm not sure that's relevant. The point of this, Clare, is that sadomasochistic behavior often masquerades as kindness. I've resolved to see systematically through all s/m's disguises. If my 'kindness' is motivated by the desire to feel like a good person, or to get someone else's approval or to reassure them of mine—if it's a means to some end—then it's suspect and I oust it.

"I knew Jean had just vacuumed the bathhouse, and it occurred to me that when I hauled the hose back out there she might think I was vacuuming again because I didn't approve of her work. But really, how do I know what she's thinking? And what business is it of mine to be trying to guess? Do you see what I mean?"

"I guess so," Clare answered reluctantly.

Sonia folded her arms on the table and leaned toward Clare. "You have to understand, Clare, that getting out of sadomasochism is the most important work of our lives. The first step is to be aware of when it happens, every single time, and clarify and exorcise it by saying it aloud as soon as we see it.

"A few weeks ago Jean and I and the dogs were on our daily walk up the old forest service road, and as you know, there are two gates to get through, and you have to crawl through the bars of the second one. Now usually Jean slips through faster than I. But this time I beat her through, and as I did, I thought how much better I did it than she, how graceful I was in comparison. It's a small thing, but the sadomasochism is as virulent as if it were huge: I compare myself favorably to her and get a zing of superiority from it."

"It just seems so insignificant to me. I mean, who cares about who's better than who?"

"Only every single one of us every single living second," Jean answered. "It's so profoundly become our way of being that we're hardly ever conscious of it anymore. You know competition is the core of maleness—sports, wars, business, love; who's most talented, smartest, strongest, biggest, powerfulest, sexiest. Everything in mensworld is hierarchical, comparative, sadomasochistic. But by now it's also become women's way of being. It seems 'natural' to us, too. But it's not. In women, it's an inversion, a gross perversion. What Sonia and I are doing here is excavating our depths and throwing out all male artifacts.

"Clare, you've been out there. Look at what we do to each other even in our so-called women's movement: we get high about ourselves at one anothers' expense. We love hearing that another woman is having a hard time because that makes us feel better. We love it especially if that other woman is well-known, because that ups the sadomasochistic ante."

Sonia laughed. "I get letters of condolence every once in awhile: 'I heard from a friend that you were having a hard time. I'm so sorry.' Where does that come from? Not from my reality, but from women's necessity to perceive me as down. Remember when the rumor got started that a certain famous feminist had a brain tumor? It became so popular that, to many women's serious disappointment, she finally had to publish a disclaimer that she was and had always been tumor free."

Jean grimaced, and turned back to Clare, "We willingly—and happily—trash one another so that we can experience that rush of excitation that in patriarchy is the only way we know to feel alive. Perceiving others as down so that we can be up is all we know of self-esteem. Every good feeling can be traced back to it. Well, it's destructive and hateful and sick and I'm getting it out of me so that I can discover my womanly way of being again."

They were interrupted by the ringing of the phone, but before Sonia or Jean could react, Clare was up and headed for the study. In a moment, she reappeared and dashed for the mudroom.

"That was UPS," she told them, pulling on her parka. "I'm going to meet him at the gate." She hurried out the front door.

They looked at each other and shrugged. As they cleared the table together, Jean remembered. "Oh, Barb called to welcome us home. She wanted to talk but I was in the middle of making the soup. I invited her to dinner tonight."

"Good, I've missed her."

"Me, too. But," she mused, "it was a strange conversation. She talked about Clare the whole time, how wonderful she is, how competent, how much fun to be with. I mean, it isn't that I disagree with her, but it seemed like she was promoting her. Anyhow, it didn't feel right."

Sonia nodded. "I've been feeling strange ever since we came home. The dinner, the decorations, breakfast this morning, flowers, and now this UPS thing. I hate the analogy, but it reminds me of being fattened for the kill."

"Yeah, almost cloying, like she's wooing us. I like her better as just Clare, not my suitor. I have to talk to her when she gets back."

"Ditto."

But they didn't get a chance until later in the afternoon, when the phone mercifully stopped ringing. For Jean, the delay was welcome. She hated unpleasantness, and she felt that telling Clare she didn't want her to do unsolicited favors for her was going to be very much so. Sonia also hated confrontations, but unlike Jean, she preferred to get them over with quickly. So she was boiling with impatience by the time they got to it.

But it wasn't as difficult as either of them had feared. Clare was defensive at first, then quickly recognized what she had been doing. She admitted that she was trying to show them how much she loved Wildfire and how much she wanted to be part of it. She said she realized that she had gone overboard, but that she was desperate to have them see how important it was to her.

Then came the hard part. Jean plunged in.

"I like you a lot, Clare. If I didn't, I wouldn't have invited you back. I'm glad you were here the three weeks we were away. Knowing how competent and reliable you are, I never once worried about the place or the dogs.

"But I learned a lot from my first attempt at community living. Most important, I learned what I do and don't want. I'm not interested in simply living with a group of women to make our economic lives easier—I know I've said this before, and that you've agreed. My all-consuming desire is to get patriarchy out of me—is this the millionth or billionth time I've said that? But it's the deepest truth of my life. It's why I've been willing to do difficult and frightening experiments, why I've been willing to put myself through some pretty rough moments, why I would rather die than go on with my illusions and conditioned mind.

"I don't think there are many women out there willing to do what Sonia and I are doing. I'm not saying that because I think we're superior or better than anyone else. It's just that this seems to be a rare passion, or purpose. I know you've been interested in our life here, and I've enjoyed talking about it with you, but it isn't enough just to be interested, or to be willing to experiment *up to a point*. Women who join us have to be ready and willing to go beyond anything any of us dreams is possible, willing to face the unmitigated terror of renouncing maleness in our deepest souls. I don't have that sense with you. This isn't a judgment. It's simply my feeling, and I've learned that I have to trust that."

Clare held up her hand. "I admit that I'm not ready for some of the experiments the two of you've done. In some cases, I'm not even convinced they're necessary, and in others they're a little too radical for me right now. But it doesn't mean I won't get there. It just means that right now I'm not. And I feel I can learn a lot from the two of you. I'd like to be given a chance."

Sonia shook her head. "One of the things I'm very clear about is that I don't want to teach anyone. That stance is blatantly sadomasochistic. I want women who are doing this on their own, Clare, who are figuring it out for themselves. Jean and I haven't had any teachers through this. We've figured it out, step by step, and we did it because it mattered enough, because it was all that mattered, because our lives depended on it. Ultimately, that's the only reason any woman will ever do it."

"But you've had each other. I don't have anyone else."

"We found each other because we were in the same internal space, because we were longing for freedom with the same passion. Though we've had each other now for awhile to experiment with, before we met, we'd cleared our own personal decks enough that when we got together, we each knew exactly what we wanted and could see immediately how we could do it faster and better together. Without our own individual work and desire, our life of experimenting together couldn't have materialized, let alone be worth a damn."

"I think you're asking too much of most women. Your conditions are almost impossible to meet. I don't see how you're ever going to attract any other women here."

"Then so be it. This is what I want, and all I'll settle for. As Jean pointed out, Wildfire is not about numbers. It's about creating women's world on this planet. Women's world doesn't just automatically spring into being because a group of women get together on a piece of land. Without rigorous self-examination and grueling personal work, we're no better off together on land than we are living separately in the cities."

"I guess I have your answer then." Clare stood up. "I'll leave first thing in the morning."

27

"She's leaving tomorrow?" Barb exclaimed incredulously. "I thought she was going to stay."

Sonia and Jean exchanged looks. "What made you think so?" Jean asked.

"Well, she fits in so well. I told you on the phone how efficient she was, how capable. My gutters came down off the south side of the house with all this rain, and she was over in a flash to help me fix them. And you've told me how much you like her."

"It's true. Clare's capable and helpful and very pleasant, Barb. But that's not enough."

"I don't understand you," Barb said plaintively. "I thought the idea of a community was to have a lot of women. How can you have a community with two?"

Sonia suppressed a smile; Barb sounded so aggrieved. "You can't. But that's irrelevant, really, because I'm not interested in having just a community. I want women's world, and there's a universe of difference between the two. Clare understood that. She may not have liked it, but she understood it."

"Is she mad?"

"I don't know. She didn't say."

"Hell, I'm sorry she's going. I looked forward to having her in the neighborhood." She added impulsively, "She can come and live with me, if she wants." Then, still bemused, she shook her head again. "You know, I don't get it. I really don't get it."

"And I don't expect many women will," Jean said.

Clare left the following morning. If she was angry, she didn't show it. They wished her well and welcomed her back for visits, but neither Jean nor Sonia felt they would ever see her again. Clare was going to find her community or die trying; this was her passion.

Barb was deeply upset. She had approached Clare after dinner with her proposal that Clare come live with her. She had plenty of room, she had argued, and Clare would have total freedom. Clare had thanked her, but explained patiently that it was community living she craved.

"But we have a sense of community here," Barb had protested. "Sonia and Jean are almost next door, we have our Murder Maids group, there are always women visiting Wildfire. And if all goes well, we'll have two more women in the neighborhood soon." While Sonia and Jean had been in Canada, two women had looked seriously at the twenty acres adjoining Barb's property.

"I know that, Barb. And believe me, I appreciate the offer. If I wanted to, I could buy land up here and build a house, but that isn't what I want. It isn't enough. I want to live on land with other women. Lots of them."

"You've been trying to find your Garden of Eden for over twenty years now and haven't succeeded. What makes you think you're going to now?"

Barb's words stung, and Clare abandoned her efforts to explain. She understood Barb's unhappiness but knew she couldn't do anything about it.

Driving home by herself that night, Barb waxed nostalgic about the good old days, when women weren't so damned complicated. "Just a bunch of spoiled brats," she mumbled to herself, and vowed to stick with pigs for the rest of her life.

○ ○ ○ ○ ○ ○

Jean shivered as Sonia brushed her fingertips up and down her spine. "Your fingers feel like feathers," she said, "like the downy underfeathers of a baby bird." She shivered again as the nerve endings along her spinal cord sang. She couldn't remember ever before experiencing such sensations, such pure, uncensored delight. Her body felt powerful, vital, full of energy.

Women are the real body lovers, she thought. *In our uncorrupted state, body, spirit, mind, and emotions are unified, never separate, and all simply power. And our bodies are at the core of that power. Male bodies have no such core of power, so men envy and hate women's bodies, envy and hate our power. No wonder they have to control our bodies, no wonder they have to make us do sex—it's the only way they can separate us from our bodies and our power. It's only when women get out of our sex minds, when we can't even think of sex anymore, let alone do it in any of its forms, that we can reclaim and know our bodies, what they're capable of, what female power is.*

As Sonia pulled the blankets over them and curled her warm body around her, Jean breathed a sigh of contentment. She was almost asleep when from light years away she heard Sonia's voice.

"What?" she asked, struggling up from the fog.

"I asked you what you thought of Ellie." Ellie was a middle-aged woman who had attended their Michigan workshop and had written, asking if she could stop by on her way through New Mexico to Arizona. Liking her letter, they'd agreed to let her visit. She had arrived only a few hours earlier, exhausted from a marathon drive across the country, and had gone almost straight to bed.

"I don't know yet," Jean answered slowly. "She seems nice, but beyond that, I don't have any real impressions."

"I was wondering why you put her in Marcy's old room instead of upstairs."

"It's warmer here on the second floor, for one thing, and for another, the toilet up there needs a new valve. I've shut it off until

I can get one." Jean cuddled closer. They were in Sonia's bed tonight.

"I think Ellie's going to suggest that she join us here. I thought I'd warn you. She asked me a lot of leading questions while I was helping her get settled."

"Oh, great," Jean moaned. "I sure didn't get that impression from her letter. She'll have to bring it up herself, of course. Maybe we should send her to Barb."

"Barb's pretty upset right now. As much as I like her, I have to struggle against feeling impatient and even irritated with her sometimes. It's not her fault. She's not really interested in what we're doing. I have to remind myself of that, and not always foist unwanted explanations onto her."

Jean kissed her softly, then turned over and snuggled into her belly. "I'm off to sleep, dear bump."

"Me, too, beauty." Sonia yawned.

Jean dreamed the night away, wild, vivid dreams of women walking hand in hand through the trees, across the mountains, women singing, dancing, laughing, totally free within themselves and together. She dreamed of a fire that warmed them and cooked their food and invited them to tell their stories. She could smell the food, almost taste the marvelous concoctions that bubbled in pots over the fire.

She awakened with a start, the dream still very much with her, so much so that she could even smell the food. As her mind cleared and her eyes focused, however, she realized that the smells were coming from their real kitchen.

Even without checking to see where Sonia was, she knew the cook had to be Ellie. Sonia wouldn't be caught dead cooking if she could help it.

She glanced at the clock. Six twenty-two. What was Ellie doing up at this hour? Last night she told them she wanted to be in Los Gatos by early afternoon, but Los Gatos was at most only two hours away. She yawned hugely. Normally an early riser, she had slept soundly, well past her usual rising time. But, she admitted to herself, her rising time had changed considerably since she and Sonia had started sleeping together. She loved their morning cuddles and quiet talks and rumpuses so much that it was hard for her to leave the bed. Almost 6:30 now.

Stretching, she slipped out from under the blankets and tiptoed across the wooden floor to the bathroom. She peed, shivering in the early morning cold, and then hurried into her

bedroom, where she gathered up jeans, clean socks and underwear, and her favorite sweatshirt, the one with the singing coyotes
on it. Downstairs, she turned on the shower in the bathhouse, and
while waiting for the water to get hot, jumped up and down to
keep warm. Her shower jig, Sonia called it.

She washed quickly, not wanting to waste a drop of water, then
stood at one of the large, thermal-pane windows to towel off. The
winter birds were there in flocks, jostling for position at the
thirteen feeders. She made a mental note to buy more seed, then
turned back to the mirror and her hairdryer. As she did, her eyes
passed quickly over the two black plugs on the floor where the
toilets would someday go. She lacked the confidence to do it
herself, and although Sonia had decided to figure it out and do it,
other things had gotten in the way. Actually, Jean was in no hurry.
Once the toilets were in, there would be another experiment
waiting for her. The awful one.

In the kitchen Ellie was setting out plates. A large, towel-
covered basket held a jumble of fresh, hot muffins. "Apricot," Ellie
told her, hugging her close. "And tofu scramble, with mushrooms
and peppers and soy cheddar."

"It's a banquet!" Jean exclaimed, breaking off a piece of muffin and trying not to feel uneasy about Ellie's behavior. "Oh, Ellie,
this is delicious." She finished the muffin. "I'm glad you found
everything all right."

"This kitchen is a perfect dream. Everything seems so effortless
in it. And the space!"

"What space?" Sonia asked, coming tousled-headed and
bleary-eyed into the kitchen.

"Outer." Jean embraced and kissed her. They held each other
for a long moment before Sonia went in to shower.

Later, forced by a cold rain to stay in the house, and full of Ellie's
good breakfast, they drifted into the library. There, the gas log fire
had chased out the chill and damp. Sonia threw herself down on
the hearthrug, Jean sat cross-legged in the papasan chair, and Ellie
sprawled on the couch.

"I should call Harper and Lauren," Jean said, making no attempt to get up. "And Dana. We haven't talked to them since we
left for Canada."

"Right," Sonia agreed, not moving. "Good idea."

"I got up during the night to pee," Ellie said. "I was creeping
through your room to the bathroom, trying to be quiet, Jean,

when I ran into something hanging from the ceiling. It scared the hell out of me!"

"My hammock chair," Jean laughed. "Sorry about that. I should have warned you."

"I didn't get hurt," Ellie assured her, "but I was afraid I'd wakened you. Then I discovered you weren't even there."

"No, I slept with Sonia last night."

Ellie's eyebrows rose in surprise. "I thought you two weren't having a relationship."

"We aren't. Sleeping together doesn't constitute a relationship."

"Now wait a minute," Ellie protested. "That's not what Sonia said in *The Ship*. She said that when you live together, sleep together, and do almost everything together, you're having a relationship—and that's what you two do. It's obvious that you love each other."

Sonia winced. "I'm very leery of that word, Ellie. In mensystem it doesn't mean a thing. I don't use it and won't until I know that what I'm feeling is what love was in women's world."

"Okay, okay. But what I was saying was you're doing all the things you yourself say constitute a relationship."

Feeling too lazy to go into the lengthy explanation required to refute this, Jean said hopefully, "I don't suppose you'd just take our word that we're not?"

"Let's say I believe that you *think* you're not. But it looks to me like you're doing exactly what the rest of us do. So I'm inclined to think that it's a matter of semantics."

Hearing this yet again, Sonia felt suddenly tired to the bone, as if there were no way she could find the energy to explain it one more time. But willing herself to do so, she began.

"This isn't about semantics, Ellie. A relationship is a very distinct set of behaviors. You can recognize it by its basic rules and conventions, its basic assumptions and expectations. You've read *The Ship*, you know that one of the major rules, assumptions, and expectations is that you'll do things for each other. So maybe it's enough to say that Jean and I aren't having a relationship because neither of us does anything for the primary purpose of pleasing the other or of making the other feel good or loved. We don't try to meet each other's needs or make each other happy. If, say, I do something because I want to and it also happens to please Jean, that's dandy. But we're each responsible for our own happiness and capable of obtaining it. We take that very seriously around here."

"Well, I know you explained that in the book, but it still sounds pretty selfish and cold to me."

"You couldn't be more wrong. It's the freest, most delightful existence imaginable, for me at least. Knowing and being truly my Self and taking total responsibility for me is what I want more than anything. I know this isn't the case for everybody, and I'm sure you're right that this would make many women miserable."

Ellie looked obstinate. "We all want to be ourselves. You make it sound as if you're extraordinary."

Inwardly, Sonia groaned. "I know women think they do, but obviously it isn't true or they wouldn't still be so actively involved in patriarchy. Hell, just what they do to their bodies is enough to show how enslaved they are: drinking coffee and tea and alcohol, eating meat, dairy, and sugar. And they're having all kinds of relationships, mucking around in politics, fighting with other women about racism, ageism, able-bodyism, classism; in other words, facilitating patriarchy with their every heartbeat."

"Not all women, Sonia. I'm very careful with my diet, as you can see by what I fixed for breakfast this morning. I don't do dairy, meat, sugar, or caffeine. I do allow myself a little treat a couple of times a week, and that's a glass of organic wine with dinner, especially if I've had a hard day. I figure I deserve it."

Jean shook her head. "What a strange, upside-down argument. As often as I've heard it, I still don't understand how women can deliberately do something harmful to their bodies and think of it as a 'little treat'. It's total reversal: the label of 'treat' implies that it's good for you, but alcohol is not good for you. For your body, it's the opposite of a treat—it's abuse. And no body deserves abuse."

Ellie sulked. "Look, I gave up cigarettes, sugar, coffee, and relationships. The first three were excruciatingly difficult." She smiled as Jean and Sonia laughed. "That one glass of wine a few nights a week is the only comfort I've held onto. And even that's changed. I used to have a couple glasses of wine every night."

"So your reasoning is that because you've suffered and are so much better than you were," Sonia summarized, "you deserve to have your one little vice. The illogic of this is that for doing what men tell you is good—suffering—you then punish your body. That's the sadomasochistic voice of the Fathers inside you encouraging you to find reasons to destroy yourself."

"I understand what you're saying, but damn it, it's so hard out there. You two have lost track of what that world's really like. You're up here in the mountains together, loving each other, doing work you enjoy. I'm alone in a hostile city with a job I hate. I figured out a long time ago that I had to get rid of most of my vices if I wanted to have half-way decent health. I used to drink a lot in order to cope. Now I've stopped, except for a few glasses of wine a week. Those few glasses help me survive. I have to have something to get me through this shit."

"Women used to say that very thing to me when I had my practice," Jean said. "That they had to have something to help them survive the horrors of their lives. I'd sit down with them and together we'd try to figure out harmless substitutes, like meditation or affirmations. But now I realize that coping mechanisms like those are not harmless. They keep us from facing the truth, that our lives are intolerable. The hideousness of our lives is what we have to change."

"Being called a survivor has always been a positive thing in patriarchy," Sonia said thoughtfully, "but it's not actually a compliment at all. Men have spawned an abomination and they get us to tolerate it by giving us strokes—we're strong and good if we can survive it. It's the only badge of courage women ever get in mensworld. But surviving is no big deal, really. Anyone can do it. If we can't do more than survive, if we can't find the gumption to flourish, why stick around to suffer?"

"Obviously because men have made suicide taboo," Jean answered.

Sonia nodded. "Smart guys. If suicide were sanctioned, women by the millions would be getting out of here, and mensworld would collapse."

"Well," Jean shrugged, "as I often say, I *do* think women are getting out of here, but in socially acceptable ways—cancer, for one."

Ellie was finding this conversation very unsettling. "But back to the question of whether the two of you are having a relationship," she said, changing the subject. "Can you be more specific?"

Sonia pondered a moment.

"Okay. An example of not relating is that Jean and I don't try to protect each other from unpleasantness. When a bad book review came the other day, Jean handed it to me immediately. Her assumption was that if I were to decide to read it, I could handle it, or—more than that—that if I couldn't, that was my problem. She's not going to try to spare me, she's not going to rescue me or take care of me."

"This hasn't been easy for me," Jean smiled ruefully. "I was a premier rescuer."

Sonia reached over and touched her face. "True," she said affectionately. "But not any more, thank goodness."

Turning back to Ellie, she said, "When Jean first moved here, we were in the process of remodeling this house. One day she and I were moving some heavy pieces of sheetrock out of one of the downstairs rooms into the yard. Since she was carrying the front end, she walked out across the old crumbling deck first and called back to me, 'Watch out, Sonia. There's a big hole here.'

"As soon as we put the stuff down, I asked her not to do that sort of thing any more. I could watch out for myself, I said, and I'd rather break an ankle than establish that kind of relationship with her."

Ellie knitted her brows. "But that's just being thoughtful. We'd do it for anyone."

Considerateness again, Sonia thought with a sigh. "No, it's relationshipness, and yes, in the malestream we do it with practically everyone. What society calls consideration and thoughtfulness are always fittings of the Ship, how we've been taught it's best to be with others."

"I must be a little dense," Ellie said stiffly. "Tell me what's the matter with it."

"It's matronizing to take care of each other in such ways. In this case, especially since I'd lived in this house for several months and crossed that deck thousands of times, I could be assumed to know to watch out for the holes. Jean understood instantly, and since that day has done her damnedest not to take responsibility for my safety or health."

Clearly unconvinced, Ellie shrugged.

"Another evidence that we're not doing a relationship—and you know, these are just a few of literally thousands—we don't try to comfort each other and we don't give each other unsolicited advice or opinions. We let each other suffer through our sadnesses and problems, and ask for help or comfort if we want it, in the way we need it. We let each other be. This is not easy—either for the one with a problem or the one who has simply to stand by and watch. But part of allowing each other to come to grips with our true feelings is not to blur or obscure them with static.

"We say what we want. This may sound easy, but it's been a humdinger. In relationships, we often get in the habit of saying things like, 'You must be hungry. Let's stop at this restaurant and get something to eat', instead of, 'I'm hungry'. We say, 'You must be cold. Would you like me to shut the window?' instead of, 'I'm going to shut the window because I'm cold'. It's another protective measure, a way of not revealing ourselves, of not being vulnerable.

"Except for now and then when we regress, Jean and I don't check things out with each other, or give or get permission, either overtly or tacitly. For instance, if I want to spend the day with a friend, I do it. I don't tell Jean my plans, I don't check it out with her to make sure it's okay, I don't worry that she may have made other plans for that day that include me. In that sense it's as though we live alone, because nothing either of us does is in relation to the other.

"Most important of all, we don't do things we dislike in order to please the other. When I was with Marcy, we went to several movies a week because Marcy liked to go to movies. I didn't think about it, really. It was something to do together and so I did it. But since we ended our relationship, I haven't seen a single movie. When I realized this, what it told me was that I didn't really like movies, that I had only gone to please her, to keep our Ship afloat. Obviously, left to myself—as I am—I would never go to a movie, never watch a video. But I didn't know that until I was out of the relationship and on my own."

Jean put her hand over Sonia's on the table. "I'm totally free to do as I wish," she told Ellie, "to come and go as I please, without having to 'work it out' with Sonia. There's no bargaining, no exchange, no compromise. In relationships, doing something for the other person often takes the form of compromise. Believe me, I know all about it, having been the prize compromiser of all time in my relationships.

"For instance, I hate meat, hate having it in my house, but when a lover asked if it was all right for her to cook some once in a while, I said, 'Sure!' But it wasn't all right. I resented every second of it.

"Another one. I fiercely dislike television, but one of my lovers wanted it, so I agreed to have it if she would use earphones. Even without the noise, I hated the intrusion, the ugly *energy*, of the thing. There were hundreds of these, so by the time we broke up, I was full of resentment. And it was all my own doing."

"I don't understand what you mean when you say you don't have to work things out with Sonia."

"Let's say I'm in town, doing errands, and I see an ad for a movie and decide on the spur of the moment to see it. I don't have to call Sonia and find out if it's all right. I don't even have to call her and tell her I'm going to be staying later in town than I thought. I'm totally free to do that.

"But if I had done that in any of my relationships, there'd have been big trouble. One lover would have resented my staying later than I'd said. Another would have resented my seeing a movie without her. A third probably wouldn't have minded if I'd called and told her first.

"In relationships we have to negotiate for our own time. We have to work out something, even if it's minor. I was involved with a woman named Alice who was an avid tennis player. She played several times a week, and was good enough to compete in meets. Most of those were held in Las Palomas, but several times a year, she'd travel to some other city, and be gone anywhere from five days to a week.

"I have a good friend that I like to visit a couple of times a year. Alice wasn't crazy about my doing that, but she had to let me because I let her go away to her tennis meets. We had an exchange going. One year, after I'd already met my friend twice and Alice had been to her two meets, I had a chance to go birding on an island off the coast of Florida with my friend. Alice was furious. It was unfair, she said, because I'd already been gone my two times, and so on. I had to offer her something else in exchange to pacify her."

"But your examples are unusual," Ellie protested. "This sort of behavior isn't the norm."

"Oh, yes it is, Ellie," Sonia said. "Relationships demand that we account for our time to our partners, regardless of how liberated we might think we are. We negotiate and compromise all the time. Compromise is essential to relationships. So Jean and I don't do it. Each of us does exactly what we want without feeling as if we have sometimes to do things one way and sometimes the other, or reach some sort of acceptable middle position. Compromise is control and we avoid it like the plague. It has no place in women's world."

"What do you mean, compromise is control?"

"Pretend that Hazel and Rita are in a relationship, and that they disagree about the frequency with which they should go to movies. Rita wants to go at least four times a week, whereas once a month would be more than adequate for Hazel. Let's say Rita tries to get Hazel to change, but that Hazel refuses. If they don't want their Ship to sink, they're going to have to compromise. Or pretend to—most compromise is so grudgingly entered into that it doesn't last long.

"Anyway, compromise demands a solution that allows both women to hold on to the illusion of control. So Rita and Hazel settle on going to the movies once a week. Neither woman is really happy, but since relationships are about control, not happiness, and they each got some of it, they feel okay about the deal.

"Jean and I don't do that. We believe that if you're compromising, you're not getting along. It's easy for us not to. Being outside relationshipness, neither of us feels obligated to please the other or to contribute in any way to her well-being."

Jean spoke up. "Fortunately, it's turning out that when Sonia is least externally motivated, most attuned to herself, least focused on me, everything she does pleases me. She's so darned adorable I can hardly stand it."

"And vice versa," Sonia grinned at her.

"I see what you're getting at," Ellie spoke hesitantly, "but it seems to me that the urge to couple is innate."

"No," Jean said firmly. "Not for women. For men, maybe—though I doubt it; I think they have to be socialized to do it so that they don't just constantly rampage, pillage, rape, and destroy everything. For women, that 'urge' is definitely a learned, conditioned response. Not so we won't rampage, but so that we'll use our power to keep men afloat and somewhat under control. Coupledom is a bedrock essential of patriarchy's survival. That's why we've all been heavily brainwashed to believe it's normal and natural and necessary. But it totally strips women of power. It and all other relationships numb us to the point where we scarcely know who we are, what we feel, what we want, or what we're doing. They make Stepford wives of us all. This is a state men find highly desirable in women."

"Well," Ellie said, "I don't do relationships anyway. I prefer instead to have sex occasionally with some consenting woman."

Sonia shrugged. "You're just having very short relationships, Ellie. We can't have sex without doing a relationship. They're one and the same."

"But sometimes I only see a woman once or twice. How can that be a relationship?"

"You have a very specific goal in mind when you go to bed with that woman. When you have a goal, there's no room for spontaneity, for authenticity. The minute you start sex, regardless of how long you intend to continue it with a particular person, you fall automatically into the rules that govern relationships. Sex is sadomasochism is relationships. They're synonymous and can't be separated. And they're lethal for women."

"The way you talk everything in this world is bad for women," Ellie said bad-temperedly.

"Ah, now you're getting it!" Sonia laughed, then became instantly serious. "It's a man's world, Ellie, through and through. Not for a single instant in five thousand years has it reflected or supported women as female beings. Every moment since maleness appeared on earth, it has tried in millions of ways to destroy the power that is femaleness. That's what keeps therapists in business: helping women tolerate this otherwise intolerable reality."

"So you'd agree that therapists are necessary."

"To patriarchy, oh yes, absolutely. But to women, deadly. They sustain women's illusions about men and society. They help women find ways to bear their despair and anguish instead of having nervous breakups with maleness. Therapy was instituted by men to prevent women from breaking through into their power.

"You can know this because men value therapy so highly. Without it, without the illusion it helps maintain, women might leap out of their mental and emotional straitjackets and make courageous dashes across the borders of men's world."

Ellie bristled. "I take issue with that kind of generalization, knocking all therapy and therapists. Therapy has helped me. I don't know that I'd be alive today without it."

"It depends on your definition of 'help'. Obviously, therapy has helped you bear your bondage with less awareness of its degradation and therefore with less pain. If therapy didn't keep women from recognizing the truth, finding their power, and breaking free, you'd better believe there'd be a law against it—and a brutally-enforced law. But the men in control recognize how essential it is to keep the slaves quiet. Like opium in China."

Agitated, Ellie stood up. "I think I'm on overload," she said, trying to sound apologetic and only managing to convey how angry she was. "I assure you that I'm going to think carefully about everything you've said. But right now I can't take in another word." She reached for Sonia's hand and squeezed it. "It's been wonderful meeting you, Sonia. I appreciate your letting me visit." She turned and took Jean's hand. "It's a marvelous house and I've enjoyed being here." She left the room to get her things.

"Well, we don't need to worry about her wanting to live at Wildfire," Jean said.

Getting up from the floor and snuggling down beside Jean in the double papasan chair, Sonia sighed. "I knew it was pointless before I started. She didn't get it, not one word. I don't know why I persist like that. Except that there's always such hope in my heart that something I say will trigger a woman's memories of her wild anarchic self."

Jean nodded sympathetically. "But you know, I don't even care anymore. I used to want more than anything for all women to be free, to be our original selves. But I know now that most women aren't going to choose freedom. What matters to me, Soni, is that you and I have made that choice."

Smiling, Sonia kissed her. "Let's call our friends and tell them we're home."

o o o o o o

Dana was glad to hear from them, and before she hung up, reminded them that the Murder Maids would be meeting at her house the following night. "I haven't heard from Harper or Lauren for a few days," she said. "Do me a favor and remind them."

Sonia gave Jean Dana's message while she dialed Harper and Lauren. The phone was answered on the first ring.

"Lauren!"

"Lauren?" Sonia was startled. "No, this is Sonia, Harper. Are you all right?"

Harper broke down. Sobbing, she managed to tell Sonia that she and Lauren had had a fight last night, that Lauren had told her she wanted to end the relationship, and that this morning she and her two suitcases were gone.

"I don't know where she is," Harper sniffled. "Please call me if you hear from her."

Sonia hung up, troubled. When she told Jean what was going on, Jean said, puzzled, "I wonder where she went?"

Sonia shook her head. "*I* wonder what the hell happened last night."

What happened was that Harper came home from work angry. Not at anything in particular, but it had been a difficult day and, like a good businesswoman, she had kept her anger out of the workplace. Home now, it was easy to find a focus for it. Like Lauren's muddy boots, right there inside the back door. Although they were off to the side, out of the line of traffic, their presence infuriated her. She was fastidiously neat, whereas Lauren tended to be sloppy. On rare occasions, Harper would admit that Lauren had improved over the years, but today was not one of those days.

Then there was the issue of food. Between relationships, Harper ate all her meals in restaurants—when she ate, that is; during her bouts of anorexia, she never spent all her food budget. In most of her relationships, her partners had assumed the role of housewife and, like Lauren, had been expected to do the cooking. The problem was that Lauren didn't like to cook and didn't do it well. That night when Harper saw the pot of split pea soup on the stove again, her fury erupted.

"What do you need?" she shouted at Lauren. "Cookbooks? Cooking lessons? Whatever it takes, damn it, get it! I'm sick of split pea soup and grilled cheese sandwiches!"

Lauren lowered her head and kept quiet through Harper's tantrum, having learned early on that it was best to let her get it all out. She also knew that afterwards Harper would want to take her in her arms and kiss her as she always did, then lead her to the bedroom and have sex with her.

Lauren waited until Harper had finished, then looked up, met her eyes, and said, "I'm leaving."

Harper did a doubletake. "You're *what?*"

"I'm leaving you. I'm through."

Harper laughed harshly. "What a joke you are, Lauren. Leaving. You couldn't survive five minutes on your own. Just who are you going to run to? Tell me, come on, tell me," she taunted.

Despite her shaky insides, Lauren sat still. It wouldn't do to let Harper see how agitated she was. Knowing she couldn't trust her voice, she remained silent.

When her gibes and threats failed to get a response, Harper grabbed the pan of soup and hurled it against the wall.

"Go ahead, run to your sisters!" she screamed, storming towards the door. "You deserve each other!"

Lauren watched, detached, as the soup dripped slowly down

the wall. She stayed where she was until she heard the bedroom door slam, then rose quickly, crossed to the study, and locked herself in. Leaning against the door, her hand over her thudding heart, she let out her pent-up breath in a long, ragged sigh. She listened carefully for a minute. When she was quite sure that Harper wasn't in the hall trying to figure out a way to get at her, she checked the closet to make sure her bags were still where she had left them. Then she stood at the study window and stared intently across the dark yard, waiting for the bathroom light to go on.

In the bedroom, Harper flung off her office clothes and threw them into a corner. Kicking a ladderback chair out of the way, she sat on the edge of the bed. She was trembling with rage and frustration. Jerking open the bottom drawer of her night table, she pulled out her vibrator, plugged it in, and turned it on. Within seconds she had an explosive orgasm, followed quickly by another. Without waiting for the waves of orgasm to subside, she jerked the plug out of the wall, and headed for the bathroom. Minutes later she was standing beneath the shower, hot water beating on her head.

Stupid cunt, she thought angrily. Who needs her.

She didn't hear Lauren leave.

28

"I had a terrible dream." Jean sat up and stared out the window at the vast expanse of snowy whiteness, while Sonia struggled to open her eyes. "I dreamed my Aunt Louise was trying to drown me in the bathtub. When I fought her, my uncle came and held my head down against the floor of the tub."

"That's a bona fide nightmare, Jeannie."

Jean frowned, trying to sort out the jumble of thoughts that crowded her mind. "I've got a funny feeling about this dream. I think I'm ready to remember some things that have been buried for a long time." She gave Sonia a quick kiss and leapt out of bed, sucking in her breath as her feet hit the icy floor. Grabbing her clothes, she sprinted downstairs.

The sky was leaden and the thermometer registered -10. Pulling on her boots and coat, she picked up the pail of birdseed and plowed out through the snow to the feeders. It was crucial not to let the feeders run out in this weather. Glancing at the mesh bag hanging from an oak branch, she made a mental note to make another batch of peanut butter/seed balls for the nuthatches and woodpeckers. She broke the thin layer of ice in the bird bath. Even its heater wasn't able to keep the water totally thawed.

The year of snow. It was only the second of January, and already they had had over fourteen feet of it. Jean could see how snow was the focal point for the Eskimos. She was beginning to feel that there was not much more to life than shoveling it and knocking it off the pine branches before they broke under its weight. Beautiful, yes, but overstaying its welcome. She longed for spring.

Her thoughts turned to Lauren. It had been a full three days after Sonia's conversation with Harper before they had heard from her. She had simply shown up, driving a rental car, and asked if they could talk. Barb had been there, helping Jean build a snow-proof bird feeder. They had abandoned the project and joined Lauren and Sonia in the kitchen, a full pot of tea in front of them.

"I'd had enough abuse," Lauren had told them. "The thing is, it wasn't even her bad mood that night that set it off, although I'm sure she thinks it was. I'd already packed my bags and was planning to tell her after dinner."

"Where are you staying?" Barb had asked.

"A little motel on route 31. But I've signed a lease on an apartment in town, on Calle del Sol. I move in next week."

"You can stay with me," Barb had offered. "I'd love having you, and there's plenty of room."

"I appreciate that Barb. Dana made the same offer, and there's a vacancy in her complex, too. But I've got to be on my own. I've been dependent on someone else all my life." She had picked Nikki up and begun rubbing her little pink tummy.

"I've always believed I couldn't do it myself. You know, live alone, take care of myself. The first thing Harper said when I told her I was leaving was 'Who're you going to run to'? She knew that had to be the first thing that entered my mind when I thought of leaving her. Where will I go? Who will I stay with? As soon as she threw it in my face, I knew the answer: I had to run to me."

"Are you scared?" Barb had asked.

"Terrified. So what's new? I've been terrified since I was a child. At least I'm finally growing up, and maybe someday I'll stop being afraid."

"I hope you'll let us know if there's anything you need," Sonia had told her.

Jean shivered and released the branch she'd been liberating. It was too cold to be out more than a few minutes, and she hurried back inside the house. Sonia was sitting on one of the counter stools eating her oatmeal. Seeing her there . . . that stool. No, not a stool. A kudu. Kudu? She shook her head. I must be going crazy, she thought. But that stool looks so familiar . . . .

Later, chopping vegetables for the soup, the same thing happened with the soup kettle. It seemed familiar, yet different. She searched her mind, trying to pull it out, but it wasn't ready to let go. So close, though, so close.

Another major storm ripped through the mountains late that afternoon, knocking out power lines. She and Sonia retired to the library, where the smallness of the room coupled with the fireplace guaranteed warmth and snugness. With a couple of kerosene lamps for light, they curled up on the couch to read. At least Sonia did. Jean, wrapped in a Scottish wool shawl, closed her eyes and dozed.

She heard his footsteps in the hall, and wrapped her arms around Tippi, pulling the little dog closer. Tippi growled when he approached the bed, but he grabbed her by the collar and flung her on the floor. He smelled bad, a mixture of oil and grease and stale beer. Years later, friends and family would wonder at her refusal to ride the trains. She could not have told them that the smell reminded her of her Uncle Jack, who had been a train mechanic.

He didn't talk to her anymore. In the beginning, he had stroked her long hair and told her how pretty she was, how happy she made him. Now he didn't bother. She waited for his hand under the blankets, on her knee, then her thigh . . . but not tonight. Pulling the blankets off her, he lifted her from the bed and carried her to the bathroom.

Aunt Louise was there, the bag in hand, waiting. Stripping off Jean's nightgown, her uncle laid her in the bottom of the tub and stood back. Aunt Louise slipped the bag over a hook in the wall, then knelt on the floor next to the tub. The narrow tube always hurt when she pushed it in. It was meant for an adult, not a three-year-old. No matter how hard she fought not to, she could not stop the gasp that escaped her as the cold water surged into her bowels.

He lifted her out and, holding her under one arm, put the stool into the tub and set the glass pot on it. She could see Aunt Louise crossing the hall to her room and closing the door. He placed her on the pot, still naked, and tied her ankles to the legs of the stool with two lengths of rope.

Then he unzipped his pants and pulled out his penis, big and swollen, and started stroking himself. She could smell him, sour, sweaty, surrounding her in a cloud of fumes.

She fought releasing the water. She always did: this time it wouldn't come out, it wouldn't. Squeezing her legs together, shutting her eyes tightly, don't look at him, don't think about him, don't let the water out! But the water won again, and as it did, a thick, viscous liquid hit her in the face, in her eyes, running down across her mouth and into her lap.

She wouldn't look at him. She could hear his breathing, she knew he was leaning against the wall, and she hoped beyond hope that he would go now, that he would leave her alone. But not tonight. He crossed to the toilet and urinated, then closed the lid and sat there, waiting, watching her, waiting. She wouldn't look at him. She knew he would start touching himself again, soon.

She felt him loosen the ropes around her ankles, then jerk her arms as he lifted her off the stool and removed the pot of water and excrement. Setting it on the floor of the tub, he laid her, belly down, across the stool and retied her ankles, and this time, her hands.

She knew she had to leave her body. She knew she had to get out of it before he pushed his penis in her. SHE HAD TO GET OUT!

Her hands flew up to her mouth as she stifled the scream. Slowly, slowly she realized where she was. She wasn't in his house. He was dead. She was in the library, with Sonia and the three dogs. Sonia, book beside her, was watching her, her eyes as unlike his as possible. They were filled with love and empathy.

"I know what happened," Jean said simply. "I remember what he did."

It was all she needed. The next morning she walked into the bathroom while Sonia was brushing her teeth and emptied her bowels effortlessly.

Sonia and Jean both knew, from their readings and from talking with women all over the world, that it is a rare woman who makes it to adulthood without experiencing some form of sexual abuse. Jean knew that her experience was not rare, although men would have her think so, would encourage her to believe that her uncle was a very sick man, a pervert. They didn't want her, or any woman, to figure out that perversion is what men are, that perversion is their norm. Women have to believe that experiences like Jean's are few and far between, that few men would have done what her uncle did. The truth is that most men, even if they do not act on it, are sexually turned on by what her uncle did and would give a great deal to have been in his shoes. She stopped him, finally, after three years of continual sexual assault. One night, as he was lifting her off the floor of the bathtub after her aunt had given her the enema, she relaxed her sphincter muscle and splattered him with water and excrement. Disgusted and furious, he never came near her again. But the damage had been done.

Nevertheless, on that second day of January 1992, the day after her fortieth birthday and thirty-four years later, she purged him from her bowels forever.

29

One of the advantages of the long, harsh winter was that it gave Sonia and Jean time to think and talk, especially after Sonia returned from her teaching stint at Stanford. It wasn't unusual for them to fall into bed talking and still be at it four, five, or six hours later. They were figuring things out.

For Jean, the eating disorder phenomenon proved a recalcitrant puzzle, one to which she returned again and again. She knew there was a direct answer to the question of its etiology, and she knew that that answer was not going to be found in psychiatric journals. Bit by bit, she began to piece it together out of her own history, starting with her uncle's sexual abuse and ending with the demise of sex and relationships in her life.

"When I was six," Jean told Sonia deep in one black freezing night as they lay warm together in bed, a Suzanne Ciani tape playing, "I heard my father telling his sister that if she didn't lose weight, she would never get a man. He said she was so fat that no man would want to touch her." She shifted onto her back.

"That did it. When I heard those words, I knew I had to get fat, so fat no man would ever want to touch me, even look at me except in disgust. So I started to eat.

"I ate and I ate. By the time I was eight years old and in fourth grade, my mother was so alarmed she took me to a doctor. He decided my thyroid was sluggish and gave me thyroid medication and diet pills—uppers.

"The diet pills definiteiy took away my appetite and I started to lose weight immediately. But they also made me jumpy and nervous and unable to sleep. That was all right with my parents and the doctor so long as I lost weight. But none of it was all right with me, particularly the weight loss. Panicky, I only pretended to take the pills, and kept eating. Soon I gained back the weight I had lost, then surpassed it. My mother put locks on the cupboards, hid the fattening foods, and made sure there were plenty of carrot and celery sticks around. The truth is I preferred those, but they didn't pack the fat on, so I'd go down to the corner store and buy candy and cookies and hide them in my room. For years I stuffed myself, and for years I hated my body and was totally miserable."

Sonia, nestled against Jean with her arm across her sharp hip bone, tried to imagine her friend fat and miserable. But she couldn't do .t. Jean, with her copper hair, green eyes, and vivid coloring, was too vibrantly healthy and happy in her trim, now 115-pound body. Too thin, Sonia thought, conscious of the hip bone under her arm, but certainly not the gaunt, 90-pound-skeleton she had apparently been at the nadir of her anorexia.

"Then I got married. He didn't seem to care that I was fat. Or at least he never said anything. I think it came up once, and he told me he thought I looked fine. And I slowly came to believe him. I didn't try to lose weight for my wedding, like so many women do. And as soon as I was married, I felt safer, as though the wedding band would protect me from other men.

"Brad and I were both students and had little social life, but one night we decided to go to a party being given by a married cousin of his. I won't go into the details, but when the party ended, there were six of us who stayed behind, three couples. We decided to play cards. At least the guys decided to play cards. The wives just went along as wives do. We had all been drinking, though for once I was relatively sober and functional.

"I had noticed that Brad seemed very interested in one of the wives. I'll never forget her name: Fawn. By men's standards, she was very beautiful—long blonde hair, high cheekbones, and thin body. Very thin.

"Anyhow, as the game progressed and the guys got drunker and drunker, they also got raunchier and raunchier. At some point, Brad's cousin brought out another deck of cards, this one with pictures of naked women in bondage on them. That did if for me. I left the game, and my leaving gave the other two women an excuse to leave, too. The men stayed on in the living room for a long time getting off on their cards.

"When Brad finally came to bed—we were staying at his cousin's, and so were the other couples—he was obviously stirred up and wanting sex. It was the furthest thing from my mind, but I was a good wife. The problem was that he was so drunk he just couldn't do it. He was sort of halfway there, but not enough to count, if you know what I mean." She gave a short laugh.

"After poking and prodding for about fifteen minutes, he rolled off me, reached over and grabbed my belly in his hand, and squeezed it hard. 'You've got so much fat down there I can't even find you.' Then he turned over and went to sleep.

"I didn't sleep that night. The next day, I didn't eat anything, only drank black tea and diet coke. I did the same thing the next day, and the next, because I knew he was really disgusted with my fat, and I knew he was very interested in Fawn. I decided that if that's what he wanted, I'd give it to him. In three months I went from 185 pounds to 125."

"Did that please him?"

Jean shook her head. "I don't think he even noticed. He was preoccupied with school and Fawn. I think they had a brief affair, although I'm not certain. Then he got a job two thousand miles away and I didn't go with him. Our marriage was over, anyhow. After he left, I started to eat again, and in a few months was back to my pre-diet weight of 185.

"Then one night at work in the library, my boss raped me. He was waiting for me at quitting time. Everyone else was gone. I had no warning at all—he simply jumped me. I tried to fight him off, but he pinned me to a table and started hitting me in the face. When I kept struggling, he slapped me even harder and hissed, 'Don't give me that shit. A fat girl's gotta get it somewhere.' I froze. When it was over, I went home and locked myself in my apartment and stayed there for five weeks. I didn't answer the door or phone. And I didn't eat. When I came out, I weighed 105 pounds."

"And that was the beginning of the serious eating disorder."

"Yep. This time it was for real. Since fat didn't keep men away, somewhere inside me I decided that if I stopped eating, I'd get so small they couldn't see me anymore. I'd just disappear, cease to exist. I remember walking down the street and feeling immense satisfaction at the horrified looks on people's faces when they saw me coming. I looked like a walking corpse. But I felt powerful, knowing that no one would want to touch me as long as I looked like that. I felt in control. I knew people thought it wasn't okay to starve to death, and I was telling them to go to hell, I'd do whatever I wanted."

"You almost died doing it, though."

"I didn't care, Sonia. I really didn't care. I was so full of despair. I couldn't see any way to be happy. By this time I was having relationships with women and there really wasn't any significant difference. I was binging and purging and starving with a vengeance. I tried all kinds of therapy. I tried hospitalization. Nothing worked. I was on a roll—rolling right toward my grave.

"But I guess something in me was stronger than my death wish because I managed to stop the destructive behaviors. But as I told you before, I couldn't stop the thoughts. Even though I was no longer binging and throwing up, even though I was eating enough to keep me alive, I still thought about it all the time, still ached to do it. I had to fight it every step of the way."

"Until you stopped doing relationships and sex."

"Right. That worked like pure magic. The desire, the urges, the obsessions left instantly. I stopped eyeing every piece of food as though it were poison. My 'forbidden foods list' disappeared— the list of foods that I couldn't keep from throwing up. I began to feel normal for the first time in my life, and I really mean for the first time.

"I don't think there's a woman in the western world who doesn't have some kind of eating disorder, some kind of strange relationship with food and eating. She may not even be conscious of it, but I think it exists."

"I certainly didn't think I had one, but of course I did—always rigidly monitoring my weight; that's unnatural as hell," Sonia said. "Anyway, you're free of yours."

"I am. The last time I even felt the urge was nearly a year ago, when we did the vulva-and-breast-touching experiment. But I know that when I tell an audience that it's over, there will always be at least a handful of women who can't believe me. In their place, I wouldn't either. They really believe they can't stop. Unless you've had a life-threatening eating disorder, you can't begin to imagine what I'm talking about. The obsession, twenty-four hours a day, seven days a week. It's like a cancer, eating away at you, gnawing at you every second, ruining your entire life. I couldn't think of anything *but* food: eating it, not eating it, buying it, preparing it, throwing it up. I pored over cookbooks, especially the ones with pictures, and thought how wonderful that food looked and how wonderful I was that I could resist it. I was very proud of myself. I was in control."

Stroking Jean's side softly, Sonia murmured, "Sounds like that was the most important thing to you."

"Oh, absolutely," Jean said. "And not only to me. In men's world, women mistake control for power, and in this world, in sex, we are out of our power. It's this, this being out of our power, that sends us into a tailspin of despair and illness, into bizarre kinds of controlling behaviors such as anorexia and bulimia."

She paused a moment, then said thoughtfully, "I didn't know any of this consciously, of course. As you know, I did everything I could think of to make myself like sex, to make my body respond. But in the end I couldn't keep it up. It was killing me. The lies, the half-truths, the incredible energy it took to try to keep it all together. And the battle against self-destruction."

She fell silent, inwardly shuddering a little, and held Sonia closer. "It's hard to believe it was all just sex, Sonia. That paltry, feeble experience mensystem tells us is so wonderful. That perversion all women are supposed to be able to do so naturally. All lies. Sex isn't wonderful or natural, we aren't able to do it, and ultimately we can't. No woman can be really successful at relationships and sex because none of us can stay happy doing them.

"And when our spirits suffer, so do our bodies. That's why we're dying of despair by the millions, only calling it breast cancer, cervical, ovarian, and uterine cancer. And if we're not dying outright, we're dying as much as we dare with chronic fatigue and environmental illnesses."

She put her arms around Sonia, getting as close to her as she could, reminding herself that it was really all over, feeling a poignant mixture of relief, joy, and sadness.

After a while she asked sleepily, "Think we'll ever hear from Harper again?"

"Maybe if she gets over her anger at all of us. She thinks we betrayed her."

"That's ridiculous. Lauren told her where she was and what her plans were the very same day she told the rest of us."

"Yeah, but we found out first, and Harper had asked me to call her as soon as I heard, remember. I would have, if Lauren hadn't made us promise not to talk to Harper until she did. But there's more to it than that. I think she's particularly angry at you and me because we always talk against relationships, and she thinks we influenced Lauren to leave her."

"Typical Harper, assuming Lauren couldn't do anything on her own," Jean said. "I'm not sorry she went back to Boston. I haven't missed her. Funny, I expected Lauren to go back, not Harper."

"So did I. I never expected Lauren to do half of what she's done. Her determination and perseverance have been pretty impressive. And the way she stood up to Harper right to the histrionic end. I'm glad it's Lauren who stayed, too. I like having her come to walk the dogs or just hang out and talk. I don't want to live with her full time, but I enjoy her company."

Jean gave her a squeeze. "I enjoy *your* company and want to live with *you* full time." Suddenly she remembered something. "I had a dream last night, about your jade plant—the one over there by the sliding glass door—and I dreamed I changed my name to Jade."

"Jade." Sonia thought it over a moment. "I like it, very much. I didn't know you'd been thinking about changing your name."

"I haven't, at least not consciously. But I think I want to, and I think I want to try Jade for awhile. I'll need to change my last name, too—Jade Tait isn't going to cut it. I've been thinking about DeForest."

"Jade DeForest," Sonia repeated. "It's beautiful—but I'm going miss Genius."

Jean grinned. "Don't worry. I'll always be a genius." Then seriously, "If I decide I like the name Jade, I have no idea of how to go about making it legal."

"I don't think it's hard. Two of my ex-children did it, and I think it was just a matter of filing it with some court. We'll find out. Anyway, I hope you do like it and decide to keep it. It's exotic, it's elegant, it's perfect—just like you, Jade-lo."

30

Jade shivered, but resisted the urge to put her clothes on. Although the house was its usual early–morning cool, she knew the shivering was more than a response to cold. It was nerves.

This was The Naked Experiment. She had been pleased that she'd been able to shower in the open space of the bathhouse without feeling too embarrassed. But toweling off one day she had asked herself the fatal question: what would be harder? Answer: walking around the house naked for an hour.

To be sure they would really do it, not just talk about it, she and Sonia immediately made it into an experiment. On the first day, she held her arms stiff and slightly in front of her. When she sat, she crossed her legs and folded her arms over her belly, a belly that was larger and more off-putting to her than it had been in a long, long time. When she finally realized that she was trying to hide herself, she began walking around the house with her arms out, as if she were ballet dancing. It wasn't easy for her.

But it was for Sonia. Even with breast implants, she had always been more at ease with her body than Jade had. Nevertheless, both of them were delighted by the sensory deliciousness of nakedness, how it heightened their physical awareness: the slightest breeze riffling the tiny hairs all over the skin, the hot sun streaming through the kitchen windows onto a bare back, the softness of Nikki's fur as she cuddled into them, and each other's sweet, gentle touches in passing. The Naked Experiment opened up a whole new dimension of freedom.

One thing became absolutely clear as they moved from experiment to experiment: the body was central to women's power. Sonia had known it for a long time. "The journey into the body is the journey to the stars," she had written. Jade's Hopi friend had said it a decade earlier, and now—after almost a year of experimenting—they were beginning to understand the depth and scope of it.

Sonia continued her love affair with her breasts, talking to them every night as she stroked them. Then in May of 1992, the media exploded with horror stories about breast implants. Of the millions of women who had received them, almost none had been warned of the potential hazards of silicone poisoning. Law suits sprang up all over the country, and for the first time implant dangers were being taken seriously.

One night, Sonia and Jade were lying in bed, Sonia loving her breasts, Jade reading. Suddenly, Sonia said, "I've got to have them out, Jade-lo."

Jade put down her book and looked over at her. It had been clear for some time that Sonia's breasts were getting smaller, a sign that silicone was leaking out. But the Palo Alto surgeon's warning that it would be a massacre to remove them had kept her resigned to living with them. She had not wanted to hurt body any further. But now her body was giving her another message: get rid of them!

So they began the search for a surgeon who would be willing to remove them. But most doctors, finding out how old the implants were, refused to deal with them. Finally, after more than a dozen phone calls, they located a plastic surgeon who agreed to do it.

On June 9, 1992, Sonia checked into a Las Palomas hospital. The surgeon had already told her that he would not even attempt to remove the dacron patches that were now imbedded in the muscles of the chest wall. He also warned her that most likely all that would be left was scar tissue. He was chagrined at her refusal to have cosmetic surgery afterwards, assuring her that although there might possibly be problems with *silicone*—though he thought not—*saline* implants were perfectly safe and would at least leave her with something besides two little empty bags hanging on her chest. But she was adamant. Regardless of how she looked afterward, she wanted her body free of men's atrocities.

As expected, during the operation the implants burst. The surgeon told Jade he had done twenty-five saline flushes on each side in an attempt to clean it out.

"Did you get it all?"

He smiled patronizingly. "I'm sure you've never worked with silicone caulk, but if you had, you'd know that if you spill it or get too much on, it's impossible to clean it up with water. It's not water soluble. The silicone flushes got some of it, but most is still in there."

"What happens to it then?"

He shrugged. "The body takes care of it."

"I don't see how," she persisted. "You know the nature of silicone. I'm afraid it will get into the liver and kidneys and lymph system and clog them."

He shrugged again, and hurried off for a radio interview on the merits of breast implantation.

But the implants were out, and that was all that mattered to Sonia. The first week was a searing hell of pain from the cutting and general trauma. But almost as bad was that she was wrapped so tightly around the chest that she could scarcely breathe and had to sleep sitting up in a chair. The nausea from the anesthesia was fierce, too, for a few days, and her back ached from lying motionless for hours on the operating table. She was exhausted and sore, but very peaceful. She had her body back.

When the bandages came off two weeks later, Jade immediately began hot packs and compresses. Every pack she removed was covered with clear, sticky silicone. It oozed from the incisions and nipples. They continued hot packs and hot soaks for several months in an attempt to pull out as much of it as possible.

Three weeks after the implant removal, Sonia agreed to do a radio show about her experience. The calls that pored in as a result, as well as of the news zinging through the grapevine, were heartbreaking. Many were from women who were desperate to have their implants removed but had discovered that their insurances would not cover such 'elective surgery'.

"Elective, my eye!" Jade snorted. "These are major emergencies, lifesaving procedures." Sonia had not had any health insurance, and because the money for the operation had to be paid *before* she went into the operating room, she and Jade had had to sell their truck and trailer. But not every woman could raise the necessary money so quickly.

Several women reported that their husbands left them when they made the decision to have them out. Others revealed that they had received the breast implants as high school or college graduation gifts from their fathers, who feared that their lack of mammary endowments would make them unmarriageable.

They all spoke of shame and guilt. They all said they wished they had known what they were getting into before it had been too late. They all regretted having done it. And those without the finances were stuck with their implants—like asps at their breasts, killing them.

One young woman, barely twenty-four years old, sobbed into the phone. Her father and husband-to-be had pressured her into having implants. Ironically, the surgery had occurred exactly two years to the day of her having been raped by one of her father's co-workers. "It felt the same," she wept. "When I came out of the anaesthetic I felt raped."

"She's right," Sonia concurred. "That's what it is, sexual assault. Breast implants, face lifts, tummy tucks, liposuction, stomach stapling, electrolysis, collagen injections—all sexual abuse. Because men get off on big breasts. Because they don't like wrinkles, or stretch marks, or full bellies, or hair. To the tune of billions of dollars and incredible suffering, women subject themselves to knives and tools of torture for sex' sake."

"But women—and only women—can stop it," Sonia later assured a large audience in Missouri. "Men certainly aren't going to. They're going to keep on trying to convince us that we'd look better without our wrinkles, without our gray hair and small breasts. They're going to get us to diet ourselves to death. They're going to go on hating and trying to destroy us. Until we stop being their victims. Until we decide to love ourselves just as we are and tell them to go to hell!"

This is why the body experiments were so critical. If they didn't free themselves of the pernicious conditioning about women's bodies, nothing else they did would ultimately matter.

In August, Jade's friend Pam, a therapist from the Bay Area, came to see them. One morning just after breakfast, the three of them were in the lounge area of the kitchen. Jade was lying naked on the floor, arms outstretched, realizing that while she was almost comfortable being naked with Sonia, she was still very embarrassed in front of other women. *Yet another experiment,* she sighed to herself.

Remembering a story, she said, "Just before I left the health practice, a woman came into the office in tears. She told me that as she was driving to the clinic, she suddenly understood everything. Men were building new condos north of town, and had had to bring bulldozers in to rip out hundred-year-old pinon and juniper trees. There wasn't a single tree left, she told me. Just torn, ripped-open earth. As she continued to drive, she saw nothing but signs of destruction and hatred—cement slabs and roads, ugly buildings, overgrazed lands, erosion, old strip mining sites. She said that what hit her hardest was the realization that the earth is female. 'This is how they treat women. This is what they think of us, of femaleness. They hate us as we really are. They have to change us, destroy us. I want out of this world'."

Sonia was sitting cross-legged on the floor with Maggi's head in her lap. "I don't blame her. It's very painful, seeing the truth as clearly as that. I want out of it, too."

Pam, a robust, red-headed woman, sat bare-footed in one of the rockers, holding Nikki. "Men's world is a grim place," she agreed. "And they do hate us. It's a fact." This reminded Jean of Coral and her two-fact night at Wildfire. It seemed like centuries ago that they had all laughed and played together in this kitchen.

"That workshop you gave on shame last fall really shook me," Pam said to Sonia. "I thought I'd done most of my shame work and was mostly free of it, at least the big stuff. I mean, I could walk around naked, pee with other women in the bathroom, that kind of thing. But when you started talking about bowel movements and vulvas, I knew I'd better get to work.

"So I started doing my own experiments with a housemate who had also gone to the workshop and was all fired up. I got over bowel-movement phobia pretty fast, and having my vulva looked at while I watched.

"But a couple of weeks ago a friend showed up at the house, sicker than hell. She'd left work to go home but hadn't been able to make it that far, so she'd stopped at our house. I told her to get in my bed and I'd bring her some tea. When I walked into my room with the tea, I nearly died—I'd left my vibrator on the bedside table. I'd used it the night before and had forgotten to put it away. To make matters worse, she was lying on her side facing the table so there was no way I could slip it into the drawer without calling her attention to it.

"I gave her the tea and made sure she was comfortable, then left her alone to sleep. My cheeks were burning and I was trying to think of some excuse to give her, like muscle cramps in my shoulders. Then it hit me. What was I ashamed of?

"So I talked to my housemate about it, and started carrying my vibrator into the living room and using it right there. That was hard. It would have been hard even if we'd been in a relationship. But being just friends and housemates, it was excruciating."

Jade sat up. "I'm impressed, Pam, and believe me, I know what you mean by excruciating. Sonia and I have been doing a vibrator experiment, too. Actually, several of them. The first was to use the vibrator when we were together. And as you said, this wasn't easy, but after awhile we both got used to it. Then I tried to think of what would be harder. Up until this point we'd been using the vibrator only in the bedroom. We realized that this made it hard for us not to think of what we were doing as sexual. You know— sex happens in the bedroom. So we moved out of the bedroom into the kitchen, the lounge, and the library."

"And when we were comfortable with that, you said . . ." Sonia grinned wickedly at Jade.

"I said, 'What would be harder than that?' and realized that what would be harder would be simply to walk into a room where Sonia was and without saying a word, pick up the vibrator and begin."

"Explain why that would be more difficult," Pam asked, brow furrowed.

"What was—and still is—so hard about it is that there's no way to soften it, to prepare others for it. I mean, it's easy now when we both do it, it's a joint decision, we're both going to do it, and we get ready for it. But simply to walk in without saying a word and pull that thing out and start moaning . . . I don't know. I feel very exposed and foolish. Terribly embarrassed."

Sonia laughed. "One night I was lying in bed wide awake trying to think of how to get to sleep. I wasn't sure if Jade was asleep or not. Suddenly, I thought how nice it would be to use my vibrator, but with Jade lying next to me I was so reluctant to use it that at least a half hour passed before I was actually able to bring myself to look for it. I opened my drawer and felt around in there, but it wasn't there. So I felt on the floor, thinking maybe I'd left it there. No luck. By now I was pretty sure Jade was awake so I stopped worrying about making noise, but I still couldn't find it. Finally I muttered, 'Where is that darned thing?'"

She grinned sheepishly. "Of course, I knew immediately what I'd done. Following the rules of the experiment, I hadn't told Jade directly that I was going to use the vibrator, but by asking myself the question aloud, I had effectively announced my intentions. Which cut the embarrassment in half, at least."

"I see what you mean. When I've used mine in front of Loni, I've always warned her ahead of time. I don't think I could do it otherwise. It's shame, all right."

Sonia touched her vulva through her jeans. "We all know who made our vulvas shameful. I want to reach the place where nothing I do feels shameful, nothing about my body causes me embarrassment."

She stood, pulled off her shoes, jeans and underpants, and sat back down on the couch with her legs wide apart. "I want to be able to sit here naked like this, both sets of labia flapping in the wind, clitoris, urethra, vagina, and anus fully exposed—aren't they gorgeous?—and feel as comfortable as if I were fully clothed. I'm never going to give my body the message again that there's anything indecent about her."

Pam said she understood, but that for her, the hard part was finding other women who felt the way she did, who wanted to do the experiments and were not in their sex minds about them. Her housemate was fine—to a point. But she didn't dare ask Loni to touch her vulva, or her breasts, because for Loni, that would be sex. She was limited in what she could do with Loni, and limited in what she could do herself.

"That reminds me. I'm curious about your vulva experiments and what you've learned about orgasm," Pam said as she matter-of-factly pulled her shirt over her head and stepped out of her sweatpants and underwear.

Jade flipped over onto her stomach. "That's right, we hadn't figured that one out when we saw you last. Well, we've learned a *lot*, but I'll try to condense it. I discovered that when I didn't try to force my body to feel some predetermined sensation, or to have sex, she had orgasms effortlessly, one after the other, until I was ashamed to be seen with her, the hussy! That's what's been hard for me, to feel as if it's not just all right but wonderful that my vulva loves so much to be touched, that she's so wild and playful and alive."

Sonia reached over and patted Jade's rump. "This lucky woman didn't take on the conditioning about sex that most of the rest of us did," she explained to Pam.

"Yeah, you talked a little about that in the workshop."

"Well, it's because she couldn't force her body to feel sexual—though heaven knows she tried. So, unlike mine, hers hasn't had to relearn how to be its original self."

"The last time we talked you were pretty discouraged about the whole thing," Pam recalled.

Sonia nodded. "It's true. At the beginning of this most amazing time with Jade, I sometimes did have orgasm when my vulva was touched even after I gave up control of her. But she was very cautious. It's taken her this long to really believe and trust that I won't use her for sex ever again. Now my clitoris and vagina, like the rest of my body and soul, are in an almost constant state of arousal, wild as the wind, free and full of joy, eager for pleasure."

"Great!" Pam grinned. "Congratulations! I've been working on it, trying not to be orgasm-oriented when I touch my vulva. When I touch her without a goal, though, I usually end up going to sleep. I certainly don't have orgasms. It takes more than just touching myself mindlessly for that to happen."

"It's because your body—like mine used to be—is accustomed to excitation and to responding only in sex."

"Well, I hope mine gets over it soon. I worry about her sometimes. Stroking her without thinking of anything in particular is very relaxing and soothing, and I do it a lot, especially when I read in bed before I go to sleep. I like that feeling, but it seems that that's the only response she has to my touching her." Pam was dodging Nikki's persistent tongue.

"I think she'll wake up when she's convinced that neither you nor anyone else is going to sex her anymore."

"I have to admit that I envy you two. I don't want to have relationships. I've suffered over them enough for a dozen women. And I sure don't want sex. I never did, although I always managed to convince myself I did. Whatever desire I stirred up fizzled out fast, though, like in a few weeks. My honeymoons were short-lived!"

She paused, remembering something, then laughed. "I was in therapy years ago, after my divorce and just after my last relationship with a man. The therapist was male." She held up her hand quickly. "I know, I know. I was terribly unenlightened in those days. Anyhow, I was talking about my anger at men, my fear of them and of relationships and sex, and he said to me pompously, 'I don't think most women experience what you're reporting'. I shot back, 'I don't think most women report what I'm experiencing!'"

"Good for you!" Jade laughed. "You're absolutely right. Women don't tell the truth because they're made to feel like freaks if they do. Damn, I wish women would wake up to their real feelings, instead of going around like wombots."

"Hey, I like wombots even better than fembots," Sonia said. "I may be one in some ways, but I'm less of one now than I was a few weeks ago."

Pam waited expectantly.

Sonia shrugged. "Just the same old story, I'm afraid—I remembered the years of physical and sexual abuse I suffered as a child at the hands of a male relative. I'd always thought I was one of the lucky ones, that somehow I'd escaped that most necessary of men's terrorist tactics. But I'd just buried it deeper. Anyway, now I'm carrying a lot less heavy psychic baggage around than I did for half a century, and feeling very light and free."

Pam reached down and shook Sonia's foot. "More congratulations! I love to hear about women's personal victories. They give me courage."

Sonia was quiet a moment, examining a gray pubic hair. Then she looked up. "Well, then I have another one for you. Not so dramatic, but to me just as much a victory.

"Jade and I started an experiment late last fall, 'The Weight-Gaining Experiment'. All my adult life I'd been under the impression that I didn't worry about my weight, that I just ate what I wanted and didn't gain. And I often said to Jade how lucky I was that I hadn't ever had an eating disorder.

"But I realized one day that that wasn't true, that though I hadn't been conscious of it, I had watched my weight very rigorously, that I had always been in control, telling my body what and how much she could eat and how much she could weigh. After listening to Jade's stories, I realized that I was doing this and that it was an eating disorder. Massive s/m—my assumption that I knew better than my body what was good for her. So I decided to let her be."

Sonia stood up, scratching her hip. "This carpet makes me itch." She sat down on the couch. "Ah, this is better. Come on, Maggi. Resume your position." Maggi jumped up next to her and put her head in her lap.

Sonia took up her story. "This may not sound like much, letting your body be. But for me it was the most frightening of all the experiments—next to taking off my shirt at Michigan. When we first thought of it, I moaned to Jade, 'I can't do this one, and that's that!' I believed that if I didn't keep her firmly in check, my body would get so fat I'd have to be rolled around the room. I was sure that all that was between me and massive obesity was my will power. To give that up felt like dying."

"The thought almost froze me with terror, too," Jade remembered. "I could barely stand myself at the enormous weight I already was—112 pounds. To let my body go completely, well, that was almost unthinkable. But that alone told me I had to do it, had to trust her, had to get out of my mind all the false notions about how much I should weigh and what to do to achieve that.

"So we both began. Every day we both had to tell our bodies that we were letting them go, that they could be whatever they wanted to be. If they wanted to be bigger, then fine, we could accept that. We were both convinced that we would gain weight—a lot of it."

Sonia nodded. "I kept telling mine it was dandy if she wanted to be fat, that it was irrelevant to me. Every time I said that, I nearly fainted from fear, but I wanted her to be free."

"Did you gain weight?"

"Oh, yes," Sonia said. "I went from 118 to 132 pounds."

"Jade?"

"I went from 112 to 122. I weigh most during the winter months, when my body always adds a few pounds anyhow. But that's not the end of the experiment." She looked at Sonia.

Sonia resumed the story. "One day, we realized something very important. You see, we had both assumed that if we stopped trying to control our bodies, we would gain weight. That assumption was just more evidence of control."

Pam shook her head. "I'm lost."

"What we should have told our bodies was something like, 'I'm not going to control you any longer. You're free to do what you want'. Instead, we were assuring them that it would be fine with us *if they gained weight*. By making that assumption and by preparing ourselves for weight gain, we forced them to gain weight."

"So what happened?"

"As soon as we really stopped relationshipping them, really dropped all expectations and assumptions and gave them total freedom, we both lost weight. They had never really wanted to be as heavy as we had forced them to be."

Sonia turned to Jean. "But you know, Jade-lo, I'm glad I did the wrong thing first, because otherwise how would I ever have had the experience of really loving this body when she weighed more even than when I was pregnant? I could have lived with her like that forever, you know. And I'm glad to know it, glad to be free of my fear of fat."

"I don't know what I'm doing with that one," Pam sighed. "I like to think I don't worry about my weight, either, but now I'm not so sure. I like my body the way she is, but I'm not sure I'd like her as much if she got a lot heavier."

Jade nodded. "Like us before this experiment, your acceptance of your body is conditional. She's fine the way she is now, but if she starts getting it into her head to get bigger . . ."

"Then I'm not sure I'm going to like her," Pam finished, nodding at Jade. "You're right, it's pretty conditional."

"I think almost any woman who thinks she loves her body unconditionally is fooling herself," Jade said thoughtfully. "As long as she stays within certain patriarchally-induced boundaries, she's fine. But once she starts going over the line, she changes her tune, and fast."

"The truth is," Pam said, "that women's bodies are beautiful. Period. And men's are disgusting. They smell bad, they're often covered with coarse hair, they are almost constantly walking around with this hard, grotesque thing sticking up in the middle, trying to find a place to put it. Their bodies are simply a mechanism for hauling this monstrosity from place to place.

"I mean it when I say women's bodies are beautiful—unless we're deliberately abusing them, deliberately trying to harm them. I was at the West Coast Women's Music Festival a few years ago, and there was a woman at the pool. She was so anorexic I nearly fainted when I saw her. I couldn't look at her."

Jade said nothing, but she knew how it felt from the other side.

"I've got to pee," Pam stood in one swift, graceful motion, depositing Nikki on the floor as she strode towards the bathhouse. "I love this room!" she called back to them.

Sonia had finally gotten fed up with the fact that their toilets were sitting in boxes in the shed. Armed with a do-it-yourself plumbing book, she had hauled the toilets into the bathhouse, and step by step installed them according to the instructions and diagrams. Their shiny black enamel matched the sinks and the support beam. And even Jean, who had been so reluctant at first, loved the way they looked and loved using them.

Pam came back, wiping her nose with a wad of toilet paper. "Allergies," she explained, flopping back in her chair. "No matter where I go I manage to find something growing out there to be allergic to."

Jade nodded in Sonia's direction. "She has a wonderful allergy story," she said.

"I had terrible allergies for years," Sonia told Pam, "ever since my breast implants. They were so severe that I had to go for shots and take drugs. But even then, I suffered horribly.

"Then last spring when the pinons began sending out clouds of golden pollen and the misery began, I realized I needed to review the truth about my allergies. I turned on the most beautiful music I could find, lay down on my bed, closed my eyes and conferred with myself. 'Women and plants are not separate,' I remembered. 'We are one another, fully, literally. So pollen, the life force of plants, can't possibly harm me. It can only vitalize me, enlarge me, give me health and joy.'

"I imagined walking through the forest on that slope over there, imagined a great gust of pinon pollen enveloping me, gilding me, pouring energy into me, making me feel lightheaded with life."

"I'll bet you're going to tell me that your allergy disappeared instantly," Pam said cynically.

"Yes, in fact I am," Sonia laughed. "When I first lay down, I could hardly breathe. My eyes and ears and skin and the roof of my mouth itched ferociously, and I was an ambulatory mucous factory. When I got up, I could still feel a little tickling in my nose, but that was about it."

Pam looked disbelieving.

Sonia shrugged. "I couldn't believe it either. I don't think of myself as a person who has such powers. I was sure it was temporary, that by the time I got back downstairs, it would be back in red-pepper savagery. But to my amazement, it wasn't. I ran out of the house and up the hill among the pinons. A gusty breeze was swirling the pollen in billows off the trees and along the ground. I stood still, letting it embrace me, raised my face into it and breathed deeply. And just as I had imagined, I felt energized and enlivened."

"Mind over matter," Pam concluded.

"Not at all," Sonia corrected her. "Nothing over anything. Simply reviewing the truth of femaleness."

"You mean, you think men can't do this?"

"I'm sure they can't do what I did. Maybe they can rid themselves of allergies by repeated suggestion, by dint of incredible will power and practice. But not effortlessly. Not by reviewing the truth, because the truth is that men's bodies are not connected to life.

"In fact, I was so indoctrinated to believe I was man-like that it never occurred to me that just fifteen minutes of conferring with myself would rid me forever of a fierce, quarter-century-old allergy. I thought I'd have to meditate every day several times, maybe for months, maybe years, before I noticed any significant improvement."

"Well then, do you think all women could do this if they believed they could?"

Sonia shook her head. "No, I don't. I believe that the power came from my returning at least partially to my original state— that is, from escaping the sex mind, remembering and practicing unconditional touch. The power is in being female—unconditional, nonsexual. I don't know any woman besides us who is consciously trying to be this way."

Affronted, Pam said defensively. "I hear stories like this all the time in my practice. Women do amazing things."

"Of course. But rarely, and non-reproducibly for the most part. I can now do this at any moment about anything. For instance, I've always had excessively dry skin and thought that because of my hypothyroidism, I couldn't do anything about it. After the allergy experiment, I reviewed the truth with my thyroid. I apologized for having made limiting assumptions about her for so long, for having slathered my body with lotions in the belief that she was too disabled to do her job of skin moisturization. I told her she was now free of all my assumptions, free to function fully *if she wanted to.* I wasn't expecting her to change and I wasn't expecting her not to. I was suspending expectation. But I gave her the option by putting only a tiny bit of lotion on my body after bathing.

"Apparently, she wanted to be free of the life-long constraints I had imposed on her, because almost immediately she began moisturizing like mad. I hardly need to use lotion at all anymore."

Jade spoke up. "Having watched Sonia do these remarkable things, I decided one day to see if reviewing the truth with my body would affect my life-long wheat allergy. It's almost anticlimactic to say that that allergy's totally gone. Along with several others."

Jade got up and sat next to Sonia, kissing her gently on the lips. Twining her arms with Sonia's, she turned to Pam. "Neither of us can tolerate victimhood anymore, in anyone or anything. We told Tamale, that brown dog there, that what was keeping us from respecting and loving her fully was her victim behavior, being very specific about what that behavior constituted. She changed overnight."

Sonia took it up. "Then I went to the ficus tree that has been my companion for nearly a decade and told her that I wasn't going to spray her for scale anymore. She didn't have to be a victim, I told her, but if she wanted to be, if she got so much satisfaction from it that she didn't want to change, she couldn't live in this house, I would find another home for her. I told her this wasn't meant as a threat, simply a reality. There are no victims in women's world, only peers.

"For ten years, no matter how hard I'd battled it, scale had flourished on that ficus. I'd never been able to rid her of it entirely even for a few days. The day after I reviewed the truth with her, she began to free herself of parasites. That was three months ago. After a week, she didn't have a single live scale on her.

"I repeated this with three other houseplants that had had trouble with parasites. Once they realized that they didn't need to be victims, that they couldn't live outside patriarchy if they were, two of them chose not to be.

"Effortless, all this. That's one of the major differences between men's world and women's world. Because there's no time and space in it, everything in women's world is totally effortless."

Not being able to take in the effortless part, Pam changed the subject. "What did you think about the Marianne Littleton scandal?" she asked.

Jade shrugged. Marianne Littleton, a well-known author and therapist, had recently been convicted of malpractice charges for having had sex and a relationship with a client.

"I don't know the details," Jade said, "but I know she was had."

"But the testimony found that she had entered into a sexual relationship with the woman while she was still a client," Pam protested.

Irritated, Jean waved her hand. "They had a two-year relationship. It was only when it broke up that the 'client' filed suit—obviously a case of vengeance and greed. I can't stand victims, Pam, and the 'client' sounds like a victim to me. A nasty one, too."

"But you agree that Marianne was wrong to enter into a relationship with someone who was her client? I mean, therapy puts you in a very vulnerable position . . ."

"Which is one of the reasons I dislike it so much. You're right, we are vulnerable when we're in therapy because it's pure sadomasochism—therapist on top, client on bottom. We're already in a relationship with them, we're already having sex. This is the nature of therapy. So every single damned person in therapy is being sexually exploited. Let's take all the therapists to court! They're all guilty, so why pick on a few?"

Hitting her stride now, she expounded. "I hate the assumption that women are weak and vulnerable, that we aren't able to make good decisions for ourselves, that we need help, need 'support'. I'm sick of all the sniveling, cowardly women out there taking the victim role instead of standing up powerfully and refusing it. I'm sick to death of them!"

Pam was silent. She wondered if Jade remembered that she was a therapist. She felt momentarily shocked, then hurt. She would never have sex with any of her clients! Never! There had been numerous occasions when a client had shown more interest than was appropriate. And, she had to admit, she had had her share of attractions. But she had never acted on them, and in the cases of clients showing interest in her, had gently maintained her professional distance.

But of course, she realized, Jade wasn't necessarily talking about physical sex. She was talking about hierarchy, about sadomasochism, which she called sex. She needed to think about this long and hard.

"Men want women to believe we're victims, Pam," Jean went on. "Because you can't control power-full people. But it's not just men telling us we're victims. It's women, too. In fact, almost more so.

"I had a relationship with a woman who was quite a lot older than I. Unfortunately, it didn't have a happy ending, especially for her. She wasn't able to let go of me and I finally had to be brutally honest with her to get her to detach.

"I was telling a mutual friend about it later. I thought the friend was pretty neutral about our breakup, but when I got to this part, she was shocked and upset. 'But she's an old woman', she remonstrated. 'It's hard for old women to start over, harder than you can imagine. If she'd been forty years younger, I think what you said to her would have been fine. But she's not. She's old. You hurt her unnecessarily'.

"Do you see what I mean? What Della was saying to me is that old women are weak and fragile and have to be handled with kid gloves. They aren't strong and powerful and capable of taking care of themselves. We—meaning me, in this case—have to take care of them, have to be 'easy' on them. And this from a woman who claims to love and respect women! How can she, if she goes around feeling this superior to them?"

She looked a little shamefaced. "I do go on, don't I? But it's so sick! I guess that's why I've reacted as strongly as I have to the Marianne Littleton case. The woman she got involved with is not taking responsibility for her part in the affair. Without even knowing her, I know she's a victim."

"Or just damned shrewd!" Sonia muttered sleepily, lying down on the couch and pulling an afghan over her.

"I hear you," Pam nodded slowly. "I can tell in my practice which women are going to do well, and which aren't. The victims never do well, because, as you pointed out, they don't take responsibility for their actions. They come to me to try to figure out how they can get the people in their lives to change, or how they can make them see what they're doing wrong, not how they can change themselves. It's true that they thrive on victimhood."

"Reminds me of something a friend of ours always says: 'I refuse to make a career out of being an incest survivor'."

Pam stood up and began getting dressed. "You've given me a lot of think about. My mind is teeming." She looked around for her shoes, found them under her chair, and pulled them on. "I need to take a walk and let it rest. I wanted to do some exploring before I left tomorrow, anyway. But when I get back, I'd love to cook dinner."

"The kitchen is yours." Jade inclined her head in the direction of the couch. "I think we've lost Sonia." Sonia, with Maggi curled against her stomach, was fast asleep.

"I'll see you in a few hours," Pam whispered, leaning down to hug Jade.

31

But Pam was in no condition to cook dinner when she returned from her walk. Or rather, her hobble. Stopping at the creek on her way back, she had removed her shoes and socks and waded, enjoying the cold rushing water on her feet and legs. Tying the shoe laces together, she had flung her shoes around her neck and continued towards home, socks in hand. A moment later she had been viciously attacked by a prickly pear cactus.

It had taken her close to thirty minutes to remove the obvious spines from her right foot. By then, the foot had swollen to twice its normal size and was throbbing with pain. She had just hoped she would make it back to the house before she passed out.

One look, and Jade immediately gave her a dose of Rescue Remedy, the Bach Flower miracle formula for shock and pain. Then she extracted the spines Pam had missed and wrapped the foot in a clay pack to draw out the poison and any recalcitrant spines. A cup of umemboshi plum tea took care of the nausea, and by the time Jade had finished, Pam was ready for the supper Sonia had prepared—English muffin pizzas. She carried them on a tray to Pam's room, where they picnicked on the bed.

"I thought you didn't cook," Pam teased Sonia, reaching for her second muffin pizza.

"I cook excellent peanut butter sandwiches, but we're out of peanut butter. Then I saw the muffins in the fridge and a jar of spaghetti sauce . . . slapped some soy cheese and a few olives on 'em and, Voila, our repast. I wasn't a mom for 28 years for nothing!"

"I'm going to keep these in mind for the nights I can't face the stove." Pam wiped a smear of spaghetti sauce from her nose and took another muffin half. "Isn't it hard, just the two of you here? I mean, this is such a big place. I notice that many communities have ads in women's publications almost begging women to join them. Have you thought of doing that?"

"No!" Sonia and Jean yelped in unison.

"Guess I hit a sore spot!" Pam laughed, a little chagrined.

Seeing her embarrassment, Sonia explained quickly. "Since we can manage this place ourselves, financially and physically, numbers aren't important to us." She began to clear the bed, talking as she went. "And as you can imagine, we're certainly not interested in having women live here in the same way they live out there. There's nothing new about living on the land with other women so long as sadomasochism in all its guises is still the modus operandi. Why limit inhabitants to women, if women are thinking and behaving like men? Frankly, I don't believe women are ready to live in community."

"You said that at the workshop, Sonia, and it made sense to me, if only because of your idea of doing what you want to do all the time. I can't help but wonder what would happen if a woman's doing what she wants to do infringes on other women's freedoms. I can't see how you or anyone can resolve that."

Setting the dishes on the floor, Sonia lay down on the bed and put her head in Jade's lap in such a way that she could look at Pam as she spoke.

"Yep, you're right. That's why women aren't ready to live together again as we did before patriarchy. I know as well as I know anything that when women are free of our conditioning, when we are most ourselves, our desires and behavior are perfectly harmonious with one anothers'. We aren't there yet. Few—and I mean very few—women want to undertake the rigorous deprogramming that Jade and I have undertaken, for example. Most women still want to believe that it's enough to get together with other women, that somehow when they do, magic will happen and everything will be lovely. Nothing could be farther from the truth."

Jade made a face. "The only magic is that we haven't killed one another off in our communities. But we've come darned close to it." She continued stroking Sonia's forehead.

Pam put a pillow behind her back. "There's a small group of women in the Bay Area who purchased a house in Oakland. They decided that since it wasn't feasible for any of them to live on the land, they would try it in the city."

"And?" Jade raised her eyebrows.

"Not doing well. Two of the women have a five-year-old boy, so the main focus of this group is on the child. They're determined to prove to the world that this boy is going to be extraordinary because he was raised by five women."

"The old belief that nurture, not nature, is men's problem," Jade sighed. "I'm so tired of it. Especially since it's such a blatantly woman-hating theory."

Pam frowned. "I don't follow you."

"There's no way in hell that women can win with this one. When their boys turn out to be jerks—and they will, given long enough—they'll be accused of not having loved them enough. Or of having spoiled them. Or of not providing them with good male role models. I wish women who have sons would turn them over to their fathers and leave town."

"Tell her the story about the university women and their experiment with raising children in a totally female environment, Jade," Sonia urged her.

The experiment had begun years before when five women professors had received a grant that would enable them to live together with other like-minded women, creating a totally non-sexist, nurturing environment for their children. Their hypothesis was that what were perceived as gender differences were totally attributable to socialization; that if boys and girls were reared by women without reference to gender, boys would exhibit the same behavior as girls. With grant money they purchased a farm not far from the university and moved onto it: five women, a two-year-old girl, and two infant boys. Within the next two years, three more children were born, two boys and one girl. A sixth woman joined them, bringing with her her infant daughter.

They had no television, no radio, no external reminders of the outside world. Men were permitted to visit, but not to stay even for one night. The men were carefully chosen by the women for their sensitive, non-macho demeanors.

The children were home schooled and all were treated equally, receiving massive amounts of positive reinforcement and love. They grew in an environment where there were no sex-specific roles, where boys learned to cook and sew along with girls and girls learned to use tools, and where all jobs were given equal importance.

One of the requirements stipulated by the grant was that the children have bi-annual psychiatric examinations as a way of monitoring their progress. The reports that came back were always glowing: the children were above average in intelligence and in maturity, and showed extraordinary sensitivity and cooperative abilities. This was especially noteworthy among the four boys. The child psychiatrists were impressed.

The trouble began when, within months of each other, the eldest boys turned twelve. They started teasing the older girls in what was first perceived as a playful way. It soon became obvious, however, that this teasing had a tinge of cruelty to it. The women were quick to pounce on this and, they thought, eradicate it.

But shortly after the boys turned thirteen, they were discovered in the tool shed with one of the younger boys and the two oldest girls, ages eleven and nine. They had forced the two girls to strip, and had raped the oldest one. Although the younger boy had not participated in the actual rape, he had urinated on the nine-year-old girl.

The community fell apart, the women at first shocked, then horrified. *How could this have happened?* These boys had known nothing but love and nurturance. Unlike other children, they had been protected from the cruelty and violence of the outside world, from the all-pervasive viciousness of it. Where had this come from?

Only one of the women was able to look at what had happened in an even semi-objective way. She had been forced to realize that nurture had little or nothing to do with it, that nature—in this case male nature—was absolutely the key. While the other women were blaming themselves and searching for what they had done wrong, she realized that there was nothing they could have done differently. It was clear to her that maleness was innate and could not be changed.

"That's a terrible story," Pam said when Jade finished.

"The real tragedy is the illusion those women lived with for all those years."

"But Jade," Sonia interrupted, "this illusion is what all women have about their sons; I was no different. The tragedy is that women refuse to see men as they are and waste their lives trying to change them."

Pam was adamant. "Boys belong with their fathers. But you'll never get women to agree to that, not in a million years. They're never going to let go of their precious sons. Sons are what give them status, give their lives meaning."

"But Jade and I have met several women in our travels who have given their sons back to their fathers. Not a lot, but certainly more than in my child-rearing days. It was practically unheard of then."

"Yes, I actually know a couple of women who have," Pam admitted, leaning forward. "You know, somehow I can handle heterosexual women being hooked into men. But when I see lesbians having sons and sacrificing themselves for them, I want to barf. What's the point of being a lesbian if you're still squandering your energy on males?"

"What's the point of being a lesbian, period?" Jade asked. "The more I'm around women who call themselves lesbians, the more I realize I'm not one."

"Me, either," Sonia said dreamily, nearly blissed out by the head massage she was getting.

Pam frowned. "That upsets me, because I do identify as a lesbian. I mean, I'm certainly not heterosexual."

"But you've said you don't want to do sex with women," Jade reminded her.

"That's true, but being a lesbian isn't just about having sex with women."

"Oh come on, Pam," Jade said impatiently. "You know better than that. No matter what the popular line is, lesbianism's about having sex with women. Let me tell you a couple of stories.

"Three years ago I organized a group of lesbians to come together at my home in Ojo Caliente to talk about buying land and living in community. On the second day of the three-day weekend, a woman showed up who was staying at the hot springs nearby. Her name was Jerri. She sat through the rest of the second day and all of the third. I liked her. Although she didn't say anything during the meetings, I spent some time with her on Saturday night during dinner.

"She was in her late fifties, had divorced her husband, bought a travel trailer, left her family, and taken off on her own. There was something very strong about her in spite of her quiet ways.

"On Sunday afternoon, the last day of the gathering, we went around the circle and talked about our feelings, what we wanted, and so on. When it came to Jerri, she asked the group how they would feel about having a non-lesbian in their community. She told us she was celibate and totally uninterested in having relationships with men. But she was also uninterested in having them with women.

"I felt good about her and told her I wouldn't mind. One other woman agreed. But the rest of the group—and we're talking thirty-plus women—were very put off. Many of them told her directly that they only wanted to live with other lesbians, and because she was not sexual with a woman, had never been, and had no intention of being, she would not be welcome."

Pam sighed. "Yeah, okay. Sound's familiar."

Jade nodded. "There are hundreds of examples. I knew another woman who started attending our lesbian gatherings. She came to the potlucks, the coffee house, the dances, the meetings. She kept saying she thought she was a lesbian, but wasn't sure. At the time she was sharing a house with a man she had once been involved with, so no one took her seriously, and some women were noticeably uncomfortable with her in the meetings and discussions.

"When she moved into her own place, everyone waited for her to get involved with a woman. When she didn't, many of the women became outright hostile to her. They didn't want a 'straight' woman in their midst. Even though she had decided she was a lesbian, she hadn't 'proved' herself by having sex with a woman. When she finally did, everyone was immensely pleased. Now she was a real lesbian, and they welcomed her with open arms.

"And yet these same women will tell you that they don't believe being a lesbian is only about having sex with women. They'll tell you it's about being woman identified. Woman identified! Nothing could be further from the truth! Most lesbians are the most male-identified women on the face of the earth!"

"You realize that this demolishes the idea of lesbian culture, don't you?"

Sonia turned over so Jade could massage her neck and shoulders. "You mean, it shatters the myths and destroys the illusions," she yawned. "Lesbian culture is simply male culture with the pronouns changed."

Jade smiled down at her, then looked up at Pam. "I had to see through the deceptions, Pam. One day I realized that the only difference between lesbian culture and heterosexual culture is that lesbians have physical sex with women. That's it. As we speak, there are lesbian couples out there getting married and fighting for the legalization of those marriages. They're having babies, or adopting them. They're still taking care of men, or becoming separatists—both reactions to men and therefore male-centered behavior.

"In women's communities, they think they're doing something radical by living with other women. They may ban television and radio and newspapers, may prohibit men on the property, may have a rule against anything that is blatantly male, such as male music. But they have rules in those communities. They have relationships. They have an exchange system.

"But more basic than that by far, the very way they're thinking is male. Several dozen times a day—at least—they engage in sadomasochism of some sort without even recognizing it. We all do, every last one of us."

Pam fidgeted and looked away. "This blows me away. I suspect you're saying some true stuff. I'm not sure about all of it, but I'm not ready to argue, either. It just makes me wonder who I am, what I am. I thought I'd made an enormous leap in becoming a lesbian, and in identifying myself as one openly and proudly."

"So did I, Pam," Jade said softly. "I was right out there on the front lines. The front page, actually, of the Las Palomas Journal, unashamed and unabashedly proud. I became deeply involved in lesbian and gay politics. I lobbied to have the same rights as heterosexuals had, I organized Gay Pride rallies, I was outspoken and at times outrageous. I believed it all, the whole fairy tale, so to speak. I believed we were doing something radical because patriarchy was so opposed to it."

"Right!" Pam sat up straighter. "I've always believed that anything they disapproved of was probably subversive as hell."

"Me, too. But now I believe they make a fuss about it in part to get us to do it, to do the very thing they say they don't want us to do. Reverse psychology, you know. By withholding the legalization of same-sex marriages, they make us want to get married. They force us to react. We give them the finger and say, 'You can't stop us from marrying, you can't stop us from having babies'. And they're delighted, of course, though they can't let on. Because that's how they trap women: marriage and children. Men have their smart moments. And of course, having babies still requires male intervention, regardless of how you do it. So they're still very involved in our lives."

Sonia reached over to stroke Pam's leg. "We said we're not lesbians. Let me tell you something even more politically incorrect: I'm not a feminist, either. Feminism is the women's auxiliary, women hanging about on the fringes of the men's club begging to be let in. As a well-known feminist said, 'Add a woman and stir'. I don't want *in* men's world. I want *out*."

○ ○ ○ ○ ○ ○

Jade surveyed the kitchen. Dishes everywhere, from lunch as well as supper. She had intended to wash the lunch dishes earlier, but was distracted by phone calls. Then Pam had come in with her wounded foot, and that had taken up the rest of the afternoon, with supper and their long talk afterwards finishing off the day. Her head ached, a dull, throbbing pain behind her eyes. She could hear Sonia's voice on the phone in the office.

Grabbing the dish pan, she filled it with hot, soapy water and dumped the dishes in. Eyeing the cookie sheet that Sonia had broiled the muffins on, she was reminded of Pam's lavish praise of Sonia's quick pizzas. They *had* been good, probably better than anything she could have made. *Sonia's just a better cook, that's all*, she thought morosely. *Even though she hates to do it, she's better at it than I am.* Hearing Sonia's laughter from the office increased her irritation. *Who the hell is she talking to so long?* She scrubbed furiously at the stuck cheese on the cookie sheet.

"I'm bad, Jade-lo," Sonia announced, sweeping into the kitchen. "Barb's been filling me in on all the latest gossip. I know, you don't have to tell me—I'm evil. But it was fun."

Jade grunted and went on with the dishes. She was surprised at Sonia's admission. She was definitely not the gossipy type and usually loathed it.

Sonia circled the countertop until she was opposite Jade and the sink. A jigsaw puzzle was in progress, and as she searched for pieces, she told Jade Barb's gossip. Jade did her best to keep her comments to a minimum. Couldn't Sonia tell that she wasn't feeling well and needed help with cleaning up? Couldn't she tell that she wasn't interested in Barb's stories? As she cleaned each dish, she flung it into the drainer. Her frenzied washing sent splatters of water onto the counter, enough so that Sonia slid the puzzle away from the sink.

"I thought Barb had more intelligence than that," Jade snapped. "I didn't think she was the type to believe every piece of garbage that comes out of the women's community."

"I don't know that she believes it," Sonia replied. "She was simply repeating what she'd been told, and we were making a comedy routine out of it. Barb can be hilarious."

"I don't know what's funny about getting your kicks at other women's expense," Jade muttered crossly. "I'm amazed you spent so much time on the phone, with all the work there is around here. I've got a lousy headache."

Okay, Sonia said to herself, *so you're trying to guilt-trip me into helping you with the dishes and clean up. If that's what you want, you have to say it, not just go all passive aggressive on me.*

"Damn!" Jade yelled, as a glass shattered in the sink. "Double damn these cheap glasses! Who the hell bought them anyhow!" Angrily, she searched the water for broken glass. Sonia neatly slipped a puzzle piece into place, then headed up to the quiet of her room and a good mystery. The dogs followed close at her heels, casting backward glances at their furious friend.

The dishes done, Jade ran a wet cloth over the counters and wiped down the stove. Her head was worse now, so she went to the pantry and searched the herb shelves for white willow bark. Swallowing four tablets, she returned to the kitchen, where she evicted the cat from her bed and covered the bird for the night. Climbing the stairs, she noticed that Sonia's door was closed. *Fine. Let her be mad,* she thought. She wondered briefly about the dogs, then decided they could be Sonia's responsibility for a change.

She undressed quickly and got into bed. She knew that once she fell asleep, the headache would go. Normally, sleep came easily when one of these struck. But not tonight. She was upset and angry. Even after Sonia knew about her headache, she hadn't offered to help out. The hell with her.

An hour later and still awake, she sat up and turned on the light. She knew why she couldn't sleep, and she knew that until she went in and let Sonia know she wasn't angry anymore, sleep would evade her. So getting out of bed, she crossed the room to their shared bathroom and quietly pushed open the door to Sonia's room. Seeing her sitting up and reading, she approached the bed and, after a moment's hesitation, slid in beside her.

Sonia looked up briefly, then went back to her reading. Jade reached a tentative hand out to her arm, and, receiving no rebuff, started to stroke her very lightly, very gently. When Sonia didn't recoil, Jade took it as a good sign. At least she was open to her being here. She continued to stroke her arm, then her shoulder and side, her legs, all the way to her feet and back up again. She did this over and over, waiting for some sign, some clue that Sonia was willing to accept her silent apology.

She got nothing.

Finally she sighed and, pushing the blankets back, returned to her room. If Sonia was determined to stay angry, then fine. There was nothing she could do about it. Flipping her light off, she tried to focus her attention on sleep. It was futile. Tossing and turning, it was well after three a.m. when she finally drifted off.

The early morning light wakened her and, squinting at the clock, she suddenly remembered the night before. She felt terrible. Although the headache was gone, in its place was a depression that threatened to spoil the day. As she flung off the blankets and headed for the bathhouse, she wondered if Sonia were still angry.

The hot water beating on her head and face helped. Dressing, she looked for signs of Sonia. Her cereal bowl was in the drainer, which meant she was up and had eaten, and the absence of the dogs told her they were all outside. She was right. Sonia was out front, working in the flowerbed.

As Jade crossed the deck, the dogs miraculously appeared and covered her with affection. She spent more time with them than usual, dreading the actual confrontation with Sonia and yet sure to collapse if she did not do it soon. As she walked up to her, Sonia looked up, nodded, then returned to her weeding.

"Sonia? I'd like to talk to you, if it's okay."

Sonia's eyes met hers.

"I'm just sorry you're still angry with me, that's all. If you don't want me around, I'd like you to tell me and I'll stay away."

Sonia laid down her trowel. "I don't know why you think I'm angry. I'm not."

"But last night when I came in to see you, you never said a word to me. Except for a quick glance when I got in bed, you didn't even acknowledge my presence."

"You never said a word to *me*, you mean."

"But I did. I mean, maybe I didn't use words but I spoke to you with touch. I lay there for a half hour touching you, and you acted like I wasn't there."

Sonia straightened. "That's true. You did come in and you did touch me for a long time. And that touching of yours was loaded. And I mean *loaded*."

She took off her gloves and sat down on one of the built-in deck benches. She looked solemn.

"Jade, for well over a year we've lamented that in men's world all women have had available to us has been men's touch—

conditional touch, sex touch, means-to-ends touch, stimulus/ response touch. For over a year we've remembered and talked about how, before men, women *only* touched unconditionally. For over a year we've been seriously, dedicatedly, passionately experimenting with unconditional touch.

"Then last night you come in and start touching me *to get a response*, touching me to get something from me, touching me with expectation, *sexing* me.

"I want to tell you something about that touch and I hope you can hear it: it was almost unendurable. It made me feel sick. Not just because I could tell instantly that you weren't touching me simply because you loved doing it. But also because my body can't stand sex any more. I would have preferred silence and distance, even anger, to what you did last night."

Jade recoiled as if she had been slapped. Before she could speak, Sonia went on.

"Last night when I came into the kitchen, I knew something was wrong because you were slamming and banging dishes all over the place and looked madder than hell. You told me you had a headache, and you mentioned that there was a lot of work to do. And I knew you were trying to get me to help.

"But you didn't *ask* me, Jade, and I was damned if I was going to let you control me that way. If I had come in and you were just being your usual self, of course I'd have plunged in and worked. It was hard not to, at least for the first few minutes, but under the circumstances I couldn't. I decided that if you wanted to play martyr, that was your business."

While she had been speaking, Jade had sat down on the bench beside her. Now Sonia reached over and put her hand on her knee.

"But angry at you? No, not for a second. Put off by your behavior? A little. But not angry. If there was any anger last night, it was coming from you. Maybe you projected yours onto me. When you came into my room, I almost said something to you, but I stopped myself. In my relationships, I was always the one to speak first about what was happening between us, the one who made the first move, who suggested that we sit down and talk about it. Though you and I have had almost no tense moments until last night, I decided not to get into this habit with you."

She got up and went back to weeding. Jade stood up too, very sobered. Resting against the edge of the deck, she thought about what Sonia had said, and knew it was all true. She hadn't wanted to face those dishes alone. In fact, she hadn't wanted to do them at all. And there was no rule that said she had to. But she had chosen to, of her own free will.

Then instead of asking Sonia directly for help, she had tried to coerce her into it through guilt. When this had failed, she had become angry and resentful and, unwilling to own these feelings, had projected them upon Sonia.

She stepped off the deck and knelt down beside her. "You're right on all counts, Soni. I'm sorry I behaved the way I did. Talk about regression! I was angry at you because you didn't respond to any of my garbage. I wanted a fight and you wouldn't give it to me and it made me mad."

Sonia sat back on her heels and regarded Jean with deep blue eyes, eyes set off by her tanned, healthy face.

"I'd like to hug on it and let it go," Jade said, reaching for her.

"Well, I don't know," Sonia drawled. "Check with my secretary and see if she can work it into my schedule." She held out a hand to Jade, who pulled her to her feet and enveloped her in an enormous, rib-crushing hug.

"Shoot, I had a hideous night," she murmured into Sonia's hair. "I missed you fiercely, Soni."

"Well, I missed you too, but not so much that I was willing to risk any more sex."

Jade laughed. "I don't blame you a bit. I did even more sado-masochism last night, though, which I might as well confess. I started thinking about how much Pam enjoyed your pizzas and decided you were a better cook than I was and that I might as well throw in the towel right now."

Sonia moaned into her ear. "Oh, great. I slap a few things on muffin halves and suddenly I'm a gourmet chef and you're a flophouse cook! But as I know as well as anybody, competitiveness isn't logical."

She bent and picked up her gloves and trowel and started for the house. "Well," she said, linking her arm with Jade's, "I've got a good one for you. Remember yesterday when I walked into the bathhouse and found you watering the plants? Immediately, I thought you must be unhappy with the way I've been taking care of them. Until I realized that I'd slipped back into sadomasochism, I was getting quite a charge out of being 'bottom'."

"But it was just a couple of droopy ones. I know nothing whatever about plants."

Sonia shook her head. "That isn't the point, as you know, anymore than my making pizzas last night is the point. It's just habit, this automatic comparison. But our telling each other every single time it occurs is getting rid of it."

"True. We don't have nearly as many of these confessions as we did at first. But I've got another one," she groaned, remembering. "Last night I decided you would rather sleep with the dogs than me. I was sure they were more fun and cuddly and that you'd probably never want to sleep with me again."

Sonia shrugged. "They're all right, but Maggi snores and wants my pillow. And Sneakers barks out the window at every creature for miles around that so much as stirs in the dark."

She sat at the counter and watched as Jade got the cooler out, added a thing or two to her grocery list, and stashed a bottle of orange juice in her bag.

"Well, I'm off to town, Soni," she said, "and I'd sure love your company."

"I'll pass, thanks. I really don't think I can stand town again so soon."

"It's been a week, believe it or not. But I'll make it quick, and maybe this afternoon we can start on the book."

They had decided to write a book together and were eager to begin.

Sonia nodded. "It's time." She paused a moment, then said, "Want to hear something peculiar? I miss you already."

"I know the feeling," Jade said. "I've never felt anything like it before, never wanted to spend every minute of my life with someone like I do you. Since we're not in a relationship, there's never any tension—except," she added sheepishly, "for isolated instances like last night. Being with you is pure pleasure.

"Also I have choices I wouldn't have if we were a couple. And what I choose, Soni, is to be with you all the time."

32

One July afternoon a year later, Jade turned off the road, waved good-bye to Barb and Ashley, and headed up the driveway with the dogs. When the house came into view, she stopped for a moment as she often did just for the pleasure of looking at it.

She remembered the first time they had set foot on this place. Fortunately, its natural beauty had offset the ugliness of the house and yard or they would never have bought it. It had been a nightmare—dark brown paint peeling off the sides of the house, trash carelessly piled everywhere, the front yard ravaged by backhoe attempts to improve on nature. They had despaired of ever undoing the damage done by previous owners.

But they had. New windows and doors in the house, bright teal blue paint on all the exterior wood, new stucco on the walls, the beautiful deck, bright flowers and shrubs to enhance what was naturally there and to attract birds and butterflies.

In the thick hedge of glossy-leafed gamble oaks encircling the deck and the front yard, Jade had placed bird feeders of every description and Sonia had hung wind chimes. In front of the trees, a three-tiered fountain splashed with water for the birds. From dawn to dusk, flowers, bird play, bird song, falling water, and wind chimes—a sensory paradise.

Jade crossed the deck to the walled-in lawn area where she had last seen Sonia, and found her sitting in the grass near the flowerbed she had been weeding. At Jade's approach, she carefully held out her hand. On it rested a giant swallowtail butterfly. Jade knelt for a closer look.

Slowly opening and closing its elegant black and gold wings, the butterfly vibrated against Sonia's hand, sending shivers up and down her arm. Then stretching her wings out to their fullest, she performed a perfect slow-motion pirouette on Sonia's hand. Jade sat back on her haunches and savored the picture before her.

That spring they had rolled sod out onto the dirt that covered the new septic tank, and stuccoed the wall around it the color of the house—desert rose, a delicate shade of salmon. In a purple tank top and cut-off jeans, Sonia was barefoot in the now lush grass. Behind her, her wildflower garden was a tumult of color: magenta, violet, and white globemallows, buttery-yellow desert marigolds, blue desert phlox, rich purple starflowers, spicy-sweet lavender, orange butterfly weed, and scarlet Indian paintbrush.

Jade's eyes moved beyond Sonia and the wildflower bed to the rock garden, to the purple and white petunias, lemon yellow pansies, pink, red, and orange rockroses, mauve and white alysum, and perky yellow and purple jump-ups that flanked the enormous south stone steps to the deck. On the deck, window boxes blazed with zinnias, marigolds, and dahlias.

She stood and walked back across the deck to the fountain where she had been pulling up bindweed when Barb and Ashley had stopped by looking for company for their walk. Cousin to the morning glory, bindweed was growing up through the small red lava stone she and Sonia had spread in front of the deck to solve the mud problem and give the area a clean, simple look. Despite its lovely, delicate white and pink flowers, bindweed did not belong there. There was plenty of space for it elsewhere.

Bending to pull one up, she was engulfed by a heady perfume: the Russian olives were in still in bloom up here, their yellow blossoms smothered with honeybees. As the sun touched the tips of their branches, they released their rich scent full into the wind. Taking a second whiff, she also detected the fruitier smell of the locust trees down by the creek.

The air resonated with birdtalk: black-headed and evening grosbeaks, pine siskins, mourning doves, indigo and lazuli buntings, chickadees, juncos, stellar jays, western tanangers, and bluebirds. As Jade worked near the fountain, a siskin landed on her head for a few moments before giving her hair a little tug and hopping onto the edge of the fountain for a drink. The light spray formed droplets on its tiny body.

Jade and Sonia worked contentedly for another hour, the breeze soft on their bare skin, then stopped for lunch. To go with her homemade bread, Jade tossed a salad of leafy greens, fresh tomatos, olives, cucumber, radishes, peppers, avocado, a spicy sprout mixture, and marinated tofu. They carried their food out to the deck and, the dogs sprawled in front of them, sat together on the bench, eating, touching, laughing, soaking up the beauty and sunshine around them.

The beginning of women's world, a world of love, joy, contentment, peace, and abundance. A world free of sadomasochism, of competition, of jealousy, anger and hatred. A world where all living things exist harmoniously and in balance because there is no maleness to cause turmoil and suffering. A world elegantly and exquisitely simple and pure.

Women's world: a world with no separation, no loneliness, where everything is connected to everything else—the women and the trees and the animals and the birds, all one. A world of arousal and power and infinite possibility. The world Sonia had dreamed of for years and that Jade had come to remember because of Sonia's dream.

As they had cleared out the illusions of mensystem and become peaceful and happy, their health had improved and they looked less ravaged by age. Their bodies, finally trusting that they would never again be subjected to sex, cast off their protective armor and exposed the soft, supple skin beneath it. They had been delighted to notice that injuries healed almost instantly with almost no scarring, and that simple touch took care of nearly every ailment.

The joy Sonia had longed for and that Jade had come to believe was possible, was finally their constant companion. They both awakened each morning glad to be alive, and often throughout the day said to each other, "I have such a happy heart!" as though they could still scarcely believe it. Every day they thought, "I can't get any happier." And every day, they did.

Finishing her lunch, Sonia tossed a crust of bread into the air, where it was seized by an enormous, metallic-blue jay. She watched it carry its prize to a tree limb, tear it to bits, and eat it, but her mind was elsewhere.

Everyone had warned them against trying to write a book together; it made enemies of the dearest friends, they were told. But instead it had been a marvelous experience for them, serving only to deepen and strengthen their bond. "The best year of my life," each assured the other.

"You know, Jade-lo, now that our book's finished, I've been thinking about another one. Something fun to do in the winter, but different this time. What do you say we write about the ghosts we've known in this house?"

"I'd love to. They're incredible stories."

"I've been thinking of titles. How about *Ghost Women of the Manzanos?*"

Jade smiled. "It's okay, but tame. We'll work some zing into it."

Suddenly she pointed to the cliffs on their left. There, almost invisible and moving stealthily, was a tawny mountain lion. They caught their breath as she stopped and regarded them intently with wild yellow eyes. "Soon," Sonia silently promised her. "We'll be together again soon." Motionless, the three females met outside time, and the world opened up among them like a flower. Until the big cat, remembering danger, turned, and melted into the underbrush.

Sonia, eyes shining, took Jade in her arms and held her close. "I love you, Jade-lo," she said joyously. "Oh, how I love you!"